Relative-ly Speaking

Book VI of
The Commitment Series

BADGER BLISS BOOKS

DEDICATION

Unless you were raised by June and Ward Cleaver, I believe all families are dysfunctional to an extent. Some think dysfunctional families are broken. Unless they are abusive in some ungodly way, I totally disagree. Take it from me...never try to fix what isn't broken.

Dysfunctionality (not a real word, but apropos!) makes life interesting and leads to strong character building and the ability to handle most of what life has to throw at you.

I, for one, love my family passionately, but to be honest, after growing up with them, and after raising a family of my own, I have to admit that dysfunctionality is more the norm than an anomaly. As a result, I have developed some outstanding survival and coping skills, not to mention having lived a very interesting and colorful life full of love, acceptance and support.

The best part of growing up in the midst of dysfunctionality is that life is never boring...and that is a wonderful thing!

I dedicate this book to all the dysfunctional families in the world...especially mine. Gotta love 'em!

ALSO WRITTEN BY KAREN D. BADGER AND AVAILABLE FROM BADGER BLISS BOOKS:

ON A WING AND A PRAYER

YESTERDAY ONCE MORE

THE BLUE FEATHER

ALL MY TOMORROWS

1140 RUE ROYALE

The Billie/Cat Commitment Series:

IN A FAMILY WAY

UNCHAINED MEMORIES

HAPPY CAMPERS

COLLECTIVE IDENTITY

SWEET ANGEL

RELATIVE-LY SPEAKING

www.badgerblissbooks.com

Relative-ly Speaking

Book VI of
The Commitment Series

A BADGER BLISS BOOK

By

Karen D. Badger

This is a work of fiction. All characters, locales and events are either products of the author's imagination or are used fictitiously.

RELATIVE-LY SPEAKING - BOOK VI OF THE COMMITMENT SERIES

Copyright © 2016 by Karen D. Badger
www.karendbadger.com

Cover design by Karen D. Badger

A Badger Bliss Book
Published by Badger Bliss Books
Georgia, VT 05468

www.badgerblissbooks.com

ISBN 13: 978-1-945761-10-2
ISBN 10: 1-945-761-10-5

First Edition, March, 2016
Second Edition, August, 2016

Printed in the United States of America and in the United Kingdom

ACKNOWLEDGMENTS

As usual, my beta readers provide an invaluable service. They find my mistakes, express their opinions about my characters and plot, and help me to improve my skills as a writer. I'd like to express my extreme gratitude to my wife, Bliss, my mom, Ellie Atherton and my very good friend, Carol Poynor, for your hard work and for being forthright and honest in your opinions and feedback. You guys rock!

I also wish to thank my family and friends for their unwavering support. The family dynamics on display in this book reflect the love and support I have received from my family over the years. I love every one of you! You give me the confidence to move forward with my stories.

The Commitment Series is about family… about how families come in many varieties… and about how family is not limited by blood relations. Thank you all for being a part of mine.

Part I

You Can Choose Your Friends, But...

CHAPTER 1

Sol rose over the rooftops, casting a bright orange glow over everything in his domain. Slivers of light entered every crevice, saturating, intruding, invading even the smallest slits, defeating the barriers intended to keep them out.

Soldiers of light attacked, conquering in parallel formation as they made their way through the Venetian blinds, landing on the occupants of the battleground. As the formation moved north, it became obvious that the enemy was defenseless, unable to escape the onslaught as the invading forces made their way across the hills and valleys created by the entwined bodies on the bed. Finally, victory was declared as the army of light reached its destination and planted its banner firmly in the face of the enemy.

"Billie," Cat said, nudging her sleeping wife.

"Hmmm," Billie murmured as she pulled Cat closer, wrapping her arms around her.

"Billie," Cat said again.

"Whaaaat?" Billie was annoyed at being awakened so early on a Saturday morning.

"Honey, please close the blinds, the sun is in my face. I can't sleep," Cat asked.

"Just roll over," Billie suggested, not wanting to get out of the warm comfortable bed.

"Please, love?" Cat asked sweetly.

Billie opened one eye and saw Cat looking at her with puppy dog eyes. *Damn, I hate it when she does that!*

"Oh, all right." She got out of bed and closed the blinds, effectively casting out the slivers of light that had invaded their bed. She then climbed back into bed, and gathered Cat into her arms once more.

Cat kissed Billie on the cheek then snuggled into her neck. "Thank you, sweetheart," She said.

Soon, they were sleeping once more, bodies wrapped around each other like braided rope.

***

Brrrring...Brrrring...Brrrring.

Cat groped for the phone. "Hello?" she said groggily. "Mom? Mom, do you know what time it is?" Cat asked irritably.

"Yes dear, it's ten a.m. You aren't still in bed are you?" Ida asked.

Cat shot up as if she had been goosed. "Ten a.m.? Oh, my God! Are you serious?" Cat looked at the digital clock on the nightstand to confirm what her mother had said. Sure enough, it read three minutes past ten.

Cat ran her hand through her hair and took a quick inventory of the bedroom. No Billie. *Damn it Billie, why did you let me sleep so long?* The last thing she remembered was nudging Billie awake to close the blinds.

"Caitlain, I just received a call from your sister," Ida said.

"Which one, Mom?" Cat asked, annoyed that her mother automatically thought she would know.

"Amy," Ida replied.

"And...," Cat asked.

"Well, she suggested that it was time for a family reunion," Ida explained.

"Funny you should say that, Mom. Before Laurel went back home after Sky's illness, Billie and I mentioned organizing one so she could meet the rest of the family."

"You know, sweetheart, finding Laurel closed a lot of holes in our family trees. I mean, she's my sister, and Billie's mother and Grandma Alex's daughter. It *would* be nice to introduce her to the rest of the family."

Cat threw herself back down onto the pillows. "You're right, Mom. So, whose going to organize this thing?" she asked, dreading the answer.

"Well, dear, since Laurel is *your* mother-in-law, *and* Billie's mother, we thought that you and Billie should do it," Ida reasoned.

Cat reached over for Billie's pillow and covered her face with it, swearing up a storm into its softness while holding it tightly to her face so her mother wouldn't hear the cursing.

"Caitlain? Caitlain, are you there?" Cat could hear her mother call out through the receiver.

Cat was counting to ten in her mind. *Eight...nine...ten. Calm down, Cat, calm down. This is your mother you're talking to.*

"I'm here, Mom," she said after taking a deep breath to compose herself.

"Well, dear, what do you think?"

"I think, Mom, that I need to discuss this with Billie first," Cat said, hopefully buying herself some time.

"Okay, dear. Just give me a call when you've decided where and when we'll have it, all right?" Ida said.

"Mom," Cat began.

"I'll call Amy, Bridget and Drew and tell them to expect a call from you," Ida continued talking as if Cat had not spoken.

"Mom," Cat said again.

"This will be so much fun, dear. And you know Grams and Grandma Jo are getting on in years. It may be the last reunion they'll have with the entire family," Ida finished.

That did it for Cat.

Damn! she exclaimed to herself. "All right, Mom. I'll call you when I've worked out the details with Billie," she heard herself saying.

"Okay, honey. I'll talk to you later then. Kiss Billie and the babies for me. Bye, bye."

"Bye, Mom." Cat dropped the phone onto her lap and reached for Billie's pillow once more.

Exhausted after screaming into Billie's pillow for ten minutes...not to mention oxygen starved, Cat dropped the pillow into her lap and rested her head against the headboard.

Why am I such an easy target when it comes to my mother? she asked herself. *My backbone just flies out the window where she's concerned!*

Cat inhaled deeply then closed her eyes and personally vowed not to exert such control over her own children. She opened her eyes and glanced at the picture of the kids on her bedside table. *Every day I'm amazed at the direction my life has gone,* she thought.

Almost nine years ago, it was just her and Tara…until that fateful day she walked into Billie's aerobics class and lost her heart forever. Over the course of the next few months, Billie and Cat fell in love. It wasn't until several months after they met that Cat learned Billie had a son…a son who was in the hospital in a coma after being hit by a car whose driver passed his school bus, despite the flashing red lights, and hit him as he was crossing the road.

So much had happened to them since they met. Cat's father, a neurosurgeon, was able to bring Seth back to them and they lived happily together as a family of four until that fateful day when Billie's ex-husband raped Cat while Billie was at work.

Their youngest child, Skylar was the product of that unholy act…an act that later became a blessing in disguise when Seth's paternal connection with her was her only salvation after she nearly died of leukemia two years earlier.

Cat had looked back on that time and chided herself for the way she treated Billie during Skylar's illness. She was jealous of the special relationship Billie had with their younger daughter, and she essentially pulled rank on Billie as Skylar's only biological parent when the child preferred attention from her beloved Mommy over her. She was truly grateful her relationship with Billie survived that trauma although she would not have blamed Billie for leaving after the way she treated her.

Cat smiled. When it came down to it, their love had endured every obstacle thrown in their path—including a gunshot wound to the head Billie suffered at the hands of her ex-husband, followed by a bout with amnesia, during which she had no memory of her life with Cat. Cat feared their lives would never be the same without a history to fall back on, but soon, Billie's memories returned and life became normal again.

I thank God every day for our network of friends and family, Cat thought. *I don't know what we would have done without them over the years. Mom, Dad, Jen and Fred. We are truly blessed.*

Cat frowned. *I wish I wasn't such a spineless jellyfish around my mother. Now we're in charge of organizing a freakin' family reunion!*

"Ah!" Cat exclaimed as she threw the covers back and climbed out of bed. She threw on a T-shirt and boxer shorts before going in search of her wife.

"Billie!" she yelled as she charged through the house. "Billie, where are you?" she called as she entered the kitchen.

"Chill out, Cat," Billie said, coming in from the back yard. "What's got your undies in such a wad this morning?" she asked teasingly.

"Don't go there, Billie, I'm in no mood for it," Cat said irritably, her hands on her hips.

"PMS-ing, are we?" Billie quipped.

Cat picked up a dish towel and threw it at Billie.

Billie caught the towel and grinned. "You can do better than that," she said as she lurched forward and grabbed Cat around the waist.

Cat tried to scramble out of Billie's grasp, but Billie held fast, nuzzling into Cat's neck and placing light kisses along her collarbone. Cat quickly settled down and pressed herself into Billie.

"Billie, why can't I stay mad when I'm around you?" she asked breathlessly.

"Because you can't resist my charm," Billie answered, nipping lightly on her neck.

"Hmmm, that feels good," Cat said as she arched closer to Billie. "I'd disagree, but I'm in no position to argue at the moment."

Billie stood to her full height and looked down Cat. "Wanna tell me what's got you so fired up this morning?" she asked.

"Why did you let me sleep so long?" Cat asked.

"Because, my love," Billie said. "You were tired. After last night's marathon lovemaking session, I'm surprised you're up as early as you are!"

Cat smiled, remembering how sex crazed they had both been the night before. They just couldn't get enough of each other. They had made love so many times she actually lost count.

"Actually, I still *would* be sleeping if it wasn't for my mother," Cat said.

Billie frowned. "Your mother?"

"Yeah, she called a few minutes ago. By the way, where were you? I'm surprised you didn't answer the phone."

"In the back yard with the kids. I got them started putting a fresh coat of paint on the tree house," Billie answered. "So, what did Mom have to say?" she asked.

"Billie, she did it to me again," Cat whined. "Damn it, why am I so weak around her?"

Billie raised her eyebrows, "What did she talk you into this time?" she asked.

"Us, love...us," Cat said.

"Us?" Billie asked.

"Oh, yeah. You and I are officially in charge of organizing a family reunion," Cat moaned.

Billie's head snapped up. "Cool!" she said.

"Cool? Cool?" Cat said, astonished at Billie's casual attitude. "Billie, do you have *any* idea how difficult this will be?" Cat asked.

"Cat, we're talking about your family here, how hard can it be?" Billie asked.

"Billie, we're talking about *our* families. Are you forgetting that your mother is my mother's stepsister? We're talking about you and me, our kids, Mom and Dad, Amy and Joe and their kids, Bridget and Kevin and their kids, Drew, Grandma Alex, Grandma Jo, Laurel, Dylan *and* Jim...you know—your homophobic stepfather?" Cat reminded her wife.

"Shit!" Billie said, looking down into Cat's face.

"Shit, indeed, my love. Shit indeed."

***

Cat and Billie sat at the kitchen table, fresh coffee and cheesecake in front of them. Cat scanned through her list as she tapped her pencil on the table.

"As far as I can tell, there will be about twenty-two people," Cat said. "Where are we going to sleep them all?"

"Well, we have a couple of choices, Cat. They can rent motel rooms for the week, or bring camping gear and set it up in the yard," Billie suggested.

"Camping gear? Billie, how can you even suggest camping after that horrible experience we had at Happy Trails?" Cat asked, seeing Billie visibly cringe at the mention of their disastrous camping trip with Fred and Jen.

"Maybe you're right. Sorry I mentioned it," Billie said, shuddering at the memory. "Well, there's always the motel," she added.

"That could get a little expensive," Cat observed.

"Well, I'm out of ideas, then," Billie crossed her arms on the table in front of her rested her chin on them.

Cat stood up and started pacing, tapping the end of her pencil on her chin as she walked. "What we need," she said, "is a house big enough for all of us."

Cat suddenly stopped and looked at Billie at the same exact moment Billie's head snapped up.

"SpireClyffe Acres!" they exclaimed together.

***

"Hi, Grams, this is Cat."

"Caitlain, darlin', it's so nice to hear from you. How y'all doin'?" Alex asked excitedly. "How's the baby?" she added.

"We're all fine, Grams. Skylar is doing great. She's on a very low maintenance dose of chemo, and seems to be tolerating it very well. Her hair has grown back in—curly this time! It really is very cute. So far, there's no sign of the leukemia returning. Dr. Berry is confident that we've beat it. So how are you and Grandma Jo?" Cat asked.

"Well, you know how it is. Josie is just as ornery as ever. I swear, Caitlain, that woman is gonna send me to an early grave. Just last week, she challenged the stable hands to a drinkin' contest, and they ended up tree climbin' of all things. It's a wonder she didn't fall and break that fool neck of hers," Alex exclaimed.

Cat chuckled at the thought of her rebellious septuagenarian grandmother climbing a tree.

"I do declare, sometimes I wonder why I stay with that woman!" Alex added.

"You stay with her because you love her, Grams," Cat stated matter-of-factly.

Alex smiled. "I'm pretty transparent, huh?" she said.

"Clear as glass, Grams, and you know what? Your granddaughter is just like you!" Cat added.

It was about a year ago now that they had discovered the blood connection between Billie and Alex. Billie had found Alex's daughter Laurel, and her grandson Dylan as well, in the process.

"Darlin', I can't tell you how happy I was to learn that Billie was my granddaughter. It is truly a blessing to have her in my life."

"Grams, I'm calling to ask a favor," Cat said.

"Of course, sugar. What is it that ya need?" Alex asked.

"Grams, Mom has put Billie and me in charge of organizing a family reunion, and we were wondering...," Cat began.

"A family reunion? What a good idea. Caitlain, I insist that we have it here at SpireClyffe Acres. We have plenty of room, a swimming pool, tennis courts. Why, it's perfect. I won't take no for an answer," Alex exclaimed.

"Grams, you are a gem, you know that?" Cat asked.

"Why thank you, Caitlain, but you did say you needed a favor. What was it that you needed, darlin'?" Alex asked.

"Just to hear the sound of your voice, Grams. Thanks. I'll call you when we have a date for the reunion, okay? I love you Grams, and Grandma Jo too. Give her a kiss for me, will you?" Cat asked.

"I certainly will, sugar, if you kiss Billie and the kids for us. I'll talk to you later, Bye now," Alex said.

"Good bye, Grams," Cat said smiling.

You are a devil Alexandra Spirakis. You knew all along what the favor was. Don't ever change, Grams, I love you just the way you are.

CHAPTER 2

Cat hung up the phone and walked over to Billie who was sitting at one end of the living room couch doing the crossword puzzle that came in the daily newspaper. The kids were scattered to the four winds as usual, Seth and Steve (who insisted he was too old to be called Stevie now) were in Seth's room playing video games, Tara was at Jen's, playing with Karissa, and Skylar and Missy were in the back yard playing dolls in the newly painted tree house.

Starting at the opposite end of the couch, Cat slowly crawled on hands and knees toward Billie, a seductive look firmly fixed on her face.

Billie pretended not to see her, seemingly concentrating on her puzzle as Cat moved steadily closer. Billie tried very hard to keep the grin off her face as Cat lived up to her name, slowly closing in on her prey, preparing to pounce at the last moment.

Billie, however, had other thoughts on her mind as she suddenly grabbed Cat by the shoulders and pulled her onto her lap.

"Gotcha!" Billie exclaimed, trapping Cat in the circle of her arms as Cat squealed. "Now, here's what I do to sneaks!" she warned as she formed her right hand into a claw.

"No! Not the claw!" Cat screamed, knowing what was coming.

"Yes, my dear, the claw," Billie answered, as her hand descended into Cat's side, unmercifully ticking her.

"No! Billie, no! Stop, please," Cat yelled, laughing hysterically, trying her best to get away. "Billie, please, stop!"

Cat was quite a handful as she struggled against Billie's assault, pulling them both off the couch and onto the floor. She had almost gotten away, scrambling to her feet, when Billie grabbed one of her ankles and pulled her back down, maneuvering herself so that she lay completely on top of her. Billie pinned Cat's wrists to the floor above her head, their noses a mere hair's breadth apart.

Green eyes met blue, locked in a match of wills, neither willing to give in as they attempted to stare each other into submission.

"Give!" Billie demanded.

"No!" Cat replied, stubborn determination filling her eyes as she maintained contact while trapped beneath Billie.

Billie grinned then kissed Cat's eyelids, forcing them closed.

"Give," she said again, whispering the word into Cat's ear.

"No," Cat said again.

More kisses, this time along Cat's jaw line.

"Give, my love," Billie said seductively without stopping the barrage of kisses.

"No, Billie," Cat said breathlessly.

Tiny nips on Cat's collarbone caused her to catch her breath and moan.

"Give in, Cat," Billie demanded.

"Oh, God, no," Cat replied.

The hollow between Cat's breasts was the next target. Billie ran her tongue through the ample cleavage, causing Cat's nipples to stand erect with sensual excitement. Cat arched her chest upward, straining against the hands that held her wrists to the floor.

"Are you ready to give in yet, love?" Billie whispered, nipping at Cat's nipples through the material of her shirt.

"I'll give in only if you promise not to stop," she bargained.

"Mom, can I go swim in Steve's...oh man! Are you guys at it again?" Seth said, embarrassed that he and Steve had walked in on his mothers' foreplay.

"Ah, I was just tickling Mama," Billie explained awkwardly as Cat stared up at the ceiling, her wrists still trapped by Billie's hands. "She tried to sneak up on me," Billie added, red-faced.

"Sure you were, mom. Can I go swim in Steve's pool?" he asked.

"Of course you can. Be sure that you and your sister are home for supper, okay?" Billie said.

"Okay, thanks, mom." Seth turned to Steve, "Let's go, before they start kissing again!" he exclaimed, leading his friend toward the back door.

The two ladies listened for the sound of the back door closing, then looked at each other and broke into giggles. Cat's arms made their way around her wife's neck as Billie released her wrists and gathered Cat into her arms, rolling them over so that Cat was lying on top.

Billie cupped the sides of Cat's face with her hands and pulled her down for a kiss. "Do you think he believed me?" Billie asked, her eyes full of mirth.

"Not a chance," Cat replied, sitting up grinning.

"I think you're right. By the way, how did the phone call to Grams go?" Billie asked.

"Really well, but before I tell you about it...," Cat leaned in so that she was nose to nose with Billie.

"I..." Cat placed a kiss on Billie's nose.

"Have..." Another, light kiss landed on Billie's lips.

"A message..." Cat's tongue flicked across Billie's now open mouth.

"To deliver," she finished, diving passionately into Billie's mouth, kissing her long and hard, driving her tongue deep into the moist cavern her wife offered willingly.

Billie grasped the sides of Cat's head firmly, loud moans escaping her throat as Cat ravished her mouth for a long moment. Finally, breaking the kiss, Cat sat up and looked Billie directly in the eyes, while struggling to control her own breathing.

"Wow! What was that for?" Billie asked breathlessly.

"Grams said to kiss you and the kids for her," Cat explained, her voice raspy and face flushed with desire.

"Somehow, I don't think Grams intended it to be *that* type of kiss, Red," Billie exclaimed. "Not that I'm complaining, mind you," she added.

"Well, she didn't specify, so I figured it was up to me to choose," Cat said.

"You chose well, my love," Billie replied, raising her head for more, which Cat eagerly supplied.

"So, how did the call go?" Billie asked again, highly distracted by the beautiful woman sitting on top of her.

"Grams offered SpireClyffe Acres even before I had a chance to ask." Cat placed one more, soft kiss on Billie's cheek. "Billie, make love to me," she whispered in her wife's ear. "I need to feel you inside me."

A low growl emanated from Billie's throat as she threw her head back to give Cat better access to her neck. "Cat," she panted, "God, Cat. I would love nothing more than to ravish you, body and soul right now, but are you forgetting our daughter and her friend in the back yard?" Billie asked.

Cat's head snapped up, her eyes meeting Billie's. "Shit! You're right!" she exclaimed.

The sound of the back door suddenly opening caused the ladies to jump. Cat quickly sat up, straddling Billie's stomach, while Billie's clasped her hands together and placed them under her head in a casual pose.

"Mama," a little voice called out.

"We're in here, love bug," Cat replied. *Great timing, Sky*, she thought as the little girl entered the living room, dragging Missy behind her by the hand.

"Mama, can I go to Missy's to play?" Skylar asked. "Her mom said I could."

Billie clasped her hands together and exclaimed, "Praise Hestia!"

Cat turned to her daughter and said, "Sure, honey, but be really careful crossing the street, okay? Oh, and be home for dinner at six o'clock. All right?"

"Okay, Mama. Thanks," Skylar said as she and Missy ran out the door.

Cat looked down at Billie and wiggled her eyebrows up and down. "Last one up stairs is a rotten egg!" she exclaimed, rising to her feet and getting a head start on her long-legged wife.

"Hey, no fair!" exclaimed Billie with a wide grin on her face, as she jumped to her feet and followed Cat.

***

"But you *have* to come, Mom. You are the whole reason this reunion is being planned in the first place," Billie said into the phone. "Look, it's about time that Jim did some growing up here. Your mother is gay. Your daughter is gay. That doesn't mean that you are. And by the way, Mom, homosexuality is not contagious. You certainly won't catch it by being around us. If that was the case, you would have been gay when we sent you home after your visit last year," Billie explained.

Cat was standing nearby, listening to Billie's end of the conversation, worry etched on her brow. Billie looked at the concern on her wife's face while she listened to her mother speak. She cupped Cat's cheek in her palm and leaned down to place a tender kiss on her lips before turning her attention back to the phone.

"So, you're coming then? Good. When is it? Cat and I were thinking it could be a Fourth of July reunion, including fireworks. Grandmas Alex and Jo insisted we hold it at SpireClyffe Acres. It's the only place large enough to hold the whole family. Yes, I know it's a beautiful place, the kids are gonna love it there. Okay, then. We'll see you on the fourth. And Mom, Jim is welcome to come too. In fact, I hope he does. It's time we get to know each other, and he has three grandchildren and a daughter-in-law who would love to meet him," Billie added, seeing Cat grin at the invitation. "All right then, Mom. I'll talk to you later. I love you. Bye."

Billie hung up the phone and looked at Cat. "Well, it looks like she's coming. If that man influences her otherwise, I'll personally execute his castration," Billie said.

"Billie Jean Charland! What a thing to say!" Cat exclaimed, a shocked expression on her face. She stepped close to Billie and placed both hands flat on the area above Billie's breasts. "Can I assist in the operation?" she asked, grinning.

"I insist that you do, Dr. Charland," she said, kissing Cat's nose. "Okay, so that's a confirmation from Mom and possibly Jim. How many does that make so far?"

Cat broke out of Billie's embrace and picked up the clipboard on the table by the phone. Scanning the paper attached to it, she said, "Let's see, that's Mom and Dad, Amy and Joe and family, Drew, Dylan, Mom and Jim, the two grandmothers, you, I and our kids. So far that's seventeen people. We still haven't heard from Bridget and her family," Cat said.

"Good," she said looking down into Cat's eyes. "See Cat, planning this thing isn't so bad."

Cat smiled nervously. "Billie, don't count your chickens before they hatch. Nothing is that easy, especially where our families are concerned. I won't relax until we're all there and enjoying ourselves," Cat explained.

Billie cupped the side of Cat's face. "I like the sound of that, Cat," she said.

"What do you mean?"

"*Our* family. When we met nearly eight years ago, the only family I had was Seth, and he was in the hospital in a coma. Thank God for Doc. If he hadn't been able to remove the scar tissue, who knows where we might be today," Billie explained.

"I would hope we'd still be together, Billie," Cat said. "I would have loved Seth…and you, regardless of his abilities."

"I know, but life would sure be different," Billie said. "I mean, we wouldn't have Skylar if we hadn't met. I realize her conception was pretty traumatic and painful for you, but she has brought so much love and richness to our lives, I can't imagine life without her."

Cat wiped a tear from the corner of her eye. "We came close to losing her to leukemia last year. I hope to God she's in permanent remission. I don't ever want that poor sweet angel to go through that again."

"I second that, love," Billie said.

"And now, look at us. We discovered you were adopted and found your birth mother while doing our genealogy…and to top it all off, she's Grandma Alex's daughter! Go figure."

"From the moment I met you, Cat, I knew our lives had been entwined through the generations. You felt so familiar. I believe we were meant to be together."

"So you believe the fates sent me to your aerobics class seven years ago?" Cat asked.

"Absolutely…and it appears the fates have a sense of humor as well, as demonstrated by your lovely pirouette onto your face in the middle of that first class." Billie laughed at the memory.

"Don't remind me," Cat grimaced.

Billie kissed Cat tenderly. "We have been through so much in our short time together. It hasn't been easy, but I'd do it again in a heartbeat if it meant coming out where we are at this exact moment. I love our life together, Cat. I wouldn't trade it for the world. Thank you for loving me."

"Sweetheart, we have lived through sexual violation, sick kids, brain surgery, memory loss, epilepsy, adoption and an identity crisis, and we've come out intact. If we can survive all that we can survive anything as long as we live through it together."

"Together, forever and always," Billie said.

***

"Kevin. Kevin, settle down. Kevin. Damn it Kevin, will you please shut up for a moment! Geesh, you are being such a baby about this! Look, everyone else is coming to the reunion. You and Bridget and the kids *have* to be there. It won't be the same if the whole family isn't there. I…I…Kevin, would you please let me talk?" Cat yelled into the phone.

Billie was half lying, half sitting on the bed, her back reclined against the headboard and her hands laced together across her stomach while she waited for Cat to finish talking to her sister and brother-in-law. For the last ten minutes, she had been listening to Cat's end of the conversation. Finally, losing all patience with her brother-in-law she rose from the bed and approached Cat.

"Kevin, let me talk to Bridget," Cat demanded as she looked up at Billie.

"Bridget? Bridget, honey, will you tell that husband of yours to stop being such a wiener? I can't believe he's carrying on like that!" Cat exclaimed. "Bridget, at least you and the kids have to come to the reunion, okay? It won't be the same if you don't. Please?" Cat pleaded.

"Cat, give me the phone," Billie said.

Cat saw the determined glint in Billie's eyes as she handed the phone to her.

Billie lifted the receiver to her ear. "Bridget. This is Billie. Please put Kevin back on the phone," she insisted. While she waited for Kevin, she lifted Cat's hand to her mouth and kissed the palm. Cat's eyes closed as her head dropped back, and a soft moan escaped her lips. Billie's attention was suddenly drawn back to the phone.

"Kevin, this is Billie. You listen to me, and listen good. I've been sitting here for the past ten minutes waiting to make love to my wife, while she's been on the phone, listening to you whine. You *will* get that candy ass of yours on the plane next week and bring your family to Charleston, do you understand me?" A slight pause. "Look, Kevin, stop being such a wuss-ass! For Christ's sake, even your children aren't afraid to fly! Now I don't want to hear any more shit from you, you got that?" Another slight pause. "I *said*, you got that?" Billie demanded angrily.

Cat stood there, looking at her wife with wide eyes. She couldn't believe Billie was talking to her brother-in-law like that. Kevin was basically a good guy, but a little too macho for Cat's tastes. She really didn't know how Bridget put up with his Neanderthal ways sometimes, but he was a good husband and father, and Bridget seemed to love him blindly. As macho as he was, however, he seemed intimidated by Billie, and Billie was taking full advantage of the fact.

"Kevin, I want an answer, right now, and it had better be the one I want to hear," she insisted, still holding Cat's gaze.

"All right. That's better. We'll see *all* of you next week then, okay? Okay, and Kevin—thanks," Billie finished, hanging up the phone.

Billie looked at Cat and raised one dark eyebrow into her hairline. "Mission accomplished," she said.

Cat smiled sensually. For some reason, seeing her wife act so aggressively was a major turn on. "Have I told you ye today that I love you?" she asked, hands on her hips.

"Only two or three times," Billie replied. "But don't let that stop you," she added, reaching out for Cat.

Cat stepped into Billie personal space and wrapped her arms around her waist. "Oh, don't worry, it won't," she replied, pulling up Billie's nightshirt and slipping her hands into the back of Billie's panties. She slid her hands down over Billie's bottom and squeezed hard.

Billie's arms automatically trapped Cat in an urgent embrace. "God, Cat," Billie moaned as she buried her face in Cat's neck.

"I have been aching for you all day," Cat whispered into Billie's ear. "I want to hold you in my arms and do unspeakable things to your person."

Billie chuckled. "Unspeakable is good," she said.

"Let me love you," Cat whispered before clamping down on Billie's earlobe.

Billie's control snapped as she lifted Cat off her feet and carried her through the house to their bedroom. She laid her on the bed and lowered herself on top of her, pinning her to be bed with a near-brutal kiss.

"Billie, let me up," Cat said. Seeing the look of hurt and confusion on Billie's face, she added, "Please love. I promise you will like it."

Billie rolled onto her back, and watched as Cat scrambled off the bed.

"Come here," Cat said, patting the edge of the bed.

Billie scrambled to her knees and made her way to the edge of the bed, sitting with her legs over the side. It was evident to Cat that Billie was making an effort to control herself. Billie was not very good at waiting games, especially when her level of frustration was so near the breaking point as it was right now.

Cat knew she had limited time and space to push Billie before she simply lost control. Walking over to the dresser, she searched through the CD's stacked there, until she found the one she wanted. Slipping it in to the stereo, she selected the desired track, and then turned to face Billie.

Strong bass and a steady drum beat vibrated from the speakers as Cat began to gyrate her hips in time to the music, arms out to the sides, and a seductive look on her face. Billie sat there mesmerized by Cat's beauty, grinning ear to ear and licking her lips as she watched Cat's hips sway back and forth.

Cat was wearing a button-down baseball jersey that came to mid-calf, the first two buttons left casually undone, exposing some of the supple fresh beneath. As she danced, her hands roamed up and down her body, cupping her own breasts and thrusting them toward Billie, just out of reach. Billie growled in frustration as Cat slipped away from her.

"Patience, my love. They will be yours soon enough," Cat said from a safe distance. Billie narrowed her eyes at Cat.

One by one, the buttons on the front of the jersey were undone. Cat made a point of holding the material together in the front as she undid each button, not exposing too much to her overheated wife.

"Cat, take it off," Billie said in a restrained voice as she grasped the sheets with her hands, obviously struggling to stay seated on the bed.

Cat grinned at the request and turned her back to Billie while continuing to sway her hips seductively to the music. Opening the jersey, she held the two sides out and pressed her backside toward Billie, wiggling it slightly. She heard Billie's sharp intake of breath as she gasped at the blatant teasing.

"Cat, you are in so much trouble," Billie warned.

Cat looked over her shoulder. "Promise?" she asked, as she slipped the jersey part way down her back and pulled the front together again, just above her breasts while leaving her upper back and shoulders bare. Turning around to face Billie, she put on her best innocent little girl face and took a step forward.

Billie reached out and grabbed her before Cat could take a step back, forcing her to stand in the space between her legs. She wrapped her arms around Cat's waist and buried her face in Cat's cleavage.

"God, Cat. Why are you teasing me so? " Billie exclaimed into Cat's chest.

Cat's body shuddered in reaction to the sensual onslaught.

Billie grabbed the two sides of Cat's jersey and roughly tore them from Cat's grasp, pushing the material down the length of Cat's arms, and allowing it to fall to the floor around her feet.

Cat stood there, exposed, wearing delicately laced panties, and very erect nipples. Cat looked at Billie with half-closed hooded eyelids, eyes smoky with desire. Her tongue flicked its way across her lips.

Billie was beyond her limits of control. Thrusting herself forward and pulling Cat toward her at the same time, she took in turn, first one, and then the other of Cat's nipples into her mouth, running her tongue around the erect buds, flicking them with her tongue, nipping at them gently with her teeth, each move causing a shudder of desire to pass through Cat's body as she moaned her pleasure.

The fire in Cat's abdomen was too much for her to control. Running her hands through Billie's hair, she grasped a handful on each side of her head and pulled her closer.

Cat was out of her mind with desire. She was already on the edge of orgasm, and Billie had hardly touched her yet.

Billie moved her caresses from Cat's breasts to the sensitive skin covering her stomach, working her way downward, running her tongue over the well-sculptured abs.

Cat's sharp intake of breath as each new area was explored, was testimony to the effectiveness of Billie's attack.

Billie slid her tongue into Cat's navel as she pushed the lace panties down Cat's legs to join the jersey on the floor.

Cat instinctively spread her legs to allow Billie access to the treasure between them. While still invading Cat's navel with her tongue, Billie's hands reached behind to cup Cat's bottom and pull her close, squeezing the supple flesh until Cat moaned her frustration.

"Billie, I'm sorry, I'll never tease you again, just please, take me now! Please, I need you," Cat begged as she faced her seated wife, hands on Billie's shoulders for support.

"Oh, but you *will* tease me again, my love. I insist. I'm counting on it. Promise you will," Billie demanded, her hand cupping Cat's womanhood.

"Yes, Billie, yes, I promise," she cried as Billie invaded her being.

"Ah, God, yes!" Cat cried out. "Harder, please," she added, causing Billie to increase the force of the upward thrusts as Cat rode the wave of desire.

With her free hand, Billie reached up and grasped Cat's breast, drawing it toward her mouth and taking the erect bud between her teeth. The overwhelming sensations caused by Billie mouth and hand pushed Cat rapidly and forcefully over the edge of oblivion as wave after wave of orgasmic relief flooded her body, causing her to convulse uncontrollably. If it wasn't for her firm hold on Billie's shoulders, Cat would have easily melted into a puddle of desire on the floor at Billie's feet.

Finally, after what seemed like an eternity, Cat collapsed into Billie's arms, straddling her lap and resting her head on Billie's shoulder.

Billie sat there, holding her precious cargo, rubbing her hand across Cat's back, and whispering soothing words of love into her ear. "I've got you, baby. I've got you."

After several moments, Cat lifted her head from Billie's shoulder and looked her in the eye. "I love you," was all she said, before lowering her mouth to claim Billie's lips.

Moving to Billie's jaw, Cat placed delicate kisses from her chin to ear, nipping at the lobe and causing Billie's hands to tighten their hold.

Cat moved to Billie's neck, leaving a trail of marks that would surely bruise. Billie threw her head back to allow Cat better access to her neck and throat.

"God, Cat, that feels so good," she exclaimed as Cat twirled her tongue around the hollow at the base of Billie's neck where her collarbones met. Reaching under Billie's nightshirt, Cat slid it upward and pushed the shirt over Billie's head and arms.

Billie reached behind herself and braced both her hands on the bed, supporting her upper body as Cat climbed off her lap and knelt on the floor between her legs. She watched Cat intently, her eyes wide with desire, her breathing deep and ragged, as the Cat explored her breasts, reaching out to touch and caress, squeeze and kiss each one. Cat looked up to meet Billie's eyes as she took a breast in each hand.

"They are so perfect, and so beautiful," Cat said, "just like you," she added before taking one erect nipple in her mouth.

Billie threw her head back once more, arms straining to support her upper body, her long hair nearly reaching the bed as she moaned out her desire. "Oh, my God, Cat! More. Please. That feels so good!"

Cat was more than happy to oblige as she greedily devoured Billie's breasts, alternately sucking, nipping and caressing each one.

Billie's body soon turned traitorous, her hips bucking upwards at Cat of their own volition. Sensing her need, Cat started working her way down Billie's torso, nipping and kissing the tender skin along the way. Cat too, stopped at Billie's navel and took her time investigating the crevice with her tongue.

"Cat," Billie said urgently as she reached around with one hand to push Cat lower.

Cat took Billie's hand and placed it back on the bed. "Patience, my love. I will release you, sweetheart, I promise," she said softly.

Billie locked eyes with her, pleas of urgency issued through the silent communication as Cat sat back on her heels and started orally caressing the skin on the inside of Billie's thighs. Billie's muscles quivered at the contact as Cat's tongue explored the soft sensitive skin high on Billie's thigh.

"Cat, please," Billie pleaded .

Cat rose back to her knees and leaned in behind Billie to grasp the waistband of her panties, pulling them off her hips and down her legs and discarding them in the growing pile of clothes on the floor. Leaning back in, she whispered huskily, "Spread you legs for me, sweetheart."

Billie's eyes flew open at the sensual command, spreading her legs wide for her lover.

Cat feasted hungrily, running her tongue over and between the folds of Billie's womanhood. Billie moaned and called out to a variety of gods as Cat captured the swollen pleasure point and drew it into her mouth, biting gently, then flicking it repeatedly with her tongue.

Suddenly, and without warning, Cat drove three fingers deep into Billie, causing her hips to come completely off the bed as her body surrendered to the orgasmic explosion erupting through her.

After several long moments, the convulsions lessened in severity and number.

Cat, very pleased with herself for bringing such pleasure to the woman she loved, rose to her feet and slowly crawled up the length of Billie's body, until she was lying completely on top of the semi-comatose woman.

"I love you," they said at the same exact moment, eliciting chuckles from both of them.

CHAPTER 3

The week passed quickly. As the weekend neared, Cat and Billie made last minute checks to their lists to be sure they had everything. Cat supervised packing the children's clothes, while Billie packed clothes for her and Cat. The kids were put in charge of individual items that they wanted to bring as carry-on luggage. These included Seth's I-Pod and wrestling magazines, Tara's DS and Goosebump books, and Skylar's coloring books, crayons, and Petey. Last, but not least, Cat took special care to pack their meds, including Skylar's oral chemo pills, and Billie's epilepsy medication. Finally, everything was packed and sitting by the back door, ready to load into the car the next morning.

That evening, they assembled in front of the TV in the family room to watch a movie and munch on buttered popcorn. Partway into the movie, they heard footsteps descend the cellar stairs.

"Hey, is anyone home?"

"We're down here, Jen. Come join us," Cat said over her shoulder.

Jen approached the family, noting the three children lying on the floor in front of the TV, all in a row, a bowl of popcorn in front of them, while Cat and Billie snuggled on the couch. Making her way over to the family, she squeezed in to sit between the two women, taking their bowl of popcorn from them, and holding it on her lap for all to share.

Cat and Billie looked at each other behind Jen's head and smiled at their neighbor's boldness.

"Make yourself at home, Jen," Billie said nonchalantly.

"Don't mind if I do, big guy," Jen said, shoving a handful of popcorn into her mouth. "Hey, this is good," she added.

Cat and Billie both squeezed in a little closer to Jen so that all three women cuddled together. Instead of intimidating Jen they way they thought they would with their shift in position, she just smiled and said, "This is cozy. We need to do this more often."

Cat and Billie rolled their eyes at each other.

"I'm gonna miss you guys," Jen said, looking back and forth between her friends.

"We'll only be gone for a week," Cat said.

"Yeah, a week longer than I'd like you to be," Jen replied.

"Stop being such a baby," Billie teased.

"I can't help it. I'm afraid you'll get on that plane and you won't come back. A lot could go wrong, you know," Jen said worriedly.

"Now you sound like my brother-in-law. He's a real wuss about flying too," commented Cat.

"I'm not a wuss," Jen countered.

"Jen's a wuss, Jen's a wuss," Billie teased repeatedly.

"I am not a wuss!" Jen exclaimed a little louder.

"Yes you are," said Billie.

"No, I'm not!" answered Jen.

"Enough!" yelled Cat. "Both of you. That's quite enough. Geesh!"

Jen and Billie looked at each other coyly before Jen leaned over and bumped Billie's shoulder with her own. "Sorry, big guy," she said.

"Ditto, shit head," said Billie.

Jen's eyes flew open wide. "Shit head? Shit head!? I'll show you who the shit head is!" Jen said, pouncing on Billie.

Soon, the two women were on the floor, arms and legs tangled as they rolled around, each trying to gain the upper hand. Cat remained sitting on the couch, shaking her head side to side as the children retreated to the edges of the rug, giving the two women ample room to wrestle.

"Mom, put a sleeper hold on her," Seth cheered.

The girls jumped up and down, clapping their hands and laughing as they watched their mother roll around the rug with their neighbor.

"Jennifer Swenson, hold still!" Billie demanded as she struggled to pin Jen down. "Damn, you're stronger than you look," she added.

"Get off me, Billie!" Jen yelled as she struggled against the larger woman sitting on top of her.

Cat sat on the couch, watching the exchange closely. What had started out as a friendly wrestling match was beginning to turn nasty. *Time to cool them off*, she thought as she got to her feet and went upstairs. Moments later, while still exchanging heated words, Billie and Jen found themselves drenched to the skin with cold water.

"Whaaaaa!!??" they exclaimed loudly together. Billie had thrown herself backward onto the floor as the cold water made contact with her skin.

"All right, you two, cool it. Do you hear me?" Cat demanded.

Billie and Jen looked at Cat, both wearing identically stunned expressions. The three kids stood there, totally amazed that their mother had just done something they would have been scolded for. All were holding their breaths, waiting to see what would happen next.

Jen looked at Billie. Billie looked at Jen. Both women started laughing hysterically, collapsing against each other. A collective sigh of relief echoed across the room.

Cat looked at the kids. "Hey guys, it's late. We've got a big day ahead of us tomorrow. Off to bed with you. Mom and I will be up in a few moments to say good night. All right?" she said.

"Ah, Ma," Seth said. "I'm thirteen years old. I'm an adult now. I should be able to stay up later," he exclaimed.

Cat rose from the couch and approached her son. "Seth, sweetheart, you may be a teenager now, and you might even tower over me in height, but you are still very hard to get out of bed in the morning...worse than me, in fact, and that's pretty bad, so off to bed with you. We have to leave early for the airport, so you need to get a good night's sleep. Okay, love?"

Seth rolled his eyes. "But Ma," he protested.

Cat pressed two fingers over her son's mouth. "Please, Seth, go on to bed, okay?"

Seth let out a deep sigh. "Oh, all right. Good night," he said. He kissed Cat on the cheek then offered his hands to Billie to help her up. He hugged Billie then headed up the stairs, followed closely by his sisters.

"We'll be up in a few minutes," Cat said as the children climbed the stairs.

Billie turned her attention back to Jen and reached down to help her up.

"Thanks, Billie," she said. "Look, you two have an early day tomorrow, I'd better head home," she said. "Please be careful, and come back to me, okay?" she asked, hugging them one at a time.

"Jen, we'll be back in a week, we promise. And besides, whose gonna pick up all that mail you'll be collecting for us if we don't come back, huh?" Cat asked.

"Oh, I see, you'll come back for your mail, but not for me. Is that it?" she asked, grinning.

"Something like that," Billie said. "Come on, I'll walk you home," she said, throwing an arm around her friend's shoulder.

"We'll see you in the morning, Jen. Remember, you're driving us to the airport," Cat said.

"I'll be here with bells on, sweet thang," she said to Cat in a fake Southern accent while placing a kiss on her cheek. "See you in the morning."

"I'll be back in a few minutes, love," Billie said to Cat as she left to walk her friend home.

***

Things were chaotic in the Charland household the next morning. All five of them scrambled around getting last minute things ready for their trip. The kitchen counter and table were cluttered with breakfast foods that no one had time to clean up. Cat was in a panic, reluctant to leave her house in such a state.

"Cat, we have no choice, we'll miss the plane if we take the time to clean up," Billie pointed out as she ushered the kids toward the car. "Seth, please make sure your sisters are belted in, okay? Mama and I will be right out."

Jen chose this moment to put in her appearance.

"Jen! Finally. I thought you forgot us!" Cat exclaimed, her mind momentarily diverted from the mess in her kitchen.

"Hey, I said, I would be here, didn't I?" Jen asked in mock indignation.

"Yes you did, and we appreciate it, Jen. Don't we, Cat?" Billie said firmly to her agitated wife.

"Billie, I can't leave the house a mess like this. I just can't," Cat said for the hundredth time.

"Cat, we'll miss the plane if we don't leave *now*. What part of that don't you understand?" Billie asked in a raised voice.

"All right, that enough," Jen said loudly. "Billie, take the luggage to the car. Cat, move your carcass or you're going to miss the plane. I will take care of this mess for you, okay? Don't worry about it. You can owe me *big time*, if it will make you feel better, all right? Now move your asses—both of you, *Now*!" Jen said forcefully, prompting both her friends into action.

Moments later, they were on their way to the airport.

"Mama, I gotta pee," Skylar complained from the back seat.

Cat turned around sharply. "Sky, I told you to go before we left," she scolded.

"Cat, it's probably her medicine," Billie pointed out. "Honey, can you hold it until we get there?" she asked the child.

"I don't know, Mommy," she replied.

"Try, sweetheart, okay? We'll be there in a few minutes," Billie urged.

Jen looked at a visibly agitated Cat. "Hey, I remember the last time we pulled over to let her pee? It was in the woods at Happy Trails Campground. We all ended up with poison ivy on our butts for days!" Jen exclaimed. Looking over to Cat, she saw a smile break out on her friend's face. She covered Cat's hand in her own. "Relax, sweetie, okay?" she said softly.

Cat looked at her friend and smiled. "Thanks, Jen," she said, holding the grin, and Jen's hand, all the way to the airport.

The Charlands arrived at the airport with just fifteen minutes to spare before boarding. Billie picked Skylar up and sprinted to the bathroom while Cat and Jen checked the luggage and validated their boarding passes. They were supposed to have met Doc and Ida at the ticket counter, but were told the older couple had already boarded the plane.

Billie came running across the terminal, Skylar riding on her back, hanging onto her mother's neck for dear life as the last boarding call was made for their flight. Moments later, after several hugs and kisses for Jen, they were buckled into their seats and sighing deep breaths of relief as the plane taxied to the runway.

They were on their way to Charleston.

CHAPTER 4

Cat, Billie, Doc, Ida, and the kids were met at the airport by a very relaxed Josephine and very fidgety Alexandra. Jo insisted on driving one of the cars, while their chauffeur, Chet, drove another so there would be plenty of room for the party of seven. Hugs and kisses were exchanged for several moments before Cat commented to Alex about her emotional state.

"Grams, are you all right? You seem a bit nervous," Cat said.

"Well I'm glad *somebody* noticed how upset I am," Alex said in a thick South Carolina accent as she shot impatient looks toward Jo.

"What is it, Grams?" Cat asked.

"For cryin' out loud, Alex," Jo interrupted, "It wasn't that bad!"

"Josephine Wycliffe, you nearly killed us on the way here!" Alex exclaimed. "I told ya to wear your spectacles!"

"I don't need any damned spectacles to drive Alex," she replied.

"Well I beg to differ, Josie," Alex returned.

"You can beg all you want. I ain't wearing them!" declared Jo loudly.

"Ah, Mom, Nona, let's just head home, okay? Why don't we let Doc drive so we ladies can sit together in the back seat and do some catching up on the way," Ida suggested, stepping in between her mothers.

"Now there's a smart woman!" Jo exclaimed. "Takes after her mom, she does," she added.

"I do declare. If she took after you, she'd be smokin' cigars and swearing like a sailor. I'm inclined to think she takes after her Nona," Alex countered.

Cat and Billie grinned as they watched Ida lock arms with both her mothers and lead them to the car.

"Grandpa, can I ride with you so I don't have to be in a car full of girls?" Seth asked Doc.

"Sure you can, scout. You can keep me company while the old biddies in the back seat catch up on their gossip," he said jokingly, earning him a shot in the arm from Cat.

"Daddy!" she exclaimed. "What a thing to say. Don't you be filling my son's head with such ideas."

Doc grinned and winked at Seth, who winked back as they walked to the car.

***

"Wow!" Seth exclaimed as SpireClyffe Acres came into view.

"It's so big!" Tara exclaimed. "I can't wait to explore."

All three children climbed out of the car when it came to a stop in front of the mansion. They stood there, side by side, staring wide-eyed at the massive structure.

"Is this only one house, Mama?" Skylar asked.

"Yes, it is, love. Grandma Jo and Grams live here with about a dozen people who help them take care of it," Cat explained. "Your aunts and I spent many summers here as children."

Billie lifted Skylar onto her hip then walked over to throw an arm around her son. "Pretty cool, huh?" she said.

"I'll say," Seth replied.

"This will make a great place to play hide and go seek," exclaimed Tara, who was standing in the circle of Cat's arms.

"Yes it will, as long as you play it outside," Cat replied. "There are a lot of valuable antiques, furniture and paintings in this house. There'll be no throwing yourself on the furniture here with your shoes on either. You got it?" Cat asked, looking at all three kids, who nodded in agreement.

"Can we go inside?" Seth asked, his voice cracking.

Billie looked at Cat and grinned at her son's subtle pubescent sign. Cat tried her best not to grin back, as Seth had asked that question while looking directly at her.

"Sure, honey. We'll need to ask Grams which rooms she's putting us all in. Go on inside," she urged.

Skylar ran inside after her brother and sister as soon as Billie put her down.

Cat hip-checked Billie.

"What was that for?" Billie asked.

"For almost making me laugh in Seth's face when his voice cracked."

"Well, Mama, what do you think of our little boy?" Billie asked, holding Cat in the circle of her arms.

"I'd say he's more like our little man. He's growing up Billie. I feel so old," Cat groaned, resting the top of her head on Billie's chest.

"Well, we'll grow old together then we can be crotchety like Alex and Jo. Aren't they cute?" Billie asked.

"They certainly are. If we're lucky, we'll be just like them some day," Cat replied.

"I hope so, love. I certainly hope so," Billie said, referring to the obvious love that still ran strong and true between the ladies after fifty years together.

***

"Grams, what time did mom say she'd arrive?" Billie asked Alex as she helped her grandmother prepare sandwiches for lunch.

"Laurel should be here on the six o'clock flight, just in time for dinner. I'll send Chet after them around five," Alex added.

"I'll go after them, Grams," Billie volunteered.

Alex placed a hand on Billie's arm. "Are you sure, Billie? You do know that Jim is coming too," she said.

Billie looked down as she cut the sandwich in half. "Yeah, I know. That's why I want to pick them up. I've never actually met Jim face to face. I'd rather do that without an audience," she said. Then, looking at Alex, she grinned and added, "Besides, he still has to meet you and Grandma Jo. Do you think it's fair to throw all four of us at him at the same time? Especially Josephine Wycliffe?"

Alex raised her eyebrows into her hairline. "You got a point there, darlin'," she said, grinning.

Billie placed her final sandwich on the platter then handed it to Alex while she grabbed the tray of chips and drinks. "Time to feed the animals," she said as she led the way to the patio where Jo and the kids were happily playing Marco Polo in the swimming pool.

Moments later, the patio table was surrounded by wet bodies, all clamoring to fill their dishes with sandwiches and chips.

Alex hovered around, filling glasses with soda and making sure everyone was served, when Jo snuck up on her from behind, and wrapped her arms around the taller woman. Within seconds, Jo's wet bathing suit had soaked through Alex's floral print dress.

"Ah! Josephine Wycliffe, why you have to be so ornery, I'll never know!" she yelled. "Now look at what y'all done to my dress. My word, you are goin' to be the death of me yet," she scolded.

Jo just stood there, looking at Alex with an evil glint in her eye.

"Josie, what is that look for?" Alex asked suspiciously as all eyes turned to the elderly women.

Jo took two steps toward Alex.

"Josie, I don't know what you're plannin' but...," Alex stammered, hands clenched in front of her. Her gaze darted around looking for an escape route, as Jo continued her approach.

Alex backed up, one step at a time, until she finally spared a glance behind her. "Oh, no you don't. Josephine Wycliffe, you get *that* idea right out of your head," she warned as she glanced at the pool and then steered herself toward the patio furniture behind her.

With every step Jo advanced, Alex looked backward. Finally, Jo had her backed up against the patio table. Leaning her wet body against Alex for the second time, she bent the woman backward over the table and reached out with her right hand beyond Alex's shoulder. While she had her bent over the table like that, she planted a long wet kiss on Alex's mouth then retrieved what she had been reaching for. Standing erect again, she shoved one of Doc's cigars into her mouth and winked at Alex, who was still half-reclined over the table, and quite flush from Jo's kiss.

"Your dress is wet, sweetheart," she said to Alex before wiggling her eyebrows up and down like Groucho Marx and walking away, cigar planted firmly between her teeth. "Last one in is a rotten egg!" Jo challenged as she and the children jumped back into the pool, cigar and all.

Cat, Billie, Doc and Ida just looked at each other grinning, amazed at Jo's boldness, while Alex finally composed herself enough to settle into a patio chair, wet dress and all, where she spent the next hour watching her wife play with the children, a most curious look on her face.

After cleaning up the lunch mess, Cat approached Alex, who was still sitting there watching the crew in the pool. She leaned close to her grandmother's ear and whispered knowingly, "You're gonna thank her proper-like later, aren't you, Grams?"

Alex just smiled, her eyes never leaving the woman in the pool. "Oh, yeah," she said, "Oh yeah!"

***

Billie paced back and forth in front of the arrival gate, alternately wringing her hands and chewing her fingernails.

Cat had been trying desperately to concentrate on the magazine in her lap, but was quite unsuccessful as Billie's pacing was a major distraction that she could not ignore. Finally, she put the magazine down and approached her wife.

Cat stood in front of Billie and grabbed her hands. One by one, she brought them to her mouth and kissed each one.

"Billie, calm down. Wearing a path in the tiles is not going to make this any easier," she said.

Billie's brow drew together in concentration. "Cat, this is my mother's husband, we're talking about here. You know... my *step*-father?" Billie said a bit sarcastically.

"Billie, honey, what he thinks about us is unimportant. We are who we are, and no one has the power to change that except you and me. I happen to like us just the way we are, thank you very much, and I don't give a rat's ass for what Jim Stafford thinks. I love you Billie. I love our children. I am happier now than I've been in my entire life, and I have you to thank for that," Cat professed. "How can that be wrong when it feels so right?"

Billie smiled and took a deep breath. "Maybe you're right, Cat," she said just as the flight from Flint, Michigan was announced. Billie looked nervously at Cat, then leaned down and gave her a tender kiss. "Thank you for loving me, Cat," she whispered.

"Ditto," said Cat in return.

Billie took Cat's hand and led her through the crowd to the waiting area outside security, closest to where Laurel's flight was docking. They stood on the fringes of the crowd and watched each passenger exit the secure area while waiting for the familiar dark head to appear.

"Do you see her yet, Billie?" Cat asked, standing on tiptoes and straining to see over the crowd.

Billie scanned the passengers once more. "There's Dylan...and there's mom," Billie said, waving her hand above her head to catch their attention.

Dylan saw them first. "Sis!" he called, making his way through the crowd and enveloping Billie in a bear hug when he reached her. "I've missed you, Billie," he said, planting a sloppy kiss on her cheek.

"I've missed you too, Dyl," Billie returned, hugging her brother close. *God, it feels good to have a brother*, Billie mused.

"Hey, shorty!" Dylan teased as he turned his attention to Cat. He picked her up and twirled her around in a circle before placing her feet back on the floor and hugging her hard.

Billie stood by and watched her brother's antics, her heart swelling with sisterly love for this young man.

"Just as charming as ever, hey, Dylan?" Cat replied, kissing her brother-in-law on the cheek. "It's good to see you, sweetie," she added, hugging him back.

"Look, I'm going to find the luggage while Billie meets Dad. Wanna come?" he asked Cat.

"I'd love to, Dyl, but I really should stay and support Billie during this meeting," Cat replied.

"No, Cat. Go on with Dylan. It might be better if we didn't overwhelm Jim right away with both of us standing here gawking at him. I'll make my introductions first then we'll introduce you when you come back. Okay?" Billie suggested.

"Honey, are you sure?" Cat asked

"Very," she said, bending down to give Cat a quick kiss. "Go on, I'll see you in a few minutes."

As Cat and Dylan ran off to collect the bags, Billie turned her attention to Laurel and Jim, who were finally making their way through the crowd toward her.

Laurel stopped directly in front of Billie while Jim held back a short distance. She reached out with her right hand and cupped the side of Billie's face. "Hello, sweetheart," she said.

Billie immediately enveloped her mother in a warm, affectionate hug. "Hi, Mom. I've missed you so much."

Mother and daughter held each other for a long moment, each fighting the tears that were making their way down their cheeks. After what seemed like an eternity, they broke apart and wiped each other's cheeks, laughing through their tears at their own foolishness.

Finally, Laurel introduced a very nervous Jim to Billie. Reaching back, Laurel took Jim's hand and pulled him forward toward her daughter. Jim's eyes locked on Billie's as though he was drawn to them, unable to break the gaze.

Wow! He's more nervous than I am, Billie thought. *Maybe I can use this to my advantage.*

"Jim, this is my daughter, Billie Charland. Billie, my husband Jim," Laurel said, a little awkwardly.

Jim was still unable to break the gaze.

Billie smiled most disarmingly and extended her hand to her stepfather. "Jim," she said congenially.

Jim continued to stare. Finally, Laurel elbowed him in the ribs.

"Oh, oh, sorry," he said extending his hand. "Jim. Jim Stafford. My God, you look exactly like Laurel," he exclaimed, staring once more.

Billie locked arms with her stepfather and gave him a crooked smile as she started leading him, arm in arm, toward the luggage claim area. "You know, my wife says the same thing. You'll meet her in a few minutes, but right now, I want to know more about you. Mom tells me you're a stock analyst. Tell me Jim, exactly what *does* a stock analyst do?" she asked, pretending to be totally absorbed in the one thing most men like to do, talk about…themselves.

Laurel held back and watched her daughter and husband walk away, arm in arm, grinning, and very proud of her daughter for finding his weak spot so readily.

Billie, my girl, how is it you know so much about men, when you obviously prefer women? she questioned happily as she followed them through the terminal.

Halfway to the luggage claim area, the trio met Cat and Dylan coming toward them, pushing a cart full of baggage. Billie looked across her stepfather to her mother and asked, "Sheesh, Mom! Did you bring your whole wardrobe?"

Jim grinned broadly and gave Laurel an *I told you so* look before patting the hand that Billie had hooked through his arm.

Billie flashed him another disarming smile.

Billie-girl, you're charming the pants right off him! thought Laurel excitedly. *This may be a fun reunion after all.*

As Cat and Dylan approached Billie, Jim and Laurel, Cat once again marveled at how much Billie looked like her mother, and how she was looking forward to Billie aging into the wondrous beauty they saw approaching them right now. "Damn, she's beautiful. They both are," she said to Dylan.

Dylan raised his eyebrows and nodded. "If they weren't my mom and sis, *I'd* sure be interested," he replied.

Cat elbowed Dylan in the ribs. "Sorry, curly, but the younger one is mine," she teased, causing her brother-in-law to chuckle under his breath.

Finally, the two parties came face to face. Billie released Jim's arm and went to stand by Cat. She wrapped her arm around Cat's shoulder and pulled her in close to her side while she introduced her to Jim.

"Jim, this is my wife, Caitlain, Cat for short. Cat, sweetheart, this is my stepfather, Jim Stafford," Billie said politely.

Jim was once again very nervous as his palms began to sweat. He found himself liking Billie very much, but seeing the way she was with Cat, hugging her, and calling her sweetheart just caused his stomach to do funny things. Reaching out his hand, he shook Cat's quickly, then let go abruptly wiping his hand on his trousers when he did.

Cat's eyes opened wide at the implied insult as she tightened her hold on Billie's arm. Billie and Laurel both had seen the gesture.

"Let me give you a hand with those bags, son," he said to Dylan as the two men went ahead of the ladies to deliver the bags to the curb.

Cat was livid and shaking with anger. She looked at Billie with tears of frustration in her eyes.

"Cat," Billie whispered, pulling her in close. "I'm sure he didn't mean it as an insult," she soothed.

Laurel too, wrapped her arms around Cat. "Cat, sweetheart, his palms sweat when he's nervous. He didn't mean anything by it," she added.

Cat just nodded through her sniffles and wiped her face dry, as she allowed Billie to lead her out of the terminal and to the car.

It was going to be a long week.

CHAPTER 5

The ride to SpireClyffe Acres was tense. Jim and Dylan sat in the front seat while the three women sat in the back with Billie in the middle, one arm around Cat's shoulder and the other holding Laurel's hand. Dylan sat sideways in the seat so he could talk to the ladies while Jim drove. Jim had volunteered to drive, taking directions from the GPS. During the ride, the car's occupants sat absorbed in their own thoughts.

How did I get myself involved in this situation? Jim thought to himself as his eyes focused on the road ahead of him.

He'd nearly freaked when Laurel told him she had an adult daughter. That alone was hard enough to take, but he considered himself an understanding man and found it in his heart to accept that Laurel had lived through a traumatic childhood. He was sure that some of her choices, although difficult, were probably the right ones for her at the time. What he was finding very hard to accept was the fact that his stepdaughter was gay. To top it all off, Laurel had found her mother as well, and she was also gay! All this homosexuality in his wife's family was making him wonder about Laurel. He and Laurel had argued vehemently about it for the past week or so. He felt totally ill at ease around *people like that*.

He and Laurel had several confrontations about her involvement in Billie's life. *If I had my way*, Jim thought, *she wouldn't associate with her at all*. But knowing the kind of woman Laurel is, and how wonderful a mother she is to Dylan, he knew he couldn't ask her to do that. He would have been fine with the whole thing if Laurel hadn't insisted he attend this reunion with her, and to make an effort to get to know Billie and her gay parents. Jim had serious doubts as to whether or not he could handle this. His palms were sweaty again just thinking about it!

He had been prepared to be totally turned off by Billie when he met her. He truly thought he would feel nothing but disgust and contempt, but the minute he laid eyes on her, he knew those feelings were impossible. She looked exactly like Laurel had when he met her thirty years earlier. He loved his wife dearly, and couldn't bring himself to feel contempt for someone who looked so much like the woman who owned his heart.

For several moments, he had even forgotten about her lifestyle...that is, of course, until he was introduced to Cat. At that moment, all his fears came rushing back, especially when Billie held her in her arms, and introduced her to him as her wife. His body immediately turned traitorous, sweat pouring from every crevice.

Jesus, Mary and Joseph, he thought. *I almost lost my lunch when I saw them together.* Instinctively offering his hand to the smaller woman, he shook it and then immediately wiped the sweat from his palm onto his pant leg, before it literally dripped to the floor. He was very nervous in their presence and had to get out of there as fast as possible.

Thank goodness for my son and the luggage, he thought as that convenient excuse presented itself to him. His thoughts ran along those lines during the entire ride to SpireClyffe.

Laurel sat there, holding Billie's hand as the car sped toward SpireClyffe. She shared furtive glances with Billie throughout the ride, silently apologizing for Jim's behavior.

Jim, please tell me you didn't mean to insult Cat, she pleaded silently to herself. *If you did, I'll never forgive you for intentionally hurting her.*

Laurel and Jim had argued vehemently over the past week about her family's *choice of sexuality*, as Jim put it. Laurel tried in vain to explain to Jim that homosexuality was not about choices, but about biology. At this point, Jim had actually accused *her* of being gay herself, claiming that if it was all about biology, then why had it skipped a generation? She found herself at a disadvantage, not having an answer to his question. Whether homosexuality was inherited was something Laurel was not able to explain. She only knew that in her case, it indeed had skipped a generation.

When Laurel came home from her stay with Billie and Cat during Sky's illness, she felt as if she was under a microscope. She knew that Jim was looking for signs that her daughter had somehow convinced her to join them in their *choice* of lifestyles. If it weren't so irritating, she would have laughed. After a few weeks of normal behavior, she assumed Jim was convinced that she hadn't turned gay, as the scrutiny abruptly ended.

Things appeared to be back to normal in the Stafford household, that is, until Billie called her about the reunion. All hell broke loose when she informed Jim that all of them were attending...all *three* of them. He vehemently refused to go at first, but eventually gave in when he saw how much it meant to her. Now here they were, in the car heading toward a meeting with her gay parents.

Jim's first encounter with Billie went surprisingly well, but when introduced to Cat, all hell broke loose. Laurel could only wonder what would happen when he met Alexandra and Josephine.

Holy Shit! she thought, mimicking Jo. *Jim, Mom is going to have a grand old time with you*, she mused, smiling slightly, sneaking a side way glance at Billie.

Laurel raised Billie's hand to her lips and kissed the knuckles. Billie looked at her mother and smiled. Laurel smiled back.

This is going to be a rough week, Laurel thought. *Somehow we have to make Jim see that sexual orientation is a minor part of the whole person. Jim has preached racial and religious tolerance and acceptance to Dylan since he was born. Why can't he practice what he preaches when it comes to homosexuality?* Laurel thought.

Laurel's thoughts returned to Alex and Jo, causing her to smile once more. If Jim spent the whole week with his homophobic attitude on his sleeve, Jo would make mincemeat of him.

Maybe he needs that, she thought. *Somehow, he needs to see these women as normal people, instead of messengers of the devil, as he had called them during one of their arguments over the previous weeks.*

As stressful as this week promised to be, Laurel was looking forward to spending time with her daughters and grandchildren. The few months she had spent with them while Skylar was ill were wonderful, despite the emotional upheaval their strained relationship had caused at the beginning of the visit. She was also glad that she was able to help with the children while Cat and Billie concentrated on making Skylar well again. If she did nothing else significant in her life, she would die happy knowing she was there for her daughters and grandchildren when they needed her.

Geesh, Dad, you really blew it at the airport, Dylan thought as he glanced at his very nervous father. *Poor Cat. I hope she wasn't too hurt by the gesture.* Dylan had seen his father wipe his hand on his pant leg immediately after shaking hands with Cat. *If you had done that to me, I would have decked you!*

Looking into the back seat, he watched Cat as she stared absently out the window. Billie had thrown her left arm around Cat's shoulder for support. Cat had subconsciously reached up and laced the fingers of her left hand with Billie's as it hovered over the area in front of her left breast. Dylan watched as Cat brought Billie's hand to her lips and kissed the back of it absently. The vacant stare out the window was definitely a sign that Cat was preoccupied. Dylan noticed the periodic clenching of Cat's jaw muscles as the car sped toward SpireClyffe.

Cat, I don't blame you if you're angry with him, he thought. *He certainly deserves your anger. If it helps at all, I'm glad you're part of my family. I think you're a wonderful woman, and I couldn't be happier to call you sister.*

Dylan recalled his first meeting with Cat and Billie. He had found them hovering over his mother, who was unconscious at their feet. He thought at first that they had harmed her. When he demanded they back away, Cat very curtly informed him that she was a doctor, and then ordered him to carry Laurel into the house where she could examine her. Even at that first meeting, her spunk struck a tender chord in his heart.

When he first looked at Billie...actually *looked* at her, he was awestruck at how much she resembled his mother. There was no denying that she was Laurel's daughter. He was overwhelmed by the very presence this woman radiated, learning at their first meeting that she meant business.

When he finally realized that Cat and Billie were a couple, he fully expected to be repulsed. He had grown up hearing his father preach about the evils of such hedonistic joining. Instead, he found them endearing, charming, and very much in love.

During the time he'd spent with them the last time they visited SpireClyffe Acres, Dylan took advantage of the opportunity of getting to know his sister, and he soon realized that he loved her and Cat dearly, as though they had been raised together. He was really looking forward to spending time with them again, and getting to know his nieces and nephew. It felt cool to be an uncle.

Allowing his gaze to move to his sister, Dylan once again marveled at how much she looked like his mother. A surge of brotherly love passed through him as she caught his eyes and smiled. He smiled back and made some lame comment about looking forward to the visit. He could see the hurt in her eyes for Cat. With his eyes, he silently vowed to her that his father's beliefs did not extend to him. Billie seemed to understand the message his eyes were sending as she mouthed the words, *thank you*. Dylan smiled and turned his face back to the road, wiping a tear of sensitivity from the corner of his eye.

You don't need his approval, Cat. Get over it! she told herself repeatedly as she watched the scenery fly by. *For Billie's sake, you've got to put it aside and pretend it didn't happen. Billie still loves you. She is all you need. And beside, he is just one out of how many who would be there this week?* Like she had told Billie earlier, his opinion of them didn't matter. *Then why does it hurt so much?*

Cat could feel Dylan's eyes on her as he turned in his seat to address Billie. Not wanting him to see the hurt on her face, she remained stoic, concentrating her efforts on staring out the window. She didn't want, nor did she need his pity.

Why did you suggest the genealogy search to Billie in the first place, Cat? It has caused nothing but harm, she seethed angrily at herself. *We were happy with each other and our children. We really didn't need anything more than that. No, you just couldn't leave it alone, could you?* she scolded herself.

Taking a deep breath, Cat remembered how crushed Billie was to realize she was adopted, and how angry she was at Laurel for selling her for drug money. Cat sat there and stewed at herself.

Finally, other thoughts came to mind. *Well, maybe it didn't turn out all that bad*, she thought. *Billie did find her mother...and they finally made up. And she did find out she had a brother.* Billie had always been envious of Cat's relationship with her sisters. Being an only child meant she'd missed out on all that. *And,* Cat thought, *we discovered that Grams is really her biological grandmother.* Cat smiled in spite of herself. *Well, I guess a lot of good has come out of it.*

Cat spared a glance at her wife, who sat stoically on the seat between her and Laurel. *God, Billie must feel terrible for what her stepfather did. If Daddy had done that to her, I would have died right there on the spot,* Cat thought, raising Billie's hand to her mouth and kissing the back of it in a silent message of love. Billie's hand squeezed Cat's lightly.

God, I love this woman. Well, Jim, you had just better get used to it, because I am not going to change the way I act around Billie just because you are here, she thought angrily, clenching her jaw repeatedly. *In fact, my dear sweet grandmother is going to have a field day with you,* she thought as images of what Jo would do to Jim crossed her mind. She had all she could do to keep a grin off her face. *Revenge is so sweet,* she thought.

What a mess this is, Billie thought. *This was supposed to be an enjoyable family reunion, not some gay rights demonstration.*

Billie looked straight ahead, watching the road through the windshield. A sudden thought made her smile. *Jen would be having a field day with this guy right now.* Billie fought to keep from chuckling as she remembered Jen's attack on the jogger who had made an off-colored remark about her and Cat while they were camping at Happy Trails Campground. *If I remember right, Fred had to help the guy back to his feet,* she thought, smiling once more.

Billie thought about what Cat had told her while they waited at the airport. She said that Jim's opinion of them didn't matter, that they had each other and their children, and their love. *Cat was right,* Billie thought. *We don't need his approval.*

Billie's thoughts turned to Laurel.

God, Mom must be so embarrassed by Jim's treatment of Cat. I'll need to talk to Cat...see if she's willing to sit down with Laurel and really talk about how she feels.

Billie held Cat's hand, aware that Cat was hurting inside by Jim's actions despite the lecture the smaller woman had given her at the airport. *It's so easy to philosophize when you are not the victim, Cat, and so hard to stay detached when you are,* she thought. *I know you're hurting right now, my love. I promise to make it up to you,* she silently promised, stealing a glance at her wife.

Just then, Cat raised Billie's hand to her lips and kissed the back of it. *She can feel me thinking about her.* Billie squeezed Cat's hand lightly.

Dylan telling her that he was looking forward to the visit suddenly drew Billie's attention to the front seat. She just smiled her agreement. Before he looked away, she saw something in his eyes. *What is it?* she thought. *Sympathy? Acceptance? Yeah, that's it, acceptance. He wants me to know that he doesn't share Jim's attitude.*

She found herself looking at her brother closely and hoping that she'd have a chance to get to know him better. They had missed sharing their childhood with one another. *Seth is going to love you, Dyl,* she thought. *He's been looking forward to having a guy around. Don't be surprised if he becomes your shadow over the next week,* she thought, smiling again at the love filling her heart for this young man.

Billie spared one more glance up at the rear view mirror and caught Jim's eyes. Jim looked away quickly, a look of disgust on his face.

Well, Jim, you had just better get used to it, because I am not going to change the way I act around Cat just because you are here, she thought, smiling evilly. *In fact, if you keep this behavior up, dear sweet Grandma Jo is going to have lots of fun with you,* she thought as she imagined just how Jo would react to Jim's homophobia. She had all she could do to keep a grin off her face. *Revenge is so sweet,* she thought.

***

Silence filled the car for the remainder of the drive to SpireClyffe, each occupant deep in thought, each one with a plan to survive the upcoming week. A collective sigh of relief was heard as Jim drove between the pillars at the end of the drive leading to SpireClyffe.

CHAPTER 6

Alex and Jo were waiting for them when the car pulled up to the front door of the mansion. Dylan was out of the car almost before it stopped, scooping Alex into his arms and twirling her around in a circle before putting her back down again and planting a wet kiss on her cheek.

"Grams, I missed you so much!" he exclaimed, grinning ear to ear.

"Land sakes, child," Alexandra croaked. "You sure know how to sweep a girl off her feet!" she added, pinching Dylan's cheek playfully. After planting one more kiss on Alex's cheek, he turned his attention to Jo.

"Don't you dare, if you know what's good for you," Jo said, placing a hand on the whip she wore at her side. Josephine had decided to start this week out proper-like by sending the message loud and clear to Jim that she wasn't about to tolerate any lecturing about the evils of living in sin.

"Ah, Grandma Jo, you're such a softie!" Dylan said scooping her up anyway and treating her to the same dizzy spell and sloppy kiss he left Alex with.

"So much for first impressions," she mumbled as she struggled to keep her balance.

Just then, Laurel, Jim, Billie and Cat approached the elderly women. Laurel made the introductions as Cat and Billie went to stand behind Alex and Josephine.

"Mom, Nona, this is my husband, Jim. Jim, my mothers, Alexandra Spirakis and Josephine Wycliffe," Laurel said.

Jim was soaked. His shirt was wet under the arms, and he could feel rivulets of sweat run down his back. This time, thinking ahead, he wiped his hand off on his trousers before shaking hands with Alex and Jo. Billie raised an eyebrow at him behind the elder ladies' backs. Looking up, he caught her eye as she stood just beyond Alex's shoulder. Once again, the resemblance struck him dumb, especially when Laurel turned to faced him and all three of them were aligned, one behind the other, with Laurel in front of him, then Alexandra, then Billie standing in the rear.

"My lord," he said, "the resemblance is uncanny!"

"Well, sonny, your lord isn't going to help you here, considering he doesn't like *our* kind,." Josephine said, placing her hand once more on the coil of whip hanging on her waistband of her safari pants. Reaching up, she pushed her fedora back on her head then reached into her shirt pocket to retrieve a cigar. Biting the end of it off, she spat it on the ground then clamped the stogie between her teeth. All of this was done without breaking eye contact with Jim. "I need a light," she demanded to no one in particular.

Jim gulped audibly.

Billie grinned.

Alexandra died of embarrassment.

Dylan tried desperately to keep a straight face.

Laurel bit her lip to keep from laughing.

Cat smiled broadly as she approached Josephine and put her arm around her waist. "You know you gave up smoking years ago," Cat said, grinning ear to ear at Jim's uneasiness.

Still maintaining eye contact with Jim, she said, "Yeah, you're right, I did. Guess I'll have to settle for a drink then," she said. Taking two steps forward, she stopped directly in front of Jim, within inches of his nose. Hands on her hips, she looked directly into his face, cigar still clenched in her teeth. "You man enough to have a drink with your mother-in-law?" she asked.

"Ah...ah...I...I... sure," he said

Billie quickly excused herself, beating a hasty exit before she burst out laughing. Dylan quickly followed as the siblings fell into each other's arms inside the atrium of the house, laughing their fool heads off.

***

"Billie?" Ida asked. "Honey, are you okay?" she said, noticing that her daughter-in-law was leaning heavily against a young man with the curly blonde hair.

"Mom!" Billie exclaimed, wiping tears of laughter from her eyes. "Mom," she said again, "This is Dylan, your nephew." Billie took a deep breath to compose herself as she introduced her brother to Cat's mother. "Dylan, Cat's Mom, Ida."

Ida's eyes grew wide as she hugged the young man. "Dylan," she said. "It's so good to finally meet you. My, you're a handsome one," she added, holding him by the shoulders, an arm's length away. Then, looking at Billie, she added. "That means your mother is here. Where is she?"

"I'm afraid we deserted her and Cat to Grandma Jo's antics," she confessed.

"Grandma Jo?" Ida said. "I'm almost afraid to ask what she's up to this time."

"She's up to giving Dad a lesson in tolerance," Dylan said, breaking down once more into fits of laughter, causing Billie to join him.

Ida put her hands on her hips. "You two are incorrigible!" she exclaimed. "Where are they?" she asked, heading in the direction that Billie pointed while holding her stomach through the laughter.

"I suppose we'd better get hold of ourselves and go back to rescue your Dad, don't you think?" Billie asked her brother.

Dylan suddenly turned serious. "No. I think he deserves everything he is getting right now. Billie, I saw the way he treated Cat at the airport. That was very rude. I'm actually surprised Cat controlled herself as well as she did. Had it been me, well, let's just say the only thing that might have saved him is the fact that he's my father," Dylan explained.

Billie sobered at the thought. "Yeah, you're right. Cat was pretty upset. You know, she lectured me at the airport before your plane arrived about this very thing. I guess in theory you can accept things more readily than in practice. I'll take her aside and make sure she's okay," Billie said.

"Mommy!" a voice suddenly rang from behind them.

Billie turned around just in time to catch a running Skylar in her arms. Scooping her up, she held her close and nuzzled her neck, making the child squeal.

"Hey, rugrat," she said. "Where's brother and sister?" she asked.

"They're with Grandpa, puttin' the horses away," she replied, looking shyly at Dylan, putting her head on Billie's shoulder.

Billie saw Skylar looking coyly at Dylan. "Sky," she said to the child, "This is your uncle Dylan, Mommy's brother."

Dylan reached out to the child and asked for her hand, which she extended shyly.

He bowed regally. "Princess Skylar," he said, kissing the back of her hand. "It's a pleasure to make your acquaintance."

Skylar giggled and pulled her hand back. Billie grinned.

"Mom, it was awesome!" Tara exclaimed bursting into the room as if she owned the place, drawing the adults' attention to herself. "Seth and I had a race, and I beat him! It was so cool!" she said proudly, arms flailing every which way. Eyeing Dylan curiously, she added, "Who's he?"

"As subtle as ever, huh, Tara?" Billie teased.

Dylan grinned. "Hi, Tara, I'm your Uncle Dylan." he said, extending his hand toward the eleven-year-old.

Tara shook it firmly and grinned. "You don't look like Mom," she observed.

Billie shook her head side to side at her daughter's boldness.

"Nope, I don't. I look like my dad. You mom looks like our mother," he explained.

Tara looked at Billie. "Nana's here too?" she questioned excitedly. Receiving a nod from Billie, she exclaimed, "All right!" then started to leave the room.

"Wait, Tare. I wanna see Nana too!" Skylar exclaimed, wiggling out of Billie's arms. Soon, both girls were gone in search of their grandmother.

Billie looked at Dylan. "Well, that's two of the three."

No sooner had she said the words, than Seth entered the room. Seth immediately went to his mother and hugged her.

Billie dropped a kiss on top of his head. "Did you have a good ride, honey?" she asked.

Seth pulled out of his mother's embrace, and nodded his head. "It was awesome, but of course, Tara had to be a show-off again," he said, slightly embarrassed that his sister had beat him. "Little sisters can be such a pain," he added.

Dylan laughed. "You know, I wanted a brother or sister all my life and didn't have one, until now," he said, reaching out his hand to Billie.

Billie took his hand and made the introductions to Seth. "Honey, this is your Uncle Dylan. Dylan, this is Seth."

Seth grinned ear to ear. "Cool! Finally another guy around the place!" he said, shaking his hand. Billie suddenly felt old as she looked at her son and brother together. Seth was rapidly approaching manhood. He was obviously going to inherit her height as he stood nearly 5'9" at thirteen years old, with many more years of growing to do.

"Hey, what am I, chopped liver?" Doc said coming up behind the group.

"Sorry Grandpa," Seth said. "But, well, you're kinda old."

"Seth Michael Charland! What a thing to say to your grandfather!" Billie said aghast.

Doc chuckled. "Don't worry, daughter. I understand. I was thirteen once, several hundred years ago that is," he said, winking at Seth. Then, turning to Dylan, he extended his hand, shaking it firmly. "You must be Dylan," he said. "I'm Cat's dad, so, I guess that makes me your uncle, but you can call me Doc." Then, turning to Billie he added, "So your mother and father are here too?"

Billie cringed slightly at the mention of Jim being her father. "Yeah, they're here," she said. Then looking to both Doc and Dylan, she added, "I guess we've left Jim at the mercy of Grandma Jo long enough, huh? We'd better go see how things are going, don't you think?"

"You left that poor man with Josephine?" Doc said in astonishment. "You are a cruel woman, Billie," he added jokingly, a huge smile plastered on his face.

Dylan placed a hand on his uncle's shoulder. "Believe me, Doc, he deserves it!" he said, chuckling. "But you're right, maybe we should go rescue him."

***

They found the rest of the crew in the parlor. Josephine still had her unlit cigar in her mouth, and whip on her hip. Pacing back and forth in front of her audience, she recalled how she successfully broke the Viet Cong code used to set up ambushes against US troops during the Vietnamese War fifty years earlier. Ida and Cat, having heard the story about a hundred times over the past thirty years, had politely excused themselves to check with Maggie on dinner, while Laurel, Jim, and the children sat captivated by Josephine's story…at least Tara was captivated. Skylar sat curled up in Laurel's lap sound asleep.

Opening the door to the parlor, Billie peeked in and raised her eyebrows when she saw her daughter asleep in Laurel's arms. Silently closing the door, she relayed to the others what she had seen.

Doc smiled broadly. "Don't tell me…the Viet Cong code?" he asked. Looking to Dylan and Seth, he said, "You'll love this one. Josephine is a natural born story teller." He ushered them into the parlor as Billie excused herself to look for Cat.

Billie found the object of her desire in the pantry, where Maggie had sent her to retrieve a new package of napkins. Ida and Alexandra were in the dining room discussing seating arrangements for dinner.

Billie snuck up behind Cat and clamped her hand around her mouth. "Don't make a sound if you know what's good for you," she purred into Cat's ear,

Cat grinned behind the hand covering her mouth then nodded her head rapidly.

Removing her hand, Billie wrapped both arms around Cat's waist and started a tactical exploration of the smaller woman's midriff, while Cat pressed her head into Billie's shoulder and closed her eyes.

Making their way up Cat's sides, Billie's hands rested on her shoulders as she turned the smaller woman around to face her. Cat's cheeks were flush with desire as Billie lowered her face and claimed her lips, tilting Cat's chin upward with two fingers. Breaking the kiss, Billie looked into her wife's eyes and said, "Hi!"

"Hi, yourself," she replied.

Billie took Cat's face between her hands and traced the bone structure across finely chiseled cheeks with her thumbs. "Are you all right?" she asked.

"I am now," Cat said, pressing herself into Billie.

Once more, Billie lowered her head and placed gentle kisses on Cat's lips. Cat closed her eyes and moaned as Billie made her way across Cat's jaw to the sensitive skin behind her left ear.

"Cat, I'm sorry for the way Jim treated you today," Billie whispered into her ear.

Cat's heart was racing wildly with desire. "Who?" she asked, causing Billie to grin.

"I love you, Cat," the tall woman said, nipping lightly at her wife's earlobe. Tremors ran through the body that had surrendered itself into her arms.

"Oh, God, Billie. You're making me crazy," Cat said shakily as her hands made their way behind Billie and pulled the T-shirt out of Billie's waistband. Within seconds, Cat's hands were under Billie's shirt, kneading the muscular flesh on her wife's back.

Billie reached behind Cat and shoved her hands into the waistband of her shorts, cupping Cat's bottom and pulling their lower bodies together as she buried her face into Cat's neck. Billie sunk her teeth into the corded muscle of Cat's neck, causing her to moan loudly.

"Sweet Aphrodite!" Cat exclaimed loudly.

"There you are!" Maggie exclaimed. "I should have looked here first. You two certainly have Wycliffe/Spirakis blood running through your veins! This is one of your grandmothers' favorite places for makin' out too!" she teased.

Hands quickly found their way out from under the other's clothing as Cat buried her face in Billie's shoulder, embarrassed beyond belief.

"Now, there's no reason to be blushin', Miss Cat. Old Maggie here still remembers what it's like to be young and in love, and I'm long past being shocked by public displays of affection. Heaven knows, Miss Josephine has seen to that!" she exclaimed, causing Cat and Billie to chuckle.

Maggie turned to go, then stopped and looked over her shoulder. "By the way, child, did you find the napkins I sent ya in here for?"

Billie reached up to the shelf and grabbing the bag of napkins that Cat would have needed the step stool to retrieve. Giving them to Cat, she grinned evilly.

"I don't want to hear anything about being vertically challenged, got it, Miss Show-off?" Cat said, a twinkle in her eye.

Billie leaned over and whispered in Cat's ear, "How about *horizontally* challenged, huh?"

Cat grinned seductively. "I'll take that challenge later, my love," she said.

***

Dinner was an exercise in controlled chaos. Having had to prepare meals for Alex and Jo's frequent dinner parties, Maggie was well versed in handling large crowds, so a group of 12 people was relatively easy. What she found difficult was the need to constantly chase Ida and Laurel out of the kitchen. Finally, after politely asking the ladies to leave for the fourth time, she picked up a large cleaver and waved it around in the air.

"Now I'm gonna say this just one more time, then heads are gonna roll! This is *my* kitchen. You are here to enjoy yourselves, not help prepare the meals. You two ladies may be the mistress' daughters, but this is *my* kitchen, understand? Miss Ida, you should know that by now, having grown up in this house. Now scoot your behinds outta here, and don't come back!" she shouted.

Ida and Laurel looked at each other with shocked expressions.

"Scoot!" Maggie shouted once more.

Both ladies turned on their heels and practically ran out of the kitchen, into the dining room where Jo and Alex were helping to organize the seating.

Hearing the commotion in the kitchen, and seeing the two ladies exit in haste, Josephine chuckled and said, "I see you two have been introduced to Maggie's cleaver."

"Mom, that woman is nuts!" Laurel said in disbelief.

Josephine walked up to Laurel and patted her on the cheek. "No, sweetheart, she's just real possessive about her kitchen. Hell, even Alex and I don't dare go in there during a dinner party!"

"All right, everyone, let's take our seats and enjoy this wonderful meal that Maggie has seen fit to prepare for us," Alex said, flitting around like the perfect hostess, waving her hands about.

After a few moments, everyone was seated. Jo and Alex at the ends of the table, Jim, Laurel, Dylan, Doc and Ida on one side, Billie, Cat, Seth, Tara and Skylar on the other. They were seated such that Jim was sitting on Jo's right, Cat on her left. Seth and Dylan, and Laurel and Billie sat opposite each other.

"Josie, darlin' would you like to say a few words before we enjoy this fine meal?" Alex asked.

Jo stood at the end of the table and picked up her wine glass. Before she could say a word, she noticed Alex at the opposite end of the table gesturing wildly. She looked like she was grabbing for something on top of her head. After a few seconds of not understanding what Alexandra was getting at, Josephine became impatient.

"For the love of Zeus, Alex, what is it?" she questioned loudly.

"Josephine Wycliffe, where are your manners? Please remove your hat at the table," Alex replied.

"Oh, sorry," she said, grabbing the fedora off her head and placing the hat directly on the plate in front of her.

Alexandra lowered her head in her hands and shook it side to side.

Billie and Cat glanced at each other and grinned.

Dylan looked down at his plate and tried hard not to laugh.

Ida kicked Doc under the table as a warning to keep his mouth shut.

Jim stared open mouthed at his crass mother-in-law.

Laurel chuckled under her breath.

The kids thought Grandma Jo was so cool!

Josephine was oblivious to the commotion around her. Lifting her wine glass, she began. "Fifty years ago, a very young and naive Josephine Wycliffe was working on a mission for the US government deciphering enemy code..."

Doc leaned in to whisper in Ida's ear, "Naive? Josephine was born with a cigar in one hand and a whip in the other...ooomph!" he exclaimed as Ida kicked him under the table once more.

"I had resigned myself to being alone. Considering I was one of *those* women," she said pointedly to Jim, "I accepted the fact that I would never marry and have a family."

Billie reached over and took Cat's hand under the table. They exchanged a warm and loving look.

"Then one day, a tall, dark-haired, blue eyed beauty was brought in by my commanding officer to assist me. She took my breath away with her presence," Josephine said, making eye contact with Alex at the other end of the table.

Alex blushed profusely.

"I was captivated...a willing prisoner trapped in the depth of blue eyes," she continued. "We fell in love and decided to spend the rest of our lives together. Then, by the grace of God we had Ida, and from her she saw fit to bless us with Cat and her sisters, and eight beautiful great grandchildren."

Ida smiled at Cat and the children, acknowledging that she too, considered them gifts from above.

Josephine paused for a moment to take a deep breath before continuing. "Just when we thought we had been graced with all the wonderful things life could bring, along came Billie, who helped us to find the one missing piece of our souls.

Jo looked around the table to be certain she still had everyone's full attention before continuing. "Laurel, sweetheart," she said, directly addressing the woman who was fighting to keep tears from her eyes. "Your mother had a void in her heart for many years, believing that you had died as a baby. Finding not only you, but two beautiful grandchildren has made both of us complete."

Billie and Dylan looked at each other and smiled. Billie reached her hand across the table and took Laurel's, squeezing it for a moment before releasing it.

"So, for all these things, I am grateful. Fifty years ago, I was content to live my life alone. Today, I can't imagine how I would have survived without my Alexandra. And now we have all of you. Thank the gods," she said, raising her glass.

"Thank the gods," rang out a chorus around the table as they all sipped from their glasses.

"Let's eat!" Josephine exclaimed. "I've got plans for after dinner. All this mushy talk has made me horny!"

Jim spat his wine across the table…all over Cat.

Cat stood up, fuming, and stomped away, Billie right on her heels.

Laurel sat there dumfounded.

"Grams, what does horny mean?" Skylar asked innocently.

Three more mouthfuls of wine flew across the table from Doc, Ida and Dylan.

Alex dropped her head into her hands and died of embarrassment.

It was going to be a long week.

CHAPTER 7

Cat leaned against the window frame of their bedroom overlooking the courtyard and watched Dylan play football with the kids. It was Dylan and Skylar against Seth and Tara. Cat smiled as Skylar caught the ball and started running toward the goal, only to have Dylan come up behind her, pick her up and run the rest of the way with her in his arms. Seth and Tara piled on top of him as they made a touchdown.

A pair of arms suddenly circled Cat's waist from behind. "Hmm, you smell good," Billie said, burying her nose in Cat's freshly shampooed hair. Looking over Cat's shoulder, she chuckled as Dylan accidentally on purpose missed a tackle on Tara, allowing her to score.

"I really like your brother, Billie," Cat said. "And your mom."

Billie's arms instinctively tightened around Cat's waist. "And Jim?" she asked.

"Jim will take some work," Cat admitted. Turning around in Billie's arms, she wrapped her own arms around Billie's waist. "Hold me," she said, laying her head against Billie's chest.

"Forever," came the reply as Billie rested her cheek on top of Cat's head.

Billie's hands roamed up and down Cat's back, rubbing gently in a sensual rhythm.

Cat's hands dropped lower to cup Billie's bottom, squeezing it gently.

"Billie," Cat said.

"Yes, love?" Billie responded, a feeling of sexual pleasure starting to permeate her being.

"Do you think he'll come around? I mean, I don't ever expect him to support our lifestyle, but it would be nice for him to at least accept us the way we are," Cat explained.

"I don't know, Cat. I know that he loves Laurel very much. He wouldn't be here if he didn't. I'm hoping for her sake that he at least makes an effort to accept us. It will drive a wedge between them if he doesn't," Billie replied.

Cat turned her face toward Billie's chest and placed kisses on the bare skin above her tank top.

Billie's chin rested on top of Cat's head. "That feels good, Cat," she purred.

Cat tightened her hold on Billie's bottom as she lowered her kisses to her wife's breasts through the material of the shirt.

Billie moaned out her pleasure, pressing her breasts forward.

Removing her hands from Billie's bottom, Cat placed them on Billie's shoulders and pushed her up against the wall next to the window.

Billie's hands instinctively flattened against the wall on both sides of her hips, as she gave Cat total access to her body.

Seeing that Billie had cleared the way for her, Cat immediately cupped her wife's breasts in her hands and gently squeezed, pinching the nipples through her shirt.

Billie's head flew backward, contacting the wall with an audible thud. "God, Cat!" she exclaimed.

Cat leaned in and whispered in Billie' ear, "Bend your knee for me, love."

Billie did as she was told, as Cat straddled her wife's knee. Rocking back and forth. The material of her jean cutoffs rubbed on her sensitive skin, raising her own level of excitement several degrees. While keeping a steady rhythm, Cat lifted Billie's shirt upward, exposing two full, firm orbs that were just waiting to be feasted upon. Cat wasted no time as she took one of the precious gems into her mouth and sucked hard.

Billie moaned loudly, again, banging her head into the wall.

Moving to the other breast, Cat once again took her fill, sucking, biting, teasing, while Billie pressed her breasts toward, and the rest of her body back against the wall. While suckling at one breast, Cat reached up and snapped at the other nipple with her thumb and middle finger.

Billie came off the wall as the combination of pleasure and pain from the action nearly caused her to collapse on the spot. She wrapped her arms around Cat for support, her knees too weak to hold her on their own. "Cat, I need to lie down," she said in gasping breaths as they made their way to the bed.

Lying Billie on her back, Cat climbed on the bed and knelt down between her wife's legs. Cat positioned herself so that Billie's center was pressed into her abdomen as she lowered her body down over her prone wife and continued to administer to Billie's breasts, pushing the tank top high above the voluptuous mounds. Billie grasped the comforter on either side of herself as her chest strained upward toward Cat's willing mouth, and her head pressed backwards, pushing her chin toward the ceiling. Her eyes were closed as she called out Cat's name repeatedly, interspersed with several gods and goddesses. Once again, Cat reached up and snapped at Billie's nipple. Billie's whole body convulsed at the sensation, pushing her very near the edge of oblivion.

Cat repeated the action several times until Billie just couldn't take any more. Reaching up, she grasped the sides of Cat's head and said very loudly, right into her face, "Take me, please!" ... just as the door to their room opened.

"Cat, I came to apol...Oh, my God!" Jim said as he took in the sight before him. There on the bed was his daughter-in-law, lying between the legs of his stepdaughter, whose shirt was pushed up, exposing very full and inviting breasts, nipples erect with desire. Cat's head was clasped between Billie's hands, erotic desire written across both of their faces. There was absolutely no doubt about what he had walked in on.

***

Dylan stoked the embers in the fireplace before adding another log. The adults were all sitting around the fireplace in the parlor, drinking snifters of brandy, all except Jim and Laurel, who were curiously absent. The kids had been put to bed a short while earlier.

Billie was sitting on the floor, leaning against the couch with Cat sitting between her legs, wrapped in her arms. Doc and Ida were sitting on the couch, Doc's arm around Ida's shoulder. Alex and Jo were in their favorite chairs, hands resting clasped on the small table between the seats, while Dylan stood at the mantle, watching the fire.

Cat yawned, resting her head back on Billie's chest. Billie brushed the hair from Cat's face then leaned down to kiss the top of her head. "Tired, love?" she asked.

Cat nodded her head as she yawned once more.

"You're not the only one," Dylan said as the nodded his head in Josephine's direction.

Jo was sitting there, with her chin on her chest, snoring lightly.

"I guess I'd better get her to bed," Alex commented, squeezing Jo's hand and calling out her name until she woke up. "Josie, darlin', come on dear, time for bed," she said.

Josephine mumbled something about deciphering the ambush code as she almost nodded off again.

"Come on, sugar, let's go to bed," Alex said as she helped Jo to her feet and directed her toward the parlor door. "G'night everyone."

"Good night Nona, Mom. Goodnight Grams," came the chorus of replies.

"Mom, what time are the girls coming in tomorrow?" Cat asked.

"Bridget should be here around ten, Amy around noon, and I think Drew's plane arrives at about three. They should all be here in time for dinner," Ida replied.

"The kids are kind of excited about seeing their cousins again. They haven't seen them since our wedding. How long has it been?" Cat said, looking up at Billie. "Five years?"

"Almost," Billie replied, smiling.

Cat yawned for the third time. "Goodness!" she said.

Billie pushed Cat into a sitting position as she climbed to her feet. Reaching a hand down, she said, "Come on, time for bed."

Cat went willingly, saying her good nights to her parents and brother-in-law before following her wife to bed.

Dylan was the next to turn in after tamping the embers down to ash, followed by Doc and Ida, who turned out the lights as they went.

Tomorrow would be a busy day.

***

Rising early as usual the next morning, Billie went directly to Dylan's room. Rousting her brother out of bed, she informed him that he was going on her run with her.

"What? Are you crazy? Billie, it's only six a.m.!" he exclaimed, looking at his watch through sleep-ladened eyes.

"Come on, move it. It won't kill you. Beside, I need to talk," she said.

Dylan paused for a moment then begrudgingly complied. "Oh, all right," he said, throwing his feet over the side. "Give me a minute, okay?" he asked.

"All right. I'll meet you in the kitchen in five," Billie said.

As promised, Dylan showed up five minutes later, dressed in running shorts, muscle T-shirt and running shoes. Billie remarked to herself, not for the first time, how handsome her brother was. *He's a good guy too. He'll make some lucky girl a good husband some day*, she thought.

"Ready?" she asked.

"As ready as I'll ever be," Dylan replied. "You're insane doing this so early in the morning, you know that?" he said to his sister.

Billie chuckled. "Gotta beat the heat and humidity. Morning is the best time to do that," she replied.

"You could skip it all together," her brother suggested.

"Yeah, but then how would I keep my girlish figure?" Billie teased.

Dylan looked her up and down and once again noted how sexy she was. The sports bra, spandex running shorts and running shoes left little to the imagination. *Too bad she's my sister,* he chuckled to himself. To Billie, he said, "Yeah, you may be right. You gotta work extra hard to keep fit when you're as old as *you* are!"

"You little shit!" Billie said, chasing her brother out the door.

Billie and Dylan ran for five miles then spent some time walking and getting to know each other better.

"He walked in on you and Cat?" Dylan exclaimed in disbelief. "Holy shit. He must have had a coronary."

"Him? What about us? Believe me, Dyl, we were in no position to take visitors…literally in no position," Billie grinned.

"Wow. Did he apologize later?" Dylan asked.

"Actually, we haven't seen him since it happened. He and Mom were suspiciously absent last night in the parlor. Did you notice that?" she commented.

"You know, you're right," Dylan remarked. Then looking at his sister, and blushing slightly he asked, "Billie, do you think he was, you know, turned on by what he saw?"

Billie grinned. "You know, Cat and I wondered the same thing. He probably was," she said. "There doesn't seem to be any other excuse for *both* of them disappearing after it happened," she remarked.

Dylan just nodded and visibly shivered…a fact not missed by Billie.

"Disturbing…huh?" Billie asked.

"You got that right! The thought of my parents having sex is just… just so not cool."

Billie grinned and an easy silence fell between them.

"Dyl, can I ask you something?" Billie asked after a few moments.

Dylan looked at his sister. "How do I know I won't like this particular question?" he asked, grinning.

Billie gave her brother a hip check in response.

"All right, sis, what would you like to know?" he said.

"Well," Billie said, reaching up to tuck her long hair behind her ears, "What is it about men? I mean, I know why *I* am turned on by seeing two women together, but why men? What is it about two women that is such a turn on for them?" she asked.

Dylan looked everywhere but at his sister.

Billie sensed his discomfort and reached out to touch his arm. They stopped walking and looked at each other. "Dyl, I'm sorry if I'm embarrassing you, but I'd really like to know. I mean, men are so quick to condemn our kind, yet they seem to enjoy watching two women make love. I just don't get it," she said.

Dylan placed his hands on his hips and sighed deeply. "Well," he said, "I think there are two reasons. First, seeing a woman in the throes of passion is very stimulating. Seeing two women in the throes of passion is doubly exciting. But I think the main reason men get off on seeing two women together, is that most of them fantasize about being in the middle of them, you know, making love to two women at the same time," he answered, blushing to the roots of his hair.

Billie raised her eyebrows high into her hairline as she listened to her brother's explanation. "You're kidding, right?" she asked incredulously. "I mean, I don't believe there's a man alive that can last long enough to satisfy two women. Hell, some of them don't last long enough to satisfy one!" she exclaimed.

Dylan grinned at his sister's amazement. "I hate to admit it, sis, but you're right. It doesn't hurt to dream, though," he said as they resumed their walk. A short time later, he looked over at Billie who was still deep in thought. "You know, whoever designed men and women must have had his head up his ass!" he said, chuckling to himself.

Billie looked at Dylan and smiled. "Oh, I don't know about that, Dyl. I kind of like Cat just the way she is. Come on, I'll race ya back!" she said, getting a head start on her brother.

"Hey, no fair!" he said taking off behind her.

***

Billie and Dylan arrived back at the mansion around eight. Walking into the kitchen, they saw Tara and Skylar enjoying a blueberry pancake breakfast, happily dished up by Maggie.

"Good morning, Miss Billie, Mr. Dylan," Maggie said cheerfully, placing another pancake in Tara's plate.

Billie walked over and kissed Maggie on the cheek. "Maggie, I really wish you'd drop the Miss thing, okay?" she asked the jovial cook.

"Anything you say, Miss Billie," Maggie replied, causing the girls to giggle.

Billie swooped down on her daughters, tickling them each unmercifully. "Hey, rugrats, whose side are you on here, anyway?" she asked the laughing children.

"Maggie's!" Tara exclaimed. "She makes great pancakes!"

"Yeah, Maggie!" Skylar repeated.

Billie threw her hands up in the air and looked at Dylan. "Traitors! My children are traitors! Well little Miss Benedict Arnolds," she said, "do you happen to know where Mama is right now?" she asked.

"Shhtill shleepin'," Tara mumbled around a mouthful of blueberry pancakes.

"Oh, she is, is she?" Billie said, wiggling evil eyebrows up and down at Dylan. Then re-addressing her daughters, she added, "You girls enjoy your breakfast, all right? I'll see you in a little while." Kissing both girls on the head, she left in search of Cat.

Billie slowly pushed open the door to their room and peered in. There, sprawled across the bed, was Cat, lying on her side, one arm under her pillow, her legs askew over and under the blankets. Her nightshirt had crept its way up around her waist. The morning sun had made its way into the room, falling across the foot of the bed and bathing Cat's lower body in yellow brilliance.

Quietly slipping into the room, Billie closed the door and leaned against it. *My God, Cat, you are so beautiful*, Billie thought as she watched her wife sleep. Quickly showering away the sweat from her run, Billie returned to Cat several moments later. Reaching for the nightshirt she had discarded earlier that morning, she slipped it over her head and climbed into bed behind Cat. Rolling onto her side, she spooned herself behind the smaller woman and pulled her in close.

Cat stirred in her sleep. "Hmm," she moaned, pressing herself back into Billie, who wrapped her arms even tighter around the sleeping beauty.

"I love you, Cat," Billie whispered in her wife's ear.

Cat smiled in her sleep.

"You are the most beautiful woman I have ever laid eyes on," Billie said softly.

Cat rolled over, her eyes still closed, as she snuggled deep into Billie's embrace.

Billie placed several kisses on the redhead's face. "You are my reason for living," she said, kissing Cat's nose.

"As you are mine," Cat smiled flashing emerald green eyes at the tall woman lying beside her.

Billie claimed Cat's lips in a searing kiss, ending up by lying on top of her prone wife. "Good morning, love," she said, kissing her tenderly once more.

"Good morning," Cat said, lifting her mouth to Billie's, hungry for contact. "Kiss me, Billie," she demanded.

Billie was happy to oblige as she lowered her face once more to Cat's.

Suddenly, a knock came to the door.

"Damn!" Cat whispered under her breath.

"Cat, Billie, may I come in?" Laurel just asked from behind the door.

Billie rolled onto her back and sighed. "Come in, Mom," she called out.

Laurel pushed the door open and looked in. Cat scooted up and sat with her back against the headboard, patting the bed beside her for Laurel to sit down.

Walking across the room, Laurel approached the edge of the bed and sat down. Looking at Cat and then at Billie, she said, "I came to apologize for Jim's behavior since we arrived, especially toward you, Cat," she began.

Cat looked at her sympathetically while Billie stared at the ceiling.

Wringing her hands together, Laurel continued. "Jim told me what happened last night...how he walked in on you two. He was totally unprepared for what he saw. You have to understand that his upbringing was very strict. He was taught that your kind of love was forbidden. It will take a while for him to come to terms with it. Please be patient with him," Laurel finished.

Laurel finished her little speech then looked at the women on the bed.

Billie looked over at her mother. "Apology not accepted, Mother," she said coldly.

"Billie!" Cat exclaimed.

Rising onto her elbow, she placed her hand on Cat's thigh and looked into her eyes. "No, Cat. This is not acceptable." Then, turning to her mother, she added, "Mom, I'm grateful that you're here, really I am, but this apology has to come from Jim, not you. Does he even know you're here?" she asked.

Laurel shook her head and looked down at her hands. Cat reached out and placed her hand on top of Laurel's clasped ones.

Billie took Laurel's chin and turned her face toward her. "Mom," she said, making eye contact with the older woman, "Do you feel the same way Jim does, about us, I mean?" she asked, holding her breath waiting for the reply.

Laurel looked into Billie's eyes for several moments before shaking her head loose and looking at Cat, then down at her hands. She opened her hands to take Cat's smaller one inside, squeezing it gently.

"Billie, I won't pretend to understand your lifestyle, but I do know that when I'm around you and Cat, I see a magic between you that I could only dream of having with Jim. I understand the emotional fulfillment you get from each other. I can't say I am comfortable with the physical aspect of it," she said, blushing as she looked at her hands once more, "But I can see how happy you are together, and how much you complete each other. How can I argue with that? So, do I understand it? Not entirely. Do I embrace it? Not exactly, but you are my daughter,

Billie, and I love you and Cat, and I *so very much* want you to be happy," she finished, her eyes misty with unshed tears.

Cat smiled and hugged her mother-in-law.

Billie placed her hand on Laurel's upper arm and rubbed it up and down. "Mom, could I interest you in a little group cuddling?" she asked.

Laurel grinned as she climbed into the bed between the women and lay on her back. Soon, she had two heads resting on her shoulders, one dark, one light, as her arms wrapped around her daughters. Turning her head side to side, she kissed one then the other on the head, and closed her eyes. Soon, all three were sleeping peacefully, wrapped in a cocoon of love.

CHAPTER 8

Laurel, Cat and Billie rolled out of bed later that morning to a relatively quiet house. Doc and Ida had left moments earlier to meet Bridget's ten a.m. flight. Meandering through the quiet house, they made their way to the kitchen, where Maggie was starting preparations for the crew that would be there at lunch time.

"Good morning, Maggie," Cat said as they entered the kitchen.

Turning around, Maggie placed her hands on her hips. "Land sakes! The day is nearly over, and here y'all are just getting out of bed. Why, in my day, I'd have a full day's work in by now!" she scolded. "Sit you down at the table and I'll fetch the coffee."

Laurel looked a little fearfully at the small woman who had threatened her and Ida with a meat cleaver the night before.

Billie grinned and caught Maggie in a bear hug. "Come here, woman!" she said, hugging her tightly.

Maggie wiggled herself free from Billie's embrace and swatted her on the bottom. "Why, you insolent little pup! Get your butt over there right now, or no breakfast for you!" she warned.

Billie laughed and placed a kiss on Maggie's cheek. "At least let me help with the coffee, okay?" she said.

"You aren't gonna go away less'n I let you help, are ya?" she said, looking at Billie with mock indignation.

"Nope!" Billie replied as she grabbed four mugs from the cupboard and filled them with the rich dark liquid. She carried two of them to the table and placed them in front of Cat and Laurel, then returned to the counter for the other two. She grabbed them both in one hand and circled Maggie's waist with the other. "Come on, you're taking a coffee break with us," she said.

Maggie looked at Billie, who towered nearly a foot over her, and prepared to argue.

Before she could get a word in edgewise, Billie lifted her eyebrow and said, "I don't want to hear it! Now *you* get *your* butt over there and sit down!"

Grumbling under her breath about kids today, Maggie shuffled over to the table and sat down with the women to enjoy her break.

***

An hour later, Cat and Laurel left for the flower garden to pick a bouquet of flowers to decorate the dining room table for that evening's dinner. Billie opted to keep company with Maggie in the kitchen, leaning her tall frame against the edge of the counter, ankles crossed, while sipping yet another mug of coffee.

Before long, the house started to fill with people. First, Jim and Dylan returned from a horseback ride, entering the house through the kitchen.

"Hey, sis!" Dylan said cheerfully, kissing Billie on the cheek. "Where's your better half?" he asked.

Billie smiled. "She's out in the garden with Mom, picking flowers for the dining room. Did you have a nice ride?" she asked.

"Great!" he said. "I even got the old man out this morning, hey, Dad?" he said, turning to look at his father.

Jim looked everywhere but at Billie. "Yeah," he mumbled, finally making eye contact with his stepdaughter.

Billie raised her eyebrows at him, daring him to say more. He quickly looked away and excused himself to change his clothes.

Billie and Dylan watched him go. "Did he say anything to you about what happened?" Billie asked.

"Not directly. He doesn't realize that I know about it," Dylan replied.

"What do you mean, not directly?" she asked.

"Well, he asked me what I thought about you and Cat, and Grandmas Alex and Jo. I think he was expecting me to condemn you for your lifestyle choices," her brother explained.

Billie was a little disturbed by her brother's words. "Dyl, do you *really* think this is a matter of choice?" she asked in a slightly irritated voice.

"Whoa, chill out, sis. Those were his words, not mine. No, I don't think it's a matter of choice, no more than my attraction to women is," he replied.

"I'm sorry, Dyl," she said, running her hand through her hair, "So what did you tell him about us and the grandmothers?" Billie asked.

Before answering, Dylan grabbed a cup and filled it with coffee, then placed a kiss on Maggie's cheek and stole a cookie from the cooling tray in front of her. She swatted his hand, as he managed to get away with his prize.

"Young whippersnapper!" she cussed, trying hard to hide the grin on her face.

"Well, I told him that I thought love was love. It didn't matter to me what the package looked like, and it shouldn't matter to him, either," Dylan explained as he bit into the cookie. "Hey, these are good, Maggie!" he exclaimed drawing a cluck out of the woman at the far end of the kitchen.

"And...?" Billie prompted.

"And, nothing. He didn't say anything. He just kind of vegged out for the rest of the ride," he replied.

Just then, a commotion from the front of the house drew their attention.

"Someone's home," Billie said.

"You take that critter outside this instant," Alex said firmly.

"Aw, come on, Alex. Loosen your girdle and have some fun. It's just a snapping turtle!" Jo exclaimed as the kids fussed around the animal.

"For your information, Miss smarty-pants, I don't wear a girdle, and you know it! Now stop changin' the subject!" Alex scolded.

Josephine walked toward Alex, holding the turtle out in front of her as she neared.

"Josephine Wycliffe, get that thing away from me!" she shouted as Tara and Skylar jumped up and down clapping at the show Jo was putting on for them. Seth left them to their fun and went to the kitchen.

Seeing her son enter the kitchen, Billie asked him about the commotion in the front hall.

"Oh, Grandma Jo is up to no good again. She's scaring Grams with a snapping turtle. Do I smell cookies?" he asked, sniffing the air.

Cat and Laurel came in from outside just as Seth was making his announcement. "A snapping turtle?" they said at the same time. "Good God above," Cat added as she headed for the front hall, followed by Billie, Laurel and Dylan, arriving just in time to see Alex nearly climb on top of the telephone table to get away from the creature.

"Josephine Wycliffe, I'm warnin' you!" she cried.

"Oh, come on, Alex. You have no qualms about touching a mummy, but you're afraid of a little turtle?" Josephine exclaimed.

"Grandma Jo!" Cat exclaimed, coming up behind Jo, and causing her to jump and drop the turtle onto Alexandra's lap.

Alex screamed, and true to form, fainted.

"Seth," Billie called her son in from the kitchen.

"Yeah," Seth said as he entered the room.

"Do me a favor and carry the turtle out to the edge of the woods and let it go," Billie asked.

"No problem." Seth shoved the rest of the cookie in his mouth and did as his mother asked, followed by an entourage of sisters. On their way out, they passed Doc, Ida, Bridget and Kevin, who had just arrived from the airport.

"Good God, scout, what have you got there?" Doc asked.

"Grandma Jo's secret weapon," he said, grinning.

Doc was a little puzzled until he looked into the front hall at the circle of people around an unconscious Alexandra. Looking back at Seth, he said, "She fainted, huh?"

"Oh yeah," he said, nodding his head.

Doc smiled. "Well, you'd better get rid of that thing before Grams comes to and faints again," he noted as Seth continued his mission.

Looking back over his shoulder, he saw that he had picked up an even longer trail of followers as his three cousins joined the entourage.

"Girls!" he mumbled under his breath as he led his little harem across the lawn.

***

"Grandma Jo, you know you really have to stop torturing poor Grams like that," Bridget scolded her grandmother. "One of these days, her heart is going to give out during one of your stunts."

Dylan, and Kevin managed to pick Alex up and carry her into the parlor where they gently laid her on the couch. After a few minutes, Doc proclaimed her properly fainted, and sent Billie into the kitchen to fetch a cold cloth for her head.

"But she's just so much fun to pick on. She's such a wuss sometimes!" Josephine exclaimed defensively. "And besides, she'd think something was wrong if I didn't tease her," Jo reasoned.

While on her errand, Billie ran into Jim who had come into the kitchen by the back stairway. She stopped dead in the doorway and locked eyes with her stepfather. "Jim," she said cordially.

"Billie," he replied, then went to the counter to retrieve a cup of coffee.

Billie went to the linen closet in the corner of the kitchen to retrieve a cloth. Carrying it over to the sink, she saturated it with cold water and wrung it out. Turning to go, she was intercepted by Jim, who intentionally stood in her path.

"Ah, Billie," he said nervously, not looking directly at her. "About last night," he choked out.

"Forget it Jim. I don't want your apologies. I want your tolerance. Until you're ready to give me that, we have nothing to talk about," she said.

Jim took a step back and looked her in the eye. "I can't," he said.

"All right, look, you can think and feel any damned way you want, but I won't tolerate any more rude treatment of my wife. Is that understood?" Billie asked forcefully, her nose barely inches from Jim's.

Jim stubbornly held her gaze and nodded in agreement.

"As long as we understand each other," Billie said through clenched teeth before brushing past him and heading back to the parlor.

Billie was fuming when she rejoined the others. After handing the cloth to Jo, she walked to the fireplace in three long strides and rested her forearm on the mantle, breathing hard with anger. Cat noticed her wife's agitated state and approached her. She wrapped her arms around Billie's waist and hugged her tight. Billie lowered her arm from the mantle and enveloped Cat in a bear hug.

Josephine knelt on the floor beside Alex and placed the cloth on her forehead, then leaned in and kissed her cheek. "Come on, Alex. Wake up for me sweetheart," she said to the unconscious woman.

Alex started to stir. "Hmmm, Josie?" she asked shakily.

"Alex. Alex, honey, come on, wake up," Jo urged as she lightly tapped the side of Alex's face.

"Josie?" Alex said, slowing opening her eyes. "What happened?" she asked.

"My stupidity happened, Alex," Jo answered. Leaning in a little closer, she whispered in her Alex's ear, "I'm sorry. I am so insensitive sometimes. I do love you. You know that, don't you?" she asked.

Alex touched the side of Jo's face. "I know," she said, smiling.

"Nona, are you all right?" Laurel asked as she leaned over the back of the couch, feeling Alex's forehead with the back of her hand.

"I'm all right, sugar," Alex said to her daughter, taking Laurel's hand from her face and kissing it. Then, looking at Josephine, she asked, "Did you get rid of that critter, Josie?"

Jo smiled. "Yes, ma'am. Seth released it in the woods," she exclaimed.

"Good. Now, what does a girl have to do to get a kiss around here?" she asked.

"Keep looking at me like that, and I'll do more than kiss you," warned Josephine, raising her eyebrows up and down wickedly before kissing Alex passionately.

All eyes turned to the doorway at the sound of someone clearing their throat, just in time to see the look of disgust on Jim's face before he turned and stomped away. Laurel rose from her position at the couch and made her apologies as she went after him.

Cat felt Billie's arms tighten around her as Jim stomped away. She narrowed her eyes at Billie. "Talk to me, love."

Billie lowered her forehead to Cat's. "I don't think he'll ever accept us, Cat. I'm so worried about him making Laurel's life miserable over it," she said. "We had a confrontation in the kitchen when I went after the cloth. He is just so closed minded about this. There is no room in his heart for tolerance," Billie explained.

"There is always room for tolerance, love. We'll just have to help him find it," Cat replied confidently.

"If you can do that, you're a better woman than I am," Billie challenged.

"Well, that's a given!" Cat exclaimed.

Billie looked at her wife and grinned evilly. "Why you little devil!" she said. "I'll show you who the better woman is."

Billie wrapped her arms around Cat's waist and lifted her up, throwing her over her shoulder. Turning to Ida, she said, "We're supposed to pick Drew up from the airport at three. If we're not back by two, send someone up for us, okay?"

Smiles crossed every face as Billie carried a kicking and screaming Cat out of the parlor.

Kevin turned to Bridget and said, "Ah, hon, do you know which room we're in?" Bridget blushed to the roots of her hair at the unspoken words behind his question.

"Hot damn!" Jo exclaimed. "If we keep this up, we'll have the makings for an orgy!"

Alex, who had managed to struggle into a seated position by then, said, "Oh, my," and fainted away once more.

"Oops!" Jo said, covering her mouth with her hand.

CHAPTER 9

Billie and Cat reemerged just before one p.m. They found Jo at the kitchen table, reading the daily paper, while Alex and Laurel were decorating cookies with Maggie. Doc and Ida had volunteered to pick Amy and her family up at the airport considering Alex's unconscious state earlier.

Billie opened the refrigerator and retrieved two yogurts, one of which she handed to Cat, who in turn handed her a spoon and a coy look. Billie planted a delicate kiss on Cat's lips before going over to hug her mother and grandmother.

"Those look good," she commented, eyeing the cookies while she opened her yogurt.

"You missed lunch. You must be hungry," commented Laurel.

Billie pulled out a chair and sat down. She tilted it back, balancing it on its back legs while she braced her foot against the table leg. "Nope, we ate!" she said, grinning wickedly at Cat, who had the decency to blush.

Josephine chuckled under her breath at Billie's comment, while Alex joined Cat in her choice of facial colors.

Laurel looked blankly at Billie for a moment, until the gist of her daughter's comment sank in. When awareness came to her, she gasped and said, "For Christ's sake, Billie, do you have to talk like that?"

Billie spread her arms wide, yogurt in one hand, spoon in the other, as she plastered an innocent look on her face. "What!?" she exclaimed.

Maggie touched Laurel's arm and laughed. "Don't let it bother you, Miss Laurel. Heaven knows I've learned not to with Miss Josephine around," she said, chuckling.

Josephine looked up from her paper with the same innocent look on her face that Billie wore. "What!?" she asked.

"Hey there, is anyone home?" a voice rang out from the front vestibule.

Cat and Billie looked at each other and grinned. "Amy," they said in unison at the unmistakable sound of Amy's high-pitched voice.

"We're in the kitchen, darlin'," Alex called out, wiping her hands on her apron to greet her granddaughter.

Amy entered with a flourish; her bright yellow sundress swaying around her legs, large sunglasses perched on top of her red-gold head. "Hey, hey, everyone!" she said excitedly, hugging and kissing Alex, Josephine and Maggie before making her way to Cat and Billie. Bending down, she stole the bite of yogurt that was perched on Cat's spoon, before kissing her full on the lips. "Hey, sis! Umm, good yogurt!" she exclaimed before turning to Billie. "You're just as gorgeous as ever," she said, hugging her sister-in-law affectionately. "If you ever want to dump Red over there, give me a call, okay?"

Billie looked at Cat, grinning at Amy's bold manner.

"She takes after Grandma Jo!" Cat said.

"I heard that!" Josephine said, casting a proud, cocky look at Cat.

Amy quickly scanned the room to see if she forgot anyone. Spotting Laurel, she stopped dead in her tracks. By this time, Ida and Amy's husband, Joe had finally made it into the kitchen. Walking up to Laurel, she looked her right in the face and said, "You must be Aunt Laurel. Tall, Dark and Gorgeous over there, looks just like you. I'm Amy, Cat's oldest sister," she said, politely introducing herself while holding out her hand.

Laurel smiled. "Is that any way to greet a long lost Aunt? C'mere," she said, pulling her in for a hug.

Amy introduced Joe to Laurel then turned and looked around the room once more.

"All right, I know Bridget was scheduled to arrive before us. So where *is* Mother Superior? Amy asked.

"Amy, do you have to start on your sister so early in the visit?" Ida complained.

"I'm sorry, Mama, but, well, Bridge is so uptight. The woman needs to loosen up and enjoy herself more!"

"Amy..." Ida warned.

"All right, all right! I'll be nice. Turning to Cat, she asked, "Did she call you, whining about Kevin's fear of flying too?"

Cat grinned, remembering the conversation Billie and Kevin had on the topic just prior to a pretty passionate evening of lovemaking.

"Amy!" Ida said sternly.

Amy winced as she threw her hands up. "Okay, okay!" she said. "But the question still stands, where is Bridget?"

Alex answered. "She and Kevin took her girls and Cat's kids to the pond for a picnic."

"Kevin? Mr. Neanderthal went on a picnic?" she asked incredulously.

Once again, Cat smiled, recalling how she used that same adjective to describe her brother-in-law just a week ago.

Amy caught Ida's warning look once more. Smiling nervously, she turned to Joe and said, "Honey, maybe we should go unpack. I'm sure the girls have found their room by now and are probably making a mess of their luggage."

Joe, who never ceased to be amazed at his wife's boldness, laughed. "That might be a good idea, love. I'll get the bags in the hall," he said, heading out of the kitchen.

"Later!" Amy said, throwing a wave over her shoulder as she followed her husband out.

***

An hour later, Cat and Billie left for the airport to meet Drew's plane. Back at the mansion, the noise level raised about fifty decibels as the eight grandchildren gathered around the patio table to enjoy a snack of cookies and fruit drink.

Bridget clucked around the children like a mother hen, making sure they were orderly and well behaved while enjoying their snack.

Amy stood by, wine cooler in hand, mildly agitated that the kids were being restrained so much. "Aw, come on Bridge, let them enjoy themselves. They're on vacation for crying out loud!" she complained.

Bridget looked at her sister. "Amy, they'll just make a bigger mess if we leave them to their own devices," she said. "And my name is Bridget, not Bridge," she corrected her older sibling.

Dylan chose that moment to make his entrance.

"Wow! Who are *you*?" Amy asked, taking in his tall blond good looks.

Dylan grinned, showing off his dimples. "Hi, I'm Dylan, Billie's brother," he said, extending his hand to Amy, and then Joe.

"Is *everyone* in your family so good looking?" Amy asked, causing Dylan to blush.

"Amy, how can you flirt like that in front of your husband?" Bridget scolded her sister. "I would never do that to Kevin."

"Bridget, I stopped being jealous of Amy's flirtatious ways a long time ago," Joe said. Then, looking at Dylan, he extended his hand and he added, "She really *is* harmless, you know. I'm Joe. Glad to meet you."

Amy elbowed her husband lightly in the ribs, causing him to chuckle. Then addressing her sister once more, she said, "Sis, there's a lot of things you wouldn't do to…or probably *with*, Kevin!" she teased, causing her younger sister to blush indignantly. "By the way, where is the old redneck?"

"He's with Daddy, Jim and Grandma Jo, looking at the antique cars in the garage. He's quite the connoisseur when it comes to antique vehicles, you know," Bridget bragged.

"You must be so proud," Amy said, her sarcasm completely lost on Bridget.

Dylan covered his mouth to hide a grin. "In the garage, you say? Maybe I'll join them. Wanna come?" he asked Joe, who readily accepted. Excusing themselves, they left for the garage.

Laurel and Ida had been lounging by the pool, listening to the conversation between the sisters.

"Do they always act like that around each other?" Laurel asked.

"Since they were children," Ida replied. "Caitlain was the peacemaker in the family...always breaking up fights between those two. Having four girls so close in age was quite a challenge," Ida explained.

"How old are they now?" Laurel asked.

Ida creased her brow and looked off into the distance. "Well, let's see, Amy is Billie's age, 34, Bridget is 33, Caitlain is 31, and Drew, well, Drew was a bit of an afterthought...Doc's attempt at having a son. She is almost 27. They were certainly a handful. Sometimes I wish I had raised boys!" Ida exclaimed.

"Well, sis, boys aren't any easier. I remember when Dylan was six..." Laurel recounted as the two women sat and exchanged horror stories about raising children that most certainly had to have come from the loins of Satan himself.

***

Cat waved her hand above her head. "Drew! Drew, over here!" she called.

The cute, pixie-haired blonde smiled broadly, exposing deep dimples, as she too waved her hand above her head, acknowledging her sister. "Cat!" she exclaimed, bending over to hug her sister tightly after she fought her way through the airport crowd.

"Drew, sweetie, it's so good to see you," Cat said

Drew stood to her full five-foot-eight height, nearly a half-foot above Cat. "Where's my gorgeous sister-in-law?" Drew asked, looking around for Billie.

"She's gone to collect your luggage. She'll be back shortly."

Cat took the chance to really look at her baby sister. Drew was dressed in white short shorts and a navy blue tank top that just barely came below her breasts, showing off very tanned arms, legs and flat stomach. White socks and running shoes completed her outfit. Her hair had been dyed a very light shade of blond, and cut close to her head. "Drew, you look wonderful. I love your hair," she commented.

Drew's hand immediately went to her hair. "Really? Do you like, think it's too blond? I wasn't sure I liked it at first, but it's like, kinda growing on me," she said.

Billie retrieved Drew's suitcase from the luggage carousel and headed back to the arrival gate. She spotted her wife and sister-in-law long before they saw her. Billie stopped dead in her tracks.

Wow! Drew, you have certainly grown up since I saw you last! she thought. *If I wasn't so much in love with Cat, well...*

"Billie!" Cat exclaimed, noticing her wife coming toward them.

Billie smiled at her wife. *Nah. Cat's the only one for me. Always has been...always will be.* Her heart did flip-flops in her chest while she watched the object of her desire approach her, dragging a very blond Drew behind her.

Cat stopped abruptly in front of Billie and pushed Drew in front of her. Billie smiled and looked at her sister-in-law. Putting the suitcase on the floor, she opened her arms to the younger woman and hugged her affectionately.

"Oh, Billie, I've missed you," Drew said, touching the side of Billie's face with her hand.

Billie leaned down and kissed Drew's cheek. "Me too, little one," Billie replied.

Cat stood back and smiled at her wife and sister. "Well, we'd better get going. Everyone is anxious to see you, honey," Cat said to her younger sister.

"So, like, your mom is there, right Billie?" Drew asked on the ride to SpireClyffe Acres.

"Yes, she is," Billie replied, looking at her sister-in-law in the rear view mirror. "My stepfather and brother are there too," she added.

"Cool, like, I mean, it must have been a shock to find her after all these years," Drew said lightly.

"Well, I wouldn't have even started looking if it wasn't for Cat," Billie said, reaching for her wife's hand in the seat next to her. Lifting it to her mouth, she kissed Cat's knuckles.

Cat closed her eyes as the tender caress shot tendrils of desire through her.

Drew watched the exchange closely.

"You two are like, *so cute!*" she exclaimed, smiling broadly.

Cat looked back at her sister and smiled, thinking, *you're pretty cute yourself, dumpling.*

"We're here!" Billie declared as she pulled up to the front door. Chet came out to take the car as the three ladies went into the house.

Doc and Ida met their youngest daughter in the front hall.

"Mom, Daddy!" she exclaimed, hugging them both. Doc grinned ear to ear as Ida eyed Drew's hair color warily.

"Drewcilla, come here and let me look at you, girl!" Amy said as she barged into the room.

Amy and Drew took one look at each other and screamed, waving their arms in the air as they ran to each other and met in a fierce hug. Billie had just come into the hall, carrying Drew's luggage. Placing it on the floor near the door, she looked at Cat with a raised eyebrow as she watched the sisters' ritual greeting. Cat placed one hand on her hip, the other on her smiling mouth and shook her head side to side in disbelief.

"Baby girl, I love what you did to your hair!" Amy exclaimed, reaching up to touch the almost white hair.

"Ames, do you really like it? I mean, like, I was really afraid I would like, look old or something," Drew said.

"Sweetheart, you could never look old, why you're just a baby yet. You're all of what, twenty-six?" Amy asked.

"Almost twenty-seven," Drew replied.

"Drew?" came another voice from the doorway.

"Bridgie!" Drew exclaimed as she spotted her other sister. Crossing the room, she hugged her older sister close. "Like, how are you?" she asked.

"What *ever* did you do to your hair, Drew?" Bridget asked, eyes wide with wonder.

"Do you like it? I was kind of tired of the mousy brown. Like, I thought a change would be cool," Drew explained.

"Mousy brown? Drew, your hair was the same color as mine," Bridget pointed out.

"Oops! What-ever!" Drew said, daintily covering her mouth with her hand.

Bridget took another long look. "Well, it *does* kind of look cute on you," she admitted. "It's shorter than usual, isn't it?" she asked.

"Yeah, it's called the 'butch' look, no offense sis," she said, throwing a look over her shoulder at Cat.

"None taken, sweet pea," Cat said to her sister. "Look, your room is the third one on the left. Why don't you take your suitcase upstairs and settle in before meeting the rest of the crew, okay?" Cat suggested. "Oh, and by the way, dinner tonight is formal, Grams insists," she added.

"Cool!" Drew said, grabbing her suitcase and heading for the stairs.

"I'll give you a hand, dear," Ida said, following her daughter.

Billie walked up behind Cat and wrapped her arms around the smaller woman. "Well, cheer, cheer, the gang's all here!" she said.

"Let the games begin!" Cat said grinning.

CHAPTER 10

"*I know what you're thinking baby. I used to be just like you. You move when she's not looking baby. One sugar ain't enough for you. You, you're taking out your loans, you're burying your bone. Before you're cover's blown, you'd better take it home.....*" Drew's arms flailed around in circles, her head bobbing forward and back. "*I like the way you look. I know you like me. But one and one and one, baby makes three. Stop playing those eyes, if you want me to keep, your little secret...*" Drew sang happily along with the radio as she soaked off the exhaustion from her flight earlier in the day.

"*Tell it softly to me baby. You never mean no one no harrrr* Aaarrrgggghhh!" Drew screamed as the door to the bathroom suddenly swung open.

"Wh...wh...who are you?" she finally gasped out as her arms covered her breasts, oblivious to the transparency of the water providing a clear view of the rest of her body.

"I...I...I...I," the intruder stammered, staring at the blond pixie in the tub.

"Like, what part of that didn't you understand? *Who the hell are you*?" Drew yelled again.

"D...Dylan. I'm Dylan...Billie's brother!" he said, unable to tear his eyes away from the woman.

Drew suddenly threw her arms out to the sides and smiled widely, totally exposing her charms for Dylan to see. "Way cool! Like, why didn't you say so? I thought you were like, some kind of perv or something. I'm Drew, Cat's youngest sister," she explained, reaching out a soapy hand to shake Dylan's.

Dylan inched his way toward Drew, trying hard to look anywhere but at her generously firm breasts. He shook her hand then quickly pulled it back.

"Ah...ah...I...I," he stammered once again, inching his way toward the door.

Drew lay back in the tub, giving Dylan a full frontal view.

"Ah, Drew, I'm sorry I burst in on you. I'll just..." he began, pointing to the door.

"No! I mean, I don't mind. Have a seat. I'm done anyway. Just getting out!" she said as she began to pull herself up out of the tub.

"Ah, Drew, I've really got to go." *Cat will kill me if she finds out I walked in on her naked sister!* Dylan thought as he beat a hasty retreat out of the bathroom. When he finally made it into the hall and closed the door behind him, he leaned against the wall to regain his composure. *Wow, what a babe! I wonder if she's gay too? She sure didn't mind being seen naked by a man! This is going to be an interesting week!* he thought as he went on very shaky legs in search of another bathroom.

He was like, kind of cute, Drew thought as she toweled herself dry. *He doesn't look anything like Billie. I wonder if he looks like Billie's Mom? Hmmm, blonde, curly hair. Hey, like, the color was almost as light as mine. Cool! Dimples, too. He was like, kinda sweet the way he was so embarrassed about walking in on me. Way cool! This is like, gonna be a real fun week!* she mused as she flipped her head from side to side, then pulled a robe over her freshly bathed body combing her short blond hair with her fingers.

***

"Sky, honey, hold still while I brush your hair," Cat complained as she put the finishing touches on the child's formal wear for dinner that night. She was wearing a knee-length flower print sun dress, with spaghetti straps, white ankle socks with lace around the top, and shiny patent leather shoes.

Skylar fidgeted while her mother primped her. Looking down at the shiny patent leather, she exclaimed, "Mama! I can see my undies in my shoes!"

"Wha...?" Cat exclaimed, looking down. Sure enough, Skylar's white panties were reflecting onto her shoes.

Billie chucked nearby. "Boy, does that bring back memories!" she exclaimed.

Cat raised an eyebrow to her. "Wanna share?" she asked, imagining all kinds of things relative to her wife, undies and patent leather shoes.

"Catholic school," she said.

"Ah, Billie, a little more information would be helpful," Cat said grinning at the obvious teasing.

"Dress code. We all wore uniforms with the hems below our knees, and no patent leather shoes. For *that* very reason," Billie explained, pointing to Skylar's shoes. "The nuns were terrified that reflections of our undies would turn the boys on or something," she said, chuckling at the memory.

Cat's eyes flew open in disbelief. "You're kidding, right?" she asked. "For real?"

"Scout's honor," Billie said, raising her hand. "We couldn't walk on the railing side of the stairwells either because the boys might look up our dresses from the level below," she added.

Cat was dumbfounded by the revelations. "Billie, I'm so glad we decided to leave our children in the public school system," she said. "Imagine the message rules like that send to children," she commented.

"Well, the public schools leave a lot to be desired too, but at least they leave the warped moral ideas out of their lesson plans," Billie said.

Cat nodded in agreement as her attention was drawn to the doorway of their room.

"Tara, sweetheart, you have to get dressed for dinner or we'll be late. You know Grams wants everyone there on time," Cat said.

"I *am* dressed for dinner," Tara said, holding her arms out to the sides.

Cat and Billie looked at each other and then at their daughter. Tara was wearing a pair of oversized blue jeans, the crotch of which came to her knees, causing the pant legs to accumulate in multiple folds around her sneaker-clad feet. A T-shirt three sizes too large hung loosely on her torso, while a baseball cap sat on her head backward.

"Tara, where did you get those clothes?" Billie asked.

"From Crystal," she said, referring to Amy's older daughter. "Aren't they cool?" she exclaimed happily.

Billie approached the young lady. "Very cool," she said, "but not suitable for a formal dinner. Come on, I'll help you get dressed," she said, placing a hand on Tara's shoulder and directing her out of the room.

"But Mom, Crystal and Heidi are both dressing like this!" she exclaimed, referring to Bridget's oldest daughter as well.

Billie leaned over to look directly at Tara. "Look, sweetheart. Grams is looking forward to a nice formal dinner. We are not going to spoil it for her by dressing in these very cool, but very informal clothes. Okay? I will talk to Crystal and Heidi as well. Somehow, I don't think Aunt Amy and Aunt Bridget will like it very much either. Okay? Now let's go," she finished, taking Tara's hand and leading her out the door.

Cat shook her head side to side as she watched her wife lead their daughter away.

"Is Tare in trouble, Mama?" Skylar asked?

Cat smiled down at her daughter. "No, sweetling. Mommy is just going to set things straight with your sister and cousins. Somehow, I don't think Aunt Billie will be very popular for the next several hours," she said, chuckling.

Nearly an hour later, Billie reappeared in the doorway to their bedroom. Cat had just showered and was sitting at the vanity, blow-drying her long red-gold hair. She looked into the mirror and met Billie's eyes. "Mission accomplished?" she asked.

Billie grinned. "I won't be the most popular aunt at dinner tonight, but, yeah, mission accomplished," she said, coming up behind Cat. "You won't believe what they were going to wear," she exclaimed through slight laughter. "I think I got a little preview of what Tara will be like at age fourteen," she said, referring to the stubborn nature of Amy's daughter Crystal.

"Well, love, we're running short on time. You'd better jump into the shower," Cat said, locking eyes in the mirror with the woman behind her.

Billie kissed the side of her head. "You're right. Be right back!" she said, heading to the shower.

Towel drying her hair moments later, Billie suddenly remembered that she hadn't taken her gown out of the dress bag. *Shit! It's going to be all wrinkled!* she thought. "Cat," she yelled out into the adjoining bedroom. "Honey, did you think to take my dress out of..." she began.

Cat suddenly appeared in the doorway of the bathroom. "Yes, I did. It was all wrinkled, like mine was, so I had them both ironed. It's hanging in the cl...," Cat said, stopping short when she noticed Billie staring at her intently. She immediately thought she had something on her. Looking down at her dress, she didn't notice any stains or anything. "Billie?" she questioned.

"Cat, you are the most beautiful creature I have every laid eyes on," she said, taking in Cat's form-fitting green satin gown, and hair that had been pulled up and arranged into a loose fitting bun on top of her head, tendrils of hair curling freely along her hairline. Cat had added just a touch of blush and eye color to bring out the emerald green brilliance of her eyes.

Billie was captivated. Taking two steps forward, she was met by a hand on her chest.

"Billie, you're wet," Cat said seductively. "Now we both know I thoroughly enjoy it when you're wet...God knows I do. But water stains on satin will not look good at a formal dinner party," she explained teasingly.

Billie's breathing was very erratic. Taking a deep breath, she pulled Cat's face toward hers with a hand behind her neck, being very careful not to let her wet body come in contact with Cat's dress. "You are in big trouble, after dinner, wife," she said passionately into Cat's ear.

"Oh, I'm counting on it," Cat replied, catching Billie's earlobe between her teeth and biting gently, causing Billie to nearly double over with weakness. "I'd better leave you alone or we'll be late," she whispered, flicking Billie's earlobe once more before leaving her alone in the bathroom.

***

"Uncle Dyl, could you give me a hand with this tie?" Seth asked, struggling to fold the bow properly.

"Sure, pal," Dylan said as he folded one side of the bow in half, then wrapped the other end around the center, tucking it into the knot, then pulling it into a neat, even bow under Seth's chin. "These monkey suits sure are uncomfortable," he added as he brushed the lint off Seth's shoulders then spun him around to brush off his back. Holding him at arms' length, he said, "You look great, Seth. Are you sure you're only thirteen?" he asked. "You look at least eighteen."

Seth smiled from ear to ear. "Thanks Uncle Dyl. You look kinda neat yourself," he said.

Dylan turned back to the mirror to finish adjusting his own tie. Catching Seth's eye, he asked, "Seth, have you seen your Aunt Drew lately?"

"Sure, I saw her earlier today, just after she got here," he replied.

"What do you think of her?" Dylan asked.

"What do you mean...she's a girl!" Seth answered.

Dylan chuckled, suddenly remembering his own marginal interest in girls at that age. "Oh yeah, you got that right!" he exclaimed. "But, what do you think? Do you think she's pretty?" Dylan inquired. *Damn, I wish there was someone else here closer to my age who wasn't so close to the issue. Joe and Kevin are a little biased, and Doc, well, I can't say, 'Hey Doc, I've got the hots for your daughter ... waddaya think?'. Maybe Billie? Yeah, I'll talk to her later,* he decided as he turned his attention back to Seth.

"Yeah, I guess she's pretty, for a girl," Seth commented. Then, finally realizing what Dylan was getting at, he grinned. "You like her, don't you?" he teased, causing Dylan to blush.

Look at me! Blushing! I haven't blushed since I was…since I was Seth's age! Damn! I've got it bad! he thought as he answered his nephew. "Well, she is kind of nice. Hey, it's late, we'd better get going," Dylan said, quickly changing the subject.

Dylan and Seth gave each other the once over, one more time brushing imaginary lint off each other's tuxedoes before heading to the dining room for dinner.

***

Cat went to the dining room to seat the children while Billie was dressing. Tara had taken a little more time than they thought, leaving Billie limited time to get herself ready for dinner.

The dining room was abuzz with noise. Cat and Amy scurried around the table, trying to determine the seating arrangements and making last minute adjustments among the children so they could sit next to their favorite cousin. The men and Josephine, all dressed in black tuxedoes, stood around enjoying snifters of brandy while waiting for the signal to be seated. Ida, Bridget and Drew were drafted by Maggie to help pour champagne at each place setting in preparation for the evening toast. Although standing with the men, Dylan's mind and eyes were elsewhere, namely, on the shapely legs and bottom of one Drew O'Grady as she leaned over the table pouring champagne. Seth elbowed him periodically to draw his attention back to the conversation.

Just as Cat turned to head up stairs in search of her wife, the door to the dining room opened wide. All eyes turned as three regal beauties entered, Billie first, followed by Laurel and then Alex.

Cat's knees suddenly weakened as she grabbed the back of Tara's chair for support.

Jim's eyes opened wide, his cigar hanging out of his mouth as he stared at the women.

Josephine grinned ear to ear, licking her lips in anticipation of the after-dinner treat she was sure to enjoy.

"Oh, my God," Cat whispered hoarsely as she took in the vision before her.

The three women were wearing matching gowns, all of the same design, but of varying colors—Billie in a deep burgundy, Laurel in navy blue, and Alex in emerald green. The cut was directly out of *Gone With The Wind*. The neckline of the dresses ran low and straight across full breasts, exposing deep cleavages. Billowy peasant sleeves pushed off the shoulders, trimmed in lace, a lighter shade of the base color, proudly displayed an expanse of creamy skin and delicate collarbones, while high-cut bodices highlighted slim waists. Full skirts fell around long legs, while gathers of satin and lace accumulated at the back of their waists in pleated layers, trailing to the floor in short trains. All three women wore their hair pulled up into loosely arranged buns on top of their heads, cameo collars around their necks held on by bands the same color as their dresses. Delicate shades of blush and eye color accented high cheekbones and brilliant blue eyes, while red lipstick highlighted full lips. The result was breathtakingly stunning. Three women...identical in appearance...the only discernible difference, being age. Three generations of beauty, flesh and desire.

Cat, Jim and Josephine all stepped forward at the same time as the rest of the family looked on in awe. All three approached their respective wives, lifting bejeweled hands to their mouths for a delicate kiss, eyes never breaking contact with identical seas of blue. Leading their ladies to the table, they held out chairs as the southern belles were seated.

Before seating herself, Cat whispered into her wife's ear, "Someone else I know is in trouble after dinner, my love."

Billie smiled, but kept her eyes trained to her plate in front of her. "Oh, I am counting on it," she replied.

***

The entire family was there, all twenty-two of them, sitting around the formal dining table. Jo and Alex took their traditional places at the ends of the long table. Along one side, to Jo's left, sat Cat and Billie, their three children, Bridget's three girls, Kevin and then Bridget on the end to Alex's right. On the other side, to Alex's left, was Laurel and Jim, Dylan, Drew, Amy's two daughters, Joe, Amy, Doc and finally Ida on Josephine's right. Alex had intentionally seated the table's occupants in order to keep Josephine and Jim as far apart as possible without making it seem obvious.

Once everyone was seated, Maggie and a couple of hired caterers served the salad, followed by a filet mignon entree. Once all the salad dishes were removed and the entree delivered, Jo rose from her seat and walked to the other end of the table to stand behind Alex. Alex's face dropped progressively with each step Jo took toward her. *So much for best-laid plans of mice and men!* she thought as Jo came closer and closer to Jim, and a potential confrontation.

Josephine stood there behind Alex, her hands on the southern belle's shoulders, looking over the table at her family seated there dressed in formal attire, men in black tuxes, women in beautiful gowns. Taking a deep breath, she felt a rush of happiness and satisfaction at what lay before her.

Alex sat there tensely, waiting for Josephine to say or do something that would upset the proverbial apple cart.

Jo looked down at her wife and smiled. *She is still a beautiful woman,* she thought. She bent over and whispered in Alex's ear, "Alexandra, you still have the power to take my breath away. I love you," she proclaimed, causing Alex to blush profusely. Jo shifted to one side of Alex and turned her wife's face toward her, softly placing a kiss on Alexandra's lips. Alexandra was beyond caring what Jim thought at that moment.

Twenty faces turned to the end of the table. Nineteen faces smiled. One sat there focusing on the entree until the commotion was over.

The smile on Cat and Billie's faces faded quickly as they saw Jim's reaction to Jo's affectionate gesture. Righting herself again, Jo looked down the expanse of table and locked eyes with Cat, immediately knowing the cause of the frown on her granddaughter's face. Glancing at Jim, she took in the man's erect spine, stoic face and focused eyes. Grinning wickedly, she started nonchalantly pacing back and forth behind Alex.

"Ah, families. You gotta love 'em," Jo began. "You know, the world is made of a lotta different people. Alex and I found that out very early on in life. It takes all kinds to make the world go 'round, to quote an old cliché," she said, her right hand shoved deep into her trousers pocket, her left hand gesturing as she paced back and forth. "Alex and me, well, we've been blessed through the years with lots of loving family, family that has always been *open-minded*," she stressed, coming to stand behind Jim, "Accepting of all situations, and of all people. Heaven forbid if one of them had turned out to be *prejudiced* against someone because they were *different* from themselves," she stressed once more, bending over to make the last point directly into Jim's ear. Jim just sat there, spine ramrod stiff, staring at his plate.

"Josie honey, please," Alex said softly. The entire room was silent. All eyes were turned to Jo.

Jo looked at Alex and took a deep breath. Shoving both hands into her trouser pockets, she dropped her chin to her chest and let out a sigh. Leaning down once more, she whispered in Jim's ear, "I'm not done with you yet," then stood to her full height and walked back to Alex. Standing by Alex's side, she cupped her chin, tilting her face up.

"Alexandra Spirakis, I love you with all my heart," she said, "and as much as I want to do otherwise, I will behave for your sake, for now." Leaning down once more, she kissed Alex tenderly, then stood and looked across the expanse of table. "Well, what are you all looking at? You're just jealous because I have the prettiest girl at the party, aren't you? Well, find your own. This one's mine!" she said proudly, throwing her arm around Alex.

Bending down to place one more kiss on Alex's lips, she once again looked out across the silent table. "Can't a woman kiss her best girl without an audience?" she exclaimed, a big grin on her face.

"Josephine Wycliffe, I'd better be your *only* girl!" Alexandra said in mock anger, hands on her hips, causing the room to break into laughter. Soon, the diners resumed eating as the rest of the meal proceeded pleasantly for all except Jim, who knew that his trials with Josephine Wycliffe had just begun.

CHAPTER 11

"You know, Billie, I kind of feel sorry for Jim," Cat said. "I mean, I think he's basically a nice guy, he's just been raised with a set of beliefs that don't fit into this family," she explained as she unzipped the back of Billie's gown. Leaning in, she kissed the space between Billie's shoulder blades.

"Hmm, Cat, that feels good, but if you keep that up, we won't make it to the pool with the rest of the family," Billie said, eyes closed, head thrown back, as she reached behind her to pull Cat closer.

Cat snaked her arms around Billie, laying her cheek against her back and drawing lazy circles on Billie's stomach with her fingertips. "I'd rather be getting wet with you right here, than in the pool," she said wickedly, causing Billie to gasp for breath.

Billie turned around in Cat's arms, the sleeves of her dress falling further. "You are an evil woman, my love," Billie said. She kissed Cat tenderly while pushing the spaghetti straps off her shoulders.

"Mom?" Seth said from the hall.

Billie winced. "Damn!" She gathered her dress back to her chest and left the comfort of Cat's arms to answer the door. She opened the door wide enough to stick her head out, yet keep the rest of her body hidden behind the door as she spoke to her son. Cat took this opportunity to molest her wife behind the door.

"Seth, honey, what is it?" she asked, brushing Cat's hands away as they snaked under the bodice of the dress.

"Mom, Aunt Amy sent me up to get you and Mama. She said to tell you there was time for that later, what ever *that* means!" he said a bit confused. "So, hurry up, okay?" he said grinning.

Cat lifted Billie's skirts and pulled down her panties. Billie wiggled her hind end in an attempt to help Cat slip the panties off, as she struggled to maintain a straight face while talking to her son.

"Okay, honey...and Seth, tell your sisters to mind Grandma in the pool. Mama and I will be down shortly," she promised.

Cat slid one hand between Billie's legs, sending a jolt of electricity through her. "Oh!" Billie retorted.

Seth had turned to go, but stopped at his mother's exclamation. Turning back around, he looked at her with a raised eyebrow. "Did you say something, Mom?" he asked.

"Ah...ah, yeah...tell Aunt Amy that there's never enough time for *that*. Okay? She'll know what you mean. See you in a bit, love," Billie said, finally dismissing her son.

"Okay, Mom! Hurry up. You'll miss all the fun!" he said, running off down the hallway.

Billie shut the door and leaned back against it. Cat was all over her, immediately reaching up and pushing the gown off Billie's shoulders and letting it fall to the floor. Billie noticed that she too, had shed her own gown, and was now in a similar state of undress.

Allowing herself to be pressed against the door, Billie locked eyes with the smaller woman and said, "You know they'll just send someone else if we don't get moving."

Cat smiled. "I know. This is just a preview of coming attractions," she said, clamping down on one of Billie's nipples.

Billie arched her body toward her wife. "I sure hope the rest of the show is X-rated!" she exclaimed.

***

Some time later, Billie and Cat arrived at the pool area, hand in hand, sporting skimpy bathing suits, sarongs, towels, and big smiles. Not only had they previewed the coming attractions but had taken the time to read the Cliff Notes as well. Amy raised both eyebrows and smiled knowingly at her sister's late appearance.

Jim, who was in the pool actually playing with the children, looked at their locked hands with distaste. Billie met his gaze with one of her own then squeezed Cat's hand tighter before releasing it so she could check on Skylar. Kneeling down, Billie spread her towel out on the edge of the pool and laid down flat on her stomach, her hands crossed under her chin. She was mere inches away from where Jim was playing with the children.

"You know, there's something I've always wondered about," she said to no one in particular, "Just what does love *look* like? I mean, I guess I know what if *feels* like, but what does it look *like*?" she asked.

Jim turned to look at her. "Love is an emotion, not a concrete object. It doesn't have an appearance," he said.

Billie lifted her head and raised her eyebrows. "Oh, really? Other emotions have appearances," she said. "For example, happiness can be represented by a smiley face, anger by a frown, sorrow by a tear...but what about love? Is it black, white, blue, red? Is it hard or soft? Is it male or female? Is it one thing at a time, or several things?" Billie paused for a moment before adding, "Jim, you're a man of the world, what do you think?"

Jim faced his stepdaughter and said, "Look, Billie. I know what you're trying to do here. I'm sorry, but I don't support your lifestyle. It's unnatural," he finished.

Billie narrowed her eyes and nodded her head up and down. "Unnatural," she said. "Natural between, say...you and Mom, but not between Cat and me. Is that right?" she asked. Watching him nod his head in agreement, she added, "So what you're saying then, is that love is a multifaceted emotion. It can be many different things at the same times. It can take on lots of different meanings depending on the situation."

Again, he nodded. Billie rose to her knees then paused before climbing to her feet. "Jim?" she asked. "Do you think love is ever a bad thing?"

"No. How can something that feels so good be bad?" he asked quite vehemently.

Billie's eyebrows were perched high on her forehead. "How indeed. How indeed! Thanks, Dad. You've just verified what I've known all along," she said, leaning in to place a kiss on his cheek before rising to her feet and walking away, a wicked grin on her face.

Jim stood in the pool, dumbfounded by the corner his stepdaughter had just maneuvered him into.

***

Josephine watched the scene in the pool between Billie and Jim with great interest. When Billie rose to her feet and walked away from the pool, Jo followed her. Slipping an arm around her tall granddaughter's waist, she led her out onto the patio for a private conversation.

"Grandma Jo, is everything all right?" Billie asked when they finally stopped at the far end of the patio.

"Everything is fine, Billie-Girl, and about to get better if I have my way," Josephine said.

"What's up?"

"Billie, forgive me for eavesdropping, but I overheard your conversation with Jim. You know, I really don't think he's a bad guy...a little misguided maybe, but not really a bad guy. And it's obvious how much he loves your mother, which is why I wanted to talk to you," Jo explained.

"You know, Cat said the same thing," Billie chuckled.

"Cat said what?" the object of the conversation said, coming onto the patio to join her wife and grandmother.

"Cat! I was just telling Grandma Jo, here that you don't think Jim is such a bad guy," Billie explained.

Cat sided up to Billie and wrapped an arm around her waist. "No I don't. I didn't much like him at first, but now I realize that his initial reaction to me was out of nervousness, not dislike. According to Laurel, he was raised in a really strict, religious family that preached male dominance and heterosexual relationships for the purpose of procreation, not love. He's just not used to accepting different kinds of love. We need to help him see that love is love, regardless of the wrappings," she explained.

"Male dominance?" Jo snorted. "He doesn't seem to throw his weight around with Laurel," she observed.

"I don't think Mom would let him get away with it, even if he tried!" Billie exclaimed. "And you'll notice that Dylan doesn't share his beliefs. I think that's another one of Mom's influences," she added. "The point is if he can give up some of his beliefs because he has found them to be too restrictive within his own family, then maybe there's hope for getting him to accept other alternatives."

Billie paused to take a breath.

"Look, I'm not saying he has to embrace us with open arms. He has to decide for himself how much of our life style he can accept. What I am saying is that to be a well-rounded person, he needs to learn tolerance, and to accept the fact that every family does not fit into the mold he has built for himself...*and* that's its okay to live outside that mold," Billie finished.

"Yeah. I think there's hope for him yet. We've just got to help him see the error of his ways," Jo said, smirking.

Billie threw her free arm around Josephine's shoulder and hugged her. Chuckling, she said, "Why do I get the feeling that you are really going to enjoy this little lesson?"

***

Alex watched Jo, Cat and Billie come back to pool-side and join into the family activities. She had been sitting with Ida and Laurel, talking about the fireworks they had planned for the next evening, "...bein' as it *is* our country's birthday and all," Alex emphasized. Doc and Jim were still in the pool, throwing the children high into the air to splash down noisily into the water.

Kevin and Joe sat by lazily on loungers, with Kevin making comments about voluptuous hips and full breasts as the various wives and sisters-in-law strolled by.

"Hey, chickie-baby!" Kevin clucked, making kissy noises with his lips as Amy walked by.

Amy looked at her sister. "Bridge, your husband is a pig!" she exclaimed, grinning ear to ear, and swaying her butt side to side a little more dramatically, winking as she passed her own husband. Joe restrained himself, although his wife's actions wanted him to make Kevin's pig status look tame.

"Kevin! You stop that this minute. What are your daughters going to think?" Bridget exclaimed.

Kevin continued his macho ways, that is, until Billie stepped into his line of vision, legs spread apart, hands on her hips, a stern look on her face as she peered down at him on the lounger.

For some reason, Billie had the power to stop Kevin cold. When he saw her, he instinctively covered his private areas with his hands, and grinned. Joe laughed as Billie walked away smirking.

Finally, the hour approached bedtime for the younger children as their mothers scurried to ready them for bed. The seven girls had planned a slumber party in one of the two rooms they were sharing, so no arguments were heard about an early bedtime. Cat had been talked into telling several stories to the girls and their mothers before turning in, and soon it was near midnight when Skylar started drifting off to sleep. After tucking the girls in and kissing them all a good night, Alex, Cat, Amy, Bridget and Billie crept out of the room and returned to the parlor.

Seth, being a ripe old man of thirteen, joined Jo and the men in the parlor for an evening of drinks and discussion while the ladies busied themselves with organizing the girls' slumber party. While he wasn't happy about being served grape juice while the adults drank wine, he at least had the opportunity to visit with them, and not sent to bed like some kid, so he relented and did not complain.

Little did the adults know, Seth stealthily refilled his juice glass with wine whenever he was sure the adults weren't looking. By the time Cat, Billie, and the rest of the women returned to the parlor, he was quite happy and feeling no pain.

"Hi Mommy!" he said staggering over to Billie as she walked in. "I love you, Mommy!" he said, placing his head on her chest just below her chin. Her arms instinctively wrapped around her son.

Billie and Cat looked at each other with creased brows. Cat took the glass out of Seth's hand and sniffed the contents, then held it under Billie's nose.

All eyes turned toward Billie as Mount Charland erupted. "What the hell is wrong with you people? Who gave my son wine? For Christ sakes, he only thirteen!" she shouted.

Confusion lit up the faces of the accused.

"Billie, wait!" Cat instructed. Then, turning to Seth, she said, "Seth, honey, where did you get the wine?"

Seth grinned, goofily. "I snuck it!" he bragged. "I didn't get caught, either! Cool, huh?" he said.

"No, *not* cool!" Billie exclaimed. "We'll talk about this tomorrow, young man. Right now, you need to go to bed," she said, as she directed him to the door. Looking back over her shoulder, she said sternly, "I'll be back. We're not finished talking about this!"

Cat and Billie led Seth to the room upstairs that he was sharing with Dylan. Throwing the door open, they proceeded inside, only to be stopped short by the sight of Drew and Dylan in bed together, in the throes of passion. Cat instinctively slapped a hand over Seth's eyes as she stared agog at the occupants of the bed.

"Great! Just great!" Billie shouted. "I've got a drunken kid and my brother is in his bed porking my wife's sister! Isn't life grand?" she exclaimed. "Come on Cat, we'll need to put him in Drew's room," Billie instructed.

Drew and Dylan had been startled into attentiveness and now sat side by side on the bed, Drew holding the bed sheets up against her breasts. On their way out the door, Cat looked back and said to her sister, "You are in big trouble, Missy. We need to have a talk!"

Ten minutes later, with Seth settled in Drew's bed, Cat and Billie stopped off at their room to collect their sanity before dealing with the situations presented to them this evening.

Closing the door behind them, Cat strode across the room, her arms flailing in all directions. "Shit! Shit! Shit!" she exclaimed. "What the hell is happening around here? Drunken kids, bigoted parents, promiscuous brothers and sisters! Shit, Billie!" Cat ranted.

Billie let her rant, leaning against the door and taking the time to compose herself before speaking. Finally, she took a deep breath. "Cat. Calm down. We need to look at this rationally." Billie started to pace back and forth as Cat sat on the edge of the bed.

"First, Drew and Dylan." Billie stopped in front of Cat and knelt on one knee. She placed a hand on Cat's thigh. "Cat, it didn't take us long to jump into bed together after we met," she said, holding a hand up to quell the tide that was about to erupt from Cat's mouth. "I know...we were together much longer than one day before doing the deed, but *I* was ready to do it from day one, weren't you?" she asked pointedly.

Cat looked down and blushed. "Yeah, I guess you're right," she said smiling coyly at her wife.

"All right, now about Seth. Somebody in that room needs a lecture. Maybe all of them, and I plan on providing it. They should have been keeping an eye on him. I'm sure our son will wake up with one colossal headache tomorrow morning. In fact, I hope he does...and I don't want you making it easy on him, okay? He needs to learn a lesson from this," Billie instructed.

"Me? Billie, you are the one who turns to mush when the kids are sick. I think you need to lecture yourself about that particular topic," Cat retorted.

Billie looked down at the floor and grinned, then peeked back up at Cat, still from bent knee. "You know me too well, wife. Well then, remind me tomorrow to give him a hard time about it, okay?" she asked.

"Deal!" Cat said.

Billie rose to her feet. "Now, what to do about my bigoted stepfather," she said.

Cat rose to her feet and wrapped her arms around Billie's waist. "Do we really have to do *anything* about him, Billie?" she asked.

"If we plan to have any kind of future relationship with my mother, I think we do," Billie replied. "We need to do this without casualties. That's the hard part," she explained.

"Well, I guess we start by treating him the same as everyone else. He was there when Seth drank the wine. He's just as responsible as the rest. Let's go kick some ass!" Cat exclaimed.

***

Moments later, Billie barged into the parlor. By then, the entire family except the children, Drew and Dylan were there. Doc, Ida and Laurel, who had gone on an evening stroll earlier, had joined the family shortly after Seth was led to bed.

"Okay, let's talk about being responsible adults," Billie started as Cat stood by her side, her arms crossed in front of her. "Our thirteen-year-old son is going to have one whiz-bang of a hangover tomorrow morning because several adults were too busy drinking and visiting to keep an eye on him," she stated.

Jim immediately became defensive. "I didn't see *you* here watching him," he accused.

"I was putting my daughters to bed, Jim. Seth asked if he could join all of you, and you collectively said yes. That makes *you* responsible for him," Billie reasoned.

Most of the men in the room had the decency to act sheepish at their shortcoming, all except Jim, who was primed for a fight after an entire day of badgering from the family on his moral beliefs. The wine in his system fueled his courage.

"Who are you to question my sense of responsibility and morality?" Jim questioned. "You, who live in sin on a daily basis in front of your children?"

Cat grasped Billie's arm firmly as she watched her wife's knuckles clench into fists.

"I think that's quite enough," Jo said, stepping between Jim and Billie. "I happen to like Billie's sense of morality. She's a very good wife and mother."

"You *would* think that. You are just like her!" Jim exclaimed. Now it was Laurel's turn to grab Jim's arm. He looked back sharply at who had hold of him arm. Seeing it was Laurel, his eyes immediately softened.

"I think I've had quite enough of this for one night," Alex piped in. "All this arguin' is gettin' us nowhere. Why don't we discuss this in the mornin', like southern genteel people," she suggested.

Jim shook off Laurel's arm and walked up to Alex. "As for you, madame, the southern aristocracy is not one I would stand by in times like these. After all, it was *they* who encouraged the immoral and hedonistic act of slavery!" he shouted.

Jo cringed as Alex's face turned beet red. The one thing that she had learned early on in her relationship with Alex, was to *not* insult her southern heritage.

Alex rose to her full height, and took a step forward. "You, Sir, are a rogue and a bore, and I kindly ask you to leave my home at the first opportunity in the mornin'!" she demanded.

"With pleasure!" Jim shouted as he stomped out of the room, followed closely by Laurel.

"Oh, my!" Alex said faintly as Kevin and Joe helped her to her favorite chair. Josephine was immediately by her side, holding her hand.

CHAPTER 12

After Jim stomped out of the parlor with Laurel tight on his heels, the rest of the family quickly dispersed to the far corners of the mansion, turning in for the evening, hoping that things would blow over by morning.

Six members of the household put in a very strenuous night. Three pairs of silhouettes stood in stark contrast to the raging storm outside the estate. Near hurricane winds invaded the region overnight, downing trees and cutting off electricity. There would be no planes departing the Charleston airport the next day.

Jo and Alex sat in bed, their backs against the headboard as they stared into the lightning-filled darkness. Alex reclined against Jo, her head on Jo's shoulder. "Josie, darlin', was I too rough on him?" she asked.

"No sweetheart, you weren't," she replied. "I understand how he could be upset with me and Billie. Sure, we were kind of rough on him earlier in the day, but that was no excuse for his rude behavior toward you. I'd say you handled the situation quite well, my love," Jo said proudly.

"The airport will be closed tomorrow, you know. He'll have to stay here for at least another day or two," Alex observed.

Josephine just nodded. "I know." She kissed Alex on the forehead and motioned for her to scoot down into a lying position. Taking Alex into her arms, Jo held her close and rubbed a hand up and down her forearm until she was asleep. Moments later, she too drifted off to the sounds of the storm raging outside.

***

"Jim, come to bed," Laurel said from her seated position against the headboard. Jim was standing by the window, staring into the rainy and windy night.

Jim turned his back to the window, leaned against the frame and placed both hands on the sill beside him. "Laurel, do you think I am too rigid and inflexible?" he asked.

Laurel pulled her knees up to her chest and hugged them close. "Sometimes you are, Jim." A pause. "Are you asking if I think you are being inflexible about this particular topic?" she asked.

Jim nodded.

Laurel took a deep breath and extended her legs straight out in front of her, leaning back on her hands. "Jim, I can't tell your heart how to feel. We are talking about my daughter and parents here. I love them, even the way they are. I won't say that I totally understand or embrace their lifestyle, but they are my flesh and blood and I love them regardless. I wish you could find it in your heart to at least accept them, but I can't ask you to do that. That is a decision you will have to make on your own, if you are even capable of it," Laurel explained.

Jim nodded again, then rose to his feet and leaned against the window frame. "The airport is sure to be closed tomorrow," he said into the silence.

"I know. Come to bed, Jim," Laurel said, holding the sheet open for Jim to crawl into.

***

Billie and Cat stood wrapped in each other's arms in front of the window, watching the raging storm outside. Cat's head lay on Billie's chest. Billie's cheek rested on Cat's head, her long arms wrapped around her. Bolts of lightning highlighted their forms on the wall behind them.

Long moments of silence filled the space, save for the random cracks of thunder.

After a time, Cat spoke.

"Billie?"

"Hmm?"

"I'm sorry things aren't working out with Jim. I know how much you wanted them to for Laurel's sake."

Billie nodded and pulled Cat closer. "I think we're being given another chance, Cat. This storm will definitely close the airport tomorrow," Billie observed.

"Do you think so?" Cat asked.

"Yeah. I'm going to try to get through to him one more time. I think I'll ask Dylan for some help," she explained.

"Billie, what did you think about finding Dylan and Drew together tonight? I mean, they're both adults, but...," Cat started.

"But she's your baby sister," Billie finished for her wife.

Cat smiled against Billie's chest. "Yeah, something like that."

"Well, I think it's pretty cool. But I am concerned that it was kind of sudden. I hope they've thought beyond their raging hormones," Billie explained.

Cat just nodded and squeezed Billie tighter while trying to stifle a yawn.

Billie pushed Cat slightly away from her and tilted her chin so she could look into her eyes. "Come on love, let's go to bed."

Climbing into bed, Billie lay on her back and opened her arms to Cat. She rolled onto her side and promptly wrapped her long frame around the smaller woman. Within moments, their bodies were entwined like braided rope, as they drifted off into the dreamscape.

***

The family woke the next morning to a freshly washed earth, the rains having cleansed the air, leaving a pungent odor of seawater and salt. The breeze had calmed and the sun was shining, ushering in a new day. Unfortunately, the midnight storm also brought with it random debris, strewn all over the grounds of the estate from fallen branches to garbage cans that once stood by the back door.

On this, their third day at the estate, the family pitched in to clean up after the storm, working all day to collect and stack strewn branches and debris into a large pile in the middle of the field beyond the house. Everyone pitched in. Of course, Billie had to drag a very hung-over Seth out of bed, and roust Dylan and Drew, but by mid-morning, they had a full crew, and between them all, they managed to clear the property of debris by the end of the day.

Considering the airports were indeed closed for the day, Jim and Laurel readily pitched in to do their share, not speaking directly to Alex or Jo about the events of the previous evening. Throughout the day, Alex and Laurel stole secretive glances…silent apologies made on the fresh ocean air, but other than that, no other contact was made.

The pile was easily fifteen feet high when they finished.

"Hey, why don't we have a bonfire after the fireworks tonight!" Tara exclaimed while standing at the base of the tall debris pile.

Jo came up beside her and pushed her fedora back onto her head. She had been sporting an unlit cigar between her teeth all day. When doing yard work, she typically donned her work clothes as Alexandra called them…loose pleated trousers and short sleeve shirt, both tan, leather knee-high boots into which she tucked the pant legs, and the ever-present fedora.

Jo placed both hands on the small of her back and looked up at the debris pile.

"Good idea, scamp. A bonfire is a very good idea. Maybe we can have a real Amazon type party. Heh, heh, heh. It's been a long time since I've been to one of those," she chuckled.

"Amazon?" Tara asked curiously.

"Oh yeah," Josephine grinned wickedly as she thought of scantily clad women gyrating around a bonfire to the steady beat of drums. "Amazons." With a definite mission in mind, she ran off to find Alex, and to assemble the women for an Amazon war council.

***

Jo had the women's full attention.

"Josephine Wycliffe, where on earth did you get that idea?" Alex asked, hands on her hips.

"From Tara," Jo said, a twinkle of excitement in her eye.

"It figures," Cat said between her teeth, causing Billie to grin and elbow her lightly in the ribs.

"Ah, Grandma Jo, exactly what do Amazons do at a party?" Amy asked, her curiosity piqued.

"Well in the time of the ancient Amazons, parties were organized to celebrate successful hunts, or bountiful harvests. Sometimes they were used as pep rallies, to emotionally prepare the women for going to war, and sometimes, they were used as religious or initiation ceremonies," Jo explained.

"And we would be celebrating...why?" Bridget asked.

"We would be celebrating family," Jo said. Walking around the group of women she had assembled near the pool, she added, "Look, humor an old lady. The last Amazon ritual Alex and I witnessed was ages ago, and it was so phony, it was laughable. We have the opportunity here to recreate history!" Josephine said excitedly, looking up at the sky and waving her hand in front of her as if creating the vision from her mind.

"Well, I think it's like, a cool idea," Drew said perkily. "Do we get to wear costumes?" she asked.

Jo looked at Alex with a wicked glint in her eye. Alex just dropped her head into her hands and moaned.

"Why do I think I'm not going to like this?" Bridget asked.

"Oh Bridge, loosen up. Have some fun," Amy urged.

"You know, this just might be fun," Cat added.

"Now let me get this straight," Billie said, leaning back to support her body with her arms. "We dress in scanty costumes, including masks, smear war paint all over our bodies, then seduce our partners by drinking wine and dancing around a bonfire until everyone is worked up into a sexual frenzy. Does that sound accurate?" she asked.

"Exactly!" said Jo.

"Count me in!" Billie said, grinning ear to ear, causing Cat to blush to the roots of her red-gold hair.

"I don't know about this," Bridget whined.

Ida and Laurel had been sitting quietly, listening to the proposal and subsequent conversation, trading opinions only with each other, until finally Ida spoke up. "We think it's a grand idea," she said, speaking for herself and her sister.

Bridget's eyebrows went out of sight. "Mom?" she said incredulously.

Ida walked over to her second oldest daughter and cupped her face between her palms. "Bridget, dear, there's still a glow in this old woman's heart. I'm not going to miss the chance to rekindle it into a raging fire."

Bridget was flustered speechless as Amy thrust her fist into the air and said, "You, go girl!" to her mother.

"Okay, it's settled then. It will take a day or two make the costumes, so we'll have the fireworks tonight and schedule the bonfire for the day after tomorrow." Jo looked around, collecting nods of approval from all the women.

"Grams, what about the children?" Cat asked.

"Well, they can certainly join in. We'll just save the good stuff for after they're in bed," Jo explained, wiggling her eyebrows up and down seductively.

Billie draped her arm around Jo's shoulder. "Bless your wicked heart," she said, chuckling.

As the group of women dissipated, Josephine detained Laurel. "Laurel, sweetheart, Nona and I would like to talk to you," she said.

Laurel approached her mothers, a sad look filling her eyes. Alex opened her arms to her daughter and held her close as Jo stood by rubbing the younger woman's back.

"Sweetheart," Alex began, "we don't want you to leave tomorrow. Things got out of hand yesterday. Things were said that shouldn't have been. Josie and I want you to know that we're sorry, and that we plan to talk to Jim as well."

"I don't want to leave either. I've just found you," she said tearfully.

For a long moment, mothers and daughter held each other.

Billie and Cat had walked a few paces away, before stopping and looking back at the trio. "Cat, I need to do something about this right away. This rift is breaking my mother's heart," Billie explained, looking down into the love-filled eyes of her wife.

Cat just nodded her head. "What can I do to help?" she asked.

"You're already helping, love. Your support is all I need."

***

"Dyl!" Billie shouted out across the yard to get her brother's attention. Once she had it, she waved him over.

"What's up, sis?" he asked, running toward her and Cat, slightly out of breath.

"Dylan, we need a big favor from you, one that may be very difficult for you to do. I want you to think about it, and if you are really uncomfortable with the idea, then we'll find another way," she began.

"Whoa, Billie, wait a minute. Maybe you should start with telling me what you're trying to accomplish, and what you want me to do," he said.

Billie looked at Cat, and then back at Dylan. "We're trying to make your father see the light," she said.

Dylan's eyes flew open wide. "And how do you propose to do that? He's been here for three days, and is holding stubborn to his beliefs," Dylan observed.

Billie cringed slightly as she prepared her brother for the blow. "Well, Dylan, I was kind of hoping that you'd help," she said sheepishly.

Seeing his sister's demeanor put him immediately on guard. "Somehow, I don't think I'm going to like this," he said, "but fire away."

Billie quickly explained her plan to her brother.

"You want me to *what*?" Dylan exclaimed.

"Come on, Dyl, it's for Mom," Billie urged.

Dylan walked a few feet away, then turned back to face his sister. "All right. All right, I'll do it for Mom, but there'd better be *no* witnesses, and I get to tell him the truth afterward. Agreed?" he demanded.

Billie flashed a crooked smile at her brother. "Agreed," she said, shaking hands with the young man.

***

Jo and Alex cornered Jim and Laurel later on that evening, just before dinner.

"Jim, may we have a word with you?" Alex asked, intercepting him in the hall on the way to the dining room.

Jim stopped short and looked at his mother-in-law, while Laurel squeezed his hand slightly. Jim briefly acknowledged the gesture before agreeing to speak with the elder ladies in the parlor.

Alex went directly to her favorite chair, while Josephine stood by the fireplace, one arm on the mantel. Jim and Laurel were directed to the divan opposite Alex's chair.

"Jim, Laurel," Alex began, hands folded daintily in her lap. "I would like to apologize for my rude behavior after dinner last evenin'. I'm afraid I let my Southern pride get in the way of my good sense," she began. "I do not wish to lose my daughter after havin' just found her, so I beg your forgiveness, and ask that you consider stayin' on for the duration of the week."

Jo clenched her fists as she stood at the mantel, her back partially turned toward her daughter and son-in-law. She hated to see Alex humble herself like that. After all, the confrontation wasn't all her fault.

Jim glanced at Laurel, and then rose to his feet. Taking one step forward, he bowed at the waist and reached for Alex's hand, which she gave readily. Kissing the back of her hand, he said, "Alexandra, I graciously accept your apology and offer one of my own. I'm afraid I wasn't on my best behavior last night either, and the wine I consumed did nothing to still my foolish tongue. Please forgive me."

Alexandra smiled ear to ear.

Jo unclenched her fists and visibly relaxed.

Laurel let out a breath she didn't realize she was holding.

All was well once more in the Spirakis/Wycliffe household as the ladies exchanged warm hugs and handshakes with their son-in-law.

***

Late that evening, after dinner was over and the sun had set, the entire family assembled on the front lawn of the mansion to watch the Fourth of July fireworks display. As was the tradition every year, Alex and Jo hosted the Independence Day celebration for the nearby community. Soon the field was peppered with lawn chairs filled with friends, neighbors and community members. Alex and Jo proudly introduced their family to the community, who returned the greetings with respect and warmth.

Jim noted the fury of activity with interest. Regardless of to whom the introductions were made...be it a city council member or the poor family from the farm down the road, Alex and Josephine greeted each person with the utmost respect, and received the same in kind. They made no pretense about the nature of their relationship. Ida and Laurel were introduced as their daughters. No attempt was made to hide the fact that they had committed their lives to each other in a loving and caring way, as a husband and wife would. And they were accepted. This fact amazed Jim the most. The community accepted them without reservation.

You have a lot to think about, his internal voice spoke to his heart. *You have to put aside the pain and humiliation and accept that what happened to you was not typical*, the voice said.

Jim shook his head to clear his mind, forcing his attention elsewhere as Jo introduced yet another neighbor to him.

Overall, the evening was a huge success. By the end of the fireworks, the individual families had migrated together; tired children lay draped across parents' arms while the grand finale lit up the sky very near the hour of midnight. Soon, friends and neighbors returned to their homes, after thanking Alex and Jo once again for hosting such a grand event as the celebration of their country's birthday. The only revelers left were the

Spirakis/Wycliffe clan, who were busy ushering small children to bed.

CHAPTER 13

The women made themselves scarce the next day, leaving the men to find their own entertainment. All six of them were sitting around the pool, Doc, Jim, Kevin, Joe, Dylan and Seth. Bored. This was the fifth day at SpireClyffe Acres and they had already seen the sights. It didn't cross their minds that they weren't there as tourists, but as family members on vacation. They were there to relax and enjoy life, not to spend their time involved in organized activities.

"We are pathetic!" Doc exclaimed. "Look at us! The women desert us, and we die of boredom!"

Kevin reclined his long legs in front of him and popped open another beer. "Yep, pathetic. That's us," he said, guzzling his beer.

It was in this state that Maggie found them when she went to tidy the area around the pool.

"Land sakes!" she clucked, hands on her hips. "Without the womenfolk around, you little puppies are lost, ain't cha?" she teased.

Rolling up the dishtowel she always carried in the waistband of her apron, she started snapping at the men's legs.

"Get your butts outta those chairs and do something! The ocean borders the property; and there's a fresh water lake just a mile down the road. Go fishing! There are horses in the stable. Go riding! Do something!" she scolded.

The men did their best to avoid Maggie's wrath as they jumped around, dodging the stinging towel.

"Okay! Okay! Fishing is good!" exclaimed Joe as he nearly jumped into the pool to avoid being snapped. Five other heads nodded vigorously in agreement.

"Good! Now be gone with y'all...and bring back supper!" she shouted after them, chuckling to herself as she returned to her kitchen.

***

"Grams, are we going to have enough material to make sixteen Amazon costumes?" Drew asked innocently.

"Well, sweetheart, since there's practically nothing to them, I'd say yes," Jo answered.

"Oh groan! What am I getting myself into?" Bridget complained.

Amy opened her mouth to reply, but was stilled by her mother's scolding look.

"Nothing to them, huh?" Billie said, directing the question at Jo, but looking at Cat with arched eyebrows.

Jo noted the look on Billie's face and swatted her granddaughter's arm. "Save it for later!" she scolded good-naturedly.

"Oh, there's plenty more where that came from," Billie said, grinning.

Cat reached up and grabbed the front of Billie's T-shirt, pulling her face close to her own. "If I'm going to run around half naked, gyrating all over the place for you, my love, you had better make it worth my while," she said seductively.

Billie placed a quick kiss on Cat's mouth. "Oh, you won't be disappointed. I promise you," she said, kissing her once more.

"Put a lid on it and get to work!" Josephine scolded once more, causing grins to cross the faces of Ida and Laurel who were busy with their own costumes.

"What are the men going to do while we're prostituting ourselves in front of them?" Amy asked.

"Oh, Amy, do you have to use that word?" Bridget said, cringing at the thought.

"Bridge, are you still a virgin?" Amy asked. "Because you sure act like one!"

"Amy Marie, stop badgering your sister. Do you hear me?" Ida scolded. "My word! Do you always have to pick at her like that?"

Amy had the decency to look ashamed. Punching Bridget lightly in the arm, she said, "Aw come on, Bridge, you know I'm just teasing, don't you?"

"Yeah, I guess so," Bridget admitted, "but you know Amy, not everyone is as loose as you," she added.

Amy's head perked up, a big grin plastered across her face. "Touché, sister dear!" she said as Bridget and Cat exchanged a high-five. Billie grinned at the sisterly exchange.

"To answer your question, dear," Alex volunteered, "Grandma Jo and I have decided to put the men in charge of the drums. Of course, we'll have to teach them the rhythm, and teach all of you the Amazon war song and dance, but you'll catch on quickly, I'm sure."

"We have to learn a song, Nona?" asked Laurel.

"Oh yes. It is a special war song, sung by the Amazons the evening before battle. It pumped them up, so to speak. Got them all excited about going to war," Alex explained.

"Do the men get to wear, like, skimpy costumes, too? I'm, like, dying to see Dylan in a g-string!" Drew exclaimed.

All eyes turned to Drew, mouths open. Cat and Billie dropped their faces into their hands.

"Ooops! I guess you all, like, didn't know about that, did you? Well, now you do!" she squealed delightfully.

Laurel raised an eyebrow at Billie, whose face betrayed the fact that *she* obviously knew about it. Billie winced out her apology.

"Well, nothing like keeping it in the family, huh?" Amy said, breaking the tension and causing general laughter to spread out across the room.

***

It was very late into the afternoon before the costumes were ready. True to Jo's word, they did not require much material.

The tops consisted of two small triangles of leather to cover each breast, held on by straps around the neck and back, and decorated with various feathers and beads. Swirling patterns were drawn here and there with gold or silver paint sticks. The bottoms were cut low, and just barely covered the essentials. Strands from a couple of old grass skirts had been sewn in sparsely around the periphery of the waistbands, falling to the knees of the wearers. In lieu of masks, the plan was to decorate their hair with more feathers and grass strands, and to add beaded necklaces, and feathery wrist bracelets, gauntlets and ankle bracelets. Their feet would be bare. The costumes for the little girls and for the older women, were of similar design, but much more modest.

Once the ladies' costumes were completed, they started on the men's. Cat and Billie worked on Seth's, Drew made Dylan's and the remaining four ladies made one for each of their husbands.

"They're not gonna wear these things, you know," Amy said.

"Hey, if I can parade my old wrinkled butt around in one of these skimpy costumes, then they can proudly display their beer bellies!" Josephine exclaimed.

"Josie, dear heart, I beg to differ, but your wrinkled old butt is kinda cute," Alex replied. "I kinda like it the way it is...aged, like good wine and cheese," she said.

"Great!" Jo said, throwing her hands out to the sides. "My butt reminds her of moldy old cheese!"

The women roared with laughter at Alex and Jo's antics.

It was going to be an interesting bonfire.

***

The men stood proudly around the dining room, holding chairs out for the ladies to be seated. The women approached cautiously, not really sure what their partners and sons were up to. Finally, all were seated and waiting expectantly for Maggie to serve the meal.

As the doors to the kitchen swung open, the men puffed their chests out, smug expressions crossing their faces as

Maggie placed a meal of blackened catfish, Cajun rice and black-eyed peas before the diners.

Alex recognized the delicacy immediately, "I do declare, Maggie!" she exclaimed. "Where on earth did you find catfish on such short notice?"

"The men-folk were kind enough to catch it for us, Miss Alexandra," Maggie replied. "That is, after I chased their scrawny, moping butts outta here this morning," she added, hands perched on her generous hips, head bobbing side to side as she made her exclamation. Laughter erupted around the table.

Alex looked around at the proud faces. "Well, thank you very much, kind sirs," she said formally, receiving nods of acknowledgment in return.

Cat leaned over to Billie and whispered in her ear, "They're all cavemen, including our son!"

Billie chuckled her agreement as she dove into her dinner, savoring every bite.

***

Bright and early the next morning, Josephine took the men into the basement where she and Alex stored artifacts and museum pieces they had collected over the years. Among the items were several tall drums and other percussion instruments. Allowing them to choose their own instruments, she finally had them organized enough to start demonstrating the basic Amazon drum beat. As she suspected, the younger men went for the drums, while Doc and Jim opted for the sticks and maracas.

It took a full two hours for the four drummers to finally get the pattern of the beat, and another hour for them to meld together so that they complimented rather than compete against each other. Finally, the sticks and maracas were blended into the music.

"Okay, fellas, one more time," Jo instructed as she led the band with the makeshift baton she had constructed out of a pencil. "One, two, three..." she beat as the song began. Jo stood there, listening intently, trying to feel the spirit of the song, to no avail.

Damn! she said to herself. *Looks like they're all tone deaf...all except for young Seth. Maybe there's something to that rap music after all.*

Josephine paced back and forth, trying to figure out how to get some umph into the beat. Finally, on the verge of giving up, she though, *Oh hell, maybe everyone will be too drunk to notice.* Suddenly, the thought hit her. "Of course!" she shouted out loud.

The men stopped playing and looked at Josephine with raised eyebrows.

"Fellas, how would you all like some cold beer? Or maybe whiskey shots?" Josephine suggested, grinning ear to ear.

Smiles broke out across all but one face...Seth's, who promptly turned green, remembering the hangover from the day before.

Well, this is one way to get them to wear the costumes. They'll be too drunk to care! Josephine thought as she poured the shots. Passing them out to all but Seth, they raised their glasses in a toast.

"Here's to the best Amazon bonfire ever. To the Amazons!" Jo shouted.

"To the Amazons!" toasted the men.

***

"Okay, ladies," Alex said, clapping her hands and lining the women in a row on the back patio. "Now ya really have to put your own style into it, but basically you hop around from foot to foot kinda like this," she said, demonstrating something that looked similar to an Indian war dance. "Then ya stop, knees bent, feet pointing out, hands on your knees, and sway your head side to side, like this." Again, Alex demonstrated the dance step. "Okay, now let me see y'all do it," she said.

Fourteen females, ages seven to fifty-five began gyrating to imaginary music. Alex covered her mouth with her hand to prevent the ladies from seeing the grin that was rapidly growing there.

"All right now, throw a little hip action into it. Yes, that's it!" Alex said to Amy as she let loose.

"Shake those shoulders, Drew. You've got it! Come on Caitlain, sway those hips! Bridget…Bridget honey, you've got to loosen up. You're way too stiff!" Alex commented, causing Amy to snort.

"Ida, Laurel, girls, you're not going to raise your husbands' spirits with moves like those!" Alex said, raising wicked eyebrows.

Finally, exasperated at the group of mannequins and robots she had in front of her, Alex called a time out. "Okay, ladies, let's take a break. All right, I'd like all my little grandbabies to come here for a moment," she instructed.

The seven little girls all gathered around their grandmother. "Okay, sweetlings," she said. "How would you like to do Grams a big favor?" she asked.

Seven heads shook in unison.

"Good! Please run in to the house and tell Maggie that Grams would like a big pitcher of her special ice tea and eight glasses for us ladies, and to give each of you some cookies and something to drink as well. Okay?" she asked.

Once the kids were out of hearing range, Alex sat the ladies down for a talk. "Okay ladies, we need to talk," she began. "I'm gonna be up front with y'all. This dance I'm teachin' you is not only a war dance, it's an Amazon mating dance."

Bridget's eyes flew open. Rising to her feet, she put her hands on her hips and exclaimed, "I thought so! Grams, how could you? Why, I never!" she said.

"That's just the problem, Bridge. You never!" Amy replied.

"Now that's enough, girls," Alex said. "Anyway, y'all need to loosen up and to put some passion and spunk into it. Your goal here is to seduce your mate."

Billie leaned in to whisper in Cat's ear. "So, should I play hard to get?"

Cat poked Billie in the ribs with her elbow.

"All right now, here comes our refreshments," Alex said, indicating the maid pushing the refreshment cart onto the patio, followed by the children.

One by one, eyes widened as they sampled Alex's special ice tea. This was going to be an interesting lesson.

***

By dusk, the estate was buzzing with activity. The entire morning and part of the afternoon was spent practicing for the evening dance. By early evening, everyone was in costume and war paint, beer bellies and wrinkled old butts included. By that time, all self-consciousness about how foolish they looked had flown out the window, thanks to the whiskey shots and special ice tea they had consumed all day.

A nice buffet dinner had been laid out on the patio, containing several food items one would expect to see at a primitive cookout, including spare ribs, corn on the cob, corn muffins, fresh fruit salad, cold baked potatoes and several skins of very strong wine.

After dinner the music began. The men were so loose from the shots and wine they had consumed that they played flawlessly. It didn't take much encouragement for the women to get up and dance to the intoxicating beat, swaying their bodies to and fro, seductively gyrating their hips, throwing their heads back and flailing their arms. It did take some effort however, to remember that the children were still awake and anxiously waiting for the bonfire to be lit.

Soon, the fire was raging as the wall of flames lit up the night sky. Within a couple of hours, the children started yawning. One by one, they were led to bed by parents anxious to get the party started. By eleven, they had all retired, including Seth. Finally, they were alone as both the bonfire and the fires within their souls were fed by the alcohol they had consumed and the atmosphere they had created by the music and dancing.

The dance started with the nine women moving in war-like fashion around the bonfire. The fire reflected off the scantily clad forms, covered with a layer of sweat produced by the heat of the fire and the exertion of the dance. The dance was intoxicatingly seductive, pulling the women into a trance-like state as they moved around the fire.

Primal urges overcame them. One by one, they loosened up and released their inhibitions, gyrating to the drumming, singing in deep guttural tones as they swayed to the music, seducing their respective mates with thrusting hips and roaming hands as they passed by them. The most surprising release of inhibition came from Bridget who, fueled by the amount of tea she had consumed throughout the day, totally let loose and openly seduced Kevin while he tried desperately to keep his tempo on the drum. They were the first couple to leave the party.

One by one, couples deserted the flock. Doc and Ida, Dylan and Drew, Jim and Laurel, Alex and Jo, Amy and Joe. Finally, Cat and Billie stood alone, wrapped in each other's arms, sweat glistened bodies melding together in front of the dwindling bonfire, Cat's head lying flat against Billie's chest, Billie's cheek resting on top of Cat's head.

"Billie," Cat whispered.

"Yes, my love?" came the answer as they swayed to the nonexistent music.

"Let's go walk on the beach," she suggested.

Billie looked up at the sky. "It looks like it might rain, Cat," she observed.

"Don't worry love, you're not made of sugar, you won't melt," chucked the smaller woman.

Billie threw her head back and laughed, taking Cat's hand. They headed across the field to the beach.

It was a very dark night, the moon peeking through at random intervals between the dark clouds that floated across the sky. Led primarily by the sound of the water, Cat and Billie made their way to the water's edge, walking along in the surf, hand in hand, savoring the feel of the warm water on their feet and the smell of the sea invading their nostrils. They would stop occasionally to share a kiss, a touch, or a look.

At one point, the sky completely clouded over, leaving them in total darkness. The couple stopped walking and just held each other, basking in the solitude their self imposed prison brought to them. No light...only sound and touch. Suddenly, it began to rain.

Falling to the sand, they huddled together, with Cat sitting between Billie's legs, resting her back against Billie's chest. The feel of the damp sand under their fingers was their only connection to the earth as they listened to the sound of the waves hitting the shore. They imagined the white cascading foam receding back into the ocean, as the smell of salt and seaweed permeated their senses. Inhaling deeply, their lungs filled with the glorious nectar of life-giving air as the spray of the ocean settled lightly on their skin, adding to the dampness brought on by the rain.

Suddenly the sky above them released the demon within, thunderous applause rolling in its wake as the sky lit up with its fire. Wave after wave of vibrations rocked the earth as the storm raged its way across the earthen stage, touching its audience with breathtaking adeptness, as baby angels cried their sorrows down upon the earth in torrents.

Cat and Billie smiled broadly as the forces of nature joined to hit the earth with a resounding crash that shook them to the very core of their beings, making them gasp for breath and filling their chests with a sudden burst of adrenaline. Billie reclined on the sand, holding herself and Cat up by her elbows. Throwing their heads back, they thrust their chins toward the traitorous sky as the rain drops pummeled their bodies and the lightning proudly displayed the slick moisture covering their skin.

Another loud clap of thunder and burst of lightning filled the darkness as a wave of near-orgasmic excitement ran through the women sitting on the beach. The excitement was too great for Cat to control. As another bolt of lightning lit up the sky, she scurried to her knees and faced a reclining Billie. Billie could see the intense passion in her face reflected by the streak of lightning.

"Billie, this is driving me crazy. Make love to me, right here...right now," she pleaded.

Billie narrowed her eyes at Cat, smiling seductively. She helped Cat to her feet then stepped in close to cup her face between wet sandy palms. Lowering her face, she kissed Cat passionately, the rain falling in torrents around them, causing their loose hair to adhere slickly to their faces, dark entwined with red-gold.

Billie reached under Cat's legs and lifted her into her arms, carrying her to the edge of the water. Falling to her knees, she lowered Cat into the surf and laid her body on top of her, propping herself up by her elbows on both sides of Cat's head. Taking Cat's face between her hands, she kissed her long and hard, driving her tongue deep into her wife's mouth, just as a wave crashed onto their entwined forms, covering them completely with water.

Cat gasped, desperately fighting both Billie and the receding tide for air. As soon as the water cleared, Billie returned for more, barely giving Cat time to fill her lungs before devouring her mouth again. Another wave hit them. In a surge of desperation, Cat pushed against Billie, rolling them both over. Sitting up straight on top of Billie, Cat threw her head back, her hair whipping the water and sand around as she gasped once more for air.

"Billie!" Cat gasped. "I need you now!" she said desperately, her hands placed firmly on Billie's shoulders, pinning her to the surf. The combination of air restriction and the storm raging around them was causing her level of desire to rage out of control.

Billie surged upward, bringing herself into a sitting position, with Cat straddling her lap. Reaching up, she grabbed the center of Cat's Amazon bra and ripped it off forcibly, breaking the straps that held it in place around her neck and back. Reaching behind Cat, she pulled her close, their cores separated only by the thin material of their outfits.

"God, Billie. Yes!" Cat screamed as Billie pounced on and roughly devoured first one breast and then the other. Cat grabbed Billie by the hair on either side of her head as she threw her own head back, forcing her breasts closer to Billie's eager mouth. Rain pummeled down, lightning highlighting their passion-filled silhouettes against the darkened beach.

Billie pulled Cat's mouth to her own. "Cat, I want you so badly. I want to kneel before you and inhale your musky scent. I want to explore your center with my mouth. I want to fill you with everything that I am. Oh, God, Cat, I want to hear you scream my name and beg me to take you over and over," Billie proclaimed passionately.

Cat was shaking out of control, her whole body in a state of sexual shock. "Do it! Billie, please. Love me," she said, her nerves strung out to the breaking point.

The clouds started to thin, allowing the moon to shine through; however, the rain continued to fall lightly.

Rocking herself forward, Billie laid Cat back down in the surf and leaned in between her legs, tenderly kissing her face and neck. Cat's core was pressed into Billie's abdomen, her legs wrapped around her waist. Sitting back on her heels, she forced Cat's bottom to lie flat on the sand, her legs still straddling her wife's lap. Billie knelt above her lover and savored the look of intense passion and pleading in her wife's eyes. Placing her hands on Cat's knees, she slowly ran them down the insides of Cat's thighs, causing Cat to convulse with desire.

"Billie, please!" Cat pleaded in a small voice. "I am so wet for you, love."

Reaching under her wife, Billie pulled the rest of her Amazon costume off, placing kisses along the length of Cat's legs as she released each one from the confines of the panties. Billie inhaled the scent of her lover from the panties before casting them away.

Cat was shaking out of control from the intensity of her own sexual desire. Her head was thrown back, hands grasping the sand by her sides, rain falling steadily onto her face.

Billie leaned in once more to place several tender kisses on Cat's mouth, neck and breasts as another tide surged in and covered their bodies.

Sitting up, Billie looked down at her Cat's naked, quivering form. Green, smoldering eyes, hooded with desire. Red-gold hair spread out around her in the sand, swaying to and fro in the tide like seaweed. Nipples became erect from desire and the effects of the cold tide flowing over them in periodic waves. A small puddle of sandy water was trapped in her navel, the hair around her treasure wet and glistening from a combination of the tide and Cat's overflowing desire. Billie's restraint was sorely tested as she took in the sum total of desire before her. She felt her own font overflow with wetness for this wondrous beauty beneath her.

Unable to restrain herself any longer, Billie reached under Cat and lifted her bottom out of the surf, raising it high out of the water, and resting in on her own chest, bringing Cat's core to with reaching distance of her mouth. Looking down over the expanse of abdomen at the smaller woman below her, Billie saw the desperation and want in Cat's eyes. Without further hesitation, Billie closed her eyes and inhaled the heady aroma, bringing her mouth to feast for long moments upon the treat awaiting her there as Cat writhed in sexual agony.

Oh, God! Billie thought, almost climaxing at the shear pleasure she was bringing to her wife. *God, Cat, you taste wonderful. I could feast on your gifts forever. How does this feel, love?* She flicked her tongue over Cat's pleasure point.

Cat responded in kind with a loud moan and an upward thrust of her hips.

You liked that, huh? I thought so. God, I love doing this to you. How about this? Billie thought again, as her teeth nipped lightly at the swollen bud of desire.

Cat's whole body stiffened in response.

Oh, no, no, no, no. Not yet, love. It's much too soon, Billie thought as she released the bud and blew cool air over the heated area.

"Billie! I am so close. Please let me come," Cat begged.

Billie responded by blowing more cool air over Cat's heated core. "Not yet love," she said, lowering Cat's bottom to the sand once more, relieving the pressure on the smaller woman's neck.

"Yes. Billie, please!" Cat begged.

"No love," Billie answered as she leaned in once more to kiss her wife. Reaching under Cat's shoulders, she gathered her into her arms just as another wave hit them.

Lifting Cat out of the water, Billie pulled her in to straddle her waist once more. Cat ground her core into Billie's abdomen in an attempt to gain some relief.

Billie looked at her and raised one eyebrow in reprimand.

Cat leaned in and placed butterfly kisses on and around Billie's left ear. "Please," she whispered to her wife.

"No," Billie whispered back.

Wrapping her arms tightly around Cat's waist, Billie rose to her knees and then to her feet. Cat remained locked around her wife, arms around her neck, legs around her waist, tongues firmly entwined in her mouth, as Billie walked into deeper water. When the water came to just below Billie's breasts, she relaxed her hold on Cat and allowed it to provide buoyancy.

Billie grasped Cat's face between her hands and once more buried her tongue deep into her mouth.

Cat was on fire. She couldn't believe that she was standing there in the cold ocean with her wife, yet she was on fire...literally overheated with desire. Cat returned Billie's ardor tenfold in a breathtaking kiss, fighting for room in Billie's mouth.

Cat was so preoccupied with the kiss that she didn't feel Billie moved one hand into the water, beneath her. Suddenly, Billie thrust upward, burying two fingers deep within her wife.

Cat came out of the water like she was shot from a cannon. "*Oh, my god!*" she screamed into the night. "Billie! God, Billie! More! Please! Harder!" she cried loudly as Billie added a third finger and thrust repeatedly into Cat.

Cat was nearly comatose from the sensations coursing through her body. Never before had she felt such sudden, intense desire as she did at that moment. In the seven years she had been with Billie she had experienced nearly every level of desire possible...or so she thought. This was something totally foreign and far more intense than anything she had ever lived through. Between the intense shafts of desire shooting from her core to her brain and the stimulating temperature of the water, she was helpless to resist as she tumbled violently over the chasm of orgasmic pleasure. Down she plummeted, free falling for several moments until she finally landed on a downy pillow of love in the arms of her wife.

Shivering uncontrollably, Cat laid her head on Billie's shoulder as her body recovered from the desirous trauma it had just experienced.

Billie reached around and lifted Cat into her arms, holding her close as she slowly walked toward the shore.

God, Cat. I feel so needed right now. To be able to bring you this level of pleasure is all I ever want out of life. I will love you till my last breath, sweetheart, she thought as she approached the shore and sat with her back against a large piece of driftwood, holding Cat across her lap as the smaller woman fell asleep in her arms.

CHAPTER 14

The next morning found Billie and Cat asleep on the beach, both lying on their sides, Billie's back up against the large piece of drift wood she had used as a backrest the previous night, with a naked Cat tucked protectively within the circle of her arms. They were a mess—covered with war paint, dried mud and sand particles in places they didn't even know existed, hair tangled and littered with sand and seaweed.

"Hey," said a voice. "Hey, you two, time to get up."

Startled, Billie immediately jumped to her feet to defend herself and her charge. Clearing her eyes of sleep, she looked at the intruder and realized it was Josephine.

"Grandma Jo," she said, rubbing her eyes, effectively adding more sand to them. "Damn!" she said, brushing her hands off. "What happened?"

"I'd say, too much wine, and passion by the looks of it. Amazon bonfires...gotta love 'em!" Jo exclaimed, handing Billie the blanket she had brought with her.

Taking the blanket, Billie knelt down and shook the still-sleeping Cat. "Cat, sweetheart, come on, wake up, love. Grandma Jo is here," Billie said gently.

Cat brushed her hand away. "Go'way," she said stubbornly, causing Jo to chuckle and mumble something about it running in the family.

Billie resorted to the direct approach. "Cat, you are lying on the beach in broad daylight, naked. Now I have a blanket here for you to cover up with, but you don't get it until you get up," she said.

Cat immediately shot up into a sitting position. "What?" she said alarmed, looking around wildly.

Billie gave her a few seconds to recover before handing the blanket to her. Helping her to her feet, Billie threw an arm around the smaller woman as she steadied herself.

Cat looked around at her surroundings. "We spent the night here, didn't we?"

Billie shook her head.

Opening the blanket to look at her own state of undress, she looked back at her still-clothed wife and grinned, "Looks like I owe you one, huh?" she said.

Billie shook her head once more then leaned in to whisper in Cat's ear, "I'll expect payment in the shower this morning."

Cat grinned from ear to ear. The shower was one of her favorite places to make love to her wife. The possibilities were endless.

"Well if you two are done with your foreplay, we should be headed back. Everyone else has been up, dressed and fed for about an hour now," Jo informed them.

"How did you know where to find us?" Cat asked.

"Well, this is exactly where I would have brought Alex if we were about 40 years younger. Lucky guess, I suppose. Be grateful *I* found you and not Jim," she added as they headed back to the house.

"Grandma Jo, do you think he'll ever come around?" Billie asked. "I mean, we all go home tomorrow. If we haven't changed his mind yet, I'm not sure we ever will."

"Well, I guess you have to ask yourself if it matters if he accepts us...or not," Jo reasoned.

"For Mom's sake, I think it matters," Billie replied solemnly.

"Well then, for your mom's sake, I hope he does," Jo replied as she locked arms with Billie for the walk back to the mansion.

***

Billie and Cat returned to their room through the back staircase leading from the kitchen to the upper stories. They were in such a state of disarray, they wanted to avoid the stares and ribbing that would most certainly have come if the family had seen them. As it was they had to endure Maggie's clucking as they passed through the kitchen.

After a very long shower, Cat and Billie donned T-shirts and shorts, and climbed into bed to snuggle for a while. Cat spooned herself behind Billie's taller frame, wrapping her arms around her wife's waist and kissing her lightly between the shoulder blades.

"Cat," Billie whispered.

"Hmm?" Cat replied.

"I love you."

Cat smiled into Billie's back and kissed her again.

"I love you too," she whispered back before drifting off to sleep.

Sometime later, the ladies found themselves awakened by two small bodies perched on top of them.

"Grrrrrrrrr," Billie said under her breath.

Giggling.

"Grrrrrrrrrrrrrrrr," she said again, this time, starting to stir.

More giggling.

"Grrrrrrrrrrrrrrrrrrrrr!!!" she said one more time, rearing up and capturing the children, pulling them down between Cat and herself and pinning them with her weight. By this time, Cat was fully awake and quite ready to participate in the capture.

"Mama Bear, what do we have here?" Billie said in a deep gravelly voice.

"Looks like dinner to me, Papa Bear," Cat replied.

The children squealed with delight.

"Do you think we need to cook them first?" asked Papa Bear.

"Nah, let's eat them raw!" replied Mama Bear.

The two bears proceeded to tickle the little intruders with tiny nips to their bellies.

After several moments of torture, the two ladies collapsed on top of the children, wrestling around with them until the little girls had managed to position themselves on top, straddling the adults.

"Okay! Okay, we give up!" Billie said to Skylar and Lisa, Bridget's youngest daughter.

"What do you rugrats want?" Cat asked, pinned to the bed by Lisa.

"Grandma and Nana sent us to look for you. Said you been sleepin' long enough," Skylar related.

"Well, they're probably right," Billie said. Looking over to Cat she added, "Whaddaya think Mama Bear? Do you think hibernation is over?"

"Yep, I think it is, and beside, you need a shave, Papa Bear," Cat replied, grinning.

"Why you...," Billie said, lunging to grab Cat who moved just beyond her reach and rolled off the bed, running out of the room behind the squealing children.

***

The family gathered on the side lawn to celebrate one last afternoon of fun before they had to migrate home the following day. With twenty-two people, they easily had two complete waffle ball teams, and quickly proceeded to split into two groups. For the next few hours, they played ball, no one really taking the game very seriously, adults bumbling the plays when the younger children managed to hit the ball. The game ended with scores that resembled football more than baseball. By late in the afternoon, everyone was thoroughly exhausted, but elated with the camaraderie and sense of family that pervaded the atmosphere.

Maggie outdid herself once more with an elaborate cookout, which the family enjoyed while the children played croquet and the adults lounged by the pool. Billie and Cat were in the pool with Dylan and Drew, hitting a beach ball back and forth, while the rest of the adults were reclining in loungers or visiting at nearby patio tables.

While passing the ball back and forth, Billie and Cat simultaneously lunged for the ball. Billie's hand grazed off the side of it and came down to accidentally hit Cat right in the side of the face. Cat immediately went down into the water, holding her hand to her face.

"Cat!" Billie exclaimed, reaching into the water to retrieve her injured wife. All eyes turned to the women as Billie pulled her up and profusely apologized for striking her.

"Cat, sweetheart, I'm so sorry," she said, kissing the spot where her hand had made contact with her wife's cheek.

"I'm all right, Billie. It was an accident. I'm fine," Cat said, but eagerly accepted the gentle caresses her wife was dishing out.

Billie leaned in and kissed her face once more, then placed a delicate kiss on her lips. "Forgive me?" she asked, looking directly into Cat's green eyes.

"Oh, for crying out loud! She said she was all right!" Jim suddenly proclaimed. "Christ! Your kind makes me sick sometimes!"

Alex gasped, reaching for Jo as she felt a faint coming on.

Total silence descended as all eyes turned to Jim. Laurel held her breath, disbelief clouding her features.

Billie moved away from Cat and hefted herself out of the pool, very near to where Jim was sitting. Dylan moved quickly to intercept her.

"What did you say to me?" Billie said, venom lacing her voice.

"Billie, no," Dylan said, physically holding his sister back.

"No, Dylan. Someone needs an attitude adjustment," she said.

"Then let me do it," he said.

Billie looked at her brother, remembering the favor she had asked of him earlier. Raising her eyebrows in question, she silently asked him to explain.

"I'm beyond caring if there are witnesses, Billie," he said. Turning to his father, he continued. "Dad, do you love me?" he asked.

Jim shifted his eyes from Billie to Dylan, confusion clouding them over. "What kind of question is that?" he asked.

"Just answer it. Do you love me?" Dylan asked again.

"You know that I do, son. I would die for you," he said vehemently.

"What if I told you I was gay, Dad. Would that change the way you feel about me?" He asked pointedly.

Drew, who had moved over to stand next to Cat, gasped out loud. "You are?" she asked. Cat elbowed her in the ribs.

"Dylan," Jim stammered.

"Answer the question, Dad," Dylan shouted, causing his mother to take a step forward. Ida promptly stopped her sister's advance with a hand on her arm.

Jim was totally confused. "Why...why no. It wouldn't change the way I feel. You would still be my son," Jim said, his voice cracking with emotion as his eyes darted around in a near panic state.

"Then why can't you accept my sister and my grandmothers?" Dylan asked. "For that matter, why can't you accept all gays? Why, Dad?" he said, once again raising his voice.

"Because they're evil. Don't you understand? They corner little boys in closets, and touch them, and make them do things that...oh, God. It wasn't my fault!" Jim exclaimed, falling to his knees, crying.

By this time, Billie and Cat both realized what was happening. Taking a quick step forward, Billie wrapped her arms around her stepfather and sank to the floor with him, holding his head against her chest. Ida released Laurel's arm at the same time that Cat climbed out of the pool and approached the fallen man. Dylan fell to his knees and wrapped his arms around his sister and father. Soon, the family of five knelt in a huddle, comforting the crying man in the center, while Jo and Alex respectfully ushered the rest of the family away from the patio, allowing the stricken family time and space to heal.

* * *

The sun rose far too early for the family the next morning, knowing that this was their last day together, probably for a long time to come. The atmosphere was solemn around the breakfast table. Even Maggie had tears in her eyes as she served the family their last meal together. After they were all seated and served, Jo and Alex stood together at one end of the long table and looked out over their loved ones. Jo cleared her throat. All eyes turned in the direction of the elderly ladies.

"Ah, I'm not very good at this, but I'll take a stab anyway," Jo began, as Alex wiped the corner of her eye with her breakfast napkin. "This past week has been one of the most wonderful that Alex and I can remember. Who would have thought that fifty years ago, when I met this magnificent woman," she said, taking Alex's hand, "that we would end up with such a wonderful family."

Josephine paused to take a drink of water and to compose herself before continuing.

"Some of us came together a week ago as virtual strangers, but will depart here as family, united in love...and make no mistake, Alex and I love each and every one of you deeply. A very big piece of our heart will leave with you today. Please don't stay away too long. God willing, Alex and I will be around for many more years, and we pray they will be years filled with the presence of those before us today," Jo recited.

Several sniffles were heard around the room. Billie reached for Cat's hand under the table and squeezed it tightly. Cat looked over at Billie and allowed a lone tear to run down her cheek.

Billie leaned in and kissed it away. "Don't cry, love. We'll be back," she whispered to her emotional wife.

Josephine continued. "As part of your assurance that we'll see you often, Alex and I have decided to invite the children to spend part of their summer vacations here each year. In fact," Jo said, raising her hand to quell the squall of excitement that started to arise around the table, "In fact, we'd like to make a one-week Fourth of July vacation mandatory for the whole family every year...complete with an Amazon bonfire. What do you say?" she asked, looking hopefully around the table.

A loud cheer broke out as the children started making plans with their favorite cousins for the next year's visit. The adults rose from their seats and circled Alex and Jo, hugging them vigorously and exchanging promises to attend. Finally, Jo raised her hands, signaling for quiet all around. When the room was silent once more, she turned to Alex and said, "Alex, was there anything you wanted to say to our family before Maggie serves breakfast?"

Alexandra inhaled deeply, then rose to her full height and looked around the room. "Josie agreed to do all the talkin' cause I'm just a big mushball when it comes to sayin' goodbye. But I do want to say one thing. The sayin' goes that you can choose your friends, but you can't choose your relatives. Well, between you and me, I am so glad that it's true, 'cause I can't imagine choosin' better relatives on my own. The gods were truly lookin' out for Josie and I when they picked y'all for us. We love you, and we're lookin' forward to doin' this again next year," she finished.

The room erupted once more in a barrage of cheers, hugs and kisses before the family finally settled down for their last meal together.

***

The rest of the day was spent in tearful goodbyes as each family departed for home, promising to stay in touch with each other and the elderly ladies from Charleston.

Goodbyes were especially bittersweet between Jim and the ladies. Since his breakdown the evening before, they had spent several hours talking and coming to an understanding about the trauma that had left Jim feeling the way he did about homosexuals. After much discussion, he came to realize that he had stereotyped all gays based on that one horrifying childhood experience with an abuser he assumed was gay, but was probably in fact, not. He came to realize that pedophilia was not a gay disease, and that in fact, most pedophiles are heterosexual men.

Jim acknowledged that he needed to be more open minded and accepting. Several promises were made by all parties to spend time together working out the issues and forming new bonds. Before departing, Jim and Laurel made plans to visit with their daughter and family, specifically for that reason.

***

Billie and Cat waved vigorously as their plane left the runway, stopping only after the plane became airborne. Sitting back in their seats, Cat reached out and took Billie's hand, kissing the back of it before pulling it in close to her heart. Looking at her wife, such love shone from her eyes that it took Billie's breath away. Billie saw something else there as well...something she questioned with her eyes.

Cat just smiled knowingly, and thought of the skimpy Amazon outfits she had tucked away into their bags, as the plane soared homeward.

Part II

For Better, Or For Worse

CHAPTER 15

She lay in slumber, oblivious to the watchful eye of the woman who silently feasted on her beauty...watching the rise and fall of her shoulders as she lay face down on the bed, arms tucked beneath the pillowy down that cushioned her face.

Oh, what I wouldn't give to be the down in that pillow, that I could cradle such beauty, she thought as she smiled and delicately drew one long finger down the length of the sleeping beauty's arm.

The sleeping woman twitched as the nerve endings on her arm registered the intrusion.

Leaning in, the dark-haired woman whispered, "I love you," as her lips made contact with the soft contours of her bedmate's cheek.

A tiny smile crossed the features of the sleeping woman as she subconsciously acknowledged the caress.

Continuing her game of hit and run, the woman reached over once more and brushed golden bangs off the forehead of her victim. "You are my heart," she whispered huskily.

An arm shot out from under the pillow to shoo away the bothersome contact...but still, she slept.

A wide grin spread across the woman's features at the redhead's reaction. Reaching forward yet again, she grasped the edge of the sheet covering the slim figure and gently tugged, stopping periodically as her victim stirred, allowing her to settle in again with a false sense of security before renewing her assault. Finally, she had the bedcover pulled down to the sleeping woman's waist, exposing a creamy expanse of naked flesh, dotted with the freckles of summer.

Throwing back her mane of dark hair, the woman closed her eyes and smiled to herself, remembering the passionate encounter the night before that was ultimately responsible for the golden-haired angel's state of undress. Fueled by the memories, she rose to her hands and knees, stalking her victim like a sleek, black panther, slowly crawling forward, being careful not to alert the sleeping woman with her presence. Finally, she hovered over her prey and straddled her...her creamy white skin was within a hair's-breadth of her own nakedness.

One final time she leaned in, her long dark hair falling forward to surround her in a veil of silkiness as its owner's lips delved into the crevice of the sleeping woman's neck.

The redhead suddenly arched her back upward in a cat-like fashion, moaning loudly at the pure sensuality of the invasion. Tilting her head to the left to allow greater access, she felt her lover's body lower over her own as the assault on her neck increased. The sensation of skin against skin was overwhelming on her naked back. Within moments she had trapped her lover beneath her, pressing her into the bed as she slipped her own arms under the pillow to gather her prey completely into her arms from behind.

"I love you, Billie," she moaned as she savored the feel of her lover above her.

"I love you too, Cat," Billie replied placing butterfly kisses across the side of her wife's face.

Pressing gently against Billie, Cat silently instructed Billie to release her so that she could roll over and greet her face to face. Rolling onto her back, she wrapped her arms around the Billie's neck, and pulled her down into a sensuous kiss, driving her tongue deep into her mouth.

"Good morning, my love," Cat said as she released Billie from their shared air space.

Billie smiled broadly. "Now that's a good morning kiss!" she exclaimed as she placed one more peck on the end of Cat's nose.

Cat traced her fingertips across Billie's brow and down both sides of her face. She could spend hours just looking at her

146

wife's beautiful face...finely chiseled features, eyes the color of robin's eggs, hair as dark as night, and a smile that could light up a room with its presence. Taking a deep breath, she allowed the overwhelming love she felt to surge through her chest, manifesting itself in the form of a tear at the corner of each eye.

Billie watched the love in Cat's eyes spill out between pale lashes. Leaning in, she kissed the tears away, then lowered her lips to Cat's so that she could taste the saltiness of her own tears. "I love you so much, Kitten," Billie whispered.

Cat smiled as more tears escaped. "Why is that, Billie? How did I become so lucky as to have captured your heart?" she asked.

Billie propped herself on her elbows on either side of Cat's face. Looking down into twin pools of green, she smiled devilishly. "It wasn't luck, my love. You are a siren. I was helpless. You cast your spell on me the moment you walked into my aerobics class eight years ago. I was helpless to resist," she explained.

Cat suddenly became serious. She cupped the sides of Billie's face. "Any regrets?" she asked.

"Only one," Billie replied, drawing a worried expression from Cat. "That we didn't meet sooner," she replied.

Cat visibly relaxed. Then, in her naturally logical way, she said, "If we had met sooner, you might not have had Seth. As much as I love you, Billie, he is definitely worth the time we had to wait to find each other."

Now it was Billie's turn to become teary-eyed. Blinking rapidly, she nodded her agreement and then lowered her forehead to Cat's. "We may not have had Tara or Skylar, either," she added, soliciting a nod from Cat.

Billie rolled onto her side, bringing Cat along with her. She settled in on her back and held her wife close to her chest while both women gathered their emotions. Moments later, Cat lifted her head and looked at Billie.

"Sweetheart, as much as I would love to cuddle the entire day away with you, we did promise Mom that we'd help her pick out wedding invitations today," Cat said.

Billie groaned. She hated shopping.

Seeing Billie's grimace, Cat chuckled. "Come on now. We *did* promise," she reminded her.

"Was I drunk or something when that promise was made?" Billie asked, hoping for an excuse to back out.

Cat slapped Billie gently on the belly. "Nice try, big guy, but you're not getting out of it! If I'm stuck, then so are you!" she exclaimed good-naturedly.

"But, but..." Billie whined.

"But, nothing! After all, Dylan is *your* brother!" Cat pointed out.

"And Drew is *your* sister!" Billie countered quickly.

"You're right. So we're both stuck," Cat said, grinning.

"Aarrgghh!!! I can't win, can I?" Billie whined, throwing her hands up.

"No, you can't, so quit yer bitchin' and deal with it!" Cat laughed.

Billie raised her eyebrows into her hairline. "Oh yeah?" she said, refusing to go down in defeat. "Well, deal with *this*!" she shouted as she launched an all out tickle attack against Cat, reducing her to a helpless surrendering mass in a matter of moments.

Cat laughed so hard that she developed a severe case of hiccups. "B...hic... Billie, stop! Hic... Please!" she begged as Billie continued her assault.

The sound of the phone caused Billie to stop as Cat scampered to answer it before the caller hung up.

"Hel...hic...lo?" Cat managed to say as Billie lay on her back chuckling.

"Caitlain?" said the voice on the other end of the line. "Caitlain, is that you?"

"Mom? Hic," Cat replied, jumping to her feet while grabbing her nightshirt from the bed. It suddenly occurred to Cat that her mother had the power, even over the phone, to intimidate her into covering up her nakedness.

"Caitlain, are you all right, dear?" Ida asked.

"I'm...hic...fine, Mom. Re...hic...really. Just a case of the hic... hiccups," she explained.

"I've got just the remedy for you, dear. Put a pencil between your teeth then take a drink of water and gargle," Ida suggested. "It works for me every time."

Cat looked at the phone as though her mother had escaped the loony bin. "Mo...hic...Mom, I'm fine...hic. Ahh! I ha...hic...hate the hiccups!" she exclaimed into the phone.

"Caitlain, I'm a lot older than you, and I have many more years of experience, but then again, I'm just an old woman who probably doesn't know what she's talking about, so you go ahead and do what you think is best, dear," Ida replied, a heavy silence hanging in the air.

Cat's chin dropped to her chest. *My mother should have been a travel agent specializing in guilt trips!* she thought as she sighed and said, "Okay, hic...okay. Here, talk t...hic...to Billie while I get some...hic...water."

Billie gave her wife a dirty look as she reluctantly took the phone. "Hi, Mom!" she said brightly, sticking her tongue out at Cat and making funny faces as she held the phone to her ear.

"Billie, dear, how are you this morning?" Ida asked.

"I'm fine, Mom. How are you and Doc?" Billie returned, disfiguring her face into another hilarious mask just as Cat attempted to gargle the water while holding the pencil between her teeth.

Seeing the contorted look on Billie's face was more than Cat could take. As she erupted into a laugh, her windpipe opened, inadvertently allowing water to seep in, sending her into a frenzy of coughing, water spewing from her mouth and nose. Billie looked guiltily at her ailing wife and mouthed a silent "I'm sorry" in her direction, all the while trying hard to stifle a laugh of her own.

Hearing the commotion on the other end of the phone, Ida interjected. "Billie? Billie, is Caitlain all right?" she asked worriedly.

"She's fine, Mom. Just a little water down the wrong pipe, is all," Billie explained. "So, what time would you like us to meet you today?" Billie asked.

For the next fifteen minutes, Ida engaged her daughter-in-law in idle gossip and chit-chat while Cat recovered from her coughing spell. By the time Ida finally let her off the phone, she had the latest scoop on all of the neighbor's lives, as well as a meeting time and place for their shopping spree that afternoon. After saying her final good-byes, Billie made a show of peeling the phone away from her ear and placing it on its cradle.

"God, that woman can talk! Thank you so very much my dearest wife, for sticking me with Miss Verbal Diarrhea!" Billie joked as she stood and slipped her nightshirt over her head.

Cat approached her wife, and standing on tiptoe, met the her nose to nose. In a voice still raspy from coughing, she said, "Serves you right for making me laugh!" she said before placing a kiss on Billie's nose and backing away.

Billie grinned. "Well, at least your hiccups are gone!" she observed.

Cat stopped and did an inventory check of her facilities. "Hey! You're right!" she exclaimed. "I knew you were good for something!" she added, knowing immediately that she had gone too far.

"Oh, really?!" she mused, sauntering up to Cat and backing her against the wall. She placed her hands on the wall on both sides of Cat's head. "Are you sure that's *all* I'm good for?"

Cat nervously licked her lips. "Uhm...uhm. Well, I could think of at least *one* more thing you're good for," she teased.

"And what's that?" Billie asked seductively, her lips hovering over Cat's.

"Mama!" came a voice from the doorway. "I'm hungry."

Billie dropped her chin and leaned her head against the wall with a thud. Cat peeked around Billie to observe a still sleepy Skylar standing in the doorway, rubbing her eyes.

"Hi, baby girl!" Cat said brightly. "Why don't you go turn cartoons on? Mom and I will be right there to fix you some breakfast. Okay, sweetie?"

Nodding her head, Skylar disappeared down the hall.

Billie lifted her forehead from the wall and chuckled.

"If I had a dime for every time the kids have interrupted us, I'd be rich!" Placing a tender kiss on Cat's lips, she added, "To be continued, my love," before taking her wife's hand and heading downstairs.

***

"You know what, Mom? We have a pretty weird family," Seth commented as they sat around the dinner table.

"What do you mean, scout?" Billie answered as she lifted her iced tea glass to her lips.

"Well, Nana and Grandma are sisters, right?" he asked.

"Yes, they are," Billie replied.

"Then, that makes Uncle Dylan and Aunt Drew cousins, doesn't it?" Seth continued.

Billie sent an amused glance in Cat's direction.

"Technically, yes," Billie answered.

"So, is it okay for cousins to get married? I mean, that's pretty redneck, isn't it?" he asked seriously.

"Redneck?" Cat asked, sending Tara and Skylar into fits of giggles.

"You know...redneck. The kind of person who comes from the backwoods...toothless...looks for dates at family reunions? That's kind of what happened with Uncle Dylan and Aunt Drew, isn't it?" Seth explained.

Billie casually covered her mouth with her napkin to hide the grin that had found its way onto her face.

"Aunt Drew isn't toothless!" Skylar exclaimed in a fit of laughter.

Cat tried very hard to keep a straight face. "Seth, honey, you know it isn't nice to make fun of people," she said.

"Well, isn't it?" he persisted.

Cat wiped her mouth with her napkin and placed it on the table beside her plate. Making a teepee with her fingertips, she looked across the table at her son. "I guess you could say that, honey," she began. "When Uncle Dylan and Aunt Drew met each other at the family reunion last summer, they realized they were attracted to each other."

Billie coughed into her fist, trying hard to stifle a laugh as she remembered walking in on Dylan and Drew in bed together at SpireClyffe Acres last summer. Realizing they were attracted to each other was an understatement!

Cat shot Billie a warning look before continuing. "When the reunion ended, they realized how sad they would be apart, so Aunt Drew went to live with Nana and Papa Jim for a while so she could be closer to Dylan. Before they knew it, they had fallen in love, and now they're getting married," Cat finished.

"Cousins getting married. Yep, they're rednecks!" Seth insisted, grinning ear to ear.

"Actually, they're a redneck and a valley girl," Tara added.

"Tara Charland!" Cat exclaimed. "Why on earth would you say a thing like that?"

"Get real, Ma. Sheesh, I mean, like...really!" Tara said, imitating her Aunt Drew's mannerisms and making the entire family break down into laughter.

"Hey! Wait a minute!" Seth exclaimed loudly, drawing the attention of everyone at the table. "If Uncle Dylan and Aunt Drew are cousins, then that makes you two cousins too!" he reasoned.

Billie and Cat looked at each other nervously.

"So does that mean Mommy and Mama are rednecks too?" Skylar asked her brother innocently.

Seth looked nervously at his mothers, hoping he wasn't in trouble for prompting his sister's question.

Billie looked around the table at the tension on her children's faces, and the smirk on Cat's that she was desperately trying to hide. Reaching down, she picked up her knife from the table and started picking at her teeth with it. Sitting back, she patted her stomach and pretended to spit on the floor. Turning to Cat, she said in a backwood's drawl, "Well, Maw, that sure was a good dinner ya made. Ya done yerself proud, woman."

Falling into the act, Cat replied, "Well, thank ya, Paw. Glad ya liked it. Best roadkill stew I ever made. Did you young'uns like it?" she asked the children.

The tension around the table immediately broke as the kids got into the act. Seth got up from the table and pulled the waist of his jeans up under his armpits, messed up his hair, took his shoes and socks off and rolled up his pant legs, sending his sisters into fits of giggles.

Finally, after exhausting a nearly endless supply of silliness, Cat explained in all seriousness how Ida and Laurel were indeed sisters, but in name only, as Ida was Grandma Jo's daughter, and Laurel were Grandma Alex's, so there was no real blood ties between them. So even though Dylan and Drew were cousins in name, they weren't actually related by blood, and neither were Cat and Billie.

"Ah, shucks, Maw, I was kinda likin' being a redneck," Tara joked.

"I'd rather be a redneck than a penguin!" Seth exclaimed.

"A penguin?" Cat asked.

"Yeah. I have to wear a monkey suit for the wedding," Seth whined.

"Are you a penguin or a monkey?" Skylar asked her brother in all seriousness.

"Well at least you don't have to wear a dress like I do!" Tara interjected.

"Seth would look funny in a dress!" Skylar giggled.

"Yeah? Well, you have to wear a dress too, so there!" Seth countered.

"I *like* to wear dresses!" Skylar defended herself indignantly.

"You *would*!" Tara exclaimed, reminding Cat of how her older sister Amy constantly picked on their sister Bridget.

"All right. I think this discussion is over," Billie said, sensing that things were starting to get nasty. "Look, it's a great honor to be in your aunt and uncle's wedding. You should be proud," Billie explained.

"Ah, sweetheart," Cat said hesitantly. "You have to wear a dress too," she pointed out to Billie.

Billie's face fell as that particular realization set in. Looking at Cat, she exclaimed, "Ah, shucks, Maw, and I was hoping to wear my best bib overalls!"

A chain reaction of laughter spread like a yawn in a crowded room.

CHAPTER 16

"Billie, could you come to my office please? I have something to discuss with you," Art said in a serious tone.

"Sure, Art. What's up? Am I in trouble or something?" Billie asked, remembering the confrontation she'd had with an important client earlier in the week. He was the type of client who thought he knew more about the law than the lawyers did, and notoriously gave the firm a hard time. She had given this client some important legal advice that he was hesitant to accept, and she made it clear in no uncertain terms that he was a fool if he chose to ignore it. The meeting ended with the client stomping out of the room.

"We'll talk about it when you get here," he replied seriously.

Gulping nervously, she hung up the phone and took a deep breath. *Damn! If that asshole causes me to lose my job...* she thought, trying to put on a positive face as she walked the distance between her office and Art's. Stopping at Art's door, she took a deep breath and glanced at his secretary, who gave her a curious look. Bracing herself for the worst, she knocked.

"Come in, Billie," Art called from behind the closed door.

Forcing a smile onto her face, she greeted Art enthusiastically. "Hey Art! You wanted to see me?"

"Have a seat, Billie," Art instructed as he stood and approached her.

Billie shook with nervous anticipation as she headed in the direction of the chair Art had indicated while he shut the door firmly behind her.

She crossed her legs at the ankles and clasped her hands in her lap as she watched Art walk over to the window behind his desk. He stood there with his back to her for several moments.

Christ Almighty, she thought. *He's going to can me. I just know it!*

It seemed like an eternity before Art finally turned around and leaned his backside against the sill, his large burly frame nearly filling the entire window. He crossed his arms and cleared his throat to speak.

"Billie, how long have you been working here?" he asked.

Furrowing her brow, Billie thought for a moment. "Ah, about ten years," she replied.

Art nodded his head. "I thought so," he replied.

A long silence fell between them...a silence Billie was having a very difficult time tolerating. After several moments, she just couldn't take it anymore.

"Look, Art," she said, rising to her feet. "Just come out with it, okay? I know I pissed off that client early this week, so just get it over with. Just say it. *Billie, you're fired.* That *is* what you're trying so hard *not* to say, isn't it?" she demanded angrily.

Art broken out into a wide grin.

The look on his face infuriated Billie. "What the hell is so funny?" she said angrily, hands on her hips.

Pushing himself away from the window, he walked around his desk and confronted her face to face. Placing his hand on her shoulders, he looked her straight in the eye and said, "Actually, I was going to say, *welcome to the firm.* I've decided to make you a partner."

Billie was speechless, standing there, mouth agape.

Chuckling, Art placed two fingers under her chin and closed her mouth.

Billie stood there, wide-eyed.

Art waved his hand back and forth in front of her face. "Earth to Billie!" he said jokingly.

Shaking herself out of her shocked state, she just looked at Art and said, "But...but..."

"But what, Billie? Since you've joined the firm, we have shown continuous financial growth. Your landmark case against the state for same-sex marriage several years ago brought us significant business, especially from the gay community. You are an outstanding lawyer who rarely loses a case. The promotion is totally justified," he explained.

Billie was still numb from the surprise. "But Art, that client..." she stammered.

"That client is a shortsighted fool. Luckily for him, he finally made the right decision after he cooled off and thought about your advice. He called me just this morning, singing your praises for having the guts to stand up to him. That is one man I was convinced would never admit he was wrong. I think the experience humbled him. Hopefully, he'll be easier to deal with from now on," Art explained.

Billie lowered herself into her chair and looked up into the handsome dark-skinned face of her employer. Slowly, the realization came over her as a grin spread across her own face.

Art placed a hand on her shoulder. "The paperwork will be ready for your signature tomorrow, Billie. Why don't you take the rest of the day off and celebrate with that beautiful wife and family of yours," he suggested.

Billie was totally incapable of responding with anything but a nod.

Art helped her to her feet and guided her to the door. "I don't want to see you here until tomorrow, okay? Enjoy the rest of your day, my friend. You deserve it!" he said.

Closing the door behind her, Art leaned his back against it and smiled to himself. A chuckle escaped his lips as he heard a feminine voice on the other side shout, *yes*! He could just imagine Billie pumping her fist in victory.

***

"Cat! Cat!" Billie shouted excitedly into the room as she entered the kitchen. She was bursting at the seams, wanting desperately to share her good news with her wife. "Cat?" she called again, pausing momentarily to listen for the reply that didn't come. "Is *anyone* home?" she called.

As the realization set in that she was home alone, she set her keys and briefcase on the table, and headed to the refrigerator where she saw a note attached to the door by an assortment of magnets.

Billie, I've taken the kids into town to have them fitted for the wedding. If you get home in time, meet us at six p.m. at Applebee's in the mall and we'll have dinner together.
Love you!
Cat
P. S. As long as we're at the mall, we'll get you fitted as well. Drew has picked out the bridesmaid dresses at one of the specialty shops there.

Billie moaned. "That's just how I wanted to celebrate my promotion, shopping for a dress! I'd rather walk barefoot over hot coals!" she complained out loud.

She glanced at the clock and realized she had some time to kill, as it was only three o'clock. She wished now that she had taken the day off as Cat had asked her to that morning, but after upsetting that important client a few days ago, she didn't dare tip the apple cart. Smiling to herself, she suddenly realized that she never had anything to worry about.

Well, Billie, I guess Art thinks you're pretty indispensable, or he wouldn't have made you a partner. Nothing to worry about there. Taking in the full extent of her self-serving thoughts, she took a deep breath and brought herself back to reality. *Damn woman, you sure are full of yourself, aren't you? Don't get too big for your own britches, Billie-girl. No one is indispensable!*

She decided to take advantage of an empty house as she turned up the music and enjoyed a long soak in the tub. Nearly two hours later, freshly bathed and thoroughly pruny, she headed to the kitchen dressed in her Scooby-Doo boxer briefs, black mid-drift sports bra and white ankle socks. She plugged her smart phone into the player mounted under the upper kitchen cabinet and selected a John Cougar Mellencamp album. After turning it up loud, she danced her way across the kitchen to the tune of *Hurts So Good.*

Playing her air guitar like a pro, she slid across the floor on stocking feet, singing "Come on baby, make it hurt so good! Sometimes love, don't feel like it should, Baby, uhh, hurt so good!"

Billie totally immersed herself in the music and primitive dance as she swayed her hips and bobbed her head...her fingers sliding deftly over the strings of her air guitar while her hair flew wildly around her.

"Cute! But don't give up your day job!" a voice said from the doorway.

Startled, Billie stopped dead and turned sharply toward the voice. "Jeeeeeesus Chrrrrrrrist, Jen!" she exclaimed. "Scare the shit out of somebody, why don't ya?!"

Jen approached Billie and walked circles around her; arms crossed in front of her. "Nice outfit!" she teased.

Realizing her state of undress, Billie blushed to the roots of her hair. "I just got out of the tub," she said sheepishly as she turned the music off. She could tell Jen wasn't buying it by the look on her friend's face.

"All right. All right. I was indulging myself a bit! It isn't often that I get the house to myself!" she explained in her own defense.

"You mean...you don't often get the chance to indulge in the same behavior you admonish the kids for," Jen observed teasingly.

Billie lowered her chin to her chest and looked at her friend through thick eyelashes. "Busted, huh?" she admitted sheepishly.

"Yeah, busted!" Jen reinforced.

"If you're looking for Cat, she's not home," Billie said.

"Actually, I saw your car in the driveway while on my power walk, so I thought I'd stop in and say hi and kill some time while Fred takes the kids to Karissa's soccer game."

Billie glanced at the clock. "Well, I'm always happy to see you, but it's after five. I've got to get dressed and meet Cat in the mall for dinner at six," she explained.

Jen's eyes widened. "You're actually going to the mall without a fight?" she asked incredulously, following Billie through the living room and up the stairs as she headed to her bedroom to get dressed.

"No choice," Billie tossed over her shoulder. "We're getting fitted for the wedding. Cat took the kids shopping earlier this afternoon and she left me a note asking me to meet them for dinner before my fitting. Care to join us?" she offered as they reached the bedroom door.

Jen dropped facedown onto the bed as Billie rummaged through her dresser for an outfit to wear. "Sure, seeing that I'm at loose ends myself tonight."

"Great. We're going to Applebee's," Billie said distractedly as she picked out two waist length sweaters to go with her blue jeans. "Which one?" she asked her friend.

"That one," Jen said, pointing to the blue one.

"Thanks," she replied, shoving the green sweater back into her drawer. Oh, I almost forgot!" she said excitedly, turning toward Jen. "Art made me a partner in the firm today! Shocked the hell right out of me!"

Jen bolted to her feet and screamed in delight. She hugged her tightly and jumped up and down, obviously thrilled for her friend. "Oh, my God, Billie! Does Cat know?" she asked.

"Not yet. I'm going to surprise her at dinner," Billie replied as she pulled her sweater over her head.

"Wow! So, that's gotta mean a lot more money, right?" Jen asked.

"Yeah, I guess so. We didn't actually talk about that part yet," Billie said. "But, it's not the money so much as the recognition, you know?" she asked. "I mean, feeling appreciated is worth more to me than anything," she explained.

Jen grew contemplative for a few moments…long enough to make Billie concerned that she had said something to offend her friend.

"Jen, are you all right?" she asked after long moments of silence.

Breaking out of her trance-like state, Jen once again made eye contact with Billie. A moment of embarrassed discomfort passed between them.

Regaining her composure, Jen replied. "Yeah, sure. I'm fine. I was just thinking about being appreciated, that's all. You're right. The feeling is invaluable." Then, changing the subject quickly, Jen added, "What time did you say Cat was expecting you?"

"Six o'clock."

"Well, then, we'd better hurry if we're going to make it on time!"

***

"Mom!" shouted Skylar as she saw her mother approach.

Billie smiled and opened her arms for her youngest child to jump into, swinging her in a circle before hugging the eight year old tightly. Delighted by the sound of the child's laughter, she planted raspberries into the girl's neck, holding her firmly as she squirmed to get away from the tickling sensation.

"Mom! You're tickling me!" Skylar giggled as Billie finally released her and allowed her to slide to the floor. She immediately took Billie's hand and walked back to where Cat, Seth and Tara were waiting for them.

Cat and Billie's eyes met long before they were within touching distance. She wanted more than anything at that moment to take Cat into her arms and kiss her with wild abandon, greeting her lovingly after a long day apart. However, a public mall was hardly the place for that type of affection. Not that it mattered to Billie what people thought about her, but she knew it would make the kids uncomfortable to have people staring at them in public. So, she had to settle for warm hugs and a whispered *I love you* as her lips came close to Cat's ear. Cat's warm embrace and quick squeeze communicated all she needed to know for now. It would have to do until later, when they could be together without reservations.

"Jen! What a lovely surprise! I'm so glad you came," exclaimed Cat as she took turns embracing first her wife, and then her best friend.

"Billie insisted," Jen explained. "I went over to your house to see what you two were up to, and I found Big Guy here auditioning for American Idol!" Jen said, jerking a thumb in Billie's direction.

Cat looked at Billie. "Mellencamp?" she asked.

Billie grinned. "Sometimes it scares me just how well you know me," Billie said.

Cat turned back to Jen. "I'm so glad you came along. We're going to have some dinner then have Billie fitted for her gown. *That* ought to be fun!"

Billie looked insulted. "Hey, what is this, pick on Billie night?" she asked.

"Don't worry, Mom," Seth piped in. "You should have seen me try on that monkey suit. I felt like a total geek."

"You *are* a total geek!" Tara pointed out to her brother.

"I'd talk if I were you, *Princess*!" Seth replied sarcastically to his sister.

"Mom," Tara whined. "Tell him to shut up."

"Well, that's what Ma said. She said you looked like a little princess in that gown you tried on. *Princess*! *Princess*!" Seth teased repeatedly.

"Okay…enough," Cat intervened. Shooting a quick glance at Billie, she saw a small smile at the corners of her mouth. Cocking one eyebrow at her wife in a look that said *I'll deal with you later*, she turned her attention back to the two teenagers before her. "All right now. Let's see if we can make it through dinner without any more bickering, okay?"

Cat looked back and forth between Seth and Tara, who were both standing there with their arms crossed and their eyes averted to the floor.

"I said, okay?" she repeated with much more emphasis.

"All right, all right!" Seth agreed reluctantly.

"Tara?" Cat asked, demanding a response from her belligerent daughter.

"Yeah, yeah, yeah. Whatever you say," she replied condescendingly.

"Good. Now let's get some dinner," Cat said as she herded her group into the restaurant.

***

"I'm finished. Can I go now?" Seth asked, placing his napkin on the table.

"*May* I go now," Cat corrected her son.

Billie smiled to herself. *Cat was so...so Martha Stewart some times.*

"*Maaaaaayyyyy* I go now?" Seth said, exaggerating the correction.

Pretending to ignore the sarcasm, Cat replied evenly. "Yes, you may. Meet us in front of the food court by eight o'clock. That gives you about an hour to spend in the arcade. Okay?"

"Eight. Got it!" Seth said as he rose from the table and headed out the door.

"I guess I'm finished too," Tara said.

"All right, sweetie. Same for you, eight o'clock in front of the food court. Oh, and Tara, would you mind taking your sister along? I know she'll be bored to tears in the boutique we're going to," Cat asked.

"Ah, Ma! Do I have to?" she whined.

"I'd appreciate it if you would," Cat replied.

Tara looked at her sister and disgustedly agreed to take the tag-along with her. "All right. Come on, but you'd better not embarrass me, you got it?!" she demanded sharply from the little girl.

Skylar, totally oblivious to her idol's reluctance, happily followed Tara out of the restaurant.

"Keep an eye on her," Billie shouted as they exited through the door.

"I will," promised Tara.

"Ah, peace at last," Cat said as she looked at the other two ladies sitting before her.

"Feels like old home week," Jen remarked. "We can't make it through one meal without Stevie and Karissa nearly killing each other."

"I keep remembering the mother's curse every time the kids act up," Cat said.

"The mother's curse?" Jen questioned.

"Yeah, you know the one...*I hope you have kids that act just like you,*" she explained.

Recognition dawned on Jen's face. "Oh, yeah. I remember now. Paybacks are a bitch," she said, causing all three of them to chuckle.

Conversation momentarily stilled as the waitress refilled their coffee cups. Cat took a long sip. Enjoyment was clearly apparent on her face as the hot coffee danced across her taste buds. She looked back and forth between her companions before her gaze settled on Billie. "So, how was your day, my love?" she asked softly.

Billie smiled. "My day was wonderful," she purred. She reached across the table and covered Cat's hand with her own. "Cat, Art called me into his office today and offered me a partnership in the firm," she said softly.

Cat's eyes grew into large round emeralds as the significance of Billie's news settled in.

"Billie," she said, tears of pride filling her eyes and closing her throat. Swallowing hard, she squeezed her wife's hand and continued. "Billie, I am so proud of you! You certainly deserve it. Congratulations, my love!"

Damn this public place! Billie thought to herself as she ached to take Cat into her arms

I love you, she mouthed wordlessly to Cat across the table.

I love you too, Cat silently mouthed back.

Jen sat there, tears of pride filling her own eyes, as she witnessed this touching moment.

***

"It's purple, Cat! Purple!" Billie exclaimed.

"And your point is?" Cat said as she walked circles around Billie, checking the gown out from all angles.

"I look like Barney for Christ's sake!" Billie shouted.

"*I love you. You love me,*" Jen started singing softly from her corner of the dressing room.

Billie looked at her friend and growled.

"I'm not wearing it," Billie said firmly.

"You have to. All the bridesmaids are wearing them," Cat explained, trying hard not to laugh.

"*I love you. You love me*," Jen started singing softly once more.

"Jen, I'm warning you," Billie snarled.

Jen went from singing to humming the popular children's show tune, all while trying very hard to look innocent.

"Unzip it. I'm taking it off," Billie demanded as she tried in vain to reach the zipper.

Cat slapped her hand away. "Stop being such a baby," she admonished. "Billie, you'll only need to wear it once then you can put it away and never look at it again."

Billie covered her face with her hands and rubbed hard. Exasperated, she dropped her hands to her sides and looked at her wife.

"Cat, listen to me. I know I only have to wear it once…in front of three hundred people," she complained.

"Sweetheart, it'll be okay. Trust me. You'll look beautiful in it. Honey, this is for your brother and my sister," Cat purred sweetly.

That did it. Billie could never deny Cat anything when she talked to her like that. Sighing in defeat, she said, "Okay, okay, I'll wear it, but if *anyone* calls me Barney, they're dead meat. Agreed?" she asked.

"Agreed," Cat said grinning ear to ear.

Just then the sales lady came into the room carrying an array of shoes.

"Okay, ladies," she said placing the shoes in front of Billie. "Here's the selection of shoes the bride has picked out to go with the gowns."

Billie took one look at the shoes and raised arms up in frustration.

Cat looked back and forth between Billie and the shoes. "What?" she asked.

"Cat, look at them. They all have three-inch heels!" she exclaimed.

"Billie, I…I—, " Cat stammered.

"Like, I'm not tall enough all ready??! Christ, I'm going to be a fricken seven-foot Barney," she cried.

"*I love you.   You love me,*" came a melodious voice from the corner.

"*Jen!*"

CHAPTER 17

"Billie. Honey, are you ready?" Cat called from the second story.

After a few moments with no reply, she called again.

"Billie?"

"Hold on a minute, Art," Billie said as she covered the receiver. "Cat, I'm on the phone," she called out from the living room before turning her attention back to her employer. "Okay, I'm back. All right. Okay. All right, Art. I can be there in about 20 minutes. No problem. I'm sure Cat will understand. Okay, I'll see you in a few minutes. Bye."

Billie placed the phone back onto its cradle and inhaled deeply.

"I *hope* she understands," Billie mumbled before heading upstairs to the bedroom she shared with Cat.

"There you are! Are you ready?" Cat asked, looking up as Billie entered the bathroom that adjoined their bedroom.

Billie shifted from foot to foot and avoided direct eye contact. "Ah, Cat. I'm afraid I have to bow out of the dinner," she said apologetically.

"What? Why?" Cat demanded, meeting Billie's eyes in the mirror.

With one hand on her hip, and the other running through her hair, she replied. "Art just called an emergency meeting with a client. It's one of the cases I'm handling personally. I can't leave this one totally to Art. I really feel like I need to be there," she explained.

Cat placed both hands on the edge of the sink, her back still to Billie. Shaking her head side to side, she said, "This is the third time you've altered our plans in the month since you were promoted."

Cat turned around and leaned her backside against the sink. She crossed her arms. "Billie, Drew and Dylan were counting on us being there tonight. This the first time they'll have the whole wedding party together."

Billie placed her hands on Cat's shoulders. "Cat, honey, please try to understand. I'm a partner now. I have responsibilities."

"You have a responsibility to your family," Cat countered. "Damn it, Billie," she said before turning her back to Billie. "I'm beginning to wonder if this promotion is worth it."

Billie took a step back. She met Cat's gaze in the mirror. "I'm sorry, Cat, but I need to go to work. I'll try to wrap things up quickly and maybe I'll still make the end of the dinner. Okay?"

"Do what you think you have to, Billie," Cat said sharply, looking down into the sink to avoid Billie's eyes.

Feeling like a total heel, Billie sighed deeply and turned to leave the room. She stopped at the doorway. "I'll try to make it later, Cat."

Cat refused to answer, causing an uncomfortable silence to settle over the two women.

"I'm sorry," Billie whispered before leaving the room.

***

"Cat, thank God you're here," Bridget exclaimed excitedly as she met her younger sister in the vestibule of the restaurant.

"Hi, Bridge," Cat replied, returning her embrace. "You sound upset, what's wrong?"

"Well, Amy's up to no good again," she began, causing Cat to roll her eyes.

"*Now* what did she do?" Cat asked as she ushered the children into the restaurant. "Seth, honey, could you bring your sisters over to the table while I talk to Aunt Bridget?"

"Sure. Come on, I'm starved," he said, gently shoving his sisters ahead of him.

"Hey, there's Crystal," Tara shouted as she quickly moved ahead of her brother, not needing any prompting to spend time with her favorite cousin.

After watching the kids seat themselves at the table, Cat turned back to her sister. "So, spill it. What's Amy up to now?"

"She's just so incorrigible," Bridget replied. "The minute she arrived, she started flirting with the waiter. She's been embarrassing all of us. Poor Joe. I don't know why he stays with her."

Cat placed her hand on Bridget's shoulder and gently guided her back toward the table. "Honey, you know Amy flirts all the time. That's just the way she is. I don't think she means anything by it," Cat assured her sister.

"I don't know," Bridget said, doubt tingeing her voice as they reached the table.

"Caitlain, sweetheart, come give your mother a hug," Ida demanded as Cat approached.

Cat dutifully paid her respects to both her parents before making the rounds to each of her sisters and brothers-in-law seated around the table. Intentionally stopping at Amy, she bent down to give her older sister a hug and whispered, "I understand you're being a bad girl again, sis. We need to talk later, okay?"

Amy planted a kiss on Cat's cheek and grinned. "Mother Superior has been telling tales out of school again, huh?" she said of Bridget.

Cat smiled back and squeezed Amy's shoulders. "Just behave tonight, okay?" she asked good-naturedly before moving on to greet the bride and groom to be.

"Hi, sweetie," she said, bending over to hug Drew affectionately.

"Hi, Cat. I am so glad you're here. Bridget and Amy are like, driving me crazy with their bickering," she exclaimed.

"Drew, you know how things were while we were growing up. They've always acted that way. Don't let it spoil things for you, okay? Just ignore them," Cat advised before moving on to Dylan. "Hi, hon," she said, hugging him affectionately. Are you nervous?"

"Not too much, yet," he replied. "Hey, where's that gorgeous sister of mine?" he added.

Cat sighed as she answered what was sure to be the first of many inquiries about her absent wife. "Unfortunately, she's working...again," Cat said sarcastically.

"Uh, oh. Do I sense trouble in paradise?" Dylan astutely observed.

"You don't know the half of it, Dyl. Ever since her promotion, she spends more time at the office than she does at home," Cat complained.

"Well you know, Cat, she *was* just made a partner. She's got to do her time as the low man on the totem pole," Dylan said in defense of his sister.

"Yeah, but it always comes at such inconvenient times...like tonight for example," Cat explained.

"Somehow, I get the feeling that there's no such thing as a *convenient time*," Dylan observed.

Cat looked at Billie's brother with a tinge of resentment, wanting to accuse him of defending his sister, whether she was right or wrong, but instead, she chose to ignore his remark and changed the subject. "So, where are your mom and dad?" she asked.

"They'll arrive this weekend. Dad has a stock deal he's scheduled to close on Friday," Dylan explained.

"They're staying with us at Mom and Dad's, aren't they sweetie?" Drew asked her husband-to-be.

"Yes! It's gonna be a full house," he remarked.

"Well, Grandmas Jo and Alex will be staying with us when they arrive, so that should relieve some of the congestion," Cat said.

"Like, you get the *fun* company," Drew whined. "We get stuck with the moms and dads, and you get Grandma Jo. That's like, way no fair."

Cat laughed heartily and hugged her baby sister. "Well, dear heart, life's a bitch sometimes, huh? I love Mom and Dad to death, but I still feel like a chastised teenager when I'm around Mom. That woman still has the power to intimidate the shit out of me," she joked. "Speaking of which, she's going to break her wrist motioning to me if I don't get my butt over there."

"Okay.   It's almost time to order anyway," Dylan said, looking around the table. "Everyone is here except Bob. We'll give him a few more minutes, then order without him if he doesn't show up."

"Bob?" Cat asked.

"My best friend from home. He's going to be one of the ushers along with Kevin and Joe. We needed a third usher to walk with Billie, and he agreed to be the man," Dylan explained.

"Well, I sure hope he's tall," Cat commented dryly.

"Huh?" Dylan said.

"Oh nothing," Cat replied. "Look, Mom is going to call out the guards if I don't get over there. Have a great dinner," Cat said as she headed around to the other side of the table and sat down next to her mother.

"Caitlain, dear, you look very pretty tonight. Come, sit down and look at the menu. They'll be around to take our orders soon. So, where's Billie? Will she be joining us later?" Ida asked.

"Thanks, Mom," Cat answered. "And, no, Billie won't be joining us," she added angrily before turning her attention back to the menu.

Ida looked intently at her daughter. After several moments, Cat became very uncomfortable under her mother's scrutiny and gave up trying to hide behind the menu.

"What?" she asked defensively, looking at her mother with raised eyebrows.

"You tell me," Ida replied. "Obviously there's a problem."

Cat sat back in her chair and rubbed her temples. "Mom, how on earth could you know there's a problem?" she asked.

"A mother's intuition, dear," Ida replied. "Now, tell me what's wrong," she added while continuing to peruse the menu, seemingly uninterested in her daughter's dilemma to the casual observer.

"Ida, leave the poor girl alone. We're supposed to be enjoying a nice family dinner, not putting Kitten here through the interrogation process," Doc scolded. Then, addressing Cat, he added, "So, where's Billie tonight?"

Cat allowed her forehead to drop to the table, sighing loudly before sitting up straight in her chair and held her arms out beside her. "Okay, okay," she exclaimed. "Billie's working. Can you believe it? She's working. Art called just as we were getting ready to leave, and she chose to go to work rather than be here with her family. There. Now you know," she concluded.

"Was it important?" Doc asked.

"Was *what* important?" Cat asked impatiently.

"The reason Billie had to go to work," Doc replied.

Cat looked at her father through impatient eyes. Furrowing her brow, she asked, "How am *I* supposed to know?"

"You could have asked her," Ida suggested, leaning in toward her daughter to look at her condescendingly.

Cat locked eyes with her mother for several moments before breaking the gaze and looking at her hands folded in her lap. After sulking a bit, she replied. "Mom, she should be *here* with her family. Nothing is more important than that."

Doc took one of Cat's hands out of her lap. "Kitten," he began. "*She* is more important than that." After a short pause, he continued. "Honey, Billie has worked hard to get where she is. She's finally made it. Don't you see? All those years married to an abusive man…her only child in a hospital bed for months on end, a little more than a vegetable…finding out that she was sold for drug money after more than 30 years of believing her adoptive parents were hers biologically. Cat, can't you see that she needs this? Sure, it takes some time away from you and the kids, but the fringe benefits to her as a person…to her self esteem, are very important."

Doc paused to look at his daughter.

"Kitten, has she ever not been there for you when it's really counted? Has she ever let you down when it really mattered?"

Seeing Cat shake her head no, he continued.

"So how about giving her a break? How about realizing that this is good for her? How about putting the jealousy aside and rejoicing with her, instead of fighting against her?" he asked.

Cat's head snapped up. "Jealousy? Is that what you think this is about?" she asked sharply.

"Isn't it?" Doc replied.

Cat held her father's knowing gaze for what seemed like an eternity, stubbornly refusing to answer. Finally, prompted by the arrival of the waitress, she broke the gaze and pretended to study her menu, trying desperately to keep the tears from her eyes and the quiver from her voice as she placed her order.

Cat was saved from further questioning by a ruckus at the door of the restaurant.

"Hello, fans! No, no, don't stand. Really, it isn't necessary," came a voice from behind her.

Cat turned sharply in her seat to see who was approaching. What she saw was a very good-looking young man with sandy blond hair, medium height, and muscular build, strutting toward their table like he owned the world, one eye on the waitress's backside, the other on the table he was heading toward.

Stopping just short of the table, he looked directly at Cat and said, "Oh, baby! Someone's gonna get lucky tonight," to which Cat reacted with raised eyebrows.

"Bob!" Dylan said from across the table, a big grin spread across his face as he rose to his feet.

Bob looked across the table at his best friend. "Hey, Dyl! You didn't tell me there were so many beautiful women joining us tonight," he replied as he headed around the table to shake Dylan's hand.

Taking Bob's hand and shaking it firmly, he draped one arm around the blonde man's back and started introductions, walking around the table with him and stopping at each seat.

"Bob, you know Drew," Dylan began.

"Drew, sweetheart," Bob replied as he took a squealing Drew into his arms and hugged her tight, dipping her back until Cat was sure they would fall over. She watched Dylan's face carefully for signs of jealousy, but found none. Apparently, this was normal behavior for Bob.

"And, this is Bridget, Drew's sister," he continued.

Bob took Bridget's hand and attempted to pull her out of her seat for a hug; however, Bridget was having no part of his plan. Instead, she snatched her hand out of his and curtly said hello, before tossing a dirty look at Dylan.

Next was Kevin, who shook Bob's hand firmly...perhaps a little too firmly, judging by the grimace on his face.

"This is Joe," Dylan said, moving next to his future brother-in-law. Joe extended his hand cautiously, but a little friendlier than Kevin.

"Amy, Drew's oldest sister," Dylan continued as he and Bob moved along.

Cat grinned at the irony of the situation as she watched Amy's reaction. There before here, stood a male replica of herself...brash, outgoing, and majorly flirtatious.

Rising to her feet, Amy flung herself into Bob's arms and planted a long, wet kiss directly on his lips. "Hello, Bobby," she purred as Joe dropped his head into his hands.

"For the love of God, Amy," Bridget exclaimed.

Bob was grinning ear to ear. "Hello, Amy," he returned, a sensuous leer dominating his handsome features.

Clearing his throat, Dylan took Bob's arm and broke him free of Amy. "Moving right along," he said nervously. "Bob, this is Drew's...*and* Amy's father, Doctor O'Grady."

Bob suddenly became all business. Standing erect, he extended his hand to the older gentleman, shaking it respectfully. "Dr. O'Grady, it's so nice to meet you, sir," he said.

Doc grinned as he returned the handshake. Leaning into Bob's personal space, he whispered, "Cut the crap, young man, and stay away from the blonde over there. She's a barracuda...and so is her mother," he warned light-heartedly, referring to his oldest daughter. "Oh, and by the way, call me Doc."

Bob glanced at Ida, who was looking at him suspiciously. "Ah, good advice, sir, I mean, Doc," he returned, releasing the doctor's hand before turning to Ida. Taking her hand, he lifted it to his lips and kissed the back of it. Cat nearly choked on her drink.

"Madam," he said, bowing at the waist, "You couldn't possibly be old enough to be the mother of these women. It is a pleasure to meet you. May I say how lovely you look tonight?"

Give me a break. Cat thought as she listened to her mother coo over the praise.

"Why, thank you, Bob. I'm sorry, but I didn't catch your last name," Ida said.

"Hardy. Bob Hardy," the young Casanova replied.

"Well, it's nice to meet you too, Bob Hardy," Ida returned. "Where are you staying while you're here?" she asked.

"Well, I came straight from the airport. I'm hoping to find a room right after dinner," Bob replied.

"You'll do no such thing," Ida replied. "We have plenty of room at our house. Raising four daughters, you can imagine, they all had to have their own rooms, plus we have a couple of guest rooms. In fact, all the girls are staying with us...well all except Cat and Billie," she added. "You see, Doc. I told you we shouldn't sell the old house."

"Cat? Billie?" Bob asked Dylan.

Now it was Dylan's turn to grin. "Ah yes, Cat and Billie," he said, leading Bob a bit further around the table. "Bob, it's my pleasure to introduce to you, my favorite sister-in-law, Cat."

Bob took Cat's hand and looked directly into her eyes. "Cat, huh? Such a lovely name, and so fitting for someone with golden tiger hair," he said, making Cat's stomach turn. Leaning in close, he whispered, "Does the Cat have claws?"

Cat smiled sweetly. "Absolutely, and they come on a six-foot frame," she replied, holding her smile.

Without breaking eye contact, he asked, "I assume the six-foot frame has a name?"

"Billie," Cat replied.

"Billy?" Bob became even cockier. "Billy. And, does Billy realize what a beautiful woman he has?"

"Yes, *she* does," Cat replied, seeing the shock spread over Bob's face at the revelation. Cat looked over Bob's shoulder and saw the twinkle in Dylan's eye as her brother-in-law enjoyed what Cat was doing to his best friend. Apparently, nearly everyone present had been engaged in their encounter as well, as murmurs and giggles circled around the table at Cat's remarks.

Red-faced with embarrassment, Bob quickly recovered his composure and moved on as Dylan introduced him to the kids. Finally finished, they seated themselves on the side of the table opposite Cat.

Bob leaned toward Dylan. "You know, you could have warned me, Dyl. Christ! Is Billie *really* six feet tall?"

"Oh yeah," Dylan exclaimed gleefully.

"I'll bet she's a real Amazon...all big, ugly and hairy," Bob said, almost shivering at the image he had created in his own mind.

Dylan grinned. "Actually, no. She's quite beautiful. In fact, she's a younger version of my mom."

Bob looked thoroughly confused. "Your mom? Your mom is a fox. How can she look like your mom?"

"Considering that Billie is my sister, it's quite easy," Dylan said.

Bob's jaw nearly dropped to the table. "Your sister?" he asked.

"My sister," Dylan replied, knowing he was driving his best friend crazy with confusion.

"Wait. Wait a minute. I thought you said Cat was your sister-in-law?" Bob asked.

"She is…twice over. You see, Cat is Drew's sister, but she's also my sister's wife," he explained.

Bob sat there and stared at the table, confusion clearly written across his face. "Okay, I know I can be thick sometimes, but, your sister's *wife*? What the hell are you talking about?" he asked.

Dylan was really enjoying himself. "Yeah, wife. You see, Cat and my sister Billie are married…legally. In fact, Billie is a lawyer, and she was the one who sued the state several years ago over same-sex marriages, and won. It was all over the news when New York passed marriage rights legislation. Billie is largely responsible for that. She and Cat celebrated her victory by getting married. Cool, huh?"

"Billie is a lawyer? Shit! I just hit on a lawyer's wife?" Bob exclaimed. "Damn it man, why didn't you stop me?"

"Because I was enjoying it too much," he joked.

Shaking his head back and forth, Bob looked at his friend, "Man, you have a strange family!" he said.

"If you think Cat and Billie are strange, wait until you meet Grandma Jo and Grandma Alex," he said, chuckling. "Oh, by the way, did I ever tell you that my mom and Cat's mom are sisters?"

Bob's eyes once more popped out of his head. "Jesus! I'm on overload. No more tonight, please," he said, laughing.

Cat watched the exchange from her side of the table, a mixture of sympathy and righteousness filling her mind as she witnessed Bob's reaction to her unique family. Bob didn't really concern her. He appeared to be a little boy wearing his daddy's clothes. Unless encouraged, she was pretty sure he was harmless. What *was* bothering her though, was her older sister's reaction to this newcomer. If it was encouragement he was looking for, it was apparent that Amy was willing to provide it. Cat just hoped that wedding vows would be on Amy's mind as well as Drew's in the days to come.

* * *

"Damn," Billie cursed as the kitchen door squealed. *I've got to remember to oil the hinges on this door.*

Billie quietly made her way into the kitchen and placed her briefcase on the floor in front of the coat closet. Straightening, she reached her arms into the air and stretched her tall frame to work the kinks out of her back.

Wow. I didn't realize how hours of sitting at a desk could hurt, she thought as she kicked off her shoes into the corner. Looking up at the clock on the wall above the sink, she noted the time. Two a.m. *Umph! Cat may be right about this promotion not being worth it,* she contemplated. *I just hope I'm not in too much trouble for missing the dinner.*

Billie stood in front of the open refrigerator door and scanned the contents looking for something quick to eat. "Let's see," she said out loud. "Ah, cold pizza. My favorite," she exclaimed as she reached for the large triangular morsel with one hand and the milk with the other. She poured herself a tall glass of milk then returned the carton to the refrigerator before leaning her backside against the counter to contemplate her busy day.

The case she was working on was for a client whose daughter was denied critical health care coverage for an experimental procedure because their insurance company had yet to receive a note from the child's doctor confirming her need for the procedure. Earlier in the evening, when Art called, the child was being rushed to the emergency room and Billie was called in to do battle with the insurance company to pave the way for payment, and eliminate any delays in the child's treatment.

It had been a difficult evening, with Billie meeting face to face for several hours with the lawyers for the insurance company, arguing and debating the issue until finally, Billie lost her cool and asked them how they would feel if they had a child lying in a hospital bed, dying with very little hope of recovery without proper treatment.

During the encounter with the lawyers, tears poured down her face as she recounted her and Cat's struggle to keep Skylar alive when her tiny body was racked with childhood leukemia. Billie's impassioned pleas paid off, touching the hearts of her opponents, when finally, just after midnight, the opposing lawyers relented and agreed to at least temporarily provide coverage until the letter arrived from the doctor.

Knowing a victory when she saw one, albeit a small one, she quickly obtained their signatures, then spent the next hour preparing the documentation to make the coverage official, faxing it to the insurance company's main office just shortly before leaving for home at one-forty-five a.m.

After downing her last gulp of milk, she stood there, staring at the floor in tired contemplation.

No, Cat is not right, she said to herself. *This promotion is definitely worth it. It feels good to make a difference in someone's life,* she thought as she snapped herself back to consciousness, rinsed out her glass and placed it in the dishwasher.

Heading upstairs to bed, Billie stopped at each of the kid's rooms and tucked them in, placing light kisses on their cheeks. Tears of love and tenderness misted her eyes as she stood there taking in the beauty and joy of her children.

She couldn't help but put herself in her client's shoes tonight. She knew how helpless and fragile she had felt when Skylar was so sick, and when Seth was in the hospital at such a young age, lying helplessly in a coma for months. Just as she was thinking how glad she was that Art had chosen her for this case, the realization hit her that he had chosen for her for the very reason that she *could* put herself in the client's shoes.

"You sly dog, Art!" Billie whispered to herself as she left Skylar's room and headed for her own.

Billie slowly pushed the door open, and stepped inside. As her eyes adjusted to the darkness, she could see Cat's form on the bed beneath the blankets. She was sleeping on her right side, arm tucked up under her pillow, left leg bent at the knee. Her long red-gold hair was in wild disarray across the pillow.

Billie made her way across the carpeted floor and into the bathroom to brush her teeth and slip her nightshirt on without disturbing Cat. Moments later, she slipped in behind her sleeping wife and spooned her long frame around her, draping an arm across Cat's stomach and drawing her in close. Placing her lips close to Cat's ear, she whispered "I love you, Kitten," then laid her own head down, only to fall almost instantly into a deep sleep.

Cat waited until she heard even breathing coming from the woman behind her before she released the tension she had been holding when she first heard Billie enter their room.

She had been lying awake for several hours, not able to sleep, and wondering what was keeping Billie. All sorts of worrisome thoughts ran through her mind, from Billie cheating on her, to her lying dead in a ditch somewhere.

She heard Billie come home about a half-hour ago. She heard the car door slam, the creaking hinges on the kitchen door, Billie's cursing at the noise, sounds of her wife moving about the kitchen as she made a late night snack. All were signs that Billie was home and that she was safe. All were signs that should have prompted Cat to relax, but to no avail. All she knew was that she was mad as hell that Billie had missed the dinner and that she didn't have the decency to even call her when she realized she wasn't going to make it.

Several moments later, as she still lay awake, a nagging thought lingered in her mind.

I am not jealous!

Finally, forcing herself to relax, she allowed sleep to claim her as she joined her wife in dreamland.

CHAPTER 18

Cat passed through the living room while glancing briefly at Skylar who was snuggled on the couch watching Saturday morning cartoons with Petey her favorite teddy bear.

"Good morning, sweet pea."

"'Morning, Mama. I'm hungry," Sky answered, as she watched her mother disappear into the kitchen before turning her attention back to Bugs Bunny.

Cat grinned. "Of course you are, my love. Of course you are," Cat said. "How about Lucky Charms?" she called from the kitchen as she set the coffee pot up to brew.

"Okay," Skylar answered. "Can I eat in here?" she asked.

Cat hesitated for a moment before answering. She preferred to have meals at the kitchen table as a family, however, since she and Sky were usually the only ones up at this time of the morning, she relented. "Sure, sweetie," she said. "Go ahead and set up a TV tray. I'll bring your cereal in a minute."

Moments later, she carried a tray into the living room, laden with cereal, orange juice and coffee which she placed on the TV tray.

"Here you go, love bug," Cat said.

She grabbed her coffee from the tray and settled into the overstuffed chair with her legs curled under her.

"Good morning," a velvety voice said from the stairway.

Cat looked up to see Billie take the last two steps into the living room, sleep still apparent on her beautiful face.

"It's a little early for you, isn't it?" Cat asked sarcastically.

Billie frowned. *Shit!* she thought. *I was hoping she'd be in a good mood this morning.* She decided to ignore the sarcasm while turning her attention to her daughter. "Good morning, rugrat," she said, kissing Skylar on the head.

"Morning, Mommy. Want some Lucky Charms?" Skylar asked, lifting a spoonful to Billie's mouth.

"Sure," Billie said enthusiastically as she ate the food offered to her. "Thanks, dumpling."

"Want more?" Skylar asked, offering her another spoonful.

"No thanks, sweetheart. Mommy needs coffee right now," she replied. She stood to her full height and looked across the room at Cat, who was pointedly ignoring her in favor of watching Bugs Bunny on the big-screen TV.

She looked back at Skylar. "How about I get a cup and come watch Bugs with you?"

Skylar's face lit up. "Sure," she replied. "We can *all* watch Bugs Bunny."

Moments later, Billie returned to the living room and sat on the couch next to Sky. No sooner had she sat down, than Cat rose to her feet.

"I think I'll take my shower now," she announced, heading to the kitchen to discard her coffee cup before heading up the stairs.

Billie watched her go, a slow indignant anger building in her chest. She tried very hard not to follow her, wanting Cat to think she was immune to her cold treatment, but after several moments, it became too much for her to bear. She placed a kiss on the Skylar's cheek. "I think I'll go take my shower too," she explained before heading to the stairs.

Billie pushed the bathroom door open and leaned against the frame with her arms crossed. "Wanna tell me what the pissy-ass attitude is all about this morning, Cat?" she asked.

Cat ignored her for several moments. Finally, she reached forward to shut off the faucet then slid the shower door open just far enough to reach the towel hanging on the hook. After completely covering herself with the towel, she stepped out of the shower and toweled herself dry, all while avoiding eye contact with Billie.

"Well?" Billie asked impatiently.

"Well what?" Cat replied, as she dried her legs, still avoiding Billie's eyes.

"Don't play games with me, Cat. You know exactly what I'm talking about."

Cat hung the damp towel on the hook and looked at her wife, but said nothing before proceeding to leave the bathroom. Billie took one step to her right and blocked Cat's exit.

"Talk to me, Cat."

Cat put her hands on her hips and looked directly into Billie's eyes. "What is there to say, Billie?"

"There's plenty to say, like an explanation for the cold shoulder this morning," she replied.

"You want an explanation? All right, I'll give you one." Cat started to pace. "How about asking me how the dinner went last night? How about explaining why you couldn't call me when you knew you wouldn't make it? How about letting me know where you were and what time you'd be home so I wouldn't worry that you were lying dead on the side of the road somewhere? For Christ's sake, Billie. Is your damned job so important that you don't give the kids and me a second thought once you've walked out the door?" Cat asked.

Billie didn't know what to say. Cat was right. She had been so absorbed in what she was doing last night that she really didn't think about her family at all.

"Will you please let me out of the bathroom, now?" Cat said, exasperated.

Billie lowered her gaze to the floor and stood aside, letting Cat pass into the bedroom. Cat went directly to her bureau and proceeded to dress herself while Billie struggled to come up with an excuse for her neglectful behavior the night before.

When Cat finished dressing, she looked at Billie. "Well? Do I get an explanation as to why you didn't come home until two this morning?" she asked.

"So you *were* awake," Billie said.

Cat walked toward Billie and stopped within inches of her face. "Yes, I was, but I was so angry with you by then, I didn't dare say a word. Neither of us needed a knock-down dragged out fight in the middle of the night," she explained.

Billie cast her gaze toward the floor once more. "You're right," she said. "I'm sorry."

Once again, Cat's hands went to her hips. "So that's it?" she asked incredulously. "You're sorry? That's it? No explanation?"

Billie thought back to how she was feeling last night after her victory...after acknowledging that through her hard work and efforts, a little girl would have the best possible care for a potentially life-threatening disease. She thought back to how proud she was that she was able to help, and she thought about how helpless she felt when her own child was in the same situation and she was unable to do anything about it.

Sudden indignation filled her mind as she raised her gaze to meet Cat's.

"Cat," she began. "You almost succeeded. You almost had me regretting that I worked my ass off for nine hours last night to guarantee a very ill child the proper medical treatment so that she could live to see her next birthday. I'm sorry that I didn't think to call. For that, I take full blame, but I'll be damned if I'll let you make me feel guilty about doing my job."

Billie was so angry, all she could do was sputter as she paced.

Cat suddenly felt two inches tall. Watching Billie pace back and forth, she realized that she had jumped to conclusions. The only other time Cat has seen Billie this angry was when she discovered her ex-husband Brian had broken into the house and had brutally beaten and raped Cat.

"Billie?" Cat said softly.

Billie ignored her as she continued to pace back and forth.

"Billie, I'm sorry," she tried again.

Billie stopped and looked directly at her wife. "Why, Cat? Why has my job been such a problem for you lately? If it were *you* who had to work late, I would totally understand. I would be supportive, Cat, not suspicious and controlling. Christ, it's almost as if you're jealous of my promotion," she charged.

Cat's eyes flew open as Billie mirrored her father's sentiments from the night before. Tears filled her eyes as she looked away.

"Mama? Mommy? Are you fighting?"

Cat and Billie both swung around sharply to face the door. "Sky, honey, no, we're not fighting. We're just having a discussion, sweetheart," Cat said as she dropped to her knees to take her daughter into her arms.

From the safety of Cat's arms, Skylar looked up at Billie, looking for confirmation, and finding it in Billie's assurance that things were fine.

Cat rose to her feet and tilted Skylar's chin upward. "Hey, how about you and I watch cartoons while Mommy takes her shower?" she asked.

Sky nodded vigorously, dragging her mother toward the door. Glancing back over her shoulder, Cat was dismayed by the look of hurt on Billie's lovely face. She would have to find some way to make it up to her, but somehow, she didn't think Billie would forgive her so easily. Heaven knew she wouldn't if she were in her shoes.

* * *

Billie stood under the hot spray with her hands braced on the wall below the shower head. Though the temperature of the water was tingeing her skin a rosy red, she didn't feel a thing as her full attention was focused on the turmoil raging in her head. For the life of her, she couldn't figure out why Cat was so angry lately. Ever since her promotion, she had been snippy, short-tempered, sarcastic and generally impatient where she was concerned. At least she wasn't turning her anger on the children.

I need to stop second-guessing her and confront her directly, Billie decided as she shut off the faucet. *But I need to wait until the kids are out of the house, or sleeping. The last thing we need to do is needlessly upset them.*

Billie sighed deeply. With a sick feeling in the pit of her stomach, she resigned herself to giving up her job if it meant saving her marriage. *I hate to do it. I've worked so hard to get where I am, but I love Cat even more.* The nagging feeling at the back of her mind protested this decision, but her resolve won out as she took a deep breath and slid the shower door open.

Billie stared blankly at the wall as she dried her skin. In a daze, she walked slowly into the bedroom and fished a pair of jean shorts and a T-shirt out of her dresser. After dressing, she sat on the edge of the bed and stared at the floor.

I really don't want to go downstairs and confront Cat. Skylar is already concerned that we're fighting. I need to get out of the house for a while. I need to talk to someone about this...preferably someone who wouldn't choose sides.

Billie's head suddenly snapped up. "Jen," she said into the empty room.

***

"Billie, where are you going?" Cat asked as Billie hurried down the stairs and through the living room.

"Out," she replied, not stopping to explain herself. "I'll be back this afternoon," she added, passing through the kitchen and out the back door just as Cat made it to her feet and rushed into the kitchen after her wife.

"Billie," Cat called after her. "Damn it, Billie," she said, realizing Billie couldn't hear her as she backed the car out of the driveway.

"Mama, is something wrong? Where did Mommy go?" Skylar asked from the doorway, Petey clutched tightly in her arms.

Cat turned to her daughter and saw the worry etched on her face. She forced a smile onto her face and dropped to one knee in front of her. She rubbed Skylar's arm. "Nothing is wrong, honey. Mommy just had to go out for a while. She'll be back. I promise," she said.

"She isn't gonna go live with Uncle Art again, is she?" Skylar asked, her bottom lip quivering.

Cat was aghast. She didn't realize how traumatic it had been for Skylar when Billie moved out during the child's illness over a year ago. It was such a tumultuous time. In many ways, Skylar's illness was almost as hard on them and their relationship as it was on her. The tension, hurt and anger that passed between them was almost palpable. It took a lot of love, tenderness and forgiveness to heal the wounds and rebuild a loving relationship ...a chore both women were devoted to. And they had succeeded, or at least Cat thought they had. The past year was one of the best she could remember. Skylar was healthy, the children had all done well in school, Billie had been made a partner in her law firm. Cat stopped cold as a wave a sickness passed through her stomach at the thought.

Cat brushed the feeling aside and looked once more at Skylar, who was still standing there, looking for assurance from her mother that her beloved Mommy would be coming home again. She took the child into her arms, and sat on the floor with her, holding Skylar in the circle of her arms.

"Mommy will be back, my love. I promise. She's just gone out for a while. You just wait and see. She'll be back. I promise."

***

"Jen, I just don't get it. She's been so edgy and combative for the past several weeks. I just don't know what to do," Billie complained as she sat opposite her friend in the coffee shop.

Before leaving home so abruptly that morning, she called Jen and arranged to pick her up and go out for coffee. For the past half hour, Billie had explained her predicament to Jen.

"Maybe it's the tension from the wedding. Heck, I don't know. All I *do* know is that it's causing a hell of a lot of strain between us, and it's gotta be affecting the kids."

"So, when exactly did it all start?" Jen asked. "Have you seen any pattern to it?"

"I don't know if I can put an exact date on it, but it's been about a month. As far as a pattern is concerned, I'm beginning to wonder if it's my job. I mean, she throws the partnership in my face quite a lot," Billie explained.

Jen sipped her coffee, nodding in understanding. "And what prompts the slams?" she asked.

Billie looked confused. "What do you mean?"

"Well, what was happening at the time that caused her to attack your job?" Jen clarified.

Billie looked embarrassed. "You want an honest answer?" she asked.

Jen placed her cup on the table and looked pointedly at her friend. "Of course," she replied.

"She attacks my job most often when I'm late coming home, or just after I've canceled a date with her because of it."

Jen reached across the table and knocked on Billie's forehead. "Hello. Is anybody home?" she teased. "Jesus, Billie. I can understand why she'd be upset. How often does this happen?" Jen asked.

"Since the promotion? Let's see…canceled three dates, home late a half-dozen times," Billie confessed.

"So let me get this straight," Jen said, sitting back in her chair. "One month, 20 working days, nine of those days either late or canceled. Billie, that's nearly 50% of the time! No wonder she's pissed!"

Billie sat staring at her hands folded in front of her on the table. Long moments passed before she took a deep breath and looked at her friend.

"I never thought of it that way, Jen. You're right. That's a pretty bad track record," Billie said sadly.

Jen covered Billie's hands with her own. "So the question is, what are you going to do about it?"

Billie sat back and covered her face with her hands. She rubbed hard then dropped her hands back onto the table and looked at Jen. "It makes me sick to even think about this, but I guess I'll have to give up the partnership," she replied.

"You would do that?" Jen asked.

"Jen, Cat and the kids are my life. No job, and no amount of money on the face of this earth would be worth losing them for. So, yes. I would do that," Billie explained passionately, a tear escaping the corner of her eye.

Jen squeezed Billie's hands. "Well, sweetie, I don't think you'll have to go quite that far," Jen said.

A glimmer of hope shone in Billie's eyes. "I hope that means you have some good advice for me," she said hesitantly.

"I have some advice. I don't know how good it is, but I do have some advice," Jen replied.

"Well, spill it," Billie demanded anxiously.

"Billie, how many of the late nights were spent at the office finishing up paperwork? How many of those nights could have been spent finishing up paperwork *at home* instead of in the office?" she asked.

Billie met Jen's raised eyebrows with a pair of her own, a smile breaking out on her face. "You might have something there," she exclaimed. "You know, now that I think about it, most of the late nights were spent doing just that…filing motions in the computer, transposing notes from meetings with clients. Jen, you're right. What's to stop me from doing those things on my laptop at home?"

"Bingo," Jen said. "You see, I don't think Cat is envious of your promotion, and I certainly don't think she'd want you to give it up. But I *do* think she is concerned about the time your promotion is taking away from her and the family. So, doing some of the follow-up work at home might be a good compromise. Sure, you'd be focused on your job, but you'd be *there*, available to them if they needed you. You know, sometimes Fred and I can be in the same room for hours without saying a word to each other, but just being there together is enough. See what I mean?" she asked.

Billie grinned ear to ear. "How'd you get so smart?" she asked her friend.

"It's about time you noticed, Big Guy. Now be a good girl and pay the check. It's time you head home to your family. I'm sure Cat could use a big hug right now," Jen said.

"Now that's the best advice I've heard yet. Let's go," Billie exclaimed as she rose to her feet.

Moments later, they pulled into the driveway of Jen's house. As Jen made a move to get out of the car, Billie reached for her arm. Jen looked at her friend and watched as she struggled to find the right words to properly thank her for what she had done.

Jen touched the side of Billie's face with her free hand and whispered, "You're welcome."

"I love you. You know that, don't you?" Billie asked spontaneously.

Jen placed a quick kiss on Billie's lips. "Ditto, Big Guy. Ditto," she replied. She climbed out of the car and closed the door then leaned down to look into the open window. "Now go home before I kick your ass," she said.

"Oh, I'm scared," Billie joked as she shifted the car into reverse and pulled out of the driveway.

***

Billie pulled into the driveway exactly one hour after she had left. As she entered the kitchen, she was nearly run down by an eight-year-old bundle of energy.

"Mommy, you came back," Sky screamed excitedly as Billie lifted her into her arms. Skylar proceeded to wrap herself around Billie, hugging her tightly.

Hearing the commotion from the living room, Cat walked to the doorway separating it from the kitchen, and leaned against the doorframe.

Billie looked around the human octopus that was clinging tightly to her to cast a questioning glance in Cat's direction before addressing her daughter. "Of course, I came back, rugrat. What made you think otherwise?" she asked.

Skylar finally released Billie's neck and leaned back so she could see her mother's face. "I thought you went to live with Uncle Art again," the child explained.

Billie's eyes filled with tears. Trying desperately not to cry, she forced a smile onto her face and calmed her daughter's fears. "Sweetheart, I just needed to go out for a while. In fact, I went to have a cup of coffee with Aunt Jen, that's all. Honey, I love you, and Seth, and Tara, and Mama. Why would I want to leave?" she asked.

Sky shrugged her shoulders. "I don't know," she replied. "I just remember before when you went to live with Uncle Art, and I was really, really sad," she explained.

Billie pushed an errant lock of hair behind the little girl's ear. "Well, there's no way you're getting rid of me, partner. I'm here to stay. Don't you worry about it anymore, okay?" she asked.

Skylar grinned from ear to ear. "Okay," she said, hugging her mother once more. "Mama said not to worry too. She promised you would come back, and you did," she exclaimed, hugging Billie once more.

"Yes I did," Billie said. "Mama's pretty smart, isn't she?" she added, looking over Skylar's shoulder at Cat, who stood there with tears running down her face...very much reflecting the ones in Billie's eyes.

"Yep. Mama is the smartest person in the world," Skylar agreed.

Billie reached a free hand toward Cat, who took it instantly. She embraced both her wife and child, laying her cheek on top of Cat's head and rocking her bundle back and forth. The trio finally broke apart wiping traces of tears from their faces.

Skylar quickly grew bored with her parents and wiggled free of Billie's arms. She scrambled to the floor and ran back into the living room to watch cartoons again.

After watching her daughter go, Cat wrapped her arms around Billie's waist. "So you went for coffee with Jen?" she asked.

Billie flashed a crooked smile then lowered her forehead to meet Cat's. "Yeah," she replied. "I swear we're gonna owe her a fortune for psychiatric visits," she joked.

"So, did Dr. Swenson give you any good advice?" Cat asked softly.

Billie placed a light kiss at the end of Cat's nose. "Yes, she did." Billie paused for a moment before continuing. "Look, Cat, I know I've been neglecting you and the kids by staying at work late into the night and neglecting my responsibilities here at home," she began before Cat interrupted her.

"Billie, please," Cat sputtered.

Billie placed a silencing finger over Cat's mouth. "Shhh. Listen to me, Cat. I know what the problem has been over the past month. It's a clear as day now that Jen has opened my eyes," she said.

Billie released Cat and paced around the kitchen while Cat followed her movements with her eyes.

"Cat, I thought it was my promotion. I thought you were angry or jealous about it, but I was wrong."

In three long strides, she crossed the room and stood in front of Cat.

"I was wrong, Cat. It's not my promotion that's upsetting you, it's the *effect* my promotion has had on this family."

Cat grinned as she watched her Billie fall into lawyer mode while she paced across the room.

"I was so blind. When I actually took the time to look at what was upsetting you, I was sick with self-loathing. God, Cat, do you realize that in the past month since my promotion, I have been late nine times? And that includes three dates that I canceled on you. Damn, no wonder you've been upset with me." Billie stopped in front Cat. "Sweetheart, I'm so sorry. I'd give it all up in a heartbeat if I thought I was losing you," she added.

Cat's eyes flew open. "Don't you *dare* give it up. Are you out of your mind? Billie, you've worked so hard and have made so many sacrifices to get where you are. Don't you dare give it up. Do you hear me?" she admonished sharply.

Billie drew Cat into an embrace and held her close. "Jen said you would say that," she said, her voice thick with emotion.

"Well, Jen was right," Cat replied, clinging desperately to her wife.

"I won't give it up, Cat. I promise, but I *do* need to make some changes. I need to be home more often," Billie explained. "Jen suggested that I do more of the follow-up work here at home, on my laptop. I'd still be working, but at least I'd be here with you and the kids," she finished, scanning Cat's face carefully for her reaction.

Cat's face was suddenly lit by a smile that completely filled her eyes. She nodded her head vigorously. "Billie, that's a wonderful idea," she finally said, stepping into Billie's embrace.

"Yeah, I thought so too," Billie agreed. "I'm actually looking forward to bringing work home on Monday. It's so damned lonely there at night…all alone after everyone else has gone home to their families. Geesh. I don't know why I didn't think of this myself," Billie admonished.

Cat placed her hand on the side of Billie's face. "Well, love," she said. "Sometimes, it's difficult to see the forest through the trees."

Billie smiled. "Sky-baby was right. You are the smartest person in the world," she exclaimed.

"No, love, that would be Jen. That would *definitely* be Jen," Cat replied as she and Billie laughed.

***

"All right now, everyone come over here and sit in the first two pews. Good. Thank you for joining us. Dylan, is everyone here?" asked the elderly priest.

Dylan looked around at the group that had gathered. "Everyone except Bob," Dylan replied, sitting back down.

"He'll probably be late for his own funeral," Cat whispered to Billie.

Billie furrowed her brow and looked back at her wife. "What do you mean?" she asked.

"He was late for dinner the other night too. He made quite a grand entrance if I remember correctly," Cat explained.

"I swear he'll be late for his own funeral, Padre. Let's get started without him," Dylan instructed the priest.

Cat and Billie smiled at each other when Dylan repeated Cat's thoughts.

"All right then, I'll give you a bit of instruction, then we'll walk through it a couple of times. Okay?" the priest asked. "Now, Dylan, you'll be standing up here at the altar waiting for Drew. Seth, when you see your uncle standing over there," the priest said, pointing to the far side of the altar, "you can walk your grandmother down the aisle and seat her in the front pew next to your grandfather, then go over to join your Uncle Dylan at the altar. At that time, the music will start and the ushers and bridesmaids will begin walking down the aisle in pairs. Be sure to leave adequate distance between you. If you count to ten before starting down the aisle that should be just about right. Is everything clear so far?" the priest stopped to ask, looking around at the nodding heads. "Good. Now..." he began again before being interrupted by a noise at the back of the church.

"Yo! Sorry I'm late," Bob called loudly.

Billie and Cat simultaneously looked to the back of the church.

"Well, the prodigal son returns," Cat said sarcastically.

"*That's* Bob?" Billie asked, raising her eyebrows into her hairline.

"Yep. That's the guy *you* get to walk down the aisle with," Cat replied, grinning ear to ear.

"Wonderful," Billie replied sarcastically. "He looks like a little boy."

"It gets worse, my love. You'll be about a foot taller than him in those heels," Cat said dryly.

"With any luck, he'll make a Barney remark and I'll have an excuse to kill him," Billie joked, drawing a chuckle and a slap on the arm from Cat.

"Behave," Cat reprimanded lightly.

"Well, young man, I'm glad you could make it," interjected the priest. "I'm Father Couture, and I'll be performing the ceremony. If you'd like to join the rest of the folks here, we'll continue our instruction," he concluded.

"Sure, Father," Bob replied innocently, slipping into the pew next to Cat.

"Okay, now, where were we...oh, yes, after the three sets of ushers and bridesmaids have started down the aisle, they will be followed by the flower girl. That would be you, little one," the priest said, smiling to Skylar sitting on Billie's lap. "Be sure to throw the rose petals around as you walk down the aisle, okay?"

Skylar smiled and squirmed at being the center of attention.

"Mrs. Stafford," he said, addressing Laurel, "When the little one reaches the end of the aisle, she'll sit with you and your husband. After the flower girl, comes the maid of honor, then the bride, escorted by her father. Drew and Mr. O'Grady, be sure to leave a substantial amount of space between you and the maid of honor...at least a twenty-count. The bride and her father will be followed by the train-bearer, who I believe is this young lady over there. Tara, is it?" he asked, drawing a nod from Tara. "You'll need to be sure you keep up a steady pace behind your aunt so as to not tug on her gown. When they reach the altar, you'll need to arrange her train neatly to one side, then go to stand next to the bridesmaids. Okay, that's about it. Let's take it through a dry run to see how it goes," he finished, prompting everyone to take their positions.

At the back of the church, chaos reigned until Cat stepped in and decided that they should walk down aisle in age order, placing Amy and Joe first, followed by Bridget and Kevin, then Billie and Bob. Once that was decided, they quickly organized and began the rehearsal.

"All right, the guests have been seated and the time is approaching to start the ceremony," the priest began.

"Seth, the wedding starts promptly at ten, so at three minutes before ten, you'll walk your Grandma down the aisle, then stand by your uncle. All right. Let's begin."

Offering his arm to Ida, Seth slowly walked her down the aisle and seated her in the front pew.

"Very good," Father Couture said as Seth joined Dylan. "Now, the first set of attendants," he directed as Joe and Amy walked in step, followed ten seconds later by Bridget and Kevin.

As Bridget and Kevin began the descent, Billie positioned herself in the center of the aisle and waited for Bob to join her. Looking around for her partner, she noticed that he was engaging Cat and Drew in conversation.

"Ahem, ah, Bob, let's go, it's our turn," she called over to the group.

Bob immediately left the two ladies and joined Billie in the center of the aisle. "Sorry about that," he said, looking up at her and rocking back and forth on his heels before heading down the aisle. "So, you're Billie, huh?" he asked.

"That would be me," she replied, allowing an uncomfortable silence to settle between them as they made their way slowly toward the altar.

"Cat told me you were tall," he said.

Billie smiled to herself, knowing she was intimidating the guy. "Yep," she replied. Once again, a heavy silence fell between them.

Billie could feel the relief washing over Bob as they reached the altar and parted ways to stand on separate sides with the other attendants. Bob sent shy, uncomfortable looks in Billie's direction as they watched Skylar walk down the aisle followed by Cat, and finally Drew and Doc.

After Doc delivered Drew to the altar, and seated himself beside Ida, Tara pretended to arrange the imaginary train around Drew's feet and then stood beside Billie. Father Couture once again addressed the group.

"Very good, one and all. Now that we know what we're doing, let's run through it one more time to get our timing down," the priest instructed as the wedding party once more lined up at the back of the church.

"Amy, Joe. Good! Now, Bridget and Kevin. That's right. And finally, Billie, Bob...your turn. Great," Father Couture commented as each couple started their trek down the aisle.

"Heh-heh, Billie-Bob. We sound like a redneck," Bob chuckled as they walked side by side.

Billie narrowed her eyes at the shorter man by her side, causing him to gulp.

"Ah, sorry about that. Honestly. I didn't mean anything by it," he stammered.

After the rehearsal, the group congregated outside the church, where Bob quite brazenly flirted with Amy while Joe stood by glaring at them.

"Don't like him much, do you?" Billie said, coming up behind Joe.

Joe looked at his sister-in-law. "No, I don't. Can you blame me?" he asked.

Billie looked at Bob who had his arm around Amy and was whispering something in her ear. "No, I guess I can't. He makes one move on Cat, and he's dead meat," Billie added.

Joe grinned. "I don't think you have to worry about that. He's scared shitless of you," he said.

"I can't imagine why," Billie commented innocently.

"Like hell you can't," Joe chuckled, falling silent.

"Don't let him do it, Joe," Billie said. "Don't let him take what's yours."

Joe stood next to Billie, both of them watching Amy and Bob flirting openly. "I don't own her, Billie, any more than you own Cat. She's her own woman. I can't stop her if that's what she really wants," he said sadly.

"*Is* it what she really wants?" Billie asked. She turned to her brother-in-law and decided to openly speak her mind. She placed a hand on Joe's shoulder and turned him toward her.

"Look Joe, maybe there's a reason for Amy's behavior. I mean, when was the last time you let Amy know this kind of behavior bothers you?" she asked.

"Billie, I don't want her to think I'm trying to control her. Our marriage has never been that way. I've always treated her as an equal. I mean, I'm not a Neanderthal like Kevin," he explained.

"No you're not, but maybe she needs you to be, just this once. Maybe she's trying to get a reaction out of you. Maybe she needs some kind of confirmation that you still love her and are willing to fight for her," Billie said.

Joe diverted his gaze from his wife to look Billie directly in the eyes. "Do you think so?" he asked.

Billie shrugged her shoulders. "I don't know for sure, Joe, but my gut tells me, yes," she answered.

Joe turned his gaze back to his wife and nodded his head repeatedly, remaining silent while he contemplated Billie's remarks.

"Billie, sweetheart, the kids are getting restless. Maybe we should head home," Cat called to her.

"I'll be right there, love," Billie replied.

Sliding her hand from Joe's shoulder, Billie rubbed his back. "You think about it, Joe. I really believe she loves you. It's certainly worth a try," she said before turning to go.

CHAPTER 19

"Josephine Wycliffe, you do *not* need another drink," Alexandra Spirakis scolded from her place in the window seat.

"Alex, my dear, you forced me to get into this flying bucket of bolts, now you're gonna have to live with it," Jo replied, motioning to the flight attendant. "Another whiskey, please," she ordered.

"I swear. You act like it's the first time you've flown," Alex exclaimed.

"It's the first time I've flown in a plane I've had to duck in to walk down the aisle, and I'm only knee-high to a grasshopper," Jo complained.

Alex gently slapped Josephine on the arm while she straightened her hair with the other hand. "Now, you know that's not true, Josie. What about the time you flew that two-seater all by yerself over Cairo?" she asked.

"Ah, well, that was different. The pilot passed out," Jo defended.

Alex sat up straight and placed both hands on her hips. "He passed out for the very same reason you're gonna pass out if you keep drinking," she said loudly.

Ignoring her wife's nagging, Jo started searching through her pockets.

"Now what are you looking for?" Alex asked, exasperated.

"I'm looking for my cigar," Jo replied, straightening her fedora.

"You gave up smoking years ago, silly," Alex reminded the aging historian.

"Oh, yeah, I forgot. Ah, here comes my whiskey," Jo replied. "Thank you, my dear," she added, openly flirting with the flight attendant as she paid for her drink. "Keep the change sweetheart," Jo said, winking and handing her a $20 bill for a $5 drink.

Jo cringed when she saw the proverbial daggers flying from Alex's eyes. She took a long draw on her whiskey then grinned. "Alex, sweetheart, will you marry me?" she asked.

"Josephine Wycliffe, you're drunk!" Alexandra replied.

"Yes, I am," Jo admitted grinning. "But I'm also madly in love with you. So," she said, raising her glass to Alex and spilling a portion of the contents on herself. "Will you marry me?" she asked again.

Alex looked intently at Josephine. "Josie, darlin' in my heart we are already married," she replied.

"In my heart as well, my dear, but I thought we could do it up right. After all, we can do it legally now, thanks to the marriage equality ruling. You know, I could make an honest woman out of you," Jo explained quite seriously through slurred speech.

"I think it's kinda late for that," Alex answered. "What's gotten into you Josephine Wycliffe?" she asked.

"What's gotten into me? About six drinks, I think!" Jo chuckled.

"That's what I was afraid of," Alex replied sadly, knowing it was too good to be true. For years she had toyed with the idea of asking Jo to marry her, but Jo just wasn't the marrying kind. She always said that a certificate of union was just a piece of paper that had no affect on how they felt about each other. So, they had spent the last fifty years together, married in their hearts but legally single, attending the weddings of all their friends and family...each ceremony reminding Alex that her relationship had never been legitimized. She was quite confused now at Jo's apparent change of heart.

Jo tried to explain herself. "No, Alex. Really. I...," she began before being interrupted by the flight attendant.

"Ladies and gentlemen, the captain has turned on the fasten seat belt sign. We are entering an area of turbulence so it may become a little bumpy. Please remain seated with your seat belts fastened until the fasten seat belt sign has been turned off," the voice said over the intercom.

"Great Caesar's ghost, I need another drink," Jo exclaimed, summoning the flight attendant…all thoughts of marriage having dissolved into thin air.

***

"Do you see them?" Cat asked, standing on tiptoe to see above the crowd.

"Hold on, I think that's them over there," Billie replied, pointing to the arrival gate. "Ah, it looks like Grandma Alex needs a little help. I'd better get over there," she added.

"Wait," Cat said, not intending to be left behind. "Is she okay?" she asked, following Billie through the crowd.

"She's fine, Cat," Billie answered over her shoulder. "It's Grandma Jo who's having a problem standing up."

"Grandma Jo?" Cat questioned as they reached their grandmothers.

"Billie-girl…Cat-woman," Jo said loudly when she noticed her granddaughters walking toward her. "How are my girls?" she asked, leaning heavily on Alex, who was red with embarrassment at the attention Jo was calling to herself.

"Josephine Wycliffe, will you ever listen to me?" Alex asked angrily. "I warned you about drinking too much on the plane!"

"Put a sock in it, Alex," Jo answered boldly, nearly falling over herself before Billie caught her and wrapped a strong arm around her waist.

"Come on, Grandma Jo. Time to go," Billie said, hoping to get through the crowd quickly to the privacy of their car.

"Billie, I'll grab a cart and collect their baggage, then meet you at the car, okay?" Cat asked, anxious to get her grandmothers alone to defuse what was turning into a very embarrassing situation. "Grams, how many bags do you have?" she asked.

"I'll go with you, Caitlain, dear. Your Grandma Jo can go to the devil for all I care right now. Let her make a fool of herself. I don't want any part of it," Alexandra said angrily.

Cat flashed a worried look at Billie before taking Alexandra's arm and leading her to the baggage claim area.

"I'll be damned if I *ever* marry that woman," Alexandra said under her breath, but loud enough for Cat to hear.

"What was that, Grams?" Cat asked.

Alexandra blushed and tried to hide her guffaw. "Oh, nothing, dear. Look, there's one of our bags now," she said, pointing to a large piece of luggage sliding down the shoot onto the baggage claim carousel.

Cat made four trips between the cart and the carousel before she finally collected all of Alex and Jo's luggage, and then headed toward the car. When they arrived, they found Josephine passed out in the back seat and Billie lounging lazily against the car, ankles and arms crossed. As they approached, Billie scurried to open the trunk, and efficiently transferred the luggage into it, casting furtive glances toward Cat in the process.

Crawling into the back seat, Billie pushed Jo into a seated position and leaned her against the passenger door to make room for Alexandra to get into the car. Throughout the drive home, Alex cast disgusted looks in Jo's direction, making barely audible disgruntled sounds of discontent.

Billie looked away from the road momentarily to meet her grandmother's eyes in the rearview mirror. "Wanna tell us what happened?" she asked.

"A proper southern lady doesn't discuss her problems in public," Alex replied.

Cat turned around in her seat. "Grams, we are not the public. We're family. Come on, talking about it will make you feel better," she coaxed.

Alex looked at the handkerchief she was twisting between her hands, struggling with the dilemma of airing her dirty laundry. "Oh, all right," she said. "That grandmother of yours is gonna be the death of me. The minute we boarded the plane, she started downing the whiskey, and flirtin' with the flight attendant," Alex explained. "I swear that woman still thinks she's twenty years old."

"So, what are you most upset about, the drinking or the flirting?" Billie asked coyly.

Alexandra looked back and forth between Cat and Billie's reflection in the mirror. Blushing to the roots of her salt and pepper hair, she lowered her eyes once more to the wrinkled handkerchief she was holding.

"You know she loves you," Billie added, correctly guessing the source of Alex's distress.

"She really does," Cat added, reaching back to cover Alex's hands with one of her own.

A lone tear fell onto the handkerchief as Alex nodded silently and then cast a glance at the sleeping woman beside her.

"She asked me to marry her," Alex said softly, still looking down at her hands.

Cat looked at Billie and smiled. Turning back to Alex, she said, "You said yes, didn't you?"

"No. I told her she was drunk," Alex replied, looking up at Cat. "She was, you know. She asked after I caught her flirting again with the attendant."

"Grams, you know she's harmless," Cat said in Jo's defense.

"Maybe so, but she could at least have the decency to do it behind my back. It is extremely embarrassing to have your wife flirt with a younger woman right in front of you," Alex explained.

"So, do you think her proposal was sincere?" Billie asked.

"Billie, dear, I have pondered asking Josie to marry me for years, but she has made it painfully clear that she's not interested, so I have no basis on which to judge her sincerity. I tend to believe it wasn't," Alex replied. "Now if you don't mind, dears, I would like to end this discussion."

Feeling promptly dismissed, Cat turned back around in her seat and raised her eyebrows at Billie. Reaching for her hand, Billie squeezed it tightly, sending her own reassurance to her wife that at least their love was strongly intact.

***

"All right Grandma Jo, let's go," Billie said, pulling Jo out of the car to her feet.

"I'm all right. I don't need any help," she complained, shaking off Billie's hands.

Knowing how stubborn her grandmother was, Billie just stepped back and let go of Jo, who promptly stumbled and nearly fell on her face before catching herself.

"Oh, for heaven's sake Josie, let Billie help you before you hurt yourself," Alex scolded.

"I'm fine, I tell ya! Just as soon as the ground stops moving, that is," Josephine joked.

"What's wrong with Grammy Jo?" Skylar asked.

"Seth, would you mind getting the luggage out of the trunk and bringing it to the downstairs guest room, please?" Billie asked her son as she once more wrapped an arm around Josephine's waist.

"Sure, Mom," he replied, taking the keys Billie offered to him.

"Okay, I've got the bed turned down," Cat called from the kitchen doorway as she rejoined the ladies trying to coax a drunken Josephine into the house.

"For the life of me, Josephine Wycliffe, I'll never understand why you have to cause such a scene all the time," Alex stated, obviously embarrassed by Jo's behavior.

Cat embraced Alex as Billie finally maneuvered Jo toward the house. "Don't worry about her, Grams. She wouldn't be Jo if she didn't cause a scene. You have to admit that she's added quite a bit of color to your lives all these years," she observed.

"Yeah, I guess you're right, but most people are happy with a box of eight Crayolas, while Josie insists on the ninety-six pack," she laughed.

Cat looked at her grandmother, once again taken with her aging beauty and strong resemblance to Billie. "Well, Grams, you're pretty colorful too if I should say so myself," she remarked.

Alexandra blushed. "Oh, pshaw, Caitlain" she said, lightly slapping Cat on the arm. "You're makin' me blush."

"And so pretty in pink," Cat teased as she and Alex made their way to the house behind Billie and Jo.

"Okay, Grandma Jo, that's it, just a little further," Billie coached as she led Jo to the spare bedroom. "Here we are. Down you go," she added, lowering Jo to the bed. "Off with the boots," came the next comment as Billie unlaced and removed Jo's combat style boots.

Billie chuckled as she took in Jo's attire. Alex was right. Jo *did* think she was still twenty years old. Here she was, in her seventies, and dressed in safari wear, much like she was when she traveled the world as an historian fifty years ago when she met Alex in Viet Nam.

"There you go," Billie said as she swung Jo's legs onto the bed and pulled the blankets to her neck. She removed Jo's fedora and placed a light kiss on her forehead before putting the hat on the night stand and quietly making her way out of the room, closing the door behind her.

Alex and Cat had busied themselves in the kitchen while Billie put Josephine to bed. Returning to the kitchen, Billie found her wife and grandmother in the process of making coffee cake after putting a pot of coffee on to brew.

"She's all tucked in," Billie announced, coming up behind Cat and wrapping her arms around her. "God, that coffee smells good. What 'cha making?" she asked.

"Coffee cake," Cat replied, lifting a spoon of batter to Billie's lips.

"Umm, pecans. My favorite," Billie exclaimed, smacking her lips.

"Is Josie sleeping?" Alex asked, pouring each of them a cup of coffee.

"Passed out, is more like it," Billie replied. "Grams, has she been drinking more than usual lately?"

"No, not really. She just doesn't like to fly, and she covers up her fear by dulling it with the devil's brew. She's really not as tough as she'd like you to believe," Alex explained.

"Yeah, I kind of guessed as much," Cat chimed in, grinning. "All right, in you go," Cat added as she slipped the coffee cake into the oven.

The three women carried their coffee mugs to the table where they sat, intending to visit while waiting for the coffee cake to bake.

After more than a half hour of catching up, Billie abruptly changed the subject. "So, she asked you to marry her, huh?" she said, smiling impishly.

Alex looked directly at her granddaughter. "Yes she did, but I have no reason to believe she was serious. Darlin', we've been together for fifty years. Why ask now?" Alexandra questioned.

"Why *not* now?" Billie asked. "I mean, the recent Supreme Court decision on marriage equality has made it legal for everyone now."

"Maybe the nostalgia brought on by Drew and Dylan's upcoming nuptials have gotten to her?" Cat suggested.

"I'd like to think so, darlin', but..." Alex began.

"But, nothing," Billie interrupted. "Why not give her the benefit of the doubt? Let's see what happens over the next few days. If nothing does, I'll confront her directly," Billie suggested.

"You'll do nothing of the sort, young lady. If she can't be sincere about it without bein' pushed into it, then I don't *want* to marry her," Alex exclaimed. "A lady's got standards to uphold, you know."

Billie threw a conspiring look at Cat, silently conveying covert plans to her wife through her eyes. Cat immediately picked up on Billie's vibes as she nodded her approval.

Billie sat back in her chair and looked at Alex, sighing deeply, as though she was resigned to the older woman's stubbornness. "All right. You're the boss," she said.

Alexandra covered Billie's hand with her own. "Thank you dear. I knew you would see it my way," she replied just as the oven timer began to chime.

"Coffee cake's done," Cat said, grinning at Billie's submissiveness. *Grams, I think you're in for quite a ride. Hang on and fasten your seat belt,* she thought to herself as she retrieved the cake from the oven.

***

"Hello? Oh, hi Billie," Jen exclaimed as she recognized her friend's voice on the phone.

"Jen, I need a favor," Billie began without ceremony.

"I'm fine, Barney. Thank you for asking. And how are you?" Jen replied dryly, indirectly pointing out the lack of customary courtesy to her friend.

"Jen, I warned you about the Barney thing," Billie scolded.

Barely able to contain a chuckle, Jen continued. "What can I do for you, oh exalted purple one?"

"That is so not fair," Billie exclaimed. "Pretty brave over the phone, aren't you?" she said dangerously.

"Damn straight," Jen replied.

"Okay, since I need your help, I'm gonna overlook the comments, but just this once. You got it?" Billie warned.

"All right, all right. I'll lay off for now, Barn...I mean Billie. What can I do for you?" Jen asked.

"Well, Grandmas Jo and Alex are here and..." Billie spent the next several minutes on the phone with her friend. Finally, she hung up and grinned. *Billie-girl, you're a genius,* she boasted to herself.

CHAPTER 20

"This wedding crap is really boring," fifteen-year-old Crystal said.

Tara looked skeptically at her cousin. "I don't think so. It might be fun," she replied.

"That's because you're in the wedding. At least you have something to do," Crystal retorted. "Even if it *is* carrying Aunt Drew's dress."

"It's called a train, and at least you don't have to *wear* a dress like I do," Tara whined. "That's the worst part."

Crystal and Tara had ridden Seth and Tara's bikes to the park and were now sitting side by side on the swings, lazily dragging their feet back and forth across the worn grooves beneath them.

"You're gonna look real foo-foo you know," Crystal picked, obviously jealous that her cousin was in the wedding and she wasn't.

"I'm not foo-foo," Tara spat back. Tara prided herself on her tough reputation. Even the boys at school walked a wide berth around her when she threw them one of her looks. Being called foo-foo was like issuing her a challenge.

"Are too," Crystal argued.

"You'd better stop saying that," Tara warned.

"Prove it then," Crystal challenged.

"What do you mean?" Tara asked.

Crystal looked around to see if anyone was watching them, then reached into her pocket and pulled out a sandwich bag.

"What's that?" Tara inquired.

"Take a closer look," Crystal replied, shoving the bag in Tara's face.

Tara took the bag and looked at it carefully. It contained something that resembled cooking herbs to her. Raising it to her nose, she sniffed, then quickly pulled it away and looked wide-eyed at her cousin. "It's pot!" she exclaimed loudly.

Crystal grabbed the bag and quickly shoved it back into her pocket. "Say it a little louder, Tara. I don't think the officer two blocks away heard you," she scolded sarcastically.

Tara was feeling a mixture of excitement and fear. She had never seen marijuana up close before, but she surely recognized the odor. At the end of the last school year, one of the senior girls was caught smoking it in the girls bathroom and it left behind an odor so strong, it burned Tara's nose when she went in there.

Tara's heart was beating a mile a minute. Trying hard to calm herself and not call any unnecessary attention to her and her cousin, she took deep breaths and then looked over at Crystal who was nonchalantly swinging back and forth, quite innocent to the casual observer.

"Where did you get it?" Tara asked.

"I've got connections."

Tara didn't know what to say, so she just diverted her eyes to the ground.

"So, are you a foo-foo chicken-shit, or what?" Crystal continued to dig.

Tara turned sharply toward her cousin. "I told you not to say that."

"Well, I think you need to prove that you're not a coward," Crystal said, once more pulling the bag out of her pocket and offering it to Tara.

Tara stared at the bag, not really sure what she wanted to do. "I don't know, Crystal," she said haltingly.

Crystal held the bag in front of her. "It won't hurt you, you know."

"I...I don't think I should," Tara said softly, still staring at the ground in front of her.

Crystal jumped off her swing and started to walk away, shoving the bag into her pocket. "I thought you'd say that. So I guess you *are* a foo-foo chicken-shit," she tossed over her shoulder.

Tara had had enough. She jumped off her own swing, ran after her cousin and pushed her to the ground. She held her down by the shoulders and shouted into her face, "I am *not* a foo-foo chicken-shit. You got that?"

Crystal grinned into her face. "Then prove it," she demanded again.

Tara narrowed her eyes at Crystal. She hated being put on the spot like that. She hated being made to feel small and weak.

"All right. Give it to me," she demanded, reaching into Crystal's pocket and grabbing the bag of weed. Getting to her feet, she offered her hand to her older cousin and helped her up. "Where can we go to smoke it?" she asked.

Crystal looked around. "Well, we can't smoke it out here in the open," she said, stating the obvious. "Look. There's a gas station across the street. We'll use the bathroom," she suggested, grabbing Tara's hand and dragging her across the street.

Tara had visions of the senior at school, sitting in the principal's office while she waited for her parents to come after her. "What happens if we get caught?" she asked.

"We won't get caught," Crystal replied.

"How do you know that?" Tara questioned nervously as they reached the office of the gas station.

"Because, I never get caught. Look, all we're gonna do is borrow the bathroom key, go in, smoke a joint, then head home. If we lock the bathroom door behind us, no one will be the wiser," Crystal explained. "You wait here while I get the key."

Crystal entered the office and exited a few seconds later holding an extremely large key holder with a small key dangling from a chain beneath it. "Got it! Let's go," she said as she dragged Tara around the corner of the building to the rest rooms on the side.

Once inside, with the door locked, a very nervous Tara stood in the dim light of the fluorescent bulb, watching her cousin pull a package of cigarette papers from her back pocket and expertly roll a joint, squeezing both ends closed. "Here, take this one while I roll another for me," she said.

Tara looked at the object lying in the palm of her hand. "I thought we were going to share one," she said, never taking her eyes off the joint.

"Nah. To get a really good rush, you have to smoke a whole one," Crystal replied. "Okay, here we go," she added, shoving the remaining marijuana back into her pocket and bringing her own joint to her lips. Raising a lighter to Tara, she instructed her younger cousin to inhale deeply and to hold the smoke in her lungs for as long as possible before exhaling.

Crystal started to chuckle as she watched Tara choke, while she simultaneously took a long drag on her own joint. "Don't give up on it. Try it again," Crystal said as she continued to hold the smoke in her lungs.

Tara's second attempt was more successful, as was the third and forth. Soon, the bleary-eyed thirteen-year-old was struggling to hold onto what little remained of her joint, finally dropping it into the sink when it became too small to hold without burning her fingers. Both hands came to rest on the sides of the sink to hold herself erect.

"You okay?" Crystal asked, leaning against the wall, her legs crossed at the ankles as she finished her own joint.

Tara looked at her cousin and giggled. "I'm grrrrrrreat!" she replied, sending herself into a fit of giggles once more.

Suddenly, there was a knock at the door.

"Shit," Crystal exclaimed, pushing herself away from the wall and throwing the rest of her joint into the toilet. "There's someone in here," she called loudly, futilely trying to clear the smoke away with her hands.

"Will you be long?" the voice said from the other side.

"Yeah. We, I mean, *I* just got in here, and I'm taking a dump," she replied.

After a few minutes of silence, Crystal was satisfied the person had gone away. "Tara, we gotta get out of here. Can you walk?" she asked.

Tara tried to stand erect, but nearly toppled over backward. "Sure. I'm fine," she exclaimed, clinging to her.

"Damn it, Tara. How are we going to ride the bikes home with you in this state?" she growled.

"State? What state is this, anyway? Alaska, Hawaii??" Tara said, laughing uncontrollably at her own attempt at humor.

"Jesus Christ," Crystal swore through her own haze. "Come on. We need to get back to the park to sober up before going home."

Crystal wrapped her arm around Tara's waist and half dragged, half carried her across the street and laid her on the grass near the tree the bikes were locked to. Sitting down next to her, she pulled her into a seated position against the tree and started lightly tapping her face.

"Why are you hitting me?" Tara asked light-heartedly.

"I'm trying to wake you up," Crystal complained. "Now come on, open your eyes."

After several unsuccessful attempts to sober Tara up, she finally allowed her to fall asleep on the ground. With nothing to do while she waited for Tara to recover, she lay down beside her. Soon, both girls fell into a drug-induced sleep.

***

"Hi, Mom," Cat said into the receiver. "Is Tara there with Crystal?"

"No they're not, dear. Crystal went to your house earlier this morning. She said something about going somewhere with Tara," Ida replied.

"Well, they're not here, and Tara didn't leave me a note. That's not like her," Cat worried out loud.

"I'm sure they're fine, Caitlain. So, did you and Amy have a nice time today?" Ida asked.

Cat was caught off guard. "Amy? I didn't see Amy today," she said haltingly.

"Oh! I was sure she said…oh, well, never mind dear. It must have been my imagination," Ida explained.

No, mother, I don't think it was, Cat said to herself. To Ida, she said, "Okay, Mom. If the girls show up at your house, tell Tara to call me."

"I will sweetheart. Oh, by the way, will you and Billie be able to join Laurel and me for breakfast on Saturday morning? We thought it might be fun to have a mother/daughter shopping day," Ida asked hopefully.

"Sounds fun, Mom. I'm sure Billie would love to go," *Yeah, right,* Cat said. "All right Mom, I've got to get dinner started. I'll talk to you later. Love you," Cat finished before hanging up. *Amy, what are you up to?* she thought to herself as she turned her attention to dinner.

"Hi, love," Billie said as she entered the house through the kitchen door. Placing her laptop on the table as she passed by, she went directly to Cat and placed a solid kiss on her cheek.

Cat turned and wrapped her arms around Billie's neck, bringing their faces close together for a long and passionate kiss.

"Oh, God," Billie exclaimed, burying her face in Cat's neck, her mutinous knees refusing to hold her up as she leaned into her wife and pressed her back into the stove.

"Welcome home. How was your day?" Cat asked, accepting another kiss from Billie.

"My day was wonderful. Very busy, but very productive. I've got a few notes to transcribe later," she said, nodding her head toward her laptop on the table. "How was *your* day?" she asked, burying her nose in Cat's neck once more.

Cat tilted her head to one side to allow Billie better access. "Not bad. God, that feels good. I...I left early. My third surgery was...oh, Billie...rescheduled," she finally managed to get out before snaking her hands under Billie's shirt and allowing them to roam aimlessly across the expanse of skin covering her back.

Within seconds, Billie had Cat's shirttails pulled out of her slacks, her own hands quickly finding two full mounds to cup and knead.

Cat suddenly yelped as Billie pinched two sensitive nubs. "Oh, my God," she exclaimed, covering Billie's hands with her own and drawing them closer, clearly communicating her need.

Billie nibbled on Cat's collarbone. "Are the grandmothers home?"

"No. They're gone to Mom's for dinner," Cat replied.

Billie kissed her way up Cat's neck to her ear. "Are the kids home?" she asked breathlessly.

"No. Seth is gone to the movies with Stevie. Sky is at Missy's house. And Tara...well, I'm not sure where Tara is...only that she's with Crystal," Cat explained.

Billie pulled her head back and looked at Cat, brow furrowed.

"Yeah, I know. I'm a little worried about her too, but I'm sure she's okay," Cat said, reading her wife's mind.

"I don't know about you, Cat, but Crystal makes me nervous. I mean, she just seems a little too old for her age, and I think Amy and Joe let her run a little wild," Billie commented.

Cat nodded. "Well, I guess it's kind of tough to discipline your kids when you're basically running wild yourself," she said. "I don't know what Amy's up to, but for some reason Mom thought she was with me all day today."

"I feel sorry for Joe," Billie said. "He really loves her, but I think he's afraid of losing her if he demands that she straightens out."

"I know she's my sister, but sometimes I wonder if Joe would be better off without her," Cat added.

"Well if they *do* break up, it will be Amy leaving Joe. Joe is so taken with her, he'll never leave," Billie said.

"If she's doing what I *think* she's doing, it might just push Joe over the edge," Cat remarked. "Billie, I think she's having an affair with Bob."

Billie shook her head. She pulled Cat close to her once more. "I am so glad that our lives are uncomplicated, at least for the moment," Billie added with a chuckle.

"Hmmmm. Now, where were we?" Cat replied, pulling Billie's head down to meet hers.

$$***$$

"Tara. Tara, wake up," Crystal urged, shaking her cousin.

"What?" Tara said groggily as she lifted her head.

"It's almost six o'clock. We've been sleeping for five hours. Our parents are gonna to call the cops if we don't get our asses home."

Tara rolled to her side then climbed to her hands and knees. Sitting back on her feet, she suddenly felt dizzy. "Oh, my God, I'm gonna be sick," she complained, clutching her stomach.

Crystal climbed to her feet and looked down at Tara in disgust. "Well if you're gonna blow, direct it that way," she said, pointing away from the bikes that were still chained to the tree.

"Oh, God," Tara shouted before she doubled over and emptied the contents of her stomach on the ground.

"Ewwwww! You're gross," Crystal exclaimed.

"I don't feel so good." Tara crawled to the tree and used it to slowly make her way to her feet. Five hours after smoking the joint, she was still unsteady on her feet.

Crystal stood with her hands on her hips, watching her cousin's misery. "You are such a newbie," she said. "I can tell this is your first time."

"And the last," Tara added. Finally dragging herself into an erect position, she held onto the tree with one hand while searching her pockets for the key to the lock holding the bikes. Finding it, she fumbled with the lock, dropping the key twice before finally fitting it into the slot.

"Come on, Tara, we haven't got all day," Crystal whined, making no effort to help her.

At last, the lock was undone and the chain tucked away in the small saddlebag hanging on the back of the seat. Pulling the bikes apart, Crystal grabbed one, and Tara the other. After several attempts to swing her leg over the bar, she finally lost her balance and toppled to the ground, pulling the bike down on top of her.

"Owwww! Crystal, help me. This really hurts," Tara said as Crystal worked to untangle Tara's legs from the bike. Finally she was free and standing on her feet again, favoring her right foot. "I think I twisted my ankle," she said.

"We're not gonna be able to ride these home. We'll have to walk them," Crystal complained.

"I am never going to touch pot again," Tara mumbled under her breath as she limped behind her cousin to begin their long walk home.

***

"Billie. Billie, honey, I really need to start supper," Cat said.

"Just a while longer, Cat," Billie demanded, pulling Cat down under the blankets to snuggle.

Cat happily obliged, not really wanting to recover too quickly from the afterglow of their lovemaking. She and Billie had just spent long moments exploring each other's bodies and souls, savoring their love, figuratively and literally, neither one wanting to leave the comfort of warm loving arms.

Suddenly, Cat sat erect in bed, her mother hearing finely tuned to a noise downstairs.

"What is it Cat?" Billie asked, having learned long ago to trust Cat's instincts.

"I hear something down stairs. Listen," she whispered.

"Mom," called a voice from the kitchen.

Cat jumped out of bed and quickly pulled on a pair of gym shorts and T-shirt. "It's Tara," she said over her shoulder to Billie as she headed to the door.

Billie was right behind her, pulling her own T-shirt over her head as they made their way through the upstairs hall.

Moments later, they arrived in the kitchen to find Tara sitting at the table, her right foot propped up on a chair.

Cat immediately went into doctor mode. "Tara, what happened? Where does it hurt?" she questioned as she gently probed the swollen ankle. Before Tara could answer, Cat suddenly froze and looked her daughter in the eye. Moving in closer, she sniffed Tara's clothing, a frown growing increasingly deeper as the seconds passed.

Billie looked questioningly at her wife and daughter. She too moved in closer to check things out for herself. By the time she got within two feet of Tara, she knew exactly what Cat was frowning about.

Cat's gaze met Billie's, a knowing look passing between them. Obviously trying very hard to control her temper, Cat walked away from her daughter and started pacing the room, one hand on her hip, the other one worrying the bangs on her forehead.

As Cat paced, Billie confronted. She leaned over Tara, her nose within inches of her daughter's. "Where did you get it?" she asked firmly.

Tara looked at the floor.

"You better think about answering our questions, or you're going to spend a lot of time memorizing every inch of your bedroom," Billie warned.

Tara looked up. "Crystal," was all she said.

No sooner had her niece's name left Tara's lips, than Cat was on the phone. "Hi, Mom, this is Cat again. Is Amy or Joe there?" she asked.

"Well, yes, dear. Joe is here," her mother said.

Cat chewed on her lip and looked nervously at her daughter as she waited for her brother-in-law to answer.

"Hi, Cat. What's up?" Joe asked.

"Hi, Joe," Cat replied. "It seems that we have a problem on our hands. Could you and Amy bring Crystal over here as soon as possible?"

"Amy just got home, so sure, we'll be right over. Is everything all right, Cat?"

"We'll talk about that when you get here."

"All right, then. We'll see you in a few minutes," Joe said.

Cat hung up the phone and turned back to her daughter. "You are in big trouble, young lady. Do you understand that what you did was illegal, never mind harmful? What were you thinking?" she asked.

"Crystal was calling me names," Tara said weakly.

"She was calling you names? You smoked pot because she was calling you names!" Cat shouted, her voice raising an octave with each word.

"And just what was she calling you that would cause you to take such drastic measures, Tara?" Billie asked.

"She called me a foo-foo chicken-shit. I had to prove to her that I wasn't, so she dared me to smoke a joint and I did," Tara confessed.

"Tara, I thought you were smarter than that. Didn't we talk about being strong in the face of adversity? Didn't we talk about how other people's opinions of you were less important than that of yourself?" Billie drilled.

Tara continued to look at the floor. "Yeah," she admitted.

"Look at me when I'm talking to you," Billie shouted, reaching forward to raise Tara's chin so that their eyes met. "Do you know how many kids I've seen sent to jail for doing drugs?" Billie asked, trying to put the fear of God into her daughter.

"Crystal said we wouldn't get caught," Tara reasoned.

"Well Crystal was wrong. The smell of pot is very unique Tara. Your clothes reek of it. Just how stupid do you think your mother and I are?" Billie asked. "What were you thinking?"

Tears started to form in Tara's eyes. "I guess I wasn't," she replied sadly.

"No, I guess you weren't," Billie added, finally releasing Tara's chin and walking away, her own throat choked with emotion.

"And how did you sprain your ankle?" Cat intervened.

"We fell asleep in the park, and when we woke up, I got sick and puked, and then we tried to ride the bikes home and I fell over and twisted my legs in the bars," Tara explained.

Cat threw her hands up into the air. "This is incredible," she shouted. "You could have been attacked, raped, or even killed while you were sleeping, Tara! The park is not the safest place for two defenseless teenage girls."

"We weren't defenseless," Tara said in her own behalf.

Billie took Tara by the shoulders. "Two teenage girls who are passed out in a drug-induced sleep are *absolutely* defenseless. You are so lucky you are still here to tell us about it."

"Hello?" Amy's voice said from the doorway. "You summoned?"

"You're damned right I did," Cat said, marching over to her niece, who had come into the room behind her mother and followed by her father. Taking her by the hand, she led her to a chair next to Tara. "Sit down," she ordered, pushing Crystal into the chair.

Crystal looked at Tara through narrowed eyes.

"So what's the problem here?" Joe asked, not really sure if he should be humiliated or defensive.

"Joe, Amy, do you have any idea where our daughters were all afternoon?" Cat asked.

"At the movies?" Amy replied.

"Is that what Crystal told you?" Billie piped in.

"Where do *you* think they were?" Joe asked.

"Passed out in the park from smoking pot, that's where," Cat replied harshly.

Joe turned to his daughter. "Crystal, is that true?" he asked.

Crystal ignored her father, but instead turned to her cousin. "You are such a rat," she vehemently spat into Tara's face.

That was all Joe had to hear. "Well, that's proof enough for me. Let's go, Crystal. Starting right now, you are on a very short leash," he said, grabbing his daughter's hand and yanking her to her feet. "We'll be in the car," he said to the group as he dragged Crystal out the door.

Amy turned to follow her husband and daughter, but was stopped by the sound of Cat's voice. "Amy, I know you've been up to something. Do me a favor and don't use me as you alibi again. I won't lie for you," Cat said. "Oh, and one more thing— you should take a close look at your own behavior and ask yourself if it might be rubbing off on your daughter. If you don't do something now to fix both her problem and yours, it will mean the end to everything you hold dear."

Amy stared at Cat for long moments, contemplating what her younger sister had said, before turning wordlessly and heading out the door.

"Just where do you think you're going, young lady?" Billie asked Tara as she noticed her trying to sneak out of the kitchen while her mothers were occupied with her aunt.

Tara turned around guiltily. "To my room," she replied sheepishly.

Folding her arms across her chest, Billie narrowed her eyes at her daughter. "We are not finished with you yet, Tara. What you and Crystal did today was seriously wrong," she scolded.

"It's not my fault," Tara whined as she sat down once again. "Crystal made me do it."

"She did no such thing," Cat interjected. "*You* have control over your own actions. *You* decided to smoke the pot. Crystal may have provided the means, but it was a conscious decision on your part to go along with her," Cat explained.

Tara sat with her hands in her lap and chin resting on her chest.

"So what do you think we should do about this?" Billie asked.

The teenager looked up at her mothers, guilt and shame clouding her features. "Please don't ground me," she begged. "I promise not to do it again. It was gross anyway. It made me feel really horrible."

"This can't go unpunished, Tara," Cat said as she paced back and forth, trying to come up with a punishment that fit the crime. Finally, she stopped and faced her daughter. "Look," she said, "your trip to South Carolina is a month away..."

"Ma, please don't make me stay home," Tara exclaimed suddenly.

"No, that's not what I had in mind," Cat replied quickly, calming her daughter's fears. "What I was going to say is that for the next four weekends, you will spend either Saturday or Sunday volunteering at the homeless shelter. Drugs and alcohol can be major contributors to homelessness. I think you need to see first hand the affects of reckless drug abuse," she explained.

Tara jumped to her feet, wincing as her weight came down on her sore ankle. "No way," she exclaimed.

"Yes way," Billie responded, throwing her approval behind Cat's plan. "It's either that or four weekends of grounding. Your choice," she offered.

"This isn't fair," Tara ranted. "I'm gonna punch Crystal's lights out," she threatened.

"Just remember that Crystal is only part of the problem, Tara. You are not blameless here," Cat pointed out.

Tara sat down again and angrily folded her arms across her chest, refusing to look at her mothers.

"Well?" Billie asked, hands on her hips as the looked at her daughter.

"I guess I don't have a choice, do I?" Tara mumbled, pouting sullenly.

"No, you don't. Now, I think it might be a good idea if you wash that stench off your body and then spent some time in your room. I'll bring you an ice pack for that ankle as soon as I hear the shower stop," Cat said.

Billie folded Cat in her arms as they watched their angry daughter hobble toward her room. "Hang in there, love. They're only teenagers for nine years," Billie chuckled.

Cat looked at Billie, eyebrows etched high on her forehead. "Nine years?" she said incredulously. "Nine years times three kids, you mean. I swear Miss Clairol is going to make a fortune off me before Skylar turns twenty," she exclaimed.

CHAPTER 21

"Josie? darlin', could you fix this zipper? It appears to be stuck," Alex asked as she brushed the imaginary wrinkles from the front of her dress.

"Anything for you, my love," Jo replied after first straightening her fedora. "Turn around here and let me see."

Jo reached for the zipper and attempted to raise it into place. It soon became apparent that it was stuck fast on a piece of material caught in the teeth.

"Looks like the little bugger is attempting to take a bite out of your dress, Alex," Jo observed. "Let me try to unzip it a bit first. There, that did it," she added after freeing the captive material and successfully raising the zipper to its proper position at Alex's neckline. Before Alex had a chance to turn around again, Jo slipped her arms around her waist and pulled her close, allowing her hands to roam freely across Alex's abdomen as she pressed herself into the tall woman's back.

"Josephine Wycliffe! My word, what are you doing?" Alex exclaimed, knowing full well what Jo was trying to do as heat rushed to her smiling face.

"After fifty years, I would hope you'd know, Alex," Jo quipped dryly.

It totally amazed Alex how even in her advanced years, Jo had the power to turn her insides to mush. Never once in their fifty years together had she ever regretted becoming committed to this woman. There *had* been times when she would have quite willingly strangled the aging historian, but never did she regret their relationship. Caitlain was right—Josephine most certainly did add color to their lives. She just couldn't imagine what it would have been like without her.

Jo was in the process of driving Alex crazy with sensual caresses as Cat and Billie were waiting for them to join the picnic they had planned with their neighbor Jen and her family, and giving in to Jo's amorous advances was just not convenient.

Alex grabbed Jo's hands, which were quite brazenly making their way across her breasts. Resisting the urge to encourage the roaming hands, she firmly pulled them away and turned herself around to look into her wife's smoldering green eyes.

"Josie, dear heart, we are expected to join the family for a picnic. This is not a good time to…umph," Alex tried to say as Jo silenced her with an invasive kiss.

"Oh, my," was all Alex could say when Jo finally released her. Fanning herself with one hand, and reaching for the edge of the dresser to steady her weak knees with the other, she looked at Jo, who was standing there, hands buried deep in her trouser pockets, bouncing up and down on her toes, a smug grin spread across her still pixie-like features.

"I've still got it," Jo boasted as she stepped toward Alex and placed one more, gentle kiss on the end of her nose. Then, taking a step back, she offered her arm to the regal southern belle. "Well? Are you ready? We're holding up the party," she added, as if the delay was all Alex's doing.

"Ms. Wycliffe, I swear you are gonna be the death of me," Alex responded breathlessly as she took Jo's arm, adding as they reached the bedroom door, "I sincerely hope you plan to finish what you started when we are properly alone?"

Jo's chest puffed out with assured cockiness. "You're damned right I do, Ms. Spirakis. That, you can count on."

"Oh, I am, Ms. Wycliffe. I am," Alex replied as they joined the family in the back yard.

***

"Here they are, *finally*," Seth said as Alex and Jo stepped out of the house. "*Now* can we eat? I'm starved."

All eyes turned to the back porch as the two elderly women approached the steps. As she watched them descend the steps,

Billie whispered in Cat's ear, "That's a nice flush on Grams' face. I bet I know what took them so long."

Cat grinned and turned to look at her wife. "I believe you're right, my love. If we're lucky, that will be *us* in another forty years," she replied.

"Mrs. Charland, *that* you can count on," Billie replied, unknowingly imitating Josephine's words.

"They look so cute together," observed Cat as Jo and Alex approached them. Alexandra walked daintily at Josephine's side, her right hand slung possessively through Jo's arm as her left hand kept her flowing skirt in order, a large hat shading her creamy white features from the sun's rays. Jo walked by her side, her fedora tipped slightly to the right, back erect, head held high, leading the delicate flower attached to her arm safely to their destination.

"I'm afraid the days of the delicate southern belle, and gallant southern gentleman are quickly coming to an end with these two," Billie added sadly as the two women finally reached them.

"I'm sorry we're late," Alex began after a round of hugs. "Your grandmother here...well, let's just say she chooses the most inopportune times to misbehave,"

Jo wiggled her eyebrows up and down at Billie as a knowing look passed between them.

"Not a problem, Grams," Cat said as she took Alex arm and led her toward the array of chairs arranged under a large canopy. "We're still waiting for Jen to come back. She had to run a quick errand. As soon as she arrives, we'll begin."

Seeing that the grandmothers were finally present, Seth and Stevie ran over to where Cat had seated Alexandra. "Ma, we're really starving. Can we eat now?" Seth asked.

"Honey, Jen isn't back yet," Cat replied.

"Ah come on. We're really, really, really starved. Aren't we Stevie?" Seth begged.

"Yeah, *we're* really hungry too," added Tara, mirrored by a vigorously nodding Karissa.

Cat looked over to Billie and Jo who were both tending the grill.

"Billie, honey, is there enough cooked to get the kids started?" she called out.

Billie took inventory of the items on her grill. "Yep, I think so."

The kids jumped up and down cheering at the news.

"Whoa, wait a minute," Cat said. "The salads are still in the house. You'll need to fetch them, along with the paper plates, napkins and utensils. Okay?"

"No problem," Seth replied as the four older children ran into the house to collect the rest of the food.

"Grams, I'd better go after them to make sure they get everything. Will you be all right alone?" Cat asked Alex who was sitting quite comfortably in the shade, sipping a glass of ice tea.

"Well of course, Caitlain. I'm quite content here. Go on and see to the young-uns," Alex replied, shooing her granddaughter away.

Just as Cat reached the back porch, Jen and Fred finally arrived, accompanied by an elderly gentleman. "Jen, you're here. Good. The kids are driving me crazy wanting to eat," Cat exclaimed.

"You mean there's still food left?" Jen asked incredulously. "I figured those eating machines of ours would have cleaned us out by now," she joked. "Sorry we're so late. Pops wasn't quite ready," she added. Reaching out for the hand of the gentleman beside her, she pulled him over. "Pops, this is Cat Charland," Jen said, making the introductions.

"It's so nice to meet you," Cat replied, not really wanting to call the man, Pops.

"Chester," said the older man as he extended his hand. "But please, call me Chet," he added warmly.

"Well, Chet, welcome to our home. I hope you're hungry. We have a ton of food," Cat replied.

"Ravenous," Chet exclaimed.

"Great. Ah, Jen, would you mind introducing Chet to the others while I make sure the food is ready?" Cat asked.

"No problem," Jen replied taking her father by the hand and leading him into the yard.

"Cat, where do you want the beer?" Fred asked, coming around the back of the car carrying a large cooler as his wife led his father-in-law away.

"Hi, Fred," Cat said, placing a kiss on her friend's cheek. "Put it over there by the garage. Billie and Grandma Jo are manning the grill if you want to keep them company," she added.

Fred looked over to where Billie and Jo were struggling to keep the smoking grill from getting out of control. "You're actually letting Billie cook?" Fred asked, aghast.

"Well, she's got to learn sometime," Cat replied, laughingly.

"Yeah, but I'd prefer it *not* to be when I have to eat it," Fred replied through barely controlled laughter.

"Well, you could always give her a hand," Cat suggested.

Fred looked at her as if she were speaking a foreign language. "You *do* want to be able to eat it, right?" he said dryly. "I don't know who's a worse cook—me or Billie. Either way, we're all doomed."

Cat just shook her head and chuckled as she made her way into the house.

* * *

"It's so nice to meet you, Chet," Billie said as she firmly shook the older man's hand. "I'm glad you could join us."

"Thank you for the invitation," he said, retrieving his hand and clasping both of them behind his back. "My Jen has told me so much about you and Cat. To be honest, I was a little unsure about your friendship at first. No offense intended, you understand, but when she explained to me that you were responsible for saving the lives of my grandchildren and son-in-law in that fire several years back, well, how could I object? Over the years, it has become apparent that she has really come to care for you and your family. That is a good thing. Never having had brothers or sisters, she missed that kind of closeness. Anyway, thank you for being there for her over the years," he concluded.

Billie, a little taken back at first by his subtle intonations, decided that she liked this man.

"And this is Cat's grandmother, Josephine Wycliffe. Josephine, this is my father, Chet," Jen interjected as she turned his attention to Billie's grill-mate.

A warm smile spread across Chet's features. "Ah, finally, someone closer to my own age," he replied as he extended his hand to Josephine. "It's nice to meet you, Josephine Wycliffe."

"Likewise," Josephine replied. "Call me Jo. So, what brings you here, Chet?" she asked.

"An invitation out of the blue," Chet replied. "I received a phone call from my daughter here, asking me to visit for a while. Although, in her defense, she has asked me several times in the past, but I was unable to due to my business commitments," he added.

"Really? What type of business are you in?" Jo asked, clearly making small talk.

"I was a museum curator until I retired last year," he replied, causing Jo's ears to perk up.

"A museum curator? Well, it seems like our careers are somewhat related, Chet. I am an historian; at least I was, until I, too, retired a few years ago. I'm looking forward to comparing notes with you," Jo explained.

"Well, we'll have plenty of time for that. Pops will be here for a few weeks," Jen said smiling. "Oh, where are my manners? I haven't completed the introductions yet. Come on Pops, there's someone else I'd like you to meet," she said. Pulling him away from Billie and Jo, Jen led him in the direction of Alex who was still fanning herself in the shade of the canopy.

Jo frowned as she watched Jen pull the older gentleman away from the grill.

"Something wrong?" Billie asked coyly, seeing the look on Jo's face.

"I don't know," she said thoughtfully. "Something doesn't feel right about this. Don't know what it is though," she thought out loud.

"Well, I'm sure it's just your imagination," Billie assured her grandmother. "Here, hold the plate while I rescue these burgers from an early grave," she added as she scooped the charred pieces of meat from the grill and stacked them on the plate.

***

"Pops, I'd like you to meet Ms. Alexandra Spirakis, Billie's grandmother," Jen said as she pulled her father to a stop in front of Alex.

Chet couldn't believe his eyes. There before him, was the most beautiful woman he had ever laid eyes on. Even sitting, it was obvious that she was tall and slim, with long dark hair peppered with gray. When Alex looked up at him and removed her sun glasses, he was almost floored by the intense color of her sky-blue eyes. Bending over at the waist, he reached for her hand and brought it to his lips, kissing the back of it, his eyes never leaving hers.

"I am honored to make your acquaintance Ms. Spirakis," he said formally. "Let me introduce myself. Chester McAllister. My friends call me Chet."

Alex was quite taken aback with this gentleman's formal manner. After fifty years with Jo, she was used to blunt, abrupt and quite informal introductions. This gentleman was like a breath of fresh air. Sitting tall in her seat, she tilted her head back, squared her shoulders and shook his hand daintily.

"The pleasure is all mine, kind sir," she said, smiling brightly through her thick southern drawl. "Our chauffeur at the plantation is also named, Chet. Your name should be easy to remember."

"Ah, do you mind if I excuse myself for a moment? It seems that things are getting a little out of hand on the grill," Jen interrupted, seeing the smoke billowing from the barbecue.

"Not at all dear," Alex said. "Actually, I'm a bit surprised that Billie and Josephine are doing the cooking," she exclaimed, a bit of laughter tingeing her voice as they watched Jen run to the rescue.

Chet listened carefully to the sound of Alex's voice as she spoke to Jen. "Do you mind if I ask where you are from, dear lady? I can't help but notice your accent," he inquired.

Alex motioned to the chair beside her. "Please, have a seat, Chet. Of course I don't mind. I am from Charleston, South Carolina. My family has been well established in that region for many generations," she explained.

"South Carolina. Well, that certainly explains why it sounds so familiar. You see, I am originally from Atlanta, Georgia. I grew up there as a child before my parents relocated our family to the New York area," Chet explained.

"So you're a fellow southerner, are you?" Alex exclaimed happily. "I should have guessed that very fact, based on your good manners, fine sir," she added.

"Could I ask what brings you to this part of the country, Ms. Spirakis?" Chet asked politely.

"Oh please, call me Alex," she replied, touching the back of his hand lightly. "And what brings me here…well, actually, what brings *us* here, Josie and I, that is…is the wedding of our grandchildren," Alex explained.

Chet was a bit confused at the inclusion of Jo in Alex's travel plans. "I don't understand," he said. "How is it that you know Josephine?"

Alexandra glanced at Jo, who was busy helping Jen rescue the burgers and hot dogs from the grill. A look of starry-eyed longing filled her eyes as she sighed deeply. Without removing her eyes from the scene, she recalled her first meeting with Josephine Wycliffe. "Jo and I have known each other for fifty years. We first met when I traveled to Viet Nam to help her decipher military code during the war. You see, I am a trained interpreter," she explained, moving her eyes from the grill to Chet's face.

"I sense there is so much more to your story. Please go on," Chet urged.

Alexandra looked at him and smiled. "Well, you are certainly right on that count. So, where was I? Oh yes, our first meeting. Well, Josie wasn't really interested in my help at first. She saw me as a helpless southern belle. Can you imagine? Anyway, to make a long story short, I helped her decipher the code and as the result of our work, we were able to supply key strategic information to the military that helped US forces avoid ambushes," she finished.

Chet sat back in his chair and furrowed his brow in thought. "Spirakis...Spirakis...Wycliffe. Wait a minute...Alexandra Spirakis and Josephine Wycliffe? Of course!" he exclaimed, jumping to his feet. "I remember archiving several newspapers and letters shortly after the Vietnamese war that detailed your accomplishments. Well, I am certainly impressed, and quite honored to be in the presence of such distinguished women," he concluded excitedly.

Now it was Alex's turn to be surprised. "I'm sorry, Mr. McAllister, but how is it that you were privy to those documents?" she asked.

"Please dear lady, I beg of you, call me Chet, and I was privy to the documents because at the time, I was the curator of the Museum of Modern History in Augusta, Georgia," he explained.

"Well I'll be," Alex said in wide-eyed wonderment. "Josie, Josie, darlin' come here and meet Mr. McAllister," she said loudly, motioning for Jo to join them as soon as she had the other woman's attention.

Jo cast Billie a suspicious look as she handed the plate of charred meat over to her and shoved her fedora down onto her head before sauntering over to Alex and her gentleman caller. Coming to a stop in front of Alex, she crossed her arms and narrowed her eyes at Chet, trying hard to intimidate him.

"Oh Josie, stop that and come be sociable," Alex scolded. "I want you to meet Chet McAllister. Chet, this is the acclaimed historian, and my partner of fifty years, Josephine Wycliffe," she said, making the introductions.

Chet rose to his feet and once more, extended his hand to Jo. "I have already had the pleasure of making your acquaintance madam, but that was before I realized just who you were, and the significance of your work to the history of this great country. You are known throughout the industry as a brilliant historian. It is an honor to meet you," he said, shaking Jo's hand vigorously.

Jo didn't know whether to beam under his praise, or punch him out for flirting with Alex. As it turned out, she didn't have the chance to do either as Jen came back to collect her father.

"I'm so sorry. I'm afraid I'm not being a very good hostess, dropping my father on you like that, but the burgers were in serious trouble and in dire need of rescuing," Jen explained. "So, I assume the introductions have been made?" she asked.

"Jen, you didn't tell me there would be such distinguished guests at this cookout. Do you *know* who these ladies are?" Chet asked, referring to both Alex and Jo, but obviously directing his attention to Alex alone—a fact *not* lost on Jen or Jo.

"Well of course I do, Pops. They are the grandmothers of my very dear friends Cat and Billie. The fact that they also happen to be famous in the world of history was one of the reasons I asked you to visit. I knew you'd have so much in common with these wonderful ladies," Jen confessed.

"You, my dear, are quite a sneak," Chet laughingly scolded his daughter.

"It runs in the family, Pops. Where do you think I got it from?" Jen teased. "So, is anyone hungry?" she asked, abruptly changing the subject.

At the mention of food, Chet turned to a still sitting Alex and extended his hand. "May I have the honor of escorting you to lunch, dear lady?" he asked.

Alex smiled from ear to ear as she took his hand and allowed him to help her to her feet. "Well of course, fine sir," she replied, slipping her hand into Chet's arm, feeling very much like a pampered southern belle. Looking over her shoulder, she added, "Josie, darlin', will you join us?"

"Yeah, yeah, yeah. I'm right behind you," Jo said gruffly as she followed Alex walking arm in arm with Chet toward the picnic table.

CHAPTER 22

"So when's the party?" Billie asked while transposing notes into her laptop at the desk in the corner of their bedroom.

Cat looked up from the book she was reading while snuggled in warmly under the covers of their bed. "Party?" she questioned.

"Yeah, you know, the bachelorette party. Aren't the female members of the wedding party supposed to give the bride a party before the wedding just like the guys do?" Billie explained.

"You know, you're right," Cat replied, putting the book she was reading face down on the nightstand. "The wedding is just two weeks away. We'd better get busy with the plans."

"Well, we should have plenty of help. There's Amy and Bridget, you and I, and both our moms. I'm sure they'll be all glad to pitch in," Billie pointed out.

"Where should we have it?" Cat asked.

"I'm pretty sure it's supposed to be a surprise, so I guess we'll have to have it here and invent some reason to have Drew come over. Maybe Dylan can give us a hand with that part," Billie suggested.

"Good idea," Cat said, reaching for the pad of paper next to the phone on the nightstand. "Now let's see…who to invite," she contemplated, tapping the pen against her chin.

"Well, the bridesmaids for sure, maid of honor, mothers of the bride and groom. I guess grandmas Alex and Jo should be invited, Jen, and maybe Tara and Skylar and the other nieces," Billie listed.

"Before we decide on the children, we need to decide what type of party we're going to have. I mean, if it turns out to be a little raunchy, we're not going to want the kids there," Cat explained.

Billie grinned at the thought. "I guess you're right," she said. "I *do* kind of like the idea of making it a little risqué," she added. "Maybe we should talk to Jen about having the kids do a sleepover at her house that night. I'm sure she won't mind, seeing as she'll be here with us! Fred's a big boy. He can handle a few kids for one night. Whaddaya think?" she asked, eyebrows bobbing up and down on her forehead.

Cat smiled broadly. "I think you are an evil woman, my love," Cat replied.

"Me—evil?" Billie asked innocently.

"Oh, yeah!" Cat replied. "My very own sexy devil."

Closing the cover of her laptop, Billie turned in her seat to face Cat. "Devils are supposed to be naughty, aren't they?" she asked in a sultry voice.

Cat's eye widened as Billie intentionally dropped her voice into that low sexy octave she loved so much. "Very naughty," Cat replied, throwing the covers off in an open invitation.

Billie's eyebrows jumped even higher on her forehead. "I sometimes wonder who the naughty one really is, dear heart," Billie remarked as she rose to her feet. Crossing her arms in front of her, she grabbed the tails of her shirt, and very slowly and deliberately lifted it over her stomach...over her breasts, and finally, over her head. Holding it out to the side, she unceremoniously dropped it to the floor, a look of pure mischief filling her eyes.

Without breaking eye contact with Cat, she began to run her hands up and down her abdomen, over her bare stomach, across her breasts, tracing the trail once followed by the removal of her shirt. Cat sat helplessly on the bed, watching her wife sway seductively and loving every minute of it as Billie reached behind and unhooked her bra, allowing it to follow the shirt's path to the floor.

Billie's hands slowly made their way back down, stopping briefly to cup full breasts and quickly squeeze erect nipples, causing Cat to gasp in anticipation from her position on the bed.

Slowly the hands moved, down across her stomach and back and forth across her abdomen, until finally, her fingertips slipped inside the waistband of her denim shorts, disappearing behind the coarse blue material. Cat's eyes were glued to her wife, pleading silently for those long slim fingers to work their magic and remove the clothing that was covering her treasures.

Billie tilted her head back and closed her eyes as her tongue snaked across her lips and her hands drove deeper, hips swaying to the sultry music that could only be heard in her mind. Cat was squirming helplessly as she watched her wife pleasure herself beneath the denim material, wishing with every fiber of her being that it was *her* hands administering to the beauty in front of her.

"Billie, come here," Cat pleaded, reaching out with both hands as Billie slowly removed her hands and brought them to her lips. "Oh, my, God!" Cat exclaimed, suddenly climbing to her knees and crawling to the end of the bed to where she was within a hand's reach of Billie.

Cat latched onto Billie's waist with both hands and sat back on her heels, pulling Billie close to her. Wild with passion, Cat buried her face between Billie's breasts, covering the creamy skin with kisses, alternately suckling each nipple as Billie clutched desperately to Cat's head, entwining long fingers in her hair, pulling her closer.

Billie moaned and tilted her head back, causing her long black tresses to fall to her waist. "Harder. Please, harder," she urged as Cat inhaled one swollen nipple into her mouth and caught it between her teeth, flicking the tender bud with her tongue.

Billie's body spasmed repeatedly as bolts of desire shot directly from her breasts to her groin. "Cat, I need you," she rasped hoarsely as Cat administered the same torturous treatment to Billie's other breast.

Cat fumbled like a schoolgirl as she clumsily unzipped Billie's denim shorts. Rising to her knees, the height of the bed put her at eye level with Billie. Flashes of desire jumped between them as Cat slipped her hands into the back of Billie's shorts and roughly cupped the tender mounds, pulling Billie toward her quickly and firmly. Cat squeezed Billie's bottom unmercifully until a small whimper escaped her lips.

Cat captured Billie's face between her palms. Her breath came in short pants as she fought to control a primal urge to roughly take Billie right on the spot. Not able to resist any longer, she savagely thrust her tongue deep into Billie's mouth.

A deep growl escaped Cat's throat as she pulled Billie down onto the bed and covered her tall frame with her own, continuing to assault Billie's mouth until a salty tinge of blood invaded her senses. Whether it was her blood or Billie's didn't matter as the coppery taste only served to heighten her desire. Straddling Billie's waist, she pinned her hands to the bed and leaned in close until their noses were a mere hair's-breadth apart.

"I want you," Cat growled, to which Billie responded by arching her chest skyward and throwing her head to the side to give Cat better access to her neck. Cat wasted no time as she systematically devoured Billie's neck and shoulder, leaving telltale tracks that would surely bruise. With each bite, Billie moaned and squirmed, pressing her abdomen into Cat, encouraging the savage onslaught.

Making her way across Billie's chest, Cat once more worshipped at Billie's breasts, squeezing and nipping each one in turn, pushing Billie to the precipice of desire.

"Cat, I need you—now!" Billie pleaded. "Take me. Please."

Cat lifted her head and looked into Billie's eyes, her nostrils flaring in and out in and effort to control her breathing. Billie reached up with both hands to touch Cat's face, only to find them captured and pinned back to the bed by the red-haired siren.

"I love you Billie. I want to make love to you. I want to fill you completely. Is that what you want, my love?" Cat asked.

Billie's breath came in quick pants and she vigorously nodded her approval. "Yes. Cat, please," she begged.

Cat dropped a tender kiss on Billie's nose before she moved downward once more to spread her eager lover's legs. Billie's hands quickly shot out to rest on Cat's shoulders, urging her forward. Cat had all she could do to control both her actions and her own body's response to Billie's sensual vulnerability as she savored her wife's treasures.

Billie's loud moans and gyrating hips drove Cat crazy as she reached one shaking hand. Billie's hips immediately left the bed as she accepted the invasion, thrusting herself forward to deepen the penetration.

"You like that, don't you, my love?" Cat asked seductively.

"Yes. Harder, Cat. Please!" Billie demanded as she repeatedly pressed herself onto Cat's hand.

Cat added another finger and increased the intensity and speed of the thrusts, causing Billie to scream out her pleasure.

Billie's head thrashed from side to side, tears running steadily from the corners of her eyes. Suddenly, she felt as though she would lose consciousness as an explosion started deep within her core and spread through every cell of her being.

"Oh, my, God! Cat...I'm coming," Billie yelled as Cat finally gave in to her own desire and allowed her orgasm to wash over her while bringing both herself and her lover to fulfillment.

Moments later, Billie lay wrapped in Cat's arms, both women exhausted physically and emotionally as they savored the afterglow of their love making.

"Thank you, my love," Cat said, kissing Billie lightly on the forehead.

Billie looked at Cat, surprised that she was actually thanking her.

"It's *I* who should be thanking *you*, Cat," she replied softly.

Cat smiled into her wife's face. "No, love. Thank *you* for trusting me with your vulnerability. I know that's difficult for you," Cat explained.

"You make that possible for me, Cat. I feel safe in your love," she explained.

"Always," Cat replied tenderly as Billie snuggled in once more.

"We still have a party to plan, you know," Billie murmured from her safe haven in Cat's arms, drawing a slight chuckle from Cat.

***

"I think we should hire strippers," Jo suggested as she took a large bite from her buttered toast.

"My lord, Josie! Must you always live in the gutter?" Alex asked impatiently.

"Hey! The view's great from down here! And besides, I have lots of fun company too," Jo joked. "So whaddaya say?" she added looking at the ladies seated around the large table in the diner.

"I say you need to be careful what you say in front of your daughters and granddaughters," Alex admonished.

"Nona, don't worry about Mom. You forget, I was raised by her too. I know what she can be like," Ida replied. Ida reached for Jo's hand and grinned mischievously. "Don't ever change Mama, okay?" to which, Jo replied with a grin of her own.

"So, if we did hire strippers, where would we find them?" Laurel asked.

"So I guess we've decided that this isn't going to be a nice clean social event," Billie observed, wide eyed with disbelief that her own mother actually seemed excited by the idea.

"Damn straight, it isn't," exclaimed Amy.

"Oh, for God's sake, Amy. I vote for a formal tea party, you know, like the southern belles would have...kind of a symbolic send-off for the virgin," Bridget suggested.

"Oh, please, Bridget! Do you really believe Drew is a virgin? Or Dylan either for that matter?" Amy replied.

"That is definitely more information than I needed to hear!" Ida piped in.

"Well, I like the idea. Strippers. Lots of them!" Jo reiterated enthusiastically.

"You've got my vote," Jen said. "Sweaty bodies, sleek muscles, gyrating hips. Oh, mama!"

"Have any of you been to a party with strippers before?" Laurel asked. "I mean, do they really take it *all* off?" she added, somewhat breathlessly.

"Oh, yeah!" Jo replied knowingly. "They take it off all right...exposing everything...slender waist, firm breasts..."

"Whoa, wait a minute," Amy interrupted. "Grandma Jo, we're talking about *male* strippers, not female," she corrected.

Josephine frowned and sat back in her chair, crossing her arms. "You sure know how to ruin a wet dream, granddaughter," she scolded Amy sulkingly.

"Josephine Wycliffe, you really didn't expect the ladies to hire female strippers did you? Did you forget that this party is for your *straight* granddaughter? My word!" Alex responded.

"Cat, you're being awfully quiet. What do *you* think?" Billie asked, drawing the attention of everyone at the table.

Cat looked at Billie and smiled. "I was just enjoying the exchange. You know, it's not often that we're all together like this. It's funny that when we are, it's to talk about some obscene party!" she replied chuckling. "Anyway, I think the stripper idea is great. I'm not sure Dylan will appreciate having some naked guy shaking his bootie in front of his wife-to-be, but to hell with him if he can't take a joke!" she added, grinning ear to ear.

"Cat, I like the way you think!" Amy said, giving her sister a high-five.

"Okay then, it's settled. Here's to glistening, sweaty muscles, doing the hoochie coochie in our faces!" Jen exclaimed, raising her coffee mug for a toast.

All the ladies except Bridget eagerly raised their coffee mugs to meet Jen's in the air above the table. "To naked sweaty men!" she toasted.

"To naked sweaty men!" came the reply.

"And women!" added Josephine.

***

"But, Mom! Why do we have to go to Karissa's house? I wanna stay here with all you guys," Skylar whined.

"Sorry, rugrat. This party is for the adults. You'll have a good time with your sister and Karissa. Fred is planning to camp out with you guys in the back yard. You'll have a campfire and toast marshmallows and stay up late. It sounds like fun," Billie tried to explain to her daughter.

"But, Mom! Why can't I stay? Tara can go to Karissa's house by herself," the child insisted.

"Sky, honey, I explained to you that this party is for the adults," Billie reiterated.

"But, why?" Skylar persisted.

"Because there will only be ladies here and you'll be bored. We're pretty much going to sit around and talk about how cute Uncle Dylan is, and we'll drink tea and exchange recipes and listen to Nana and Grandma talk about how Papa and Grandpa can't pick up after themselves...and then we'll talk about doing housework and laundry, then we might have another cup of tea and maybe a piece of cake...and then we'll listen to Grandma gossip about the neighbors, and maybe we'll even play a little bridge. Then the ladies will all go home and go to bed," Billie explained.

Skylar looked at her mother through furrowed brow. "That *does* sound boring!" she exclaimed.

"Yeah. Actually, I'd rather go camping with you guys in Jen's back yard! You're the ones who'll have all the fun," Billie said regretfully.

"Maybe you *can* come with us!" Skylar suggested excitedly, making Billie wince as she realized she had gone a bit too far.

Putting on her poutiest face, she sighed deeply. "I wish I could, sweetie, but Mama and I are the hostesses, so I *have* to be here!" she said.

Skylar patted her mother on the back. "Don't worry, Mom, I'll bring some toasted marshmallows home for you tomorrow," she promised.

Billie smiled. "Really?" she said hopefully. "That would be great! And I'll save you a piece of cake. Deal?" she said, extending her hand to the little girl.

"Deal!" Skylar said as she took her mother's hand and shook it vigorously.

***

"Oh baby, baby! Take it all off!" Bridget shouted as she cheered the stripper on.

Jimmy was very buff. Six feet tall, sandy blond hair, muscular build, slim-waisted, very tight glutes...and an instant success with the ladies—well, at least with most of them.

Cat sat back in her chair and thoroughly enjoyed the scene before her. There, standing on the coffee table was Jimmy, wearing nothing but a G-string, gyrating his hips to the music of Bon Jovi. All round him, were several ladies, in various states of drunkeness, all dancing...the most surprising of which was Bridget, who was whooping and hollering louder than the rest of them combined.

"Hey, sweetness!" Billie said, tripping over her own feet and landing in Cat's lap.

"Hmph!" Cat replied. "Are you having a good time, love?" she asked after regaining her breath.

"Sure am!" Billie answered. "This is a great party. Jimmy almost makes me forget that I'm gay!" she added laughingly, her eyes traveling up and down the sleek muscular body posed on the coffee table.

Cat frowned at her wife's interest in their entertainer. "Really?" she asked seriously.

Billie's eye softened as they met Cat's. "No, not really. But it sure does help me remember why I found men attractive in my younger days," she admitted.

Cat looked at Jimmy once more and grinned, nodding in agreement. "I'm kind of surprised with Bridget," she commented.

"Bridget? I'm surprised at our mothers! Did you see them earlier? They were sticking five-dollar bills in his G-string! You can dress them up, but you can't take them anywhere!" she said, chuckling.

The entire party had been a success right from the start. They had manufactured a plan to have Dylan drop Drew off at six to have dinner with Cat and Billie while he attended his own bachelor party. Drew was in a funk when she arrived, sulking over the fact that there was bound to be a stripper at Dylan's party. Billie and Cat took Drew to the local steak house where they enjoyed a nice dinner while the rest of the ladies arrived at their house and hid in strategic places to surprise Drew when they returned.

At nearly eight, Cat, Billie and Drew walked into a darkened living room and were immediately met with a chorus of *surprise* as the lights flashed on and the ladies appeared to greet Drew with cheers of congratulations. The party escalated from there when Jo broke out a large jar of maraschino cherries that had been soaking in rum for a week. Over the next hour, the ladies joked, partied, drank and ate the intoxicating cherries as Drew opened her bridal shower gifts, most of them suggestive in nature, including black crotch-less panties, negligees, vibrators, and even a large rubber dildo from Jo, which made Alex blush from head to toe as Jo's eyebrows danced up and down after Drew opened it.

At promptly nine o'clock, there was a knock on the door.

"I'll get it!" Bridget proclaimed as she rose a little unsteadily to her feet and answered the door. There before her, stood a very good-looking man in a long, dark trench coat.

"Is this the Charland residence?" the man asked.

"Yes it is. How may I help you?" Bridget asked politely.

In response, the man grabbed the front of the trench coat and ripped it open, exposing glistening tanned limbs, muscular chest, and near-total nakedness, covered only by small spandex bikini briefs.

Bridget screamed and fell back onto her rump, drawing the attention of the other ladies. Seeing the prize that was still standing in the doorway, Amy rushed forward, and stepping over a still prostrate Bridget, invited their guest in, totally ignoring her sister's plight on the floor.

"Oh, *do* come in!" Amy purred. "And your name is...?" she asked, leading him into the living room.

"Jimmy," he replied, grinning ear to ear.

"Jimmy. I like it!" Amy replied. Stopping in the doorway to the living room, she announced their presence. "Ladies, I give you, Jimmy!" she said excitedly, removing his coat and throwing it across a living room chair.

Jimmy was immediately surrounded by the ladies, all a little tipsy from the drinks and cherries, and all wanting a close-up view of their guest. Bridget, having scrambled to her feet, followed them into the living room. "I...I let him in!" she proclaimed, trying to gain one up on the ogling ladies.

After a few moments, Jimmy asked which of the ladies was Drew. When Drew was introduced to him, he took her by the hand and led her to a chair. Asking the other ladies to give him some room, he set up a portable boom box with his own pre-recorded music, and began to dance. And dance he did. As Drew sat mesmerized in the chair, Jimmy gyrated around her, bending over her to run his tongue across her face, taking her hands and rubbing them all over his body, straddling her lap and rubbing up against her. By the time his dance had finished, he had ripped off the bikini briefs, exposing the G-string beneath, and leaving a very flustered Drew speechless and a very excited group of ladies hoarse from cheering him on.

The next couple of hours were spent entertaining the ladies, who became rowdier as the night progressed, culminating in the five-dollar bills being tucked into Jimmy's G-string by Laurel and Ida as he danced.

Finally, as the last song died down, Jimmy jumped off the table and announced that he had another engagement to fulfill, calling an end to the evening amidst regretful protests from the ladies.

Climbing out of Cat's lap, Billie helped her to her feet and together, they thanked Jimmy for his services. After dutifully hugging each of the ladies, and receiving a pinch on the butt from Jo, he donned his trench coat, collected his stereo and was on his way.

"Damn! He was hot!" exclaimed Jen, who was fanning herself as she watched him climb into his car and drive away.

"He was okay, for a man," Jo replied.

"Oh, he was like...so much more than okay," added Drew as she pulled his bikini briefs out of her pocket to the delight of all the ladies. "He was like, in-fucking-credible!" she finished, starting a chorus of squeals and cheers.

"To Jimmy!" exclaimed Amy, raising her drink high.

"To Jimmy!" the ladies added as each one raised her own drink, and many more throughout the night.

CHAPTER 23

"Kill me, please!" Josephine begged, half sitting and half reclining; trying hard to get out of bed.

"Josephine Wycliffe, stop being such a baby. It's not like this is your first hangover, you know," Alex replied from her seat in front of the vanity where she was brushing her hair.

"It seems the older I get, the less I can tolerate a night out with the girls," Jo said as she finally righted herself. She rested her elbows on her thighs and dropped her head into her hands. "I need some drugs," she added, half mumbling.

"There's a couple of pain killers right there on the night stand. I kinda thought you'd need them when you finally woke up," Alex said over her shoulder.

Jo looked at the pills and water on the bedside table, then back at Alex. "Thank you, Alex." After taking the medication, she placed the glass back on the stand. "Alex, why do you put up with me?" she asked. "I mean, we've been together for fifty years, and I'll be damned if I can figure out why. I haven't been the easiest person in the world to live with."

Alex put the brush down on the vanity, and looked at Jo through the mirror. "No, you haven't been the easiest to live with, but I happen to be partial to your ninety-six pack, Josie," she replied.

Jo frowned. "ninety-six pack?" she asked.

"Yes. Josie, you add variety to my life. And beside, there's somethin' about you that's just so cute. I've grown quite fond of it," Alex tried to explain.

"Cute? Cute?" Jo exclaimed. "After fifty years, the best you can come up with is *cute*?"

"Well you don't have to be so touchy about it," Alex replied.

Jo was now on her feet. "That's cold, Alex. Damned cold!"

Alex rose to her feet and approached Jo. When she tried to place a hand on her shoulder, Jo promptly pulled away and turned her back to Alex.

"Josie?" she asked softly.

With her back still to Alex, Jo began in a shaky voice. "Alex, if someone had asked me why, after fifty years we were still together, I would say it's because we love each other." Turning to face Alex, she looked her straight in the eye. "You could have left me a thousand times over the course of our relationship, and I would have never blamed you. I know I wasn't easy to live with at times, but you stayed. As bad as things got, you stayed. I *thought* it was because you loved me. I didn't expect *cute*," she explained.

Alex reached out to touch the side of Jo's face. "Josie, I *do* love you. Truly, I do," she said tenderly.

"Then why didn't you accept my proposal, Alex?" Jo asked sternly.

Now it was Alex's turn to frown.

"On the plane?" Jo reminded her sarcastically.

"I...I...," Alex began before a knock came to the bedroom door.

"Grams, Chet is here to pick you up," Billie said from the other side of the door.

"Chet?" Jo asked sharply. "What the hell does *he* want?"

Alex wrung her hands nervously. "He called this morning while you were asleep and invited us to go to the local museum," she explained.

Jo sat down on the bed again and stared at the floor. "Well, I'll be damned," she said.

"Josie, the invitation was for both of us," Alex added hastily.

Jo looked at her with such venom in her eyes it caused Alex to gasp. "No. Don't let me interrupt your little rendezvous, Al. Have a good time," she spat before looking back to the floor.

"Josie, please, I'd like you to come," Alex pleaded.

"Grams? Chet is waiting. What should I tell him?" Billie said from the other side of the door.

Alex looked back and forth between the door and Jo. "Tell him I'll be right there, dear," she said shakily. Turning back to Josephine, she tried once more. "Josie..."

"No Alex. I'm not going. Your date is here. You'd better not keep him waiting," she said without looking up.

Sighing deeply, Alex picked up her sun hat from the vanity and placed it daintily on her head. Casting one more look in Jo's direction, she walked slowly to the door, opened it and left.

"Damn!" Jo whispered as a lone tear fell onto the carpet at her feet.

***

"Cat, I need a drink," Jo demanded as she stomped into the kitchen.

Cat put her coffee cup and newspaper down and furrowed her brow at her grandmother. "It's ten o'clock in the morning. How about a cup of coffee?" she asked.

"If I wanted coffee, I would have asked for coffee!" the Jo snapped.

Rising to her feet, Cat approached her grandmother, who was obviously distressed. She put her arm around her grandmother and led her to the table where she pulled out a chair for her. "Sit. I'll get you some coffee, then you can tell me all about it," she said.

Resigned to the fact that her granddaughter wasn't going to give her the drink she wanted, Jo slumped back in her chair and nodded, begrudgingly accepting the coffee Cat placed before her.

Reclaiming her own seat, Cat reached across the table and placed a hand on Josephine's arm. "Now, wanna tell me what this is all about?" she asked.

"'Morning, neighbor!" Jen said as she suddenly breezed into the room, immediately drawing the attention of the two ladies sitting at the table.

Jo's eyes flew open, then narrowed into angry slits. "*That's* what this is all about!" she said, pointing at Jen. "Her father! That...that...that Casanova," she accused angrily.

Jen's eyebrows took up residence in her hairline as she stopped dead in her tracks. "My father?" she asked.

"Grandma Jo, calm down," Cat said to the distressed woman. "Jen, honey, help yourself to some coffee, then come sit with us," she suggested to her friend.

Retrieving her coffee, Jen cautiously approached the table, thinking to herself that this charade she and Billie were up to may be going a little too far. "Where's Billie?" she asked, taking a sip of her coffee.

"She's gone to the store. It seems that the White Russians were a big hit at the party last night and we are now completely out of milk," Cat explained.

Jen grinned. "Guilty as charged. I believe I was responsible for putting away three or four of them myself," she replied.

"How are the kids this morning?" Cat asked.

"Oh, they're all still out cold. I think Fred let them stay up until dawn. They'll probably sleep well into the morning," Jen explained.

"Good. That will give me a chance to clean up the party debris before they come home," Cat added.

"I'll give you a hand. After all, I believe I was a major contributor to the mess," Jen laughed, remembering the handful of potato chips that ended up crushed under her feet after she dropped them in a flustered state when Jimmy ripped off his bikini briefs.

Jo sat there, following the conversation between these two women like a tennis ball back and forth across the net.

"Hello? Remember me?" she said loudly, interrupting them.

Both women looked at Jo and simultaneously replied, "What?"

Jo threw her hands out to the sides to emphasize her plight. "Chet? Casanova? Alex? Is any of this ringing a bell?" she asked sarcastically.

Snapping back to the dilemma at hand, Jen tried to calm her fears. "Jo, I wouldn't worry too much about Daddy. He's quite harmless," she explained.

"Harmless? When he's in the room, Alex doesn't even know I exist. Hell, they're gone off together at this very moment," Josephine exclaimed.

"Grandma Jo, they're gone to the museum, and you were invited as well. You just let your pride stop you from going with them," Cat observed.

"I really didn't want to feel like a third wheel, Cat," she said in her own defense. "If I could just figure out what she sees in him," Josephine wondered out loud.

"Sees in who?" Billie asked as she stepped into the kitchen and walked across the room to deposit the gallon of milk in the refrigerator. Returning to the table, she placed a kiss on Cat's cheek, then went to the counter to pour herself a cup of coffee. Bringing it to the table, she sat down as she asked her question again. "Sees in who?"

"Jo is very upset that Alex has gone to the museum with Daddy this morning," Jen explained.

"Well if you're that worried, Grandma Jo, you should have gone with them," Billie suggested.

"And just what would *that* have accomplished?" Jo asked impatiently.

"Well, it appears to me that you've left the door wide open for Chet to walk through," Billie said. "I mean, look at Chet. He's the perfect southern gentleman. He's polite, cordial, courteous, and complimentary. He has the formal manners of the South that Grams considers so important," she added.

"And what am I, dog meat?" Jo barked out.

"No, no, of course not," Cat replied quickly. "Grandma Jo, don't you see what Billie is trying to say? To Grams, Chet is a breath of fresh air, a nostalgic memory from her debutante years. She misses that."

Jo lowered her gaze to the coffee cup that she cradled between her hands. Looking up once more, the three younger ladies could see tears misting in her eyes. "I can never be that southern gentleman she is yearning for," she said with such resignation that she wasn't the only one at the table fighting the flow of tears.

Gulping to control her emotions, Billie placed her large hand over both of Josephine's smaller ones which were still holding the coffee cup. "Grandma Jo," she began. "She doesn't expect you to be. She loves you just the way you are. I think she just misses the old ways, and once in a while it doesn't hurt to let her enjoy it...even if it doesn't come from you," she finished.

"But I want it to come from me," Jo replied, her bottom lip quivering slightly.

"Then I guess we have some work to do," Billie answered, looking at the nodding heads around the table.

"Count me in," Cat said, finally allowing tears to escape as she placed her own hand on the growing tower covering Jo's coffee cup.

"Ditto," Jen added, adding her hand to the pile.

***

Billie, Cat, Jen and Jo were soon on their way to the mall to find something special for Jo to wear to the wedding. Along the way, their discussion centered on what the ladies felt Jo had to do to secure Alex's attentions.

"You want me to do what?" Jo exclaimed leaning forward in her seat.

"It won't hurt you to wait on her hand and foot for a day. Even you admit she deserves it," Cat replied.

Jo grumbled, folding her arms across her chest and pouting.

"You've got to remember that Grams was raised in the old southern style, where the ladies were pampered. It's been years since she has allowed herself that luxury. Indulge her. You want her to know you really care, don't you?" Cat asked, knowing Josephine couldn't say no.

Jo sat back in her seat and stared out the window, watching the scenery pass by. Soon, her memories brought her back to the days in 'Nam, when Alex toiled by her side, day and night, working as hard as she did to crack the secret Viet Cong code. Never once did she complain through all their years together literally sifting through the dirt and mud, trying to unearth the secrets of history. Alex had been a trooper.

Jo had to admit that the first time she laid eyes on Alex, she was tempted to put her on a plane and send her back to South Carolina. A war zone was no place for a delicate southern belle; however, the sheer beauty of the woman took her breath away. So instead of sending her back to her southern roots, she kept finding things for her to do, and reasons for her to stay. Soon, it became obvious to her that she couldn't live without this stunning beauty, not only because she had become an integral part of her success, but because she had fallen in love.

Looking back over their fifty-year relationship, Jo acknowledged that she hadn't treated Alex in the manner she was used to. The Spirakis household was one of opulent wealth, one in which Alex was used to being waited on hand and foot. It was expected that she would marry a wealthy man, settle into plantation life, and raise a brood of children with the help of several nursemaids and servants. Instead, Alexandra Spirakis took a stand and insisted on obtaining an education, and when her father died, she set off to make her mark on the world. She got more than she bargained for...she got Josephine Wycliffe.

Five years after they cracked the Viet Cong code, Jo and Alex reunited and began their lives together...constantly on the go, moving from one country to another, often spending months camped out at historical sites supervising archeologists as they unearthed historical treasures while living in tents or low-class hotels. Somehow, through all the dirt and dust, Alex always managed to look fresh. And she never complained, even when they were eating out of tin cans and sleeping on cots. Most of all, she was always there for Josephine, assisting her with historical translations, using her wealth to convince authorities to issue dig permits, and even seeing that Jo got home safely after drinking too much in the local pub.

Life with Josephine Wycliffe was a far cry from the comfortable southern plantation of her childhood, yet Alex never complained. As Jo reminisced, she once more wondered why Alex had stayed with her all these years.

"Grandma Jo?"

Snapping out of her reverie, Jo shook her head and came back to reality. "What? I'm sorry, Cat. What was it you said?" she asked.

"I said we're here," Cat replied, turning around in her seat to look at her. "Are you okay?" she added, seeing the blank look on her grandmother's face.

"Yeah, I'm fine. Just thinking about life, and wonderin' why the hell Alex has stayed with me all these years. It might come as a surprise, but I haven't been the easiest person to live with you know," she explained.

At this, Billie turned around in her seat. "You? Hard to live with? No way," she said jokingly, causing all four women to chuckle.

"Well, I don't know about the rest of you, but I'm in the mood to shop," Jen inserted, climbing out of the car.

"Me, too," Cat replied as she flung open her door.

Billie exchanged grimaces with Jo as they begrudgingly joined Jen and Cat for the short trek from the parking garage to the mall entrance.

***

"How's this?" Cat asked, holding a formal skirt and jacket set up to Jo's short frame.

Jo tried hard not to laugh in Cat's face. There was no way in hell she was putting that monkey suit on. "Ah...ah...I was kind of thinking of something a little less formal," Jo said haltingly.

"Don't you mean a little less feminine?" Billie piped in, grinning ear to ear.

"Yeah, that's it. Cat, dear, I'm not exactly a delicate flower. I need something sturdier," Jo explained.

"How about this one?" Jen said from across the room, holding up a dark blue business-type suit with a pinstriped jacket, skirt and slacks.

Josephine frowned. Still too feminine.

Billie draped her arm around Josephine's shoulder and started leading her away from Jen and Cat. "Why don't Grandma Jo and I go shopping by ourselves. I have an idea what she's looking for. You and Jen can go check out that new boutique I know you're dying to see," Billie suggested to Cat.

"You mean the one with the new body lotions and perfumes?" Cat asked, her interest piqued.

"Yeah, the one with the foo-foo smelly stuff. You go on and have a good time with Jen. We'll meet you at the food court in about an hour. How's that sound?" Billie asked.

Cat grinned. "Sounds great to me. How about you Jen?"

"I'm in," she said, hanging the pinstriped suit back onto the rack. "Let's go."

Moments later, Billie and Jo were heading in a direction opposite that of Cat and Jen. "I think I know what you're looking for. Come with me," Billie said, taking Jo by the hand and leading her through the mall.

***

"Billie-Girl, you are a genius," Jo exclaimed as she looked at herself in the tri-fold mirrors. "This is perfect. Are you sure you're Alex's granddaughter and not mine?" she asked joking.

"You look great," Billie replied, chuckling at Jo's reference to her genealogy. "Grams will certainly be impressed. You're going to steal the show," Billie added.

"I don't want to steal the show. I just want to steal her heart," Jo said, turning around to look at herself at all angles.

Coming up behind Josephine, Billie wrapped her arms around her and hugged her tight. Looking at Jo's reflection in the mirror, she said, "Well, I definitely think this outfit will do the trick—not that you'll have to work hard at it. I think you already own her heart. I think you always will."

Jo grinned. "I sure hope so, Billie. This is perfect. I'll take it."

Moments later, Billie and Jo joined Jen and Cat at the food court. Billie was sporting a garment bag. Jo was sporting a big smile.

"Well, apparently you found what you were looking for," Cat said as they approached, noting the garment bag.

"I never thought shopping could be so much fun," Jo replied, hands in her pockets, rocking back and forth on her heels, very proud of her accomplishment.

"Can I see?" Cat asked.

"I'll model it for all three of you when we get home, just as long as Alex doesn't see it. I want to surprise her on the day of the wedding," Jo answered.

"Hey, I'm starved. Are we gonna eat here or go somewhere else?" Jen interrupted.

"There's a really good Chinese place across the highway. Any takers?" Cat replied.

With three nods of approval, the women were on their way.

CHAPTER 24

After an early dinner, the Charland family retired to the living room where the kids immediately positioned themselves in various places in front of the television. Billie and Cat snuggled closely on the couch, while Jo paced the floor back and forth in front of the fireplace.

"You know, it's a beautiful day outside. The sun is shining, and it's still pretty early. You three should be outdoors taking advantage of the good weather," Billie observed as she looked at the three bodies sprawled on the floor in front of her.

"It's boring out there," Seth threw over his shoulder without looking at his mother.

"Yeah, there's nothing to do," added Tara.

"Why not hang out with Stevie and Karissa?" Cat suggested.

"They're gone out to dinner with their parents," Seth replied. "I think they're going to the movies or something after that."

"Where the hell are they?" Jo suddenly asked as she looked at her watch for the tenth time that minute. "They should have been back hours ago!" she exclaimed, drawing the attention of her two granddaughters.

"I'm sure they've just lost track of the time," Cat said in a futile attempt to pacify her grandmother. If truth be known, she too was becoming a little concerned as she noted the late hour. Jo was right...Alex and Chet should have been back hours ago.

"Humph," Jo exclaimed. "Well, I'm not waiting another minute." She walked over to Seth and prodded him lightly in the ribs with the toe of her combat boot. "Hey scout, how about you and me grab a couple of fishing poles and get outta this joint?" she suggested.

Seth looked over his shoulder at his great-grandmother. "For real?" he asked, a sparkle of interest in his eyes.

"You bet. How 'bout it?" Jo asked again.

"Sure," Seth said, jumping to his feet.

"Can I go too?" Tara asked.

"Why not?" Jo replied. "How about you, little one? Do you want to join us too?" she asked Skylar.

"Ewwwww! Fish are smelly," Skylar replied. "I wanna stay here with Mom and Mama. Maybe we can play paper dolls together?" she added hopefully.

Billie and Cat looked at each other and grimaced.

"Okay then. Where do you keep the poles?" Jo asked Billie.

"I'll get them," Seth said as she headed toward the back door. Stopping short, he turned around and added, "We'll have to stop and get some bait," before continuing on his way.

Jo turned back to the ladies. "Okay, so whose car can I borrow?" she asked.

Both ladies stiffened with trepidation, remembering Jo's driving skills from their last trip to South Carolina.

"Look, I haven't lived three quarters of a century without learning to read body language. You have nothing to worry about. Do you really think I'd drive recklessly with two youngsters in the car?" Jo asked, hands on her hips.

Billie and Cat exchanged looks then reluctantly turned over the keys to the mini-van. "Please be careful," Cat said as the keys jingled at the end of Jo's fingers.

"I will," Jo replied. "Ya ready to go, rugrat?" she directed at Tara.

"Yep," Tara replied as she followed her great-grandmother out the door.

"I'll get the paper dolls," Skylar announced as she jumped to her feet and headed toward the stairs to the upper floor.

Cat shifted within the circle of Billie's arms so that she could look directly at her wife. "You know, they really *should* have been back a while ago," she said worriedly.

"I know what you mean. I'm beginning to believe that Jo has a right to be concerned," Billie replied. "I wonder if I should go looking for them," she suggested.

"That thought has crossed my mind as well, but Grams *is* an adult after all," Cat observed.

"I'm beginning to wonder if this ruse we set up was such a good idea," Billie confessed. "I'll never forgive myself if serious harm comes to their relationship because of it."

"Healthy competition is good for any relationship, love. A little jealousy goes a long way to making one realize when you've taken your loved ones for granted," Cat replied.

Billie looked long and hard at the green orbs peering back at her. "Do you feel that way about us, Cat? I mean, do I ever take you for granted?" she asked seriously.

Cat gently cupped the side of Billie's face. "Sweetheart, no you don't. I for one believe our relationship is quite balanced. Honey, we both have our strengths and weaknesses. I'm not saying there aren't times when each of us takes the other for granted, but for the most part, our attributes tend to compliment each other. We complete one another," Cat explained.

Billie narrowed her eyes. "Is that a slam about my cooking?" she asked in mock seriousness.

"Well…" Cat replied grimacing.

"I'm back," Skylar announced as she stood before her mothers and emptied a large bag full of paper dolls on the coffee table in front of the two groaning women.

* * *

After what seemed like an eternity of playing house with the spineless dolls, Billie thought for sure she would die of boredom. Just as she was about to suggest to her daughter that they take a break, a noise drew her attention to the kitchen. Looking over at Cat, she was thoroughly amazed at how this grown woman could become so involved in child's play that she seemed oblivious to her own surroundings. Obviously, Cat had not heard the noise. Only Billie's rise to her feet broke Cat out of her spell.

"What is it, love?" Cat said, looking up from the array of paper dolls strewn all over the table.

"Someone's here," Billie replied. "I'll be right back."

Billie secretly blessed their intruder for rescuing her from the grips of paper-doll hell as she made her way to the kitchen. Billie stepped into the kitchen just as Alex stumbled into the kitchen from the porch. It was obvious that she was a bit tipsy.

"Billie, dear, give this old lady a hand, if you would," she said as soon as she laid eyes on her granddaughter.

Billie rushed to Alex's side and wrapped one arm around her waist, just as her knees gave away. Gently guiding her to the table, she lowered Alex into a chair. "Are you all right, Grams?" she asked.

Alex giggled. "Fine. I'm wonnerful," she slurred.

"Billie, who's here? Grams!" Cat exclaimed as she entered the kitchen and saw her grandmother's inebriated state. "What in God's name happened? How did you get blood on your leg?" Cat asked.

Billie looked under the table, and did indeed see a stream of blood flowing from Alex's knee.

"I can s'plain. I fell on the porch steps," Alex said. "It's no big deal."

"You fell on the steps?" Cat said in disbelief. Of Jo, she would believe it, but Alex was always so poised and careful.

"We've got to get you cleaned up. Then you've got some explaining to do," Cat scolded. "Honey, would you mind getting me some towels from the bathroom?" she asked Billie as she began to tear away Alex's battered support hose. "Oh, and bring the first aid kit too," she added.

"Grams, you had us worried sick...gone all day like that. And now look at you," Cat continued to scold as she worked. "Grandma Jo is really upset. She thinks you've gone and run off with Chet. What were you thinking coming home so late?" she asked. "And where *is* Chet? He should have seen that you made it into the house safe and sound."

Billie returned to the kitchen carrying several white hand-cloths soaked in warm water, along with a few dry towels.

"Here you go love. Is there anything I can do to help?" she asked.

"Yeah, you can talk some sense into your grandmother while I take care of her injury," Cat replied.

"Josie is upset?" Alex asked. "Whatever for?"

"Grams, you left with Chet pretty early this morning. We expected you back a lot sooner. We've all been worried," Billie explained.

An indignant look crossed Alex's face. "And just what business is it of yours if I choose to spend the day with a gentleman caller?" Alex asked sharply.

Billie narrowed her eyes while Cat widened hers. This was a side of Grandma Alex they had never seen before. Billie pulled up a chair beside her grandmother and leaned forward, resting her forearms on her thighs.

"Since when did Chet become a gentleman caller, Grams?" Billie asked. "It is totally unlike you to become intoxicated. There's only one reason a gentleman caller gets his date drunk. He better not have been disrespectful."

Alex straightened her back, a haughty manner overtaking her normally soft features. "I don't have to answer that," she declared. "Ouch! Caitlain Maureen O'Grady Charland, you're hurtin' me!" she suddenly shouted as she nearly jumped out of her chair.

"Grams, it's just a scratch," Cat responded in her best *don't be such a baby* voice as she continued to scrub the wound.

"Well, it hurts just the same," Alex whined.

"You know, Grandma Jo is pretty upset with the attention Chet has been paying to you," Billie informed her.

"Serves her right," Alex replied, hiccupping. "I'm gettin' kind of tired of standin' by while she flirts with stewardesses, waitresses, and even the cashier at the grocery store. It appears she notices everyone but me these days," Alex whined. "It feels darn right good to have someone payin' attention to me for a change."

Billie looked at Cat who was putting the final touches to a bandage on Alex's knee, a silent message of confirmation passing between them.

"Where is that crazy old woman anyway?" Alex asked, breaking the silence that had settled over the trio.

"She took Seth and Tara fishing," Cat replied.

"Oh, yeah, she's real upset," Alex said sarcastically. "She's so upset she just *had* to go fishing. If she was half as upset as you say she is, you think she would'a been out fightin' for what's hers. But, no...she went fishing instead," Alex ranted, her arms flying around recklessly.

"All right Grams, I think it's time for you to rest," Cat said as she rose to her feet and extended her hand to her grandmother.

"I'm not one bit tired, Caitlain. Besides, I have a thing or two to say to that grandmother of yours when she finally comes home," Alex said stubbornly.

"Well, at the very least, you need to rest your leg. Doctor's orders," Cat said. "Billie, would you please give me a hand walking Grams into her bedroom? She can sit up in bed and watch TV until Grandma Jo gets home," Cat said, looking pointedly at Billie.

Catching Cat's meaning, Billie quickly helped Alex to her feet while Cat wrapped an arm around Alex's waist. "Okay, Grams," Cat instructed. "Now don't put too much weight on that knee. That's it, lean on us. We'll get you there."

Within moments, Cat and Billie maneuvered Alex into the bedroom, helped her change into her dressing gown, and gently lowered her into bed, propping her up with several pillows. Cat turned on the television strategically placed on the dresser opposite the bed then sat on the edge of the bed.

"There you go, Grams. Enjoy your show. We'll send Grandma Jo in as soon as she gets home," Cat said.

Billie and Cat both planted kisses on Alex's still-soft cheek and left her to settle in, closing the door behind them.

"She'll be sound asleep in minutes," Cat said as they reconvened in the living room.

"Let's hope," Billie said. "The last thing we need is a reenactment of the Civil War when Jo gets back. I don't know what she was drinking today, but it sure did make her ornery. I just hope she didn't do something she'll regret in the morning."

"Mama, what's wrong with Grams?" Skylar asked as her parents rejoined her in the living room, where she was still playing with her paper dolls.

"Grams fell on the stairs and hurt her knee, sweetheart. Mama bandaged it up for her, and now she's resting," Billie explained.

"Oh. So, can you play with me again?" Skylar asked.

Momentary panic set in as Billie tried to think of a way out of her second visit in one day to paper doll hell. She'd rather eat broken glass than play paper dolls again. Just when she thought she had no alternative but to give in, Jo returned with the older two children.

"Cat, we need some help out here," Jo called frantically, breaking Cat away from her enjoyment of Billie's paper doll dilemma. Jumping to her feet, she ran into the kitchen, with Billie right on her heels.

"What is it?" Cat asked hastily as soon as she entered the kitchen.

There before her stood a wet Josephine, and two very sick looking kids. "For the love of god, what happened?" Cat demanded, immediately examining both children, who were quite green around the edges.

"Grandma Jo let us smoke a cigar," Tara confessed, holding her stomach.

"You did what?" Cat yelled at her grandmother.

"Hey, I promised I wouldn't drive recklessly. You didn't say anything about not letting them smoke. Besides, cigars never affected me that way. I didn't think it would be a problem," Jo said in her own defense.

"Mom, I'm gonna be sick," Seth complained.

"Not in here you aren't. Come on…to the bathroom with you," Billie said as she took her son's arm and rushed him into the bathroom.

"What ever possessed you to give the kids cigars?" Cat asked sharply, while feeling Tara's head.

"They wanted one. Hell, Caitlain, weren't you ever a kid? Can't you remember ever wanting something you knew wasn't good for you?" Jo countered.

Not wanting to argue with Jo in front of her daughter, Cat changed the subject. "Tara, honey, go upstairs and get ready for bed. I promise you'll feel better in the morning. It's nearly bed time anyway."

After Tara left the two ladies alone, Cat turned to Josephine. "Now, do you want to tell me why you're soaking wet?" she asked.

"I'd like to hear the answer to that one too," Billie said from the doorway. "By the way Cat, I just sent both Seth and Sky to bed. It's nearly bedtime anyway. Oh, and I promised Sky you'd play paper dolls with her again tomorrow," Billie added, briefly changing the subject.

"Gee thanks," Cat said dryly. Then, turning back to Jo, she folded her arms across her chest and continued. "So, spill it. Why are you wet?"

"I fell in the lake."

"You fell in the lake?" Cat repeated.

"Is there an echo in here?" Jo said sarcastically. "You heard me. I fell in the lake. Tara's line was hung up on the bottom. I was trying to pull it free and it snapped. I lost my balance, and in I went," she explained.

"And was this before or after you let the kids smoke cigars?" Billie asked.

"Before."

"So you sat on the river bank, soaking wet, smoking cigars with the kids. Did it ever occur to you that you could catch your death from cold?" Cat asked.

"Hell, no. A little water isn't going to hurt me. Geesh, you'd think I was fragile like Alex or something," she complained.

Billie resented that last remark about Alex. "Grandma Jo," she said. "It's about time you realize that your wife is not weak and fragile. Hell, Alexandra Spirakis is one of the strongest women I know. And if you don't smarten up, you're going to find out just how strong she can be," Billie scolded.

Jo did not like being chastised. "Speaking of Alexandra, is she home yet?" she asked indignantly, "Or is she still out with that nice southern gentleman you all seem to be so taken with?"

"She's home. Billie and I just put her to bed. It seems that she tripped on the steps coming onto the back porch and scraped her knee. She's in there resting right now," Cat answered.

At the mention of Alex's injury, Jo's anger vanished. "She's hurt?" Jo asked softly.

"Slightly," Billie replied. "Nothing serious."

"Well, I'd better go see if she needs anything," Jo said.

"You might want to get out of those wet clothes first and take a hot shower. I don't think Grams will enjoy sleeping next to someone who smells like dead fish," Cat added.

Jo stopped and sniffed at the sleeve of her shirt. "I guess you're right," she said, heading directly to the bathroom and leaving Cat and Billie in the kitchen alone.

Billie shook her head and grinned. "Cat, if I ever get that feisty in my old age, shoot me."

CHAPTER 25

"Good morning neighbors," Jen said as she poked her head into the door. "Is it safe to enter?" she asked.

Cat and Billie were sitting at the kitchen table, sharing the morning paper, each sporting a cup of coffee. "Sure, come on in," Billie answered.

"Now, why wouldn't it be safe to enter?" Cat asked, her curiosity piqued.

"Well, I figured that Jo might be on the warpath after Daddy kept Alex out so late yesterday," Jen explained.

"Actually, it was Alex that was on the warpath because Jo wasn't here to see her come home," Cat replied.

Jen frowned. "I don't understand," she said.

"It appears that Miss Alexandra is turning the tables on all of us, Jen. She *wanted* Jo to catch her coming home late. Unfortunately, Jo thwarted her plans by taking the kids fishing. She wasn't here when Chet brought her home. Her exact words were, *you think she would'a been out fightin' for what's hers. But no, she went fishing instead*," Billie said in her best Alexandra accent.

"Well, I'll be," Jen remarked. "And here I was feeling guilty about setting them up like that," Jen said in awe. "So, where *is* everyone this morning?"

"Well, Missy showed up bright and early. She and Skylar are in Sky's bedroom playing paper dolls, thank God," Billie said.

"Thank God?" Jen questioned.

"Don't ask," Cat interjected, holding her hand up like a stop sign.

"Seth and Tara are still sleeping as usual, and the grandmothers are still in their room. No clue as to whether they're asleep or awake. We've seen no sign of them yet, and no sounds of cannon fire coming from their room, so I'm assuming they're still alive," Billie finished.

"How is Chet faring through all of this?" Cat asked seriously.

"Well, Daddy understood what we were trying to do right from the beginning, but I'm afraid he's become a bit infatuated with Alex himself. She *is* a very charming and beautiful woman. He's quite taken with her, and more than a little regretful that her inclinations lie elsewhere, if you know what I mean…which of course you do," Jen explained, chuckling.

"Well, the last thing we want is for anyone to get hurt. The whole reason for doing this was to bring the grandmothers closer. We really appreciate what Chet is doing to help us out. I guess the ball's in Jo's court right now," Billie said.

"Josephine Wycliffe, I am not an invalid. I will thank you to stop treating me like one," a loud voice said from the living room.

"Oh-oh. There's the first cannon shot. Civil War round two," Cat whispered to Jen and Billie as they eavesdropped on the ladies' argument.

"Alex, don't get your panties in a wad. I'm only trying to help," Jo replied.

"I don't need your help. Kindly remove your hands from my person," Alex demanded.

"Ouch," Billie commented.

"Suit yourself," Jo yelled as she stomped her way into the kitchen. "Stubborn, arrogant, pigheaded…," she mumbled as she headed for the coffee pot, throwing her fedora on the table as she passed by.

"Good morning," Cat said brightly as all three ladies pretended they hadn't heard a word. "What was that you were saying?"

Jo turned around. "I said, stubborn, arrogant, pigheaded. That grandmother of yours is driving me crazy, and don't pretend you didn't hear what was said a moment ago. Hell, it was so loud, a room full of nursing home residents could have heard it from a mile away," Jo said, causing all three ladies to turn red with embarrassment at being caught. Pouring herself a cup of coffee, she joined the ladies at the table and sat down. "She won't let me help her to the bathroom. It's obvious that her knee hurts, but she's as stubborn as the devil himself."

"Sounds like someone else I know," Billie said softly.

"I heard that," Jo replied, shooting visual daggers across the table at her tall granddaughter who lifted her eyebrows in mock innocence.

Just then, Alex hobbled into the kitchen. Billie immediately rose to her feet and offered her arm for support as she guided her across the room to the empty chair at the end of the table. Seating the proud southern woman, Billie then poured a cup of coffee and placed it in front of her.

"Thank you, dear," Alex said.

"How's your knee this morning, Grams?" Cat asked after rising from her seat to kiss the older woman on the cheek.

"A little sore, but manageable," she said. "Although some people would have me believing I was an invalid," she added throwing a sharp look in Jo's direction.

"I was only trying to help, Alex," Jo said in her own defense.

"In any case, I'll be fine. I would appreciate a little something for a headache though, if you wouldn't mind, dear?" she asked Cat.

"Coming right up," Cat said as she went to fetch the pain reliever.

"A little hung over, Alex?" Jo asked coyly.

Alex avoided Jo's eyes. "Whatever makes you say that?" she asked as she took the pain relievers with the water Cat handed her.

"I could smell the booze on you last night. You seldom drink anything stronger than iced tea or wine. It was pretty noticeable," Jo explained.

"I might have enjoyed a cocktail or two while I was out," Alex replied.

"A cocktail or two? Is that why you hurt your knee, Alex?" Jo baited.

Flustered, Alex rose to her feet. "I don't have to sit here and listen to this. Caitlain, Billie, Jen…my apologies for being such poor company. I believe I need to lie down for a while—alone," she announced before once more hobbling off toward her bedroom.

Billie turned to Jo. "You're not scoring a hell of a lot of points here," she said.

"I can't help it! Just the thought of her in the arms of someone else just tears my heart out. Hurts like hell. All I want to do is strike back and then I turn into this monstrous bitch," Jo explained, tears filling her eyes and emotion choking the words in her throat.

"Maybe it's time to fight back with actions instead of words," Cat suggested.

Jo looked at the three ladies sitting around the table. "I really hate to admit this, but I don't think I'm strong enough to beat the shit out of Chet. And besides, I wouldn't want to hurt Jen like that," she replied.

All three ladies tried very hard not to laugh. It was unusual for Jo to admit a weakness.

"Grams, the only thing you need to beat the shit out of is that stubborn pride of yours," Cat explained.

For several moments, no one spoke, a contemplative silence settling over the group. Finally, Billie spoke up. "Look, the wedding is just two days away. I would really hate for it to become a war zone between you and Grams. That wouldn't be fair to Drew or Dylan," she commented.

Jo just nodded before rising to her feet. "I need some fresh air. I'm going for a walk," she announced.

"Would you like some company?" Cat asked.

"No, that's all right. I have some thinking to do. Besides, I'm afraid I wouldn't be very good company to anybody right now. I'll be back soon." With that, she planted the fedora on her head and headed out the door.

***

"Damn, look at the time. Billie, where do you think she went?" Cat asked nervously.

"It's hard to tell. She was pretty upset when she left. I can't say that I blame her. If I thought I was losing you, I'd be just about ready to cash it in," Billie replied.

Cat turned sharply toward Billie. "Don't say that. Don't you dare say that. Grandma Jo wouldn't do anything stupid, would she?"

"Desperation can drive a person to do things they normally wouldn't do," Billie said realistically. Crossing the room, she opened her arms and took Cat into them. Rubbing her hands over Cat's back, she tried to soothe away her fears. "Honey, I'm sure she's okay. She's probably sitting on a park bench somewhere trying to get her thoughts together,"

"Billie, we need to go look for her," Cat suggested.

"Look for who...Josie?" Alex said from the doorway. "I wouldn't waste your time. When Josephine doesn't want to be found, there's no sense looking. This isn't the first time she's disappeared."

"It isn't? What do you mean, Grams?" Cat asked with interest.

"In the fifty years we've been together, she's disappeared at least a dozen times, although I have to admit she hasn't done that for several years now. Most of the time she would just up and leave without warning after some big confrontation, mostly. She's usually gone for days at a time. One time she didn't return for nearly two weeks. Gradually, I began to worry less and less about her safety, and more and more about our relationship whenever the mood would strike her to run off like that. Josie can take care of herself. She's a survivor. What I *am* worried about is not *her,* but *us.* I don't know if the present state of our relationship can survive another separation," Alex explained.

Cat approached her grandmother and cupped the aging face between her palms. "The question is, Grams, do you *want* it to survive?" she asked.

Tear welled in Alexandra's eyes. Without breaking eye contact, she began to talk.

"Caitlain, I fell in love with Josie the moment I laid eyes on her. She was extraordinary. I had never known a woman quite like her before. She was brash, wild and bold. Josie wasn't afraid of anything, except maybe her own emotions, but she'd never admit that to you. She had a passion for history that surpassed any I had encountered before. She was totally dedicated to it, heart, mind, body and soul. If Josie had sent me home that first day, I would have refused to leave. Even then I knew I couldn't live without her."

Alex broke away from Cat's grasp as she absent-mindedly walked to the window to peer out. Billie took this opportunity to walk up behind Cat and surround her in loving arms.

"Josephine Wycliffe. Even her name sent chills of desire running through my veins, as it still does today." Still facing the window, she continued. "Do I want it to survive? Caitlain, if it *doesn't* survive, then I have no reason to go on. She is my sole reason for living."

"Then why...?" Cat began.

"Why the confrontations of late?" Alex asked, turning to face her granddaughters. "Cat, could you live in a relationship that was lopsided, even knowing your partner loved you with all her heart? Could you live without being formally recognized as the most important person in your partner's life? Child, I love Josie more than life itself, and I know she loves me with equal vigor, but knowing that isn't enough. I want the world to know it too, and I want Josie to be proud that the world knows it."

Alex stopped momentarily, turning her back on the duo and walking a short distance away. After a few moments, she turned around to face them once again.

"I know Josephine Wycliffe will never be the tender, gentle, passionately sincere person I would like her to be, but it would be real nice for her to even fake it once in a while, just for me. Am I making any sense?" Alex asked.

Billie's arms tightened around Cat, partially to support her now-weeping wife, and partially to keep her own emotions in check.

Cat nodded. "Grams, you are making perfect sense," she replied through the sniffles. "So you don't want the relationship to end?"

"If *it* ends, *I* end. It's just that simple," Alexandra replied.

***

Cat strained once more to see through the picture window into the darkness beyond the illumination of the front porch light. Seeing nothing, she resumed pacing back and forth across the room, each time stopping briefly to peer into the darkness. Finally, patience wore thin as she stopped dead in her tracks. "That's it. I can't take it any longer. She's been gone all day. I'm going to call Mom. Maybe she's over there."

"You're wastin' your time, Caitlain," Alex said from her position on the couch. "She'll show up when she's done poutin'."

"Well, I'm going to try anyway," Cat said as she dialed the phone.

"Hey Drew, this is Cat. How are you doing sweetie? Are you getting nervous yet? The big day is less than two days away. Yes, I remember that I need to pick up the flowers for the attendants. Don't worry about it. I'll pick them up tomorrow. Consider it done. The flower shop is decorating the church and banquet hall, right? Good. That's one less thing for us to worry about. Okay. Hey, is Mom there, honey?" Cat asked, trying hard to get to the real reason she had called her mother's house. Moments later, Cat had her mother on the phone.

"Hi, Mom? This is Cat. Is Grandma Jo with you? No? Well, she left here about nine this morning to go for a walk and she hasn't returned. Yes, I know, but she was kind of upset when she left, and we're worried about her. Yes, Grams said the same thing. Mom, I can't help but worry about her. Yes, I know she's done this before, but...okay Mom. I'll talk to you later. Love you. Bye," Cat said in defeat before returning the receiver to its cradle.

Cat ran her hands through her hair in a worried fashion before turning back to Alex. "Mom said not to worry about her, that she's done this before, and that she'll be back when she's good and ready," Cat explained.

"I told you as much, Caitlain," Alex replied.

"Grams, how can you just sit there and accept that kind of behavior from her? If Billie disappeared on me for days at a time without an explanation, well...well...I just don't think I could deal with it," Cat said, distress dictating her tone of voice. "For someone who has lived as long as she has, she sure is acting like a child," she added.

Alex chuckled. "My dear girl, you are just now realizing that? Josie will never have to worry about a second childhood because she has never left her first one behind. It's part of what makes her so charming."

"Charming? How about infuriating?" Cat blurted out.

"That, too," Alex agreed.

"I wonder if Billie's had any luck finding her," Cat pondered. "I'm going to call her cell phone."

"Don't bother," Billie said from the doorway. "No luck. She's hidden herself pretty good," Billie said as she threw her car keys on the coffee table and sat on the couch beside Alex.

"I called Mom's. She's not there either," Cat said, absent-mindedly crossing her arms and biting her lip as she resumed her pacing.

Suddenly the phone rang. All three women stared at it like a ticking time bomb, ready to deliver devastation.

Finally, Billie rose to her feet. "I'll get it," she announced as she braced herself. "Hello?" she said into the receiver. "Hello? Who is this? Joe? Joe, are you all right?" she asked. "Joe, slow down, I can't understand a word you're saying. Look, where are you right now? Yeah, okay, all right, I know where that is. You stay put. I'll be there in ten minutes. Don't leave. Okay, bye." Putting down the receiver, Billie looked at the other two ladies. "Joe's wasted. I need to pick him up before he gets himself into trouble," she explained.

"Where is he?" Cat asked.

"He's at the pub, apparently drunk off his ass. Instead of confronting his problems head on, he's trying to drown them in drink," she said, collecting her car keys from the coffee table.

Cat threw her hands out to her sides in exasperation. "What is it with this family? First Grandma Jo, and now Joe. We're all going to hell in a hand basket," she said melodramatically.

Billie rose to her feet and approached Cat. Taking the smaller woman's face in her hands, she covered Cat's lips with her own, leaving tender butterfly kisses in their wake. "Not all of us, my love," she whispered. "Not all of us. I love you. I'll be back in a few minutes, okay?"

All Cat could do was nod.

***

"Okay Joe, that's it, one foot in front of the other. Watch that step. There you go," Billie instructed as she guided her brother-in-law up the steps of the back porch. "In we go," she added, pushing him into the kitchen in front of her.

"Whoa, it sure is bright in here," Joe exclaimed as the brilliance of the kitchen bulb shot daggers of pain through his alcohol-soaked brain.

"All right, have a seat," Billie directed as she pushed him into a chair at the table.

Falling roughly into the chair, Joe immediately placed both forearms on the table and then dropped his head onto them. "Oh, my God, I'm drunk," he said.

"No shit, Sherlock," Billie answered sarcastically.

"Billie?" Cat said from the doorway.

"Hi, love," Billie replied as Cat entered the kitchen pulling her robe around herself. "Where's Grams?" she asked.

"She went to bed about an hour ago," Cat responded.

"Did Jo come home yet?" Billie asked.

"No, and I'm really worried about her. Grams said she's not concerned, but I don't believe her," Cat said worriedly.

"Well sweetie, Grams does know her better than we do. Maybe she's right. Jo will come home when she's finished sulking," Billie suggested encouragingly.

"If she *can* come home," Cat said, giving a voice to what both she and Billie were worrying about.

"Amy, Amy why are you doing this to me?" mumbled a very inebriated Joe as he rolled his head from side to side, momentarily drawing Cat and Billie's attention away from their worries of Josephine.

Cat looked from Joe to Billie. "Did he give you a hard time? It took you longer than I expected to bring him back," Cat observed.

"Oh, yeah. He decided that he wanted to beat up everyone in the bar. Accused them all of sleeping with his wife. It took me over an hour to calm them all down and convince them that he was just a raving drunk suffering from a broken heart. Then, about halfway home, he decided he was going to be sick. I managed to pull over to the side of the road and pull him out of the car just in time. Otherwise, his clothing, and my car, would have been quite a mess. He literally cried all the way home about how he thought Amy was cheating on him. Cat, what a mess. I feel really bad for him," Billie explained.

Cat just shook her head from side to side. "I'll try to talk some sense into Amy tomorrow," she offered.

"No, I don't think you should," Billie replied. "Joe needs to take care of this one himself. Amy isn't going to listen to anyone else," she finished, rubbing her hand over Joe's shoulders.

"Maybe you're right, sweetheart. Give me a minute to make up the couch, then I'll give you a hand carrying him in there," Cat said.

Moments later, after tucking Joe in, Billie and Cat snuggled closely in their bed, neither of them able to sleep, the burden of their family's woes weighing heavily on their minds.

"Billie?" Cat said softly.

"Hmmm?" Billie replied.

"Promise me our lives will never get this out of control," Cat pleaded.

"I promise," Billie said.

"Good. I promise too. I love you Barney. Goodnight," Cat said.

"I love you too, Mrs. Barney," Billie replied. "Sleep tight."

CHAPTER 26

Cat rolled over, throwing her arm across the empty space usually occupied by her wife. Realizing instantly that Billie was gone, she bolted awake and looked around. Within moments, her eyes fell on the note resting on Billie's pillow.

Cat,
Gone for a run with Jen. I'll be home soon.
I love you,
Barney

Smiling, she rolled onto her back, taking Billie's pillow with her and hugging it tightly. She loved the smell of Billie's pillow, fresh and clean, like the herbal shampoo Billie used on her hair. After several moments of basking in the scent of her wife, Cat finally decided it was time to get up.

Dragging herself out of bed, she pulled on her robe and headed for the stairs. The aroma of coffee drifted up to greet her before she even landed one foot on the top stair. *Hmmm, Billie must be back already*, she thought to herself as she scurried down the stairs and through the living room where she noticed Joe still sleeping soundly in the couch. *He's going to have one hell of a headache this morning!* she mused as she passed by.

Reaching the kitchen, Cat stopped short when she saw Alexandra, not Billie, sitting at the table, cradling a cup of coffee between her hands. "Grams, you're up early," she said.

Alex looked up, revealing red, swollen eyes to her granddaughter.

"Grams? Are you all right?" Cat asked, going directly to Alex's side.

"I lied to you yesterday, Caitlain. I *am* worried about her," Alex confessed, looking back down into her coffee cup.

Cat immediately wrapped her arms around Alex. "I know you are, Grams. We are too," she replied, feeling Alex's shoulders shaking beneath her arms.

Just then, Billie burst through the kitchen door, drawing the attention of the two ladies to her.

"Cat, Grams, good, you're up. I need your help with something," Billie said breathlessly, a slight grin creeping onto her face.

"Billie, what is it?" Cat asked, a little startled with Billie's entrance.

"Well, I just returned from my run, and I was climbing the steps to the porch, when I heard...well, it's hard to describe. You need to come see for yourself," Billie exclaimed.

Their interest peaked, Cat and Alex both rose to their feet and followed Billie into the back yard.

"There. Up there," Billie said pointing to the tree house.

"What? I don't see anything," Cat said, not really understanding what was so odd about the tree house.

"Listen," Billie said excitedly.

Both ladies stood quietly under the tree house, straining to hear the mysterious noise Billie was talking about.

"Kill me, please! I need some drugs," came the sound.

A broad smile spread across the face of Alexandra Spirakis as she realized what was behind the sounds. Then as quick as the smile came, it was gone, followed immediately by her hands perching on her hips.

"Josephine Wycliffe, you crazy old woman, come down from that tree house this very minute! Do you know what you've put us through?" Alex scolded loudly.

Cat and Billie exchanged covert grins.

"Alex? Alex, I need drugs," Jo repeated as she poked her head out of the tree house window.

"You're gonna need more than drugs when I'm through with you," Alex said through tears of relief. "You come down here this very instant," she repeated.

"I can't get down," the aging historian whined. "Help me, Alex."

"You got yourself up there...obviously in a drunken stupor, you can get yourself down. I will be in the house when you decide to act like a proper lady," she stated before turning on her heel and stomping off into the house.

Jo poked her head out one more time. "Like a proper lady?" she said in disbelief. "I guess I'm stuck up here forever."

"Come on Grandma Jo, I'll give you a hand," Billie said, propping the kids' homemade ladder up against the tree house and holding it steady for her. "How in hell did you get up there anyway?" she asked as Jo touched down onto the ground.

"Damned if I know," Jo replied. Planting both feet on the ground, she turned to look at Cat. "Kitten, could I bother you for some pain killers?" she asked.

Cat hugged her grandmother. "Sure. Come on, Grams made a fresh pot of coffee. I'm sure she won't mind giving you a cup while I fetch your drugs," Cat said in jest.

"The only thing your grandmother is bound to give me is the cold shoulder," Jo predicted sadly.

"Well then I guess you'll just have to turn on the charm and warm that shoulder up, don't cha think?" Cat suggested.

"I try hard not to...think, that is, at least not with a hangover," Jo joked.

Cat laughed and hugged her grandmother once more, elated that she was alive and well. "Grandma Jo," she said, "you most certainly have a colorful ninety-six pack."

Jo frowned. "Ninety-six pack. There it is again! What's up with that anyway?" she asked.

"I'll let Grams explain that one," Cat replied chuckling as she led her hung over grandmother into the house.

***

Joe finally rose after many futile attempts to ignore the sound of cartoons blaring from the television. Rolling over, he opened his eyes and immediately closed them again as a painful bolt seared into his alcohol-injured brain. Forcing himself into an upright position, he threw his legs over the side of the couch and immediately dropped his head into his hands.

"Morning, Uncle Joe," Skylar said cheerfully.

Joe painfully lifted his head and forced a weak smile to cross his features in response to his niece's greetings. "Morning, Sky," he grumbled. "Where are your moms?" he added.

"Mama's upstairs, and Mom is in the kitchen with Grandma Jo," Skylar responded.

"Hmm," Joe replied as he dropped his head into his hands once more, wondering how he was going to face Amy when he returned to Ida and Doc's house. Somehow, Amy had a way of making him feel guilty, even when he had done nothing wrong. Even now, after innocently spending the night at his sister-in-law's home he felt like he had deserted her, when in reality, it was Amy's behavior with Bob that was in question. Forcing himself to get off the couch, he ventured into the kitchen where Billie and Jo were obviously having a serious discussion.

"That's what she wants. That's what would make her happy," Billie said as Jo pondered her words carefully.

"That's *all* she wants?" Jo replied incredulously.

Billie just nodded, a slight smile crossing her features.

"Am I interrupting anything," Joe asked as he stumbled into the kitchen.

Billie turned around quickly. "Joe! No, you're not interrupting at all. Come join us for a coffee. How are you feeling this morning?" she asked.

Joe shuffled over to the counter and poured himself a cup of black coffee. Turning toward the ladies, he leaned his backside against the counter and sipped the strong brew. "To be truthful, lousy," he complained, running one hand through his hair.

"Join the club," Jo proclaimed. "Seems we both indulged a little too much last night. I hope when you go home, you have better luck with your lady than I'm having with mine," Jo added.

Joe looked at Jo curiously. "Is something wrong with Grams?" he asked.

"A severe case of the cold shoulder—not that I don't deserve it," she replied.

"I know what you mean," Joe commented. "When I get home, Amy will either ignore me, or kill me...not sure which at this point. However, considering this hangover, I'd opt for the killing," Joe said, causing both women to chuckle.

"Billie, do you have a writing pad and a pen? I have a few thoughts I want to put down on paper," Jo asked.

"Sure," Billie replied rising to her feet and pulling paper and pen out of the utility drawer and handing them to Jo. "Is there anything special I can help you with?" Billie asked.

Jo looked at her granddaughter coyly. "No, not really. I need to work this one out for myself. Thanks for the paper," Jo said as she accepted the items and headed into the living room, leaving Billie and Joe alone in the kitchen.

Billie looked at her brother-in-law. "Sit," she said. "We need to talk."

***

"Hi, Mom. Is Amy there?" Cat asked into the receiver as she sat on the edge of her bed.

While waiting for her sister to answer the phone, Cat looked around the bedroom. A sense of nostalgia suddenly overcame her. *God, this room has held such emotion for us over the past several years. Some of our best, and worst times have been right here*, she thought as she recalled the lovemaking, the confrontations, the illnesses and the tears.

It was here that she had found Billie comatose one morning, only to discover later that she had been afflicted by epilepsy as the result of a gunshot wound to the head months earlier.

They had lain in each other's arms, filled with fear and dread as they watched their baby girl struggle in the clutches of leukemia, not knowing if she would live or die.

It was also here that some of the most gloriously fulfilling lovemaking had occurred, each of them totally committed to loving each other and sharing the wondrous joy of living in each other's souls.

Through all their trials and tribulations, this was one place they could find sanctuary from the world. It was their secret garden, their stronghold, their nirvana. As Cat thought ahead to the pending nuptials the following day, she could only wish Drew and Dylan the same loving relationship she enjoyed with her own personal dark-haired beauty. Joys and woes included, she wouldn't trade one moment of her life with Billie, not for all the gold in the world.

Cat was suddenly drawn out of her reverie by a voice at the other end of the line.

"Hello?"

"Amy, this is Cat. Look, just in case you were *worried*," Cat said sarcastically, "your husband spent last night passed out on our couch...you know...just in case you were worried," she repeated.

"Oh, so that's where he was," Amy replied. "Go figure."

"And what's that supposed to mean, Amy? Don't you even care that he didn't come home last night?" Cat asked, exasperated with her oldest sister.

"At this point, Cat, I'm not sure what I feel. Why he chose last night to suddenly grow a backbone is beyond me. Do you know that last night he had the nerve to accuse me of having an affair? Can you imagine that?" she exclaimed obviously insulted that her husband could even think such a thing.

"Yeah, imagine that," Cat returned dryly.

"Don't tell me you're siding with him?" Amy said hotly, accurately reading her sister's tone of voice.

"Look Amy, you haven't exactly given him reason *not* to believe it," Cat replied.

"And just what does *that* mean?" Amy demanded.

"I can't believe you don't know. Amy, look at how you act. You flirt with anything in pants—men and women alike," Cat exclaimed loudly.

"And since when is flirting with women a turn off to *you* of all people?" Amy returned with a large dose of her own sarcasm.

At that moment, if Amy had been within Cat's reach, she would have surely landed the palm of her hand across her sister's cheek. Taking a deep breath, Cat consciously calmed herself, realizing her sister had yet again drawn her into a confrontation by pushing her buttons.

"All right, I refuse to let you reel me in hook, line and sinker like you did when we were kids. I just thought you might like to know where your husband is," Cat said. "Oh, and Amy, tomorrow is Drew's wedding. You and Joe are a big part of it. Don't blow it for Drew or I'll never forgive you," she warned.

"Yeah, yeah, yeah," Amy replied.

"I mean it, Amy," Cat warned again.

"Don't worry, Cat. I won't do anything to ruin the wedding for Princess," came the retort.

"See that you don't, Amy. She doesn't deserve it. I'll see you tomorrow then," Cat answered.

"Whatever. Later," Amy said before hanging up.

***

"All right Joe, remember what I said," Billie called to Joe as he climbed out of the car and headed toward his in-law's house.

Billie watched Joe walk toward the house, looking all the world like he was a dead man walking...shoulders slumped, head hung low. She felt sorry for what he was going through. She remembered a time when she thought her marriage to Cat was over. Billie sat there for several moments, recalling some of the more difficult points in her relationship with her red-haired wife.

Visions of near domestic violence sprang to her mind as she saw herself pin Cat against the kitchen door, threatening her with physical dominance.

She saw visions of Cat rejecting her during Skylar's bout with leukemia as jealousy over the little girl's love for her corrupted her common sense.

Visions of them nearly coming to blows over the amount of time Billie's job was taking away from the family.

These were all difficult times...times she would just as soon forget, as they caused her great distress. Thoughts of Cat leaving her made her physically ill. Thoughts of losing everything and everyone she loved were unbearable.

Yes, she knew *exactly* what Joe was going through.

Snapping herself back to reality, she sighed deeply before putting the car into gear and heading back home.

***

Billie entered the kitchen from the porch just as Cat entered from the living room. Both stopped dead in their tracks and locked eyes. Raw emotions flew across the room on the bridge created between them. Within seconds, they were in each other's arms, clinging desperately. For long moments, they stood there, wrapped around each other, savoring in the non-verbal love that flowed so easily between them. Finally, they parted.

Cat looked up into Billie's eyes. "Sweetheart, I will be so glad when this wedding is over and life can return to normal. If I have to solve one more person's problems, or play peacemaker one more time, I'm going to lose it," she exclaimed.

"I couldn't have said it better, myself," Billie agreed. "I just brought Joe back to your parents' after a long talk about his relationship with Amy. He is really down in the dumps, and just doesn't know how to deal with it," Billie explained.

"Well Amy has no clue as to why Joe should suspect her of having an affair. Can you believe it? How dense can the woman be? And here I thought Drew was the blond one," Cat joked, making Billie chuckle.

Billie took Cat into her arms once more. "One more day and it will all be over. Hopefully things will go smoothly tomorrow, then *everyone* can concentrate on returning to normal, whatever that means," Billie remarked.

"One more day," Cat said wistfully.

***

Alexandra Spirakis rested against the door frame of the kitchen, a glass of ice tea in her hand, watching Josephine writing furiously from her curled up position in the living room easy chair. "What is that crazy old fool doing?" Alex asked.

"I don't know. Why don't you ask her yourself," Billie suggested to her grandmother as she peeled potatoes at the kitchen sink.

Just then, Tara went running through the kitchen, heading for the back door.

"Whoa, hold on here. Dinner will be ready in about a half hour. Don't be wandering off too far," Billie warned her daughter.

Tara stopped short. "I won't. I'm just lending this CD to Karissa. I'll be back in a few minutes," the teenager replied.

"Okay. While you're over there, tell your brother he'll need to be home shortly as well," Billie shouted to Tara's disappearing back.

"I thought I made it clear that I wasn't talking to her," Alex replied.

"What's that, Grams?" Billie said, momentarily distracted by Tara.

"I said, I'm still not talking to her," Alex repeated, a little impatiently.

Billie put the potato peeler down and turned to her grandmother. "You know, I'm not sure who's more stubborn, you, or Grandma Jo," she observed.

"My word!" Alex replied, insulted. "I am *not* stubborn. I'm determined," she explained.

"Determined," Billie said dryly. "Well the end result is still the same," she pointed out.

"What result is still the same?" Cat asked, entering the kitchen from the basement door, carrying a basket of laundry.

Before Billie could answer, Alex broke in. "Caitlain, dear, would you mind findin' out what your crazy old grandmother is doing writin' away like that in the living room?" she asked.

Cat looked back and forth between Alex and Billie, a questioning frown on her face. Billie just shrugged, so Cat did as Alex asked. Putting the laundry basket on the kitchen table, she entered the living room and approached Jo. Sitting on the arm of the easy chair, she threw her own arm across the back of the chair behind the elderly woman. "What 'cha writing?" she asked.

Jo looked into Cat's face and grinned, then held the tablet of paper up for her to see. After several moments of trying to read Jo's handwriting, a wide smile covered Cat's face. Bending down, she planted a big kiss on Jo's cheek then left her to her writing. Returning to the kitchen, she went directly to the laundry basket, throwing a covert look and smile toward Billie along the way.

"Well?" Alex asked impatiently. "What is she writin?"

Cat looked at Alex and feigned innocence. "I'm afraid she'll have to tell you herself, Grams," Cat replied.

"For the love of God. What ever happened to respectin' yer elders?" Alex complained as she stomped off to her room.

Cat looked at Billie and smiled. "One more day," she said.

Billie just nodded and returned to peeling potatoes.

CHAPTER 27

"Seth, come on! You've been in there long enough," whined Tara as she banged on the bathroom door.

"Tara, please stop banging on the door," Billie said from her room at the end of the hallway.

"But Mom, Seth has been in there for an hour. I gotta get ready too, you know," she reasoned.

Billie stuck her head into the hallway. "Seth, let's get a move on," she called.

"All right, all right. I'm done," Seth announced as he pulled the door open to let his sister in.

Billie's jaw dropped as her son stepped into the hallway from the bathroom dressed in a black tailored tuxedo. "Oh, my. Seth, you look so old. Where did my baby go?" Billie exclaimed, suddenly realizing her fourteen-year-old son was more man than child.

"What's all the commotion about?" Cat said as she led a daintily dressed Skylar out of her bedroom. She too stopped short when she saw her son. Tears of pride filled her eyes as she took in his handsome blond looks. She was so dumb struck she simply could not speak.

Seth pointed to Cat. "Now don't you start crying. It's only a monkey suit," he said.

"Oh, it's so much more than that," Cat said, finally finding her shaky voice. "It's a very handsome young man in a monkey suit."

Seth's chest puffed out with pride as he strutted toward the stairway. "I'll be downstairs watching TV while you women get ready," he said boldly.

"Am I handsome too?" Skylar asked as she watched her brother descend the stairs.

"No way," Billie said, coming into the hall to scoop her daughter into her arms. "You, my little rugrat, are beautiful."

Squirming out of Billie's arms, Skylar went to great lengths to imitate her brother's strut as she too headed for the stairs. "I think I'll go watch TV too while you women get ready," she said.

Billie and Cat exchanged surprised expressions. "Looks like we've got some pretty sassy kids," Cat said.

"Josephine Wycliffe, get yourself out of that bed and get dressed," came a loud demand from downstairs.

Within seconds, Seth had re-ascended the stairs two at a time. "Ah, I think you might want to break it up before it gets out of hand," he said. "Grams is really mad at Grandma Jo."

Cat scowled and dropped her chin to her chest. "What next?" she complained as she ran her hands through her hair.

"I'll go see what's up, Cat. You go ahead and get dressed," Billie offered as she headed toward the stairs.

By the time Billie reached the living room, the volume of the exchange had increased ten-fold. As she approached their bedroom door, the cause of the problem became clear.

"Of all the days you could choose to be stubborn and pig-headed, why pick this one?" Alex demanded loudly.

"No better time than the present," Jo answered flippantly.

"Exactly why aren't you going, may I ask?" Alex continued.

"No, you may *not* ask," Jo replied sharply as Billie winced on the other side of the bedroom door. "I thought you weren't talking to me. At least that's been the case for the past couple of days."

Alex's approach suddenly softened. "Josie, please. Your granddaughter is expecting us. Please don't ruin this for her."

"She won't even notice I'm missing, Alex," Jo reasoned.

"Well, I'll notice, and so will the rest of the family," Alex explained.

"I refuse to pretend that everything is perfectly fine just for the sake of your image, Alex. I'm not going," Jo stated firmly.

Suddenly, the bedroom door flew open from the inside, startling both Billie and Alex.

"Ah, Grams, I was just about to knock," Billie stammered. "Are you two nearly ready?" she asked, trying to cover up her eavesdropping.

Regaining her composure quickly, Alex composed herself like a proper southern belle. "I am ready, Billie, but I'm afraid Josephine has declined to attend the wedding. We will just have to go and enjoy ourselves without her," she said, brushing past Billie, heading to the bathroom to repair her face.

Billie looked into the room at Jo, who was reclining comfortably on the bed. "Grandma Jo?" she asked.

"Billie, Come in," Jo exclaimed. "Take a load off," she added, patting the bed beside her.

Billie went to sit on the edge of the bed and looked Jo squarely in the face. "Why aren't you going?" she asked.

Jo grinned. "Trust me, Billie. I know what I'm doing," she replied.

"I sure hope so. You know you're not mending any fences with this kind of behavior," Billie pointed out.

"Mommy, Mama says we're gonna be late if you don't get dressed right away," Skylar said, suddenly appearing in the doorway, obviously on a mission for Cat.

Billie turned her attention to the doorway. "Okay, honey. I'll be right there," she said, rising to her feet. Before leaving the room, she paused for one last comment. "Before you do something that will change your life forever, make sure you know what you're doing, because you won't get a chance to take it back."

Jo smiled. "I have no intention of taking it back, Billie. And yes, I *do* know I'm about to change my life forever, and between you and me, it's long overdue."

Resigned to her grandmother's stubbornness, Billie just nodded and left the room.

***

The wedding ceremony went off without a hitch despite Jo's conspicuous absence, and the fact that Amy and Joe were very cold to each other. Ida and Laurel beamed with pride as they watched each member of their combined family walk down the aisle, each one just as handsome or beautiful as the last.

Ida and Laurel weren't the only mothers beaming with pride. Cat and Billie had all they could do to hold the tears of pride back at the flawless performance given by their brood. Seth stood tall and confident at the altar beside his uncle, displaying no traces of the child within. Tara's attendance of Drew's train was timely and orderly, having saved her aunt from stepping on it several times throughout her walk to and from the altar. And Skylar drew smiles and comments from all present as the dainty little princess expertly dropped rose petals in a path down the aisle during the wedding procession.

And Cat was right…even though Billie had objected to the purple gown, she was stunningly beautiful in it. Drew did make one concession on Billie's part, allowing her to wear low heels rather than the three-inch ones worn by the other bridesmaids, making Billie and Bob much more comfortable.

Even though Amy and Joe were less than friendly, their manner was polite, albeit a bit distant. Kevin, normally the Neanderthal, was actually attentive and respectful of Bridget, the nostalgia surrounding the ceremony softening his chauvinistic style. Even Bob behaved, having enough consideration for the bride and groom not to flirt openly with Amy at the ceremony. All in all, it was a beautiful wedding. Teary eyes abounded throughout the church at the beauty of the ceremony, including those of Doc, who sentimentally gave away his youngest child into the arms of her new husband.

The only real sadness was held within the bosom of one aging southern belle, who sorely missed the presence of her life partner at such a happy occasion. More than once, she reached for the hand of her beloved as something especially beautiful about the ceremony touched her heart, only to find empty space. Her tears were not only those of joy, but of sadness at what could have been, but would never be... especially now.

As the wedding party assembled on the altar to make their way back down the aisle after the ceremony, Billie noticed the door at the back of the church swing shut, its trespasser unseen. In the receiving line outside the church, she looked around, hoping to spot a familiar face in the crowd...a face that was conspicuously missing during the ceremony...but found none.

***

The wedding reception was held at a rented hall. As with the weddings of his other three daughters, Doc spared no expense to make it a joyous and carefree occasion for all involved. A meal of prime rib, baked potato and summer vegetables was catered to perfection, although neither Drew nor Dylan ate much of it with the constant interruptions by party goers tapping on their glasses with knives, a signal that prompted the new bride and groom to stand and kiss with each occurrence.

Not long after the meal was served and cleared away, the music began. Many of the party goers had started drinking as soon as they arrived at the hall, so the floor was quickly filled with dancers whose inhibitions had been chased away by the alcohol.

During the meal, members of the wedding party sat at a long table at the front of the hall, but once the dancing began, formal place settings fell by the wayside as people mingled and formed groups. In one such group, sat the immediate family of the bride and groom, along with Jen and her family, all except Tara and Crystal, who spent the entire reception casting hateful looks at each other from across the room.

"Look at them," Doc exclaimed, drawing everyone's attention to Drew and Dylan on the dance floor. "Don't they make a handsome couple?" he asked.

"They are cute indeed," Ida agreed, covering Doc's hand with her own.

"I can't wait for them to give us grandchildren," Laurel said excitedly. "Can you imagine how beautiful they'll be?"

"Grandchildren?" remarked Jim. "I'm too young to be a grandfather!" he exclaimed.

"Get used to it Jim," Doc advised. "Look at the brood we have. Why Seth is nearly a man already. Talk about feeling old!" he joked, chuckling heartily before turning his attention back to the dance floor.

Cat watched her father's eyes follow her baby sister as her new husband led her around the dance floor. "Is that a tear I see in the corner of your eye, Daddy?" Cat teased her father. "You always were a soft touch where Drew was concerned."

"Your dad is a soft touch with all four of you girls— correction, make that all *five* of you girls," Ida corrected, including a beaming Billie in the daughter head-count while Doc blushed profusely at the teasing.

"Nona, are you having a good time?" Laurel asked Alex.

Having been caught staring off into space, Alex became flustered and nearly tipped over her ice tea glass. "Oh, my. I am so clumsy some times," she exclaimed as she righted her glass before any of the contents spilled onto the tablecloth. Embarrassment reddened her face to the tips of her ears. "I'm sorry dear. What was it you asked?"

"I asked if you were having a good time," Laurel repeated, already knowing the answer.

"As good as can be expected, dear," she replied distractedly.

Ida decided to join forces with her sister to pull their mother out of a funk. "Nona, don't let Mama get you down. You know how stubborn she can be. Just because she has chosen to miss out on the fun, doesn't mean you have to. Why don't you get out on the dance floor and kick up your heels?" Ida urged.

"I agree wholeheartedly with your lovely daughter, Alex," Chet said as he approached the table, accompanied by a very exhausted Jen. "It appears my daughter can't keep up with this old man on the dance floor. Would you do me the honor of granting me your company for the next dance?" he asked smoothly, bowing at the waist and extending his open palm toward Alex.

Alexandra stammered, looking for an excuse not to allow herself to enjoy the party. "Er...I...," she began.

"I have already requested a formal waltz, to be played in your honor, dear lady. Surely you cannot deny me this one dance?" he teased, a dashing smile crossing his handsome age-worn features.

Unable to resist Chet's charm, and sorely in need of pampering, Alex relented and allowed Chet to lead her to the dance floor.

As soon as the music began, dozens of couples joined Chet and Alex on the dance floor. It wasn't long before the entire O'Grady/Stafford clan was dancing, with the exception of Joe and Amy, who were still keeping their distance from each other on opposite sides of the room. After the hangover he'd suffered a day earlier, Joe had consumed relatively little alcohol. Surprisingly, Amy was alcohol-free herself, preferring coffee and cola instead—a fact that did not go unnoticed by Cat and Billie.

"Do you see how Joe and Amy are acting?" Cat asked Billie as they glided together in tune with the music.

Billie smiled. "Yeah, like a couple of teenage lovers who have just had their first fight. Do you see how they keep looking at each other when they think the other one isn't looking?" she asked.

"Maybe our talks did some good," Cat suggested hopefully.

"I'd like to think so, but until they actually warm up to each other, this is as good as it's going to get, I'm afraid," Billie replied.

"Something needs to happen to break the ice," Cat said.

"Speaking of something happening, I'm feeling really uncomfortable about what's going on between the grandmothers. I just hope Jo doesn't do something she'll regret later," Billie told Cat. "I'm pretty disappointed with her not coming today, and I know Grams has been deeply hurt by it."

"Yeah, I'm a little disappointed in her myself. But at least Grams is starting to enjoy herself now. I'm glad Jen brought Chet along. He'll keep her mind off Jo for the afternoon," Cat mused.

As the waltz ended, the couples clapped and returned to their tables, all but Chet and Alex that is. Had Alex had her way, she too would have returned to the table to sulk, however

Chet wouldn't hear of it as he held fast to her hand and coaxed her into joining him for another dance. As that dance ended, he begged for a third. As the music began for the third dance, Alex again reluctantly gave in and halfheartedly engaged in the dancing. Moments into the dance a loud voice boomed over the PA system.

"Stop the music!"

All eyes turned to the source of the announcement as total silence descended over the room. There stood Josephine, microphone in hand, dressed to the tee in the outfit she and Billie had picked out for her in the mall. Dark gray high wasted pinstriped trousers, light gray long sleeved dress shirt, black vest that came to twin vees in front, maroon ascot, black patent leather shoes, maroon waistcoat with tails, and a black top hat and cane. Despite the fact that she was obviously a woman, Jo could have easily passed as a southern gentleman. Cat and Billie smiled at each other at the dramatic entrance that was so typically Josephine Wycliffe.

Totally captivated by the vision in front of her, Alex took two steps away from Chet and turned her total attention to the woman who owned her heart. "Josie?" she whispered.

"I have something to say," Jo said into the microphone, her eyes never leaving Alex's. "I should have done this ages ago, but I've been a damned fool, a damned fool who has wasted a lot of time. I know a lot of you noticed I wasn't by Alex's side at the wedding today, but I *was* there. Drew, honey, you were a beautiful bride," she said, confirming Billie's suspicion that the closing door at the back of the church was her.

Turning her attention to Alex, Jo continued. "As some of you know, Alex and I have been struggling of late. I'm afraid I have not been all that she needs. No, Alex, you know it's true," she said as Alex shook her head, refuting the self-incrimination Jo was putting herself through.

"I have spent several hours thinking about our situation, Alex, and I have decided that it's time for a change," Jo announced, causing Alex to close her eyes and prepare for the worse. Reaching into her pocket, Jo pulled out a piece of paper with nearly illegible handwriting. "For the past couple of days, I have been putting my thoughts on paper, and I'd like to share them with you now," she said, clearing her throat and reading directly from the page.

I WANT THE WORLD TO KNOW

I want the world to know
I'm the luckiest person on Earth.
I have my health.
I have a home.
I have loving family.
But above all else,
I have the most precious pearl
The heavens have ever made,
And her name is Alexandra.

I want the world to know
I cherish her with all my heart.
She is my reason for living.
She is why I rise each day.
She gives my life meaning.
She fulfills me in ways unimaginable.
I would be lost without her,
As I hope she would be lost
Without me.

I want the world to know
I find peace and comfort in her arms.
Her love blankets me with warmth.
Her love protects me from harm,
Even from myself.
She is my protector,
My teacher,
My friend.
I would not be whole without her.

I want the world to know
She has stood by my side

Through thick and thin,
In good times and bad
In sickness and in health
For better and for worse.
I would not be where I am today
Without her love...
Without her support.

I want the world to know
I am not ashamed of our love.
She is a prize to be treasured,
A trophy to be displayed.
I have been a fool
To have hidden it away.
Unwilling to bear the scrutiny
Of ridicule imagined,
But never realized.

I want the world to know
I am here today
To ask forgiveness...
To ask for love...
To ask for commitment.
In the presence of friends and family,
I am here today
To ask my one true love....
Alexandra Spirakis - will you marry me?

When Jo finished reading, she looked up from the paper and met the tear-filled eyes of Alexandra Spirakis, only inches from her own. Jo and the crowd held their collective breaths as they awaited Alex's reply.

Alex reached up to cup Jo's face between her hands. "Yes, you old fool. I will marry you," she said clearly before falling into Josephine's arms.

A deafening roar erupted from the crowd as dozens of well-wishers came forth to offer their congratulations to the embracing couple. Billie and Cat held back, their fingers interlaced, neither able to see through their tears to make their way through the crowd congratulating the ladies. There would be time later at home. The moment was so intensely loving and romantic that it even melted the ice wedge between Amy and Joe, who embraced warmly at the news.

Once more, Jo reached for the microphone and looked around at the crowd. "Thank you all so much for your support," she said before turning to Alex. "Alexandra, you have made me the happiest woman in the world. Now all we have to do is make it official, right here, right now," Jo announced. "That is, of course, if Drew and Dylan don't mind sharing their wedding anniversary with the likes of me."

Drew and Dylan came forward and warmly embraced the couple, assuring them it would be an honor to share such a momentous occasion with them.

"Well, I guess all we need then is a Justice of the Peace, which I just happened to have scheduled to be here today just in case," Jo said.

"Pretty sure of yourself, weren't you Wycliffe?" came a joking voice from the back of the crowd, causing a ripple of laughter to spread through the room.

"No, just pretty sure of Alex's love," Jo quipped.

Alex suddenly became impatient and took the microphone from Jo's hand. "Josephine Wycliffe, I have waited 50 years for a sincere proposal from you, and now that I've got it, I am *not* gonna wait a minute longer. Let's do this!" Alex shouted, sending the crowd once more into a fury of clapping.

***

"Ladies and gentlemen, I give to you, Josephine Wycliffe and Alexandra Spirakis, partners in love, soul mates at heart, bound together for the rest of their lives by the vows they have made before us," the Justice of the Peace announced to the crowd. To Jo and Alex, he added, "Ladies, you may kiss the bride."

As their lips touched, a deafening round of applause filled the room, and once again, the women were surrounded by well-wishers.

"Time to cut the cake," came a voice, booming from the PA system. All eyes turned to the stage where Ida was standing, microphone in hand.

Hand in hand, Drew and Dylan approached the grandmothers.

"Grams," Drew said. "We'd be honored if you'd cut the cake with us," she offered.

"Oh, darlin's, you are just so sweet," Alex exclaimed as she looked at Jo to confirm her willingness.

Alex's face drooped as she saw the evil expression on Jo's face. "Oh, no you don't!" she declared. "You are not goin' to smoosh cake in *my* face, Josephine Wycliffe."

Jo feigned an insulted expression. "Now would I do that?" she said innocently.

"In a heartbeat," came Alex's reply, causing all four of them to laugh as they headed toward the cake.

Interested in the goings on, the crowd formed a semicircle around the newlyweds as the wedding party joined them for pictures during the cake cutting.

Well aware of what her wife was capable of, Alex grabbed Jo's wrist as she offered her the piece of cake, so she had no choice but to behave. In fact, both couples managed to exchange their cake without a speck of frosting landing on any of them.

The crowd clapped once more as the newly wedded couples faced them to accept their warm wishes and pose for more pictures.

Suddenly, a loud screech rang through the room, originating from the center of the wedding party still gathered around the new couples. All eyes turned toward the source of the sound as Amy swung back and slapped Bob across the face.

"How dare you!" she exclaimed as she rubbed her backside. "Don't you ever put your hands on me again, do you understand me?" she yelled just as Joe made his way to the center of the commotion. Grabbing Bob by the front of his tuxedo, he hauled back and planted a closed fist on the young man's jaw, sending him flying directly into the cake, spewing frosting all over the rest of the wedding party.

"I have waited a long time to do that," he said, angrily pointing at the prone man. "Go near my wife again, and you're a dead man," he warned.

Bob did the only thing he could think of. He grabbed a handful of cake and threw it at Joe, hitting him squarely in the face.

"Why you little son of a..." Amy exclaimed as she lunged at Bob and pushed his face into the cake.

"Food fight!" yelled Seth as he jumped into the fray.

Unable to resist, Jo joined in, much to Alex's chagrin.

Tara saw this as a perfect opportunity to seek revenge on Crystal as she shoved her cousin's face directly into what was left of the cake on the table.

Within moments, the entire wedding party and several of the guests were involved in an all-out cake war, momentary anger with Bob forgotten as peals of laughter and cake flew around the room. By the time the din had settled, the floor, walls, and tables were covered with sticky goo, not to mention nearly every inch of the partygoers, several of them lying or sitting on the slippery floor recovering from bouts of laughter.

Cat reached down to lend Billie a hand. Somehow, during the melee, Billie found herself on the floor, her purple dress severely damaged by frosting stains. As she rose to her feet, she looked down at herself and secretly chuckled at the demise of the horrid gown.

"Hey, Barney! Looks like you forgot your bib," Jen said as she took in her friend's state of disarray.

"Okay, that's it. I've had enough," Billie exclaimed as she picked up a handful of frosting and smeared it across Jen's face. "There. Paybacks are a bitch," she said.

Jen stuck her tongue out and licked the frosting away around her mouth. "Ah, don't you really mean, revenge is sweet?" she said dryly as she smacked her lips.

Bille laughed out loud and threw her arms around her goo-covered friend. "Jen, you're a nut. Have I ever told you that?" she asked.

"Takes one to know one," Jen replied.

EPILOGUE

Cat and Billie warmly embraced the grandmothers as their final flight number was called.

"Don't forget now, the kids are scheduled to come out for the month of July," Alex reminded them. "Just like we planned," she added, referring to the yearly trip all of the grandchildren had planned to take to Charleston each summer, a tradition that had begun as a result of the family reunion they had had a year earlier.

"Don't worry, Grams, we won't *let* them forget," Seth said enthusiastically. The grandmothers were so much fun to be with, especially Grandma Jo, and especially without parental supervision.

"You do that, scout," Jo replied as she hugged him and the girls.

This is the final boarding call for Flight 1076 to Charleston, South Carolina. All passengers report to gate twenty-three, a voice announced over the intercom.

"Well, that's us," Alex exclaimed. Extending her hand to Chet, who had come to see them off with Jen, she smiled brightly. "Chet, I am so glad we had the opportunity to meet. You truly are a southern gentleman," she said warmly.

"The pleasure was all mine, dear lady," Chet said, bowing and kissing the back of Alex's hand. Turning to Jo, he extended his hand which Jo took firmly. "Josephine," he said. "Take care of this delicate flower. She deserves all the love and attention she can get."

Jo smiled. "Yes she does. I couldn't agree with you more. No hard feelings," she said, unable to resist the urge to emphasize the fact that it was *she* who had won Alex's heart.

"None at all," Chet replied. "In fact, if you're ever in the New York area, stop by. I'd love to exchange history gossip with you."

"The same goes to you, Chet. The doors of SpireClyffe Acres are always open to you," Jo replied.

"You'd better hurry, Grams before they take off without you," Cat urged. Jo and Alex were the last of the family members to return home, and she and Billie were desperately looking forward to life returning to normal.

"All right, all right!" Jo said jokingly. "If I didn't know better, I'd think you were trying to get rid of us."

Billie placed an open palm on her chest and feigned innocence. "Now would we do that?" she asked.

"Do you really want an answer to that, granddaughter?" Jo asked sarcastically.

"Ah, no," Billie replied quickly, hugging her grandmother. "Have a great flight, both of you," she added, waving as they entered the boarding gate and disappeared into the plane.

"Well, Daddy," Jen said to her father. "We'd better find your gate before you miss *your* flight."

"Chet," Billie said, extending her hand to the older gentleman. "Thank you so much. You were brilliant. Jo never caught on that she was set up. You don't know what a difference you have made in their lives. We will forever be indebted to you."

"Billie, I thoroughly enjoyed myself. Ms. Wycliffe was definitely a tough cookie. I'm glad I could help," he replied.

Cat, always the sentimentalist, hugged Chet tightly as she said her goodbyes. "We're gonna miss you, Chet. You'll have to make a point to visit with Jen more often. We'd love to see you again," she said.

"I think that can be arranged, little one," Chet said, tweaking Cat's nose.

"Okay Daddy. Is your luggage checked? Do you have your tickets?" Jen asked, fussing over her father to ward off the tears that were threatening to spill from her eyes.

"Always the fussbudget, just like your mother, bless her heart," Chet said as he took Jen's arm and led her in the direction of his gate.

"I'll see the two of you back at home," Jen said over her shoulder as she was led away by her father.

"Mom, can we go outside and watch Grams' plane take off?" Skylar asked.

"Sure, just don't go beyond the chain-link fence, okay?" Billie replied.

"Meet us in the car," Cat called to their backs. Then, turning to Billie, she sighed deeply. "Finally, alone at last," she said as Billie took her into her arms.

"This certainly has been a hectic visit," Billie mused. "But you know what? I wouldn't change a thing, well except maybe our precious daughter getting tanked on pot," she said, chuckling lightly.

Cat lifted her head off Billie's chest and looked her in the eye. "Well, we did vow to stay together for better or for worse," she said smiling.

"That we did, my love, that we did," was all Billie said as they watched the plane take off, headed to South Carolina, and to a new beginning for two very special ladies.

Photo Credit: Brad Fowler, Song of Myself Photography

About the Author

Karen D. Badger is the author of On A Wing And A Prayer, Yesterday Once More (a 2009 Golden Crown Literary Award winner for Speculative Fiction), In A Family Way, Unchained Memories, Happy Campers, Collective Identity Sweet Angel and Relative-ly Speaking (Books I, II, III, IV, V and VI of the Commitment Series), The Blue Feather, All My Tomorrows (sequel to the 2009 award winning Yesterday Once More) and her latest novel, 1140 Rue Royale...all released by Badger Bliss Books, which Karen co-owns with her wife Barbara Sawyer (aka, "Bliss').

Born and raised in Vermont, Karen is the second of five children raised by a fiercely independent mother, who remains one of her best friends to this day. Karen earned her B.A. in 1978 in Theater and in Elementary Education, and in 1994, earned a B.S. in mathematics. In addition to her novels, Karen is the author of many technical papers on photomask manufacturing, which she has presented at numerous semiconductor industry conferences, and is the holder if several technical patents. Karen is currently in her 38th year as a Principle Member of the Technical Staff with a prominent Semiconductor manufacturer in Vermont.

Karen and her wife, Barb (a retired Lt. Col., US Air Force) live in the beautiful state of Vermont—home of Ben and Jerry's. They spend their spare time with family as well as doing home improvement projects on both their homes in Vermont and New Mexico. They also enjoy camping, kayaking, motorcycling and singing Karaoke.

Please visit Karen's author website at www.karendbadger.com, or the Badger Bliss Books website at www.badgerblissbooks.com. Also like us on Facebook!

TITLES BY KAREN D. BADGER

www.badgerblissbooks.com

On A Wing and A Prayer
First edition published by Blue Feather Books, Sept, 2005
Second edition published by Badger Bliss Books – Sept, 2014
Third edition published by Badger Bliss Books – August, 2016
ISBN 13: 978-1-945761-01-0, ISBN 10: 1-945761-01-6

Yesterday Once More
First edition published by Blue Feather Books, July, 2008
Second edition published by Badger Bliss Books – Sept, 2014
Third edition published by Badger Bliss Books – August, 2016
ISBN 13: 978-1-945761-02-7, ISBN 10: 1-945761-02-4
2009 Golden Crown Literary Society Award - Speculative Fiction

In A Family Way – Book One of the Commitment Series
First edition published by Blue Feather Books, March, 2010
Second edition published by Badger Bliss Books – Sept, 2014
Third edition published by Badger Bliss Books – August, 2016
ISBN 13: 978-1-945761-05-8, ISBN 10: 1-945761-05-9

Unchained Memories – Book Two of the Commitment Series
First edition published by Blue Feather Books, Oct, 2011
Second edition published by Badger Bliss Books – Sept, 2014
Third edition published by Badger Bliss Books – August, 2016
ISBN 13: 978-1-945761-06-5, ISBN 10: 1-945761-06-7

Happy Campers - Book Three of the Commitment Series
First edition published by Blue Feather Books, Sept, 2013
Second edition published by Badger Bliss Books – Sept, 2014
Third edition published by Badger Bliss Books – August, 2016
ISBN 13: 978-1-945761-07-2, ISBN 10: 1-945761-07-5

The Blue Feather
First edition published by Blue Feather Books, July, 2014
Second edition published by Badger Bliss Books – Sept, 2014
Third edition published by Badger Bliss Books – August, 2016
ISBN 13: 978-1-945761-04-1, ISBN 10: 1-945761-04-0

Collective Identity – Book Four of the Commitment Series
First edition published by Badger Bliss Books – January, 2015
Second edition published by Badger Bliss Books – August, 2016
ISBN 13: 978-1-945761-08-9, ISBN 10: 1-945761-08-3

All My Tomorrows – Sequel to Yesterday Once More
First edition published by Badger Bliss Books – May, 2015 Second
edition published by Badger Bliss Books – August, 2016
ISBN 13: 978-1-945761-03-4, ISBN 10: 1-945761-03-2

Sweet Angel – Book Five of the Commitment Series
First edition published by Badger Bliss Books – June, 2015 Second
edition published by Badger Bliss Books – August, 2016
ISBN 13: 978-1-945761-09-6, ISBN 10: 1-945-761-09-1

Relative-ly Speaking – Book Six of the Commitment Series
First edition published by Badger Bliss Books – March, 2016
Second edition published by Badger Bliss Books – August, 2016
ISBN 13: 978-1-945761-10-2, ISBN 10: 1-945-761-10-5

1140 Rue Royale
First edition published by Badger Bliss Books – Sept, 2016
ISBN 13: 978-1-945761-00-3, ISBN 10: 1-945761-00-8

COMING SOON FROM KAREN D. BADGER
AND BADGER BLISS BOOKS

www.badgerblissbooks.com

1140 Rue Royale - Expected release – Fall 2016

Lia and Elliot are research scientists in New York City. Having met twenty-two years earlier, their lives have fallen into a 'taken-for-granted' daily routine. They agree to begin again in New Orleans, not only to further their careers, but to renew their relationship, away from the hustle and bustle of big city life in New York.

While house-hunting, they can't believe their luck when they find an historical mansion in the French Quarter of New Orleans, securing the home for much less than appraised value.

Not long after moving in, they find out why their new home was such a bargain as a series of horrid events takes over their lives, and they learn the terrifying truth about 1140 Rue Royale.

Flash Point - Book Seven of The Commitment Series - Expected release - 2017

In this seventh installment of the Billie/Cat Commitment Series, the Charlands face a series of life challenges with the potential of changing their lives forever.

In an effort to pull their lives together, they plan a trip designed to heal the wounds and solidify their family bond, but find that fate is against them as they face grave danger and events so catastrophic, the odds of them coming out alive are not in their favor. Will they survive to see another day?

1140 Rue Royale

B

A BADGER BLISS BOOK

By

Karen D. Badger

CHAPTER 1

Elliot Walker stepped into the darkened loft and dropped her briefcase by the front door. She pressed the Indiglo button on her watch and noted the time was eleven-forty-five pm.

No wonder I'm tired, she thought as she opened the refrigerator looking for a bite to eat.

"You're late again," a voice said from across the room.

Elliot jumped.

"Jesus Christ, you scared me," Elliot said. "I thought you were in bed."

"You mean, you *hoped* I was in bed."

Elliot squinted to make out the silhouette of the woman sitting in a chair by the window, subtlety backlit by the glow of the streetlight.

"Lia, I'm really in no mood to fight with you tonight."

"That's the third time this week, and it's only Thursday," Lia said.

"I'm sorry. The experiments have a way of making one lose track of time...and you know the New York City subway system—it's always running late."

"I gave up making excuses for you around nine o'clock."

Elliot frowned, then closed her eyes and dropped her head back as she remembered. "Shit," she said. "I forgot about the dinner party with your Board of Directors. Lia, I'm so sorry."

Elliot stood in the kitchen with her hands on her hips and listened to the deafening silence.

"Lia?"

Elliot watched as Lia leaned forward in her seat.

"Elliot, do you love me? I mean—do you *really* love me?" she asked.

"How can you even ask me that?" Elliot said.

Lia rose and walked toward Elliot, entering the sphere of light emitting from the still-open refrigerator.

Not for the first time, Lia's distinct African features, dark brown eyes and mocha colored skin sent waves of warmth spreading through Elliot. She loved everything thing about Lia...everything, that is, except for the icy stare that was capable of stopping her cold. The icy stare that was being directed at her at that very moment.

Elliot reached to touch the side of Lia's face.

"No. Don't," Lia said as she pushed Elliot's hand away. "I asked you a question."

"Lia, we've been together for what...twenty-two years? Would I still be here if I didn't love you?"

"I don't know, Elliot. Sometimes I wonder about that. I mean, we hardly talk to one another anymore. Hell, it's been so long since we made love, I don't even remember. You are so wrapped up in your job that you can't even make a dinner date, after you *swore* you would be there."

"I said, I was sorry."

"That dinner party meant a lot to me, Elliot. It was my chance to impress the chairman...to convince him to fund the new genome project."

"And you needed *me* there to do that?" Elliot asked sarcastically.

"I needed *you* there for moral support. You are my wife... or have you forgotten that little tidbit as well?"

"How could I possibly forget *that*?" Elliot deadpanned.

Lia walked directly up to Elliot and stopped within a hair's breadth of her.

"Who are you, Elliot?" she asked. "There are times I see glimpses of the woman I fell in love with twenty-two years ago, but they are brief and fleeting. I don't even know you anymore."

"I'm not the only one wrapped up in my job, Lia. At least I don't take my work home with me."

"People's lives depend on my research. I will never turn my back on that aspect of my career. I will most certainly take a call at home if it means saving a life. The fact is, Elliot, that I *am* taking that call from home, and not from the office or the lab. I make a point of being home for you. I purposely make time for you in my life. Can you say the same for me?"

Elliot ran a hand through her short blond hair and walked a few feet away before turning back to face Lia. "I don't know what you want me to say. You're right. I'm a horrible person," she said, holding her arms out to the sides for emphasis.

Lia shook her head. "That doesn't even warrant a response," she said.

Lia turned around and walked back into the shadows before facing Elliot once more. Elliot stood there...hands on her hips, staring at the floor.

"Elliot, something has got to change here. I cannot go on living like this. You have become a stranger to me. You couldn't even answer the simple question...do you love me."

Elliot remained silent as Lia walked toward the bedroom. She stopped before entering...her back still to Elliot.

"Just so you know, I have no problem answering that question for myself, because I still love the Elliot you used to be. I love her more than life itself."

Lia slipped into the bedroom and closed the door, leaving Elliot standing in the sphere of light emitting from the still-open refrigerator.

What the fuck? Elliot thought as she closed the refrigerator door and walked through the dark loft toward window overlooking the busy street below. She rested her forehead on the cool window pane and stared into the night.

Is Lia right? Have I changed that much?

Elliot thought back to when she first met Lia twenty-two years ago. She was twenty-five and just out of grad school with dual degrees in Kinesiology and Computer Science. Lia was twenty-eight and with a Masters degree in Chemistry, she was already three years into her employment with Lode-Star Pharmaceuticals. She saw Lia for the first time at a local Starbucks.

For Elliot, it was love at first sight. She remembered the encounter like it was yesterday. *Tuesday, May twenty-ninth, nineteen-ninety...seven-forty-five am.* Elliot had just ordered a cinnamon dolce latte and was waiting at the pick-up counter for it when Lia walked into the store.

Elliot literally struggled to catch her breath. There before her was this vision. Tall and slim, she wore a calf-length peasant skirt with a fringed scarf draped over one hip, knee-high suede boots and a cream colored blouse that highlighted her mocha skin and dark brown eyes. A wild mane of black curly hair fell to the middle of her back. The entire package reminded Elliot of an exotic gypsy. Elliot couldn't take her eyes off her as she watched this beautiful woman place her order.

As the cashier rung up her order, the woman reached for the non-existent purse she thought was hanging on her shoulder.

"Damn. I forgot my purse in the car. I'll just run out to get it."

"No! No—let me," Elliot said, reaching for her wallet as she approached the woman. She felt like Sir Lancelot coming to the rescue of the beautiful damsel.

"That's all right. It will only take me a minute to get my purse," the woman said.

"I insist. Please."

The woman tilted her head to one side and smiled. "Okay. Thank you."

Elliot nearly melted on the spot as she paid the clerk. "My pleasure," she replied. She extended her hand. "Elliot Walker."

"Elliot? That's an unusual name for a woman."

"I'm afraid my father wanted a boy. I guess with me, he got the best of both worlds," Elliot said as she held the woman's hand firmly in her own.

"Well, it's nice to meet you, Elliot Walker. I'm Lia Purvis."

"Lia. Beautiful name for a beautiful woman." Elliot suddenly blushed. "Sheesh! That was corny. Good one, Walker," she said out loud. "I'm sorry for being so forward."

"Oh, don't apologize. That was very sweet," Lia said as she collected her coffee waiting at the end of the counter next to the one Elliot had ordered earlier.

They stood facing each other as an awkward pause ensued.

"Ah...do you have a minute or two to sit and enjoy your coffee?" Elliot asked.

Lia looked around the coffee shop, then back at Elliot. She smiled. "Actually, I do."

Elliot directed Lia to the closest table and held her chair as she sat.

Two hours later, they parted company after exchanging phone numbers.

That was the first day of a relationship that would last twenty-two years...and counting.

Elliot sighed as she basked in the memory.

Lia is right. I have changed.

In those early days, we shared a passion that could not be quenched. Even as the years went by, she was the most important thing in my life. I couldn't wait to get home to her in the evenings. We would talk for hours about work and life in general. I couldn't wait to lie with her in my arms at night.

And now?

Now, our paths barely cross and few words pass between us.

What does this mean, Lia?

You asked if I still love you.

Yes. I do. So why is it so hard for me to express that love to you? I supposed I've taken you for granted, expecting you to always love me regardless of my apparent indifference.

You are still an amazingly beautiful woman, Lia...in some ways, more beautiful at fifty then when I met you twenty-two years ago. I would love to see me through your eyes...to see how much I have changed compared to that fateful day in Starbucks when you forgot your purse in the car.

You said you cannot go on living like this.

Does that mean you're leaving me?

www.ingramcontent.com/pod-product-compliance
Lightning Source LLC
Chambersburg PA
CBHW051239260626
47162CB00002B/505